Be wary around your enemy once, and your friend a thousand times. A double-crossing friend knows more about what harms you.
—*Arabic proverb*

Chapter 1

Wednesday

Ellie Carr waved her brand-new keycard at the mounted sensor a second time. Still, nothing. The updated metal door remained flush in its frame and didn't give so much as a click to indicate an attempt to open for her. As far as the door was concerned, she did not exist. She tried not to take this personally. The door was only doing its job.

But if it didn't open, she would be late for the very first day of *her* job, hardly the impression she wanted to make on those in the antique stone building now looming, impenetrable, before her. The prestigious Locard Institute would allow her to research new techniques, instruct groups of peers, and investigate unique crimes for private clients. She hadn't been this out-of-her-mind jazzed since her first day at the bureau.

With that realization came a twinge of nostalgia. The FBI might have had her tracking mob payoffs instead of developing latent prints, but at least their keycards worked. The Hoover Building had never locked her out on a concrete stoop as she held a cardboard box of pens and notepads and books and the course syllabus and silly personal tchotchkes to make her new place feel as if she belonged there. It never left her surrounded by oak trees that delighted in holding on to the morning's light rain until they could spill their leaves on unsuspecting passersby—

"Excuse me." A man materialized next to her and waved his arm. The door promptly unlocked with a mocking series of clicks. Twisting the latch, he pulled it open, but then held the chunk of steel so that she could duck under his arm if she wished. She wished. She'd ride him piggyback if it were necessary to breach that entrance.

She ducked, eye level with the winged logo on his blue jacket and noted that he had a visitor ID. Fabulous. The course attendees' cards worked, but not the new crime scene instructor's . . . She thanked him and looked around to get her bearings, having only been to the Locard a few times. Two floors plus basement, long hallways in a horseshoe shape around a central courtyard, classrooms and student labs in the far wing, staff offices down the corridor to her right. Second floor, research labs, meeting rooms, more offices. Gym, locker rooms, and cafeteria on the basement level. The floors were gleaming terrazzo that bounced and amplified every sound.

Her rescuer trotted off to his classroom and two other occupants milled about, none she recognized. Rachael, who had offered her the job, would be somewhere in the building, teaching the Crime Scene Documentation course. Ellie would take over Collecting Evidential DNA at crime scenes.

Number 11, her assigned office, turned out to be the last in the hallway on the courtyard side, a nice-size room with wide windows, plenty of filing cabinets, and a large wooden desk clearly visible through a door that had three panes of glass in the upper half. The door was, of course, locked.

The same kind of proximity pad gave her card the same nonreaction as the outer entrance. She shifted the cardboard box to her hip. Bad enough she'd already been held up that morning at the closing on a house she'd barely seen before purchasing. Rachael had said she didn't need to take over the class until after lunch, but—

"Not working?" A portly guy in a grunge band T-shirt under his open lab coat paused in the hallway, then shook his head with a sympathetic smile. "You must be Ellie. Rachael told me you'd be starting today."

"That's me."

"I'm Hector Azores. Crime Analysis. I'm not surprised Barbara locked you out. She flunked sharing in preschool and never looked back. You can set your stuff down in my office if you want." He gestured toward number 10 across the hall. *That* door wasn't even closed.

"Thanks." Nearly every surface in Hector's room already sagged under the weight of assorted folders, books, periodicals, laptops, and the odd bottle of an unidentified-colored liquid, but she found a free, if scarred, straight chair on which to deposit her items. "I appreciate the help. Who's Barbara?"

"Barbara Wright. That's her office, at least for another two days. Then she can brush us all off for the big time and present her crime analysis breakthrough to the American Academy. She can't wait, and the rest of us are pretty happy about it too. Not for the same reasons."

Ellie smiled, catching the drift.

"Where do you need to go next?"

"I'm supposed to take over a class—" She pulled her USB and some notes out of the box, all she would need to get through the next two and a half days of instruction. She hoped.

"Collecting Evidential DNA or Crime Scene Documentation?"

"DNA."

"Ah, inheriting Barbara's class, as well as her office. I can show you where the room is."

She thanked him, but he had already swept into the hall,

and she trotted to keep up. "The courses run for two weeks, so there's three days to go. It's a light month, only two courses going, twenty, twenty-five people in each one. Rachael's mostly handling the documentation one, Barbara the other, with me and Sam doing guest spots. Students are from all over, like usual. They stay at the Marriott on 261. Lunch here—you know where the cafeteria is? That's one advantage of having classes in session, we actually have cooks serving up hot lunches. When there's no classes, it's sort of an Automat, prewrapped stuff delivered daily, that sort of thing. But, hey, it comes with the job and any free food is good food."

"I completely agree. This is quite the facility." They rounded the corner into the back hallway, dodging a young woman with a metal cart and hair the color of green apples. Her test tubes clinked out a discordant tune and she focused mightily on guiding the undersized wheels to the elevator.

"Yes and no. The building started out as a private boy's school, around the turn of the twentieth century, so, yeah, it looks like Oxford and has nice touches, like large bathrooms and the gymnasium downstairs. Locker rooms—since subdivided when they let those icky girls in. The cafeteria is nice, since we are kind of in the middle of nowhere. There's Chesapeake Bay on our back step and you have to drive for about fifteen minutes in any of the other three directions to find something approaching civilization."

"I'm figuring that out." The rural setting and copious trees made quite a change from Georgetown. A welcome change.

"The disadvantage is, it still looks like a school, so if you have any past 'Mean Girls PTSD,' it might bubble up. At least they took out the lockers lining the hallway, so I stopped having nightmares about forgetting the combination. Here it is."

He gestured at the closed door to a large classroom. Through the glass she saw that individual desks had been replaced by long tables and the padded industrial chairs more suited to adult frames. Their occupants listened to a cool blonde, with tortoiseshell glasses and every hair in place, standing at the front of the room. Ellie put her hand on the knob, feeling the jazz in her head turn to unexpected needles in her stomach. She shot Hector Azores a look.

"Oh, no. Sorry, New Girl, but you'll have to brave the fish eye of death on your own."

Ellie squared her shoulders and went inside.

Chapter 2

Clearly, Dr. Barbara Wright did not appreciate even a near-silent, tiptoeing interruption. She spared Ellie one icy, and not unexpected, glare, then pointedly waited for her to take the first available seat.

Ellie's life had required walking into a great deal of new classrooms, new jobs, new friends, new families. After her mother died, and her father hadn't let the door hit him on the way out, Ellie had lived with a variety of extended family members since the age of four. Loving homes, homes she knew and people she loved, but still—new. By now, she'd become versed, and knew what to do.

She planted herself in a chair, folded her hands in her lap, and sat absolutely still. In one second flat the people around her gave up hope that she would do anything interesting and returned their attention elsewhere. Perfect.

"We're a nation of pharmaceuticals," Barbara Wright said, pacing in front of the smartboard with a swish of her dark green lab coat. "We have access to extensive medical care and twenty-four/seven television full of commercials telling us exactly what meds we need to take for common and not-so-common conditions, like irritable bowel or Tardive dyskinesia. Many conditions treated with meds are genetic. Take retinoblastoma, eye cancer. It can be crippling. It can also be readily treated if caught early, and afterward controlled by taking anticancer drugs, like cyclophosphamide. Tetrabenazine can be used to reduce some of the involuntary movements of Huntington disease. Hydroxyurea is prescribed to prevent the more painful crises of sickle cell anemia."

She projected a map of the Eastern United States on the board, the colors streaking her form as she pointed to the amorphous circles hovering above different cities. "These dots are color-coded to indicate a dispensation of medication for one of twenty-five different genetic abnormalities. I focused on larger cities with a high number of unsolved murders, where many have enough similarities to be classified as the probable work of a serial killer. With a research grant I'll be retesting any biological samples from those murders, blood, semen, urine, hair. If the drugs are detected—say, for example, we find tetrabenazine in foreign hairs on a murdered corpse in Austin—then we can search for people in the area that have Huntington's."

"How?" a woman burst out, twirling an orange-tipped dread between her fingers. "That's all protected by HIPAA. You can't make Pfizer give you a list—"

"We don't need the corporations," Barbara Wright snapped. "Or the doctors. All prescription meds go into a clearinghouse now—thank you, opioid epidemic. Law enforcement can request access to that if it doesn't involve any patient information."

"Then how do you find your serial killer if there are no names attached to the meds?" asked another student.

"That *will* require a subpoena," she admitted, fingering the ID badge hooked through a belt loop as if it were a talisman. "But when I can prove that someone who takes tetrabenazine for Huntington's has killed five women in the

Boston suburbs, I have sufficient reasonable cause to get one. No federal judge can afford to ignore that. And she hasn't— the detective in charge of that case is getting the warrant as we speak.

"Or you can reverse the equation." The doctor went on, pacing in front of the boards, while Ellie took the opportunity to let her heartbeat slow back to normal from the bustle of the morning. The surroundings were familiar—the disciplines that made up forensic science were spread too far and wide to be covered in a single degree, even a doctorate like hers. Most of a forensic scientist's education came as continuing ed.

The people sitting around her were of all sizes, ages, genders, and colors, and in various stages of interest, distraction, and boredom. Some took notes on legal pads or laptops. A bag boutique's array of purses, totes, and backpacks were scattered along tables and the backs of chairs. Pens and phones competed for surface space with travel mugs, paper cups, and water bottles, both disposable and non. In other words, like every other training class she'd ever been in.

Dr. Wright was giving another example: "In Arkansas a suspect cut himself on the knife he stabbed the victim with. His DNA wasn't in CODIS, but his red blood cells were abnormally shaped. I searched the clearinghouse for dispensed hydroxyurea and found fifteen possible subjects."

CODIS meant the Combined DNA Index System. Clearly, the attendees knew that and didn't ask, but a beefy guy in the back row scoffed: "Can they even detect drugs in a dried spot of blood? I've never heard of that."

Barbara fixed him with a cool look, one Ellie remembered well from certain teachers over the years. "Labs have been doing that for years, Sergeant Bennett, with dried blood dots from autopsies. It's even better than liquid urine or blood samples, when analyzed via ultra-high-performance liquid chromatography-ion booster-quadrupole time-of-flight mass spectrometry—or," she added, with an even more condescending tone, "UHPLC-IB-QTOF-MS, if you prefer to use shorthand."

The sergeant did not seem cowed. "But aren't they only looking for opioids?"

Dr. Wright's eyelids flickered, only for the briefest of moments. "Of course most lab analyses are geared toward illegal drugs, but restyling or adding certain analysis to look for prescription meds that are *not* what we call 'controlled substances' is an easy adjustment."

That made sense, but many faces around Ellie reflected skepticism. It might sound like a cool idea while remaining a massive long shot . . . Hydroxyurea, for example, had additional uses beyond sickle cell anemia. On top of that, a good number of people had the sickle cell trait, but only about .003 had the disease, and most of those would be children . . .

Though when it came to serial killers, even a long shot might be a good one. If it solved even one murder, wouldn't it be worth it?

"Where do you stop, though?" another student asked, swirling the liquid in his plastic travel mug. "It's often stated that many serial killers suffered a brain injury. If you round up everyone who's on clonazepam to deal with seizures, because seizures are a common issue after traumatic brain injury, then aren't you—"

"I doubt anyone would be 'rounded up' until the field has been narrowed to one specific person. And personally I'd want a correlation much more significant than *some* serial killers have traumatic brain injury and *some* might take *some* kind of medication for it. This system would be utilized only with a provable link to crime scene evidence."

"So the problem isn't stopping," the student said. "It's

starting. You have to have a killer who both leaves DNA evidence behind and has a condition requiring steady medication."

The man next to her said, "With enough analysis, finding medication is probably easy enough. Everybody's on something these days."

Barbara Wright spoke firmly, retaking control of the classroom before it broke down into individual debates. "I'm going to present this next Monday to the American Academy of Forensic Sciences. The week after that, I will be receiving my preapproved grant from Caltech to further this research there."

Ellie heard: *It doesn't matter what you think. Better minds are already going ahead.*

A man next to Ellie muttered, "Counting chickens . . ." Another sighed with apparent boredom. A few made polite and awkward noises of appreciation.

"So for your last two days of class, I will be turning you over to Dr. Carr, although after lunch I'll still walk you through your DNA samples." With one motion she unhooked her USB from the projection system and gathered up her folders, adding, "You can have the class now."

She made this announcement without so much as a glance in Ellie's direction. And then she was gone.

Some attendees looked about for this Dr. Carr to materialize, but most took the opportunity to check mobile devices for emails and texts.

"Take control," her uncle Wayne had advised in situations like this.

"You never get a second chance to make a first impression," Aunt Rosalie told her more than once. *"Get it right the first time."*

She stood, straightened her blazer, refrained from patting her hair to make sure the auburn locks hadn't budged from the chignon, and moved to the front of the room.

Ellie hadn't, in fact, aspired to be a teacher. But she had lectured to plenty of groups at the bureau—one of those "other duties as assigned" immediately foisted off on the junior agent, along with adding paper to the copy machine. She had taken to it, though, and enjoyed sharing ideas with people who wanted to hone their skills. The ones who only attended in order to get an employer-paid trip away from their desks—not so much.

Over the years she'd found the key to winning over a group's hearts and attention: snacks. The institute provided a table in the rear of the room, with an urn and a variety of Danishes, bagels, and cookies.

"Hi, I'm Dr. Carr. You can call me Ellie. I don't know how long this morning's session has already lasted, so let's take a ten-minute break for restrooms and coffee."

As a unit the attendees burst into wide smiles and two made an instant beeline for the door.

There, she thought. *Not so hard.*

Chapter 3

Dr. Rachael Davies sat at a long table in the institute's cafeteria, ate tuna salad, and listened to the conversation around her. The attendees from both courses had spent daily lunch together for eight days and even organized outings over the weekend to see all the sights of DC. Now they chatted as easily as old friends—that is, old friends whose conversations always ended up on the weirdest clue or the gooiest decomposed body they'd ever seen.

She usually ate lunch in her office, attending to paperwork during the break. As one of the institute's two assistant directors, Rachael accepted that her paperwork never ended. But with classes wrapping up, and none scheduled for another two weeks, her workload had become temporarily light. She had finished the report for the Locard's latest client, a woman in Tennessee who wanted her missing daughter found. After Rachael analyzed the stained scarf found at the scene of the teen's supposed abduction, and found equine blood and an alfalfa bud, it took no time at all to locate the girl at her online boyfriend's racehorse farm. So Rachael could take one non-multitasked lunch.

The "basement" of the Locard stretched only along the back leg of the building; built partly into the hill, its wide windows along the rear wall looked out into the deep woods. The view of the trees sufficed for décor. Purely practical terrazzo floors, laminate-topped tables, and metal chairs made up the rest of the environment. Today the air smelled like too-done toast overlaid with tomato sauce.

"She killed him with a claw hammer," Stefanie Parsons was saying over an avocado toast. Stef was a Border Patrol agent from California who seemed to exist on cigarettes, coffee, and air. "Not the head part, the claw part. It left really distinct marks."

"What was the cause of death?" Rachael, the former pathologist, asked. "Blunt force trauma or exsanguination?"

"Heart attack. I guess waking up in the wee hours to find the ex-girlfriend you forgot existed, doing her best to crush your skull, would make anyone's heart skip a few beats. Or all of them." She coughed. Rachael could imagine her alveolar septum thickening with every class break, when Stef and one or two others would return on a cloud of tobacco fumes. In thirty years the oxygen would have such a tough time getting through, the CO_2 would build up to respiratory failure—

"What is a hammer?" Farida asked. Farida Al Talel was from Saudi Arabia, all dark eyes and deeply black hair under a loose headscarf. Her English skills were excellent, but now and then a word still confounded her.

"You pound nails with it," Tony Altamonte, the New Mexico homicide detective, said, making a weak pantomime with one hand.

Oliver Suarez, from Montana, sat next to Farida. Tall and slender to the point that Rachael thought he could use more protein in his diet, the crime scene tech sketched a small doodle on the back of his notebook and showed it to her.

"Oh. *Shakush.*"

The two men on the other side of Farida looked up at the Arabic word, didn't hear more, and promptly lost interest. Bashar was Farida's cousin, and she described Irfan as "a more distant cousin." They were at the Locard only as guardians for their female relative and spoke very little English. Farida's wealthy father, from a branch of a branch of the Saudi royal family, only allowed her to make the trip if the two men came as well. He'd paid all the expenses for his daughter and the two men, even including tuition for the male chaperones, who could not understand a single word of the classes that they were attending. They were no trouble—politely quiet during class and bursting into low conversation with each other only around food.

Farida fascinated Rachael. The girl provided a crash course in Life in Saudi Arabia Today. It surprised Rachael that a country that didn't let its women drive cars until quite recently would let one travel halfway around the world to go to a coed school with an uncovered face. It turned out that cases were not as rare as Rachael would have thought. She had done some research before Farida's arrival. Women could receive a thorough education in Saudi Arabia—at gender-segregated schools—and work at nearly any job—provided their father or husband agreed. To be so free and yet not free . . . Rachael couldn't wrap her head around it. But every day with Farida provided more insights.

"We had a guy beat his pahtnuh to death with a Rossi .22." The New York City homicide sergeant, Craig Bennett, spoke around a mouthful of rib slider. He was in Barbara's DNA class. Rachael didn't know much about him except that he wanted to attend because he would shortly be promoted to lieutenant in charge of the forensic unit. "Thing was loaded. He could'a simply pulled the trigger, but no. I don't know why it didn't go off and shoot at least one of them. He told us later, 'I only wahnted him to start running the Christmas advertisements a week earlier. I didn't wahn-tuh *kill* him.' I said, 'Then maybe you shouldn'ta cracked his skull, ya think?'"

Everyone—except the two guardians—chuckled. Gallows humor, it was called, industry banter that happened to involve someone's life or death. Normally quiet Alyssa Cole, from the DNA class, described a New Year's Eve block party where two men got into an argument. The one went home to get a knife, returned, and stabbed the other. "And he went to trial. He couldn't figure out that when you walk a block away, get a knife, and come *back*, it's pretty hard to claim self-defense."

"Are we going to visit Chester today?" Oliver asked.

Rachael swallowed and said, "Of course. Temperatures dropped last night, and that can affect the insect activity. His maggots might be a bit stunned."

The Crime Scene Documentation course needed a crime scene to document, and the Locard provided one in the form of a half-buried goat in the wooded area between the parking lot and the bay. His name really had been Chester, according to the farm donating his body. He had been more of a pet than a commodity until he'd broken through a fence to feast on a pretty vine with bright flowers called yellow jessamine. Its neurotoxic alkaloid had doomed the aging goat.

Stef made a face. "They won't be the only ones. Maybe we should have dealt with the maggots *before* lunch."

"Weak stomach?" Oliver teased.

"Always. Ten years on the job and I still get queasy at the sight of blood. Vomit will make *me* vomit. I don't even like spit on the sidewalk."

"Who does?" Craig asked rhetorically. "It's just your lot. I know detectives who get to their retirement and still hafta go outside and lay down if they catch a stabbing."

Rachael said, "Besides, we couldn't go out before lunch, unless you wanted to take notes in the rain. Again."

"Does it always rain so much here?" Farida asked.

Rachael said no, but October did tend to be one of Maryland's rainiest months. The others joined in a chorus of comparing precipitation at their home locations, and Rachael noticed a new arrival. Ellie Carr crossed the gleaming floor with one of the attendees from the other class in tow.

Rachael beamed to see her. Ellie had been thrilled to come to the Locard, and Rachael had been thrilled to get her. She'd be a great addition to the Locard's panel of experts, and Rachael already had a line on a private client who could use Ellie's skills.

She opened her mouth to apologize for not finding and welcoming Ellie sooner that day, but they'd had a lot of coursework to get through, and with Ellie's late arrival—

The words died in her throat. Ellie didn't look thrilled to be there. In fact, she seemed about as thrilled as someone in a dentist's office awaiting an extraction.

Ellie gave no preamble. Putting her mouth close to Rachael's ear, she said, "We have an issue. Barbara Wright is dead."

Chapter 4

During Ellie's morning, as she reacquainted herself with the role of teacher, she spoke for an hour and a quarter about the rare but solid successes in getting DNA off fired bullet casings. Yes, when a bullet explodes inside a gun, the temperature can reach 200 degrees Fahrenheit, and, yes, metal was not a particularly cooperative substrate for DNA results, but loading rounds into a snug, stiff magazine required a lot of touching and shoving and pushing of the little buggers.

After which the woman with the orange-tipped dreadlocks tapped a jeweled pill case on the table like a judge's gavel and let Ellie know that it was time for lunch. They only needed an hour, the woman added apologetically, with the cafeteria in the building.

Ellie checked her watch, announced that Barbara Wright planned to resume the course on the next hour—one p.m.— and waited until the attendees filed out. Was she supposed to shut the doors? Lock them? But with a nonfunctioning keycard, she wouldn't be able to get back in . . . not an option.

Besides, if you couldn't trust a group of crime scene investigators to resist stealing the pencils, who could you trust?

She'd recognized one of her "students," Alyssa Cole, FBI agent, younger than Ellie, slightly underweight with mouse-brown hair. Ellie had worked with her a few times over the years when they'd been mobilized for the Evidence Response Team. They'd been friendly then, more or less, but ERT was a peripheral duty and being freed from your regular assignment to participate could be hit-or-miss. She couldn't tell from Alyssa's reaction if the woman even recognized her.

Ellie didn't close the doors, but she did turn out the light. Aunt Rosalie had been a bit fanatical about saving energy, and old habits die hard. Nor did she follow her students. "Cafeteria" brought back too many wavering nightmares of school days, of carrying around a pressed plastic tray filled with not-terribly-appetizing food, desperately sweeping the horizon for a safe place to sit that wouldn't be too near any groups' preordained territory, such as the jock, preppy, popular, or burnout sects, and murmuring the young person's mantra: *Don't let me do anything embarrassing.*

Besides, she needed a few minutes of downtime after the hectic morning, closing on her new house, throwing her hair into a messy bun while stopped at a traffic light—a moment of peace seemed in order.

Maybe the office would be open and, even better, vacant, or perhaps she could find someone to get the keycard reprogrammed. She wound her way back to Hector Azores's office, where the diet cola and peanut butter crackers in her lunch bag were calling her name.

The agenda specified that Barbara would resume after lunch, with the students running their own DNA samples, but after that, the doctor would be out the door, leaving Ellie on her own. She'd better not go far.

Barbara's office at the other end of the horseshoe remained dark and locked. Hector's stood empty, but open, and she fell upon her crackers. Not the most exciting lunch, but her still-largely-empty new kitchen had not provided a lot of options.

With three half-full coffee mugs and two Snickers wrappers scattered across his desktop, she figured Hector didn't forbid eating in his office. Two guest chairs were piled with books and folders and she wasn't about to usurp the desk chair, so she milled about, too full of first-day jitters to sit still.

The trees outside were halfway through with losing their leaves, and bursts of gold and red could still be found. As in her first high school, radiators lined the space under the windows to provide heat to the rooms. It didn't seem that much had been done to alter the place from classroom to office. Apparently, the Locard spent its money on research—from the successes she'd read of over the years—and not on décor. She liked that.

A wide chalkboard still covered the wall behind Hector's desk. He had coated it with notes she couldn't decipher at first glance: *Burglaries Meadville PA. Assaults Oklahoma. Stab Perry WI.* The information seemed straightforward enough, but what was Hector doing with it?

Ellie sipped from a can as her glance moved to the spreadsheets scattered across Hector's desk. These lists were not so general—each line began with a name: *Letitia Thomas. Wendy Chung. Alexa Ward.* These were followed by modes of death, dates, type of location (residence, vehicle, outdoor), and city. The modes were all gunshot, and the city was always St. Louis. Hector had penciled in totals at the bottom. The next sheet contained strangling deaths, also in St. Louis, but the next sheet moved on to bludgeonings in Moline, Illinois. A listing of human misery, reduced to statistics. A few cracker crumbs fell to the top layer and she quickly brushed them off with a guilty swipe.

Across the hall the man who had let her into the building that morning hovered in front of her soon-to-be office door. He peered through the glass panels at the dim interior, his hand moving toward the knob.

"Looking for someone? Dr. Wright?" Ellie asked. *Or me,* though that seemed unlikely.

He turned with a start. "Yeah, um—the next session is about to start."

"Already?"

"She said we'd need a lot of prep time—I guess we're going to run our own Rapid DNA."

"Huh. Well, she's not in there, and I've been hanging around for a bit." Ellie licked a smear of peanut butter off one finger and straightened her favorite blazer. "I'll help you find her."

He smiled, the merest suggestion of dimples framing his cheeks, and thanked her. She left Hector's office as unsecured as she'd found it and joined—

"Caleb Astor," he said, offering a hand. "Ballwin, Missouri. Don't worry if you've never heard of it. No one has."

He'd been in the class, sitting behind Alyssa, but Ellie only now noticed that he had two different-colored eyes. One was a deep blue, the other a pale brown.

She and Caleb fell into step, glancing into each office as they passed. Most were empty, but doors were open, Ellie noted. All except Barbara Wright's.

"Are you with the police department in Ballwin?"

"Sheriff's."

"Do you do crime scene?"

"Yeah, little bit of everything. It's a small department—farm country, you know?"

"You're sure she's not in the cafeteria?"

"Yeah, I went from there to the classroom. But she's not in either. I thought maybe we're supposed to meet in the lab

WHAT HARMS YOU   21

instead of the room, but clearly, I didn't pay enough attention. I was distracted by the new teacher."

He grinned at her as he said this, but only for an instant
before returning to the search. This seemed to be drive-by
flirting, quickly abandoned. Which suited her perfectly.

No sight of the other instructor in the rear hallway and
Ellie didn't volunteer to check the ladies' room, not yet. She
didn't know Barbara well enough to intrude on her hand-
washing time unless necessary.

Instead, she used the trip to continue her orientation to
the new building, to nod hello at her new coworkers nestled
in their labs and offices. The Locard, according to its website, provided services in nearly every major forensic disci-
pline—firearms, toxicology, fraud, latent prints, and so on.
A windowed anteroom held doors to the director's and assistant director's offices, gleaming in polished walnut. A muted
bang echoed down the hall, a gunshot to which no one paid
any attention; Ellie assumed some examiner had test-fired
into a water tank to determine the ballistic markings. She
recognized the document examination lab from her visit the
previous month.

"What made you decide to attend this course?" she asked
Caleb as they walked.

"Work paid for it," he said, and she laughed.

Attendees had trickled back into the classroom they'd
been in earlier that morning, once again settling in with their
notebooks and tote bags and industrial-size water bottles.
No sign of Barbara Wright.

Across the hall another classroom had four or five people
in it, checking their emails or typing on laptops. One stared
out the window at the dense forest. But no Barbara, and no
Rachael either.

Ellie noticed a light in the next room and moved to its
door. The laboratory had been prepped for something—

the counters were covered in clean butcher paper from a two-foot-wide roll mounted on the wall. At least ten workstations had been identically stocked with a box of sterile swabs on the right, latex gloves in three different sizes on the left, and a clear plastic stand full of sampling cartridges in the middle. Ellie recognized the cartridges as similar to those used for Rapid DNA analysis. The room smelled like chemicals—hardly surprising.

"Well, she's not here either," Caleb said. "I guess we wait."

But Ellie had spied a boxy chunk of lab equipment about the size of a dorm fridge on a rear counter. The flap on its lower left front gaped open, allowing a peek into the wires and tubes inside. "This must be the Rapid DNA analyzer . . . It looks like they built their own. It's been around for years, but I've never been up close and personal. This is amazing."

Rapid DNA analysis was exactly what it sounded like—a fully automated process from a swab to a CODIS-ready genetic profile, without the need for human beings to provide additional reagents, tubes, or heaters during analysis. First designed for use on the battlefield to identify soldiers killed in action, the technology quickly migrated to forensic use.

"Yeah," Caleb said. "She said something about this being the working model that they used for experiments and classroom instruction only. There's a later model they use for client work. I wonder if they're going to go for a patent. Got to be big money in that. Man, it stinks in here."

Ellie tore herself away from images of what might be going on inside the device—she'd better get Caleb back in his seat before Barbara started up again, or the woman might superglue their office door lock as a goodbye gift.

But the fumes *were* strong, tickling her nose with an acrid feel, and somehow stronger to her left than her right.

She turned. A thin bar of light showed past the bottom of a door in the west wall. The door had no identifier, but she assumed it to be some sort of closet; classrooms weren't normally designed with adjoining doors to the next space. Had something spilled?

The knob had a key slot, but moved easily when she turned it. Pulling the door open brought with it a wave of choking, stinging air, along with the sight of a person stretched out on the floor, facedown.

But from the tight bun of hair and the perfectly shaped nails, Ellie immediately recognized Barbara Wright.

The supply closet measured about five by six feet, with shelving on all three walls. The shelves had been filled with the usual accouterments: Gloves, microtubes, and disposable aprons lined half the space, and bottles and jars, most of the brown-glass type, stood along the rest. Barbara stretched out along the available floor space with her feet just inside the door, her weight resting partly on her right side, left hand up by her chest. Ellie saw broken pieces of glass near Barbara's hand, one with a partial label: FISHER SCIENTIFIC/ 1 L/ C4H1 . . .

She moved forward, but Caleb grabbed her shoulders from behind, the buttons on her jacket clinking against the door. "Stop—it's too thick. You'd better stay back or you'll pass out too."

Ellie shrugged him off. The fumes were uncomfortable, but she could breathe without choking. But to be sure, she put a hand in her blazer pocket and clapped the material over her nose and mouth. The two pens in her pocket banged against her nose, but it relieved the stinging sensation in the nasal cavity. She couldn't do much about her eyes, except keep them at half-mast. She moved Barbara onto her back and then felt her carotid for any sign of a heartbeat.

She didn't find one. Only a burning as the spilled acid singed her fingertips.

The liquid had formed a puddle under Barbara's face and upper shoulders; it left angry red patches on her skin and turned her shirt collar to a limp, partly goopy mess. Without thinking, Ellie reached out her hand to wipe her burning fingers on Barbara's left shoulder, which had stayed well above the puddle; then, instead of altering the death scene any more than she already had, she wiped them on her shoe. The Skechers were worn, anyway.

All of this took mere seconds before she turned her face to the attendee Caleb. "Call 911. Tell them I believe she's deceased."

"She's dead?" He spoke calmly. The attendees were, after all, crime scene investigators, and with a sheriff's office, he'd probably been up close and personal with more dead people than Ellie had. But it had to be a little disconcerting for the victim to be someone you were taking notes from, only a few hours before.

"There's no pulse and the eyes are fixed and open. Body temp has already cooled. Call 911 and then we'll have to find Rachael or the director."

"You go," he said kindly. "I can stay with the body."

"No, we'd better both go. The fumes *are* strong." And I don't want to add further medical claims to the Locard's problems, she thought. Not a good way to impress on my first day at the job. She left the supply room door open, but made sure the classroom door would lock behind her as they exited. That would keep out the attendees—surely, they were only given access to the building itself and not all doors within. However, she guessed that most, if not all, of the staff could get in. She'd have to hustle if she wanted to protect her new coworkers from both the unhappy sight and the toxic cloud that came with it.

She headed for the south-corner stairwell, which led down to the cafeteria, breaking into a trot. The guy from Missouri kept pace beside her.

Chapter 5

Rachael stood up before the words fully penetrated, leaving the lunch table without a word to the attendees, and committing the sin of not bussing her tray, as her mind whirled. She and Ellie strode away in silence until she realized that the student with Ellie—what was his name? Carter? Calvin?—remained behind, an uncertain expression on his face.

"Come with us," she told him in a tone that did not allow for argument, and he didn't make any. She didn't need him gossiping with the other attendees, until they could get a handle on the narrative.

Narrative, she thought. *Oh em gee, I've been in Washington too long.* The woman might be dead and she could think only of the institute's image.

The three of them remained silent until they were well out of earshot inside the stairwell before Rachael said, *"Dead?"*

Ellie spoke in a gentle tone. "Unfortunately, yes. It seems she broke a jar of hydrochloric in the supply room in the DNA lab. I locked the door to the lab so no one else could wander in there."

"Are you sure?" Meaning, of course, the dead part, and not the locking part. Ellie was brilliant, and experienced, but not a medical doctor.

"Pretty sure, yes. We already called 911."

And, indeed, Rachael became sure as well, with one glance at the body—her colleague, now "the body." After she told Carter/Calvin to wait in the hall, the fumes hit her as soon as she unlocked the door—and Barbara Wright's blank, staring eyes told Rachael that Barbara had, indeed, gone far away. Only "the body" remained. Rachael had been a pathologist for over a dozen years, had seen more corpses than she could count. There would be nothing for EMS to do.

She checked for a pulse, anyway, using a wrist after Ellie had warned her of the acid on the neck and face. The woman's extremities were already cooling.

When had she last seen Barbara? Aloud she said: "I passed her in the hall on the way to the morning sessions—about eight-thirty."

Ellie stood two feet away. The air still stunk with the acrid smell of HCl, but had dispersed too much to interfere with breathing. "I went into her class and she turned it over to me at about ten-thirty."

"She was facedown?" The red burns on the left cheek made that clear.

"Yes, I moved her to see if CPR would help." Regret tinged Ellie's voice. Moving *anything*, especially a body, without photographing first, was anathema to any crime scene tech. And any pathologist.

The supply closet had no window; the door could be locked, but never was . . . Rachael didn't even know who might have a key. Barbara Wright's feet rested at the entrance, left arm up, right one down. "I don't get it. Even if the door was closed, she must have been standing close enough to reach out and open it."

"It's hard to picture," Ellie agreed. "She knocks the jar off, or it slips out of her hand—"

"Hard enough to picture Barbara Wright dropping *anything*."

"—then maybe she gasps, or automatically tries to get a deep breath before running for it, the fumes seize up her lungs, and she collapses before she can even get out of the room."

"I guess," Rachael muttered.

It seemed much too abrupt—too *quick*—for a perfectly healthy, grown woman to be alive one moment and dead the next. But unexpected deaths were their stock in trade. Rachael would not waste time dwelling on the unfairness of fates or the vagaries of existence.

She said, "Okay. I've got to inform the director and EMS should be here in five or ten. Would you stay here, keep everyone out?"

"Of course. And I'm sorry, Rachael," she added as Rachael turned to leave. "She was your coworker. You must have known her for a while."

"Thank you. But honestly, I don't think anyone knew Barbara Wright."

She closed the lab door behind her and briefly considered Calvin or Carter or—Caleb, that was it. Leave him here as the attendees trickled back from lunch, or . . .

"Thank you for your help. Please come with me again. We have to tell the director and then I might need you to guide the EMS techs when they get here."

After a glance back at Ellie, he fell into step beside Rachael without a word. Her low heels clacked against the hard floor as she set a brisk pace to the admin anteroom. *Keep calm and flesh out the to-do list.*

So many details had to be worked out all at once. The attendees for the Collecting Evidential DNA class were supposed to be in that lab all afternoon, but she could get Ellie to move up tomorrow's lecture to keep them in the classroom. The classes had to go on. The attendees and their agencies had paid big bucks to send them, and the loss of an instructor wouldn't be a good enough reason to lop off the last bit of the course.

Then Barbara's family would have to be informed—that unhappy task would fall to the director, or, if he chose to wimp out, the sheriff's officers. They would be on their way, alerted by the 911 dispatchers. The small cities around them were not large enough to have their own police forces, so the Anne Arundel County Sheriff's Department handled all law enforcement needs. Rachael had met a few deputies over the years and had no complaints.

The institute's secretary, Carrie, would have to find Barbara's next of kin in her records—Rachael couldn't recall the woman ever mentioning a family. And Rachael would have to call a friend at the American Academy of Forensic Sciences to tell them Barbara wouldn't be presenting her theories, as well as Caltech to tell them Barbara wouldn't be taking that new job she'd been so looking forward to.

Back to the attendees. They'd be informed, of course; as trained investigators they knew something was up the moment Rachael walked away from lunch. But they were only visitors, not likely to get too upset about an instructor they'd only known since last week.

Locard staff would be allowed to go home if they felt the need. Research could wait a day, and Ellie, who didn't know Barbara, and Rachael were the only ones needed for the afternoon sessions.

Rachael doubted anyone would feel the need. If Barbara Wright had formed a close friendship during her four years at the Locard, Rachael had never heard of it.

* * *

Ellie stood guard at the door to the hallway. As attendees from both courses became bored enough to wander out into the open or head to the restroom, she told them that there had been a delay and they should just stay on break until she and Rachael could start again. Few asked a single question; a *delay* could be anything from running out of latex gloves to Barbara binge-watching TikTok videos. Their workday came stuffed with others' issues; they didn't go looking for it when off duty.

She used the sink to rinse off her fingers, though most of the burning sensation had already faded. A first aid kit had been mounted to the wall, but she didn't bother to raid it. The skin hadn't broken, and trying to bandage each one would only call attention to them. Besides, the first time she washed her hands, they'd get all wet and she'd have to start over, right?

What a way to start her Locard career. She hoped it wasn't a bad omen, then reminded herself that she didn't believe in omens. Whatever else the Beck family might be, they weren't superstitious.

Emergency Medical Services came, saw, and found nothing they could do. They pronounced Barbara Wright deceased and took all their equipment away again. The sheriff himself, a lanky man named Tom Medina, responded to the scene and now stood surveying the body and its surroundings with a thoughtful air.

"And the hydrochloric acid?" he asked. "That's what I'm smelling?"

Rachael told him yes.

"I thought that stuff just burned you."

"The fumes, if thick enough, burn the inside of the nose and mouth and lungs, just as it burns skin. The person chokes, the larynx constricts, and they suffocate."

He crouched down to take a look at the inside doorknob. There were no visible signs that Barbara had tried desperately to open it, no scratches or dents. Ellie knew, because she'd done the same thing while waiting for him to arrive.

The sheriff asked, "Why have such dangerous stuff around? What do you use it for?"

Rachael said, "A number of things—extracting DNA from tissues, working with metals, testing drugs. It's a hydrolyzing agent, among other things."

He looked up at them with light blue eyes under a mane of dark brown hair, atop a thick, but not ridiculous, mustache. It gave the fortyish man a boyish air and he had a grin to match. "I'm going to pretend I know what that means. After all, I'm just a simple country boy."

"I don't believe that for a minute," Ellie said.

This only made him grin wider, and he straightened up. "Oh, it's true. We may be less than an hour from DC, but we're a world apart. I don't know much about chemistry. I certainly didn't know you could die just from breaking a jar—I'll have to be more careful with my uncle's moonshine. Is this a common accident in labs?"

"Not that I know of," Rachael answered, her voice uncertain. "Anyone can have a chemical spill, I suppose . . . but *dying* of HCl fumes . . ."

Ellie asked, "But if her face is right in it?"

Tom said, "Her face *is* right in it."

Rachael said, "Yes, but she shouldn't have been unconscious that quickly. Anyone can go without air for a few seconds, long enough to get out the door."

Ellie had guessed the same, but she wasn't a pathologist. She truly didn't know how easy it might be for someone to die of toxic inhalation.

"Does the area figure into it?" Tom asked.

At their blank stares he clarified: "The airspace would af-

fect the concentration, right? So it would make a difference
if this little door was open or closed?"

"Yes," Rachael said. "Definitely."

"Why would she close it?"

"Don't know," Ellie said.

Sheriff Medina stood back, held the door at a 90-degree
angle to the wall, and let go. At first it didn't move, but then
it swung, silently, smoothly, until its inner edge rested
against the jamb.

"Huh. But you found it completely closed?" he asked
Ellie.

"Yes."

"Huh," he said again. "She have any medical conditions?"

"Not that I know of," Rachael said again.

"I see two possibilities," Tom theorized. "The fumes
made her choke, first. Then that brought on a heart attack
and she collapsed and either died outright or breathed this
stuff in until she suffocated. Or, she slipped in the liquid and
knocked the side of her head on the floor, passed out, and
breathed this stuff in until she suffocated. This'll have to go
to autopsy, you realize."

"Yes, of course," Rachael agreed.

"There's no sign of acid on her shoes," Ellie said. She
knew, because she'd also looked at *that* while waiting for
him to arrive.

Tom considered this. "Maybe she tripped first. That's
how the jar got broken in the first place."

Ellie thought, then nodded, and noticed Rachael doing
the same. That would explain how the very precise doctor
allowed such a messy accident. Perhaps even a sudden
aneurysm, so that Barbara had been dead before she even hit
the floor.

But what did she trip on? Ellie wondered. A small metal
bar marked the threshold. From that area the floor continued straight and even, uncracked.

"You ever see anything like this?" she asked Rachael, knowing her experience as the DC medical examiner.

"Yes," the woman admitted. "Not many, but some industrial accidents from spills and leaks—sewer workers, a grain elevator operator. People don't realize how dangerous certain fumes can be."

"What's this?" Tom pulled a latex glove from a box mounted on the wall and picked up a white plastic card from the floor near Barbara's ankle. It had a ring with a spring clip through a hole in the rigid plastic. "Her keycard?"

Ellie said, "She wore it clipped to her belt loop."

"Must have been dislodged when she fell." He handed it to her.

I wanted a key to my new office, she thought, *but not this way.*

The medical examiner's team, an investigator and two ambulance crew members—more commonly known as body snatchers—arrived. The investigator asked the same questions as the sheriff, got the same answers, and then pulled Barbara Wright's stiffening corpse from the small closet to get a better look. The acid left a smear across the linoleum.

All her clothes were intact, blouse still neatly tucked into her pants, a long-sleeved lab coat over them. The investigator pulled the blouse loose to check the lividity, but it appeared consistent with her position—cherry red on the front of her torso, where the blood had pooled and begun to coagulate, and, when turned, white across her back.

The skin damage from the acid formed angry red blotches across Barbara's chin and cheek, though one circle on her right cheek had been pressed too firmly to the tile to let the acid penetrate. The acid had also shriveled sections of her hair and stained the collar of the lab coat.

"There's no glass," Ellie said.

"True," Rachael said with a thoughtful tone. A few shards stuck to the woman's cheek and hair, but no tiny chips of brown glass could be seen on the white coat.

"It's all over there." Tom pointed to the closet's interior, and Ellie saw what he meant. The jar had not shattered into a million pieces, instead separating into a few large chunks with wickedly sharp edges. There were smaller grains here and there, but for the most part the glass could be accounted for in a foot-wide diameter next to where the head had been.

Ellie still didn't like it. It seemed too quick, too neat, and too abrupt an end for a vital, active person, but that could be Ellie's own defense mechanism. She, too, now worked in a forensic lab, in the same surroundings that had just killed Barbara Wright. Maybe she didn't want to admit how tenuous life could be.

Besides, what was the alternative explanation? Suicide? Murder? Who would try to kill themselves or someone else with such an uncertain, unlikely method? That seemed even more far-fetched than popping into a closet to grab something and never making it back out.

The body snatchers loaded Rachael's colleague onto a gurney and Tom Medina finished up his notes. Rachael called the maintenance staff to handle the chemical spill.

With an uncertain expression on her face, Rachael watched the gurney and its attendants round the end of the hallway. Ellie already knew that her new boss rarely looked uncertain.

Rachael said, "I feel like I should go with her, attend the autopsy. I, at least, owe her that. But we'd have to get Gary to take over your class and you'd have to do the body farm part with mine—"

"I can—"

"No, that's all right. I know the ME here and she's great. She doesn't need me looking over her shoulder. You have something you can present this afternoon? We need to keep them out of the lab until the spill is cleaned."

"Yes, of course. I can do the section on genealogical tracing."

"All right. We'd better get back to work, then, before we lose any more of the afternoon." Rachael sucked in such a deep breath that Ellie patted her arm in sympathy. "On with the show."

Chapter 6

Rachael led her group of attendees up the paved path from the building toward the parking lot, letting the chattering of the birds in the trees reassure her. The world went on, the day's work continued despite the accident. It seemed cruel to think of a colleague's death as simply a disruption in the workday, but that workday happened to be Rachael's responsibility. So . . . on with it.

The Locard's small "body recovery practice sites" consisted of two separate clearings in the woods off the paved walkway from the building to the parking lot. They were both thirty feet into the woods, but one or both could still make for an odiferous trip to one's vehicle during the summer months. Animals were donated to science from the surrounding farms and animal shelters, after deaths from natural causes or accidents—this made for an unsteady supply, so the Locard had to take what they could get.

Pigs were the preferred corpses due to their lack of fur and similar fat ratio to humans. Weather could affect decomposition rates, and insects and scavengers had their preferences, so the two species did not break down identically—but it was close enough for jazz, as Rachael's old music teacher used to say.

She had no interest in going through the licensing and legal hoops to work with human bodies like the original body farm in Tennessee. That was fine for their extended studies, but much more hassle than she needed for two-week courses in buried-body recovery or outdoor scene documentation.

And, if she was honest with herself, she feared community response to using real humans. Medina hadn't been kidding when he said they were an hour and a world apart from DC. The people of Fairhaven and Chesapeake Beach and Holland Point were plenty sophisticated, but lived there instead of DC for a reason—they wanted the peace and beauty and tranquility of the natural surroundings. They didn't want to drive past a constant reminder of what the evil of violence and hatred could necessitate. The Locard sat on ten acres of forest, so it *felt* as if they were in the middle of nowhere, a world unto themselves, but that wasn't quite true. At the next city council meeting, announcing the inclusion of real human corpses might bring either passionate denouncements and/or demands for removal. Additionally, local teens could sneak onto the grounds to mess with the bodies—something both disrespectful *and* not conducive to the students' training.

Although not visible from the facility or the road, the Locard sat surrounded by a ten-foot-high chain-link fence topped with barbed wire. Though a determined and agile person could get over that. As Rachael had in her teen years . . . probably still could, though she wasn't about to find out.

The rain had stopped and by now the narrow asphalt sidewalk appeared dry with the occasional puddle in uneven spots. Dampness and the songs of birds filled the air. Leaves overhead showered them with a few drops whenever the wind blew, but the temperature hovered at a balmy 70 degrees. Only Tony, the homicide detective from New Mexico, and Farida, from Saudi Arabia, wore jackets. Both were accustomed to 70 being the low for the day rather than the high.

"Have you even met him?" she heard Stef ask Farida.

"Of course I have met him!" A short pause. "Once."

They were walking behind Rachael, and she moved to the side so they would be three abreast. The Saudi's two bodyguards walked behind them, chuckling over their own conversation. They never seemed overly concerned about what Farida did, and Rachael got the impression that their presence was simply to check some box on a list of traditions, not a task that either they or Farida took very seriously. And the young woman hardly seemed a difficult charge—she kept her hair covered, wore Western but loose-fitting clothes, and never spoke of going out to bars with the other students.

"Your mother expects you to marry someone you've only met once?"

Farida spoke with both annoyance and certainty. "No! I do not have to marry anyone unless I want to. But, yes, we would not be dating for a year like you do here. It is not like that . . . and I have not said okay yet."

"Your parents think he's a catch?"

"My father wishes he had more of the Koran memorized. And my mother says she would prefer that I never marry and would stay home with her forever, but that she knows life does not work that way. I have to have a chance to make a home of my own. I do like him. I asked him what he wants to do with his life and he said he wants to work in renewable energy. We all know oil will be a thing of the past soon and the country needs to diversify."

"What about you?" Rachael said. "What do you want to do?"

"This! I want to be CSI. I want to solve crimes."

Stef asked, "What does the fiancé think of that? I've had two different guys dump me after I described some gunshot wounds."

"He said I can keep working after we get married. He thinks women should have a career. It might be hard to manage, once I have babies, but it can be done. I have plenty of little cousins who can help with day care."

A short silence ensued. Rachael could hear the birds in the trees and a rustle in the brush—probably a raccoon. Then Stef asked the tough question, because Stef always asked the tough question: "What if he changes his mind?"

Farida's smile faded. "Then I do not know. The truth is, that is how we pick husbands. Not by what they look like or how much money they have or what job they do."

She didn't finish the thought. Stef did, albeit gently. "But by how much freedom they'll allow you?"

"We have to think of these things." *Unlike you*, Rachael finished in her mind.

Farida murmured something in Arabic, ending in something that sounded like *anamoova moovavatsi*.

"What's that?"

"Something my father says: 'Be wary around your enemy once, and your friend a thousand times. A double-crossing friend knows more about what harms you.'"

"I get it," Stef said. "It's the people close to you who know what buttons to push."

Rachael said, "They're the most dangerous." The young Saudi was so bright and bubbly and bursting with enthusiasm for the world ahead . . . and sometimes, listening to her, Rachael wanted to weep.

They reached the placard in the weeds reading BODY SITE 1 and turned up the narrow path. The fallen leaves formed a carpet over the wet earth.

Stef asked, "Is he cute at least?"

This brought a smile back to Farida's face. "I think so! He has a nice smile. I . . . I have a good feeling about it."

"I wish you the best," Stef said with solemn sincerity. "I just can't wrap my head around an arranged marriage—"

Rachael said, "I don't know. The first coroner I worked under was from India and she didn't even get to meet her husband first, but she was crazy about him and they were happy as little clams."

"Clams?" Farida frowned. "The—mollusk?"

Rachael laughed. "It's a saying here, 'happy as a clam.' Which doesn't make any sense if you think about it, because I have no idea how we'd be able to tell when a clam was happy. Okay, people, here lies our dear Chester."

They gathered around, a series of strings and stakes designating the walkways. The goat had been half-buried, though falling leaves occasionally covered up the rest of him. He had been there for three weeks, past the bloating stage, well into the active decay stage in which the cadaver would lose the most mass. The skin, under the fur, had darkened irregularly. The internal organs and muscle had liquefied and begun to purge through the body's orifices, soaking into the ground around it. On top of that, maggots had been steadily working away at the flesh and tissues. In another week the body would begin to lose its identity as a body, per se, its edges literally melting into its surroundings.

It *did* smell. The sickly odor of really bad garbage wafted up in a constant layer, mixing with the damp earth scent of the usual decay of leaves and wood, the moisture in the sky, and ocean salt, yet nothing the participants couldn't handle. Working in open air instead of, say, a living room made an intense difference.

"I would think the temperature is too cool for maggots," Tony said. The homicide detective used a ruler to estimate the height of the body, making a note in the class log about how much it had changed since their first day.

Rachael said, "No, they can tolerate cold much better than you'd think. You can freeze them for about a day and thaw them out again and they'll still be active. They get dormant at around fifty degrees, but if you really want to kill them, you'll want to keep them below freezing temps for more than forty-eight hours."

Oliver, from Montana, held one end of Farida's tape measure as they noted how far the decomposition fluids had caked the dirt. "So they pass out every night when it gets cold and then wake up in the morning?"

"Maybe. Or they work on the inside tissues. The decomposition process generates its own heat."

"Yuk," Stef said. "And yuk."

Though they preferred pigs for this exercise, Rachael had been on the lookout for something else for this particular class. She'd had no idea how Farida and her bodyguards might react if presented with a pig, given Muslim edicts against pork. Technically, as long as it was not regarded as food, a pig could be viewed as simply an animal, like any other. In practice, however, there were no guarantees. Farida might have a virulent mindset against even seeing the animal—or not care a whit.

Rachael had no way to know, didn't want to ask, and didn't want to make any student uncomfortable. A goat neatly avoided all those issues. She'd told no one of these machinations. Seeing Farida's delight in all this new knowledge, Rachael felt glad she'd taken the trouble.

"We're all familiar with maggots and flies and their predictable life and migration cycles, but there are many other insects and arthropods that can give us a postmortem interval—PMI—timeline," Rachael continued. "You'll need an entomologist to examine them, but the information can be well worth the trouble."

"We don't have an entomologist," someone said.

"Your state lab system will have someone, or know someone. Try the nearest natural history museum, if nothing else. You'll need them because estimating age of some insects is not easy—in ametabolous insects, like silverfish, the young ones look just the same as mature ones, only smaller. With hemimetabolous, like cockroaches and grasshoppers, they go from egg to nymph to adult, so they look a little different, but have no pupal stage. And of course, for some insects, the pupal stage forms a black box in the middle of our timeline, since it can last days to years. It can also vary within the type of insect, depending on weather—it might last longer if the season hasn't changed. Sorry if I'm being a bit general. Normally, *our* entomologist would be covering this with you, but she's in Scotland helping out her mother this month."

A heavyset woman from Florida poked at a stick with one toe. She had a deep tan and three white patches on one arm where melanomas had been removed; Rachael absently hoped she'd become a convert to sunscreen. "How do we know what bugs are here because of the body, and what bugs just . . . live here?"

The young man next to her giggled. "Sorry—I suddenly pictured this beetle out for a stroll and getting caught up in our jars. 'I don't know anything about that body! It's got nothing to do with me!'"

Rachael laughed too. "To answer your question, we don't."

"So we have to collect every single one?" the woman asked, profound distaste on her face.

"Representative sample," Stef said, enunciating every syllable.

Rachael said, "Yes—of course you don't have to spend the whole excavation chasing every bug. Ideally, get your entomologist to come to the site with you and do their own collection. They'll know an aphid from a bedbug and have plenty of experience in collection. But if that's not an option, then . . . keep calm and pick up bugs."

She passed around jars and spread out the rest of the equipment on an empty paper bag, then demonstrated the proper collection and labeling techniques. They needed to collect insects and arachnids in two ways. Some would be put in specimen jars with air holes or maybe vermiculite for the larvae (it would allow for movement and also absorb excess liquids) so that they could live and perhaps continue to grow for entomologists to identify. A similar sampling would be put in jars with cotton balls soaked in ethyl acetate and killed, to arrest their development right at the point of body discovery. This would provide an end point to the timeline, from which they could work backward.

"Temperature and weather conditions also need to be recorded." Rachael handed a clipboard to the particularly squeamish woman, adding: "You can use this thermometer to record the ground temperature. At a real scene you have to get the air temp, the temperature at the top of the corpse, the temp under the body mass, general ground temperature from about five inches down, and the maggot mass temp if you have one. Even after you've removed the body and you're done with the scene, you're going to want to come back for a couple of days to record temperatures. If your pathologist can estimate how long the victim's been dead or, better yet, who they are, you'll need the historical data going back to when they disappeared. If your experts are local, they might have the information, but if not, you'll have to get with your closest weather station. This will be almost as important to the timeline as what bugs are present."

An attendee in charge of photography used his cell phone to take pictures of their crime scene, being sure to get the body from all angles and close-ups of anything interesting, such as a series of gashes on the goat's back. He asked what kind of animal had done that.

"A raccoon?" Stef suggested.

"Most likely," Rachael said. "We have a lot of wildlife in the area, but the fence would keep out larger types, like bears and bobcats."

"I hope so," a sergeant from Chicago said, and glanced about with sudden concern.

"We also have beavers, muskrats, foxes, even minks, but those wouldn't be interested in a dead animal."

A rustling behind them made several students jump, waiting for a crazed muskrat to attack. But a much more adorable face appeared from around a sugar maple tree, then stopped short when it saw them.

"How did you get in here?" Rachael asked the dog. "You haven't been disturbing our crime scene, have you?"

"Looks like a German shepherd," someone said.

Another disagreed. "Coloring's too light."

"Why is that here?" Farida asked, her eyes sparkling at the bundle of fur. She craned her neck to get a better look and adjusted her headscarf. Usually a solid color, this one had deep blues and greens subtly melted together. She crouched with the other dog lovers, all of them trying to entice the puppy over to their fingers. The non–dog people remained upright.

This prompted another cultural question from Stef: "You're not allowed to have dogs in your country, are you?"

"Of course we can have pets." Farida's tone grew defensive under Stef's constant scrutiny, but then she added: "Not many do."

Rachael also lowered into a squat, patting the soggy leaves in front of her. "Come here. We're going to have to find you a home that's not on a body farm."

But the puppy wasn't ready to make a friend. It skittered away from her, circled the tree, and shot from the other side of the trunk to make a beeline for the two Saudi men, waiting along the trail back to the paved walkway. They separated quickly to let the dog fly up the leaf-strewn path between them, moving with such haste it made Rachael laugh. The puppy might as well have been a mouse in an old cartoon.

All the same, she would have to speak to the maintenance crew about checking the perimeter fence—it must have wriggled under the chain link, or they had a gap somewhere. "He's a good example of the hazards of outdoor scenes, and probably not the only animal active out here since yesterday. If you noticed, some of the maggots have migrated to a piece of skin over here. I doubt the maggots carried it."

"These are smaller than the ones on the body," Farida noted.

Rachael said, "We'll have to collect some from each site and compare them to our reference charts in the lab. Who volunteers?"

No one did.

Chapter 7

Ellie lectured half the afternoon about ways to extract DNA from paper, then started in on new ways to extract nuclear DNA from hair. By five o'clock the attendees were showing signs of fatigue, and she wrapped it up.

They had, of course, been informed of Barbara Wright's death—Ellie said that she had "passed away," but made no mention of an accident. Audible guesses were made, suggesting heart attack or aneurysm. Ellie said she didn't know anything more, which was true-ish enough, and this initial buzz of conversation faded into acceptance. People died every day, and no one knew that better than this group. You just had to hope it wasn't anyone you cared about.

Caleb grabbed a cup of coffee from the classroom urn, offering to pour her one, but she turned him down. Sleeping always became enough of a challenge without caffeine after three p.m. Craig Bennett, the NYPD sergeant, asked her if adhesives interfered with DNA and she told him no, not to her knowledge. Profiles could still be obtained from fingerprints after items were treated with superglue—not ideal, of course, but possible. Alyssa left without a word; Ellie still didn't know if the woman didn't recognize her or what. Had she changed that much in five or six years? Her hair had grown out, and sure, maybe some more lines in her face, but you'd think spending four hours stringing blood spatter patterns in an un-air-conditioned apartment in Dallas would stick in someone's mind.

But Aunt Katey had always told her not to take others' reactions personally: *"Everyone lives in their own little world. Ninety-nine times out of a hundred, they're not even thinking about you."*

The attendees didn't linger, heading through the hallways in a patchy line, and Ellie went to find Rachael. The other classroom stood utterly empty, the automatic overhead lights already out. But the next lab to the west glowed, and Ellie found her there. This room smelled less of acid and more of cyanoacrylate—otherwise known as superglue.

The assistant dean of the Locard Institute had collected every piece of the broken glass jar that had killed Barbara Wright and now placed each piece, gingerly, in the superglue tank in the latent prints lab. Someone else, Ellie realized, found the doctor's death very strange.

By way of greeting, she stated the obvious. "You're printing the jar?"

"Call me crazy." Rachael moved the last shard of glass from a metal tray to the vented bottom of a vacuum tank about twice the size of a mini-fridge. "But the medical examiner's office called. A friend of mine did the post. She said Barbara had some pulmonary edema, petechiae, more or less consistent with inhaling caustics, but none of the lesions to the nasal cavities that she would have expected."

"So . . . she didn't suffocate?"

"She did . . . but from HCl fumes?" Rachael used an undersized plastic spoon to scoop powdered superglue into a flat foil dish. The dish rested on a digital scale, with powder added until the numbers satisfied her. "She also had a decent hematoma on her right temple, about here."

"Which probably occurred when she hit the floor?"

"I suppose." Clearly, the good doctor had her reservations. She latched the door of the vacuum chamber. "I described the scene, and Betsy's thinking that Barbara had a heart attack. Her coronary arteries showed blockages—Barbara didn't have the best eating habits—and some atherosclerotic lesion."

"Coronary occlusion?"

"Very good!" Rachael said with approval, and flipped a switch at the top of the chamber. It would run a preset program, sucking the air from the space so that the cyanoacrylate fumes would spread evenly over and through the target items. A water-filled humidifier added the necessary humidity, while the hot plate heated the powdered superglue to 235 degrees so that the solid changed to gas with only a brief stop at the liquid phase. "Occlusion would indicate a heart attack. *Could* indicate. And she could have hit her head on a shelf as she pitched forward. Or the floor."

Ellie said, "The part of her right cheek with no burns . . . I assume that would be the spot of skin pressed most tightly to the floor. It made me think that the acid pooled around her face after she hit the ground. She didn't land *in* the puddle."

The fume chamber began to hum. Rachael would have to wait for fifteen or twenty minutes, then turn it off.

Ellie continued, "Which could make sense if she and the jar fell at the same time. Say, for example, her heart seizes up. She starts to collapse, drops the jar, hits the right side of her head on the shelf, lands on the floor, as does the jar, which breaks and the acid spreads. She's already dead, so she's not breathing in the caustic fumes. I'm sorry, by the way. I hope I don't sound callous—how long had you worked together?"

Rachael pulled off her remaining glove. "About four years. We weren't close. I wouldn't even say we were friends. We never *conflicted*, exactly . . . other than her shuffling classes off on other instructors so she could prepare her presentation. Frankly, her theory was fairly simple—the actual work, presuming it ever gets off the ground, would be time consuming, but to describe the process can not be that difficult. I didn't see why she needed so many man-hours to get it ready. Other than that, I had no complaints about her work."

"Why would she have needed the hydrochloric acid in the first place?"

"Making up lysis buffers?"

"Oh, of course. She was planning to do Rapid DNA of all the students' samples."

"I would have expected her to have those reagents ready, not making them up during the lunch break. But like I said, she had short-timers pretty bad. She mentally checked out of this job months ago."

Ellie pulled the dead woman's keycard out of her pocket. "Thanks for letting me keep this, but I haven't even used it yet. I should go get my box out of Hector's office and put it in Barbara's before he locks up my car keys for the night."

"Hang on to it, then, but I wouldn't worry. Hardly anyone locks their offices . . . other than Barbara. I have to admit that security," she went on, with a more pensive air, "is not very tight. Beyond locked outside doors with cameras over them, there's not much. The keycards are access only, they don't record entries or exits. We have no interior cameras, though the outside ones do cover the entire perimeter of the building. I mean, we're a school for adults on a gated compound in the middle of nowhere. There's nothing to steal, unless you're a rogue scientist who covets our homemade amino acid rapid imager, and that would be a hell of a thing to tuck under your arm as you duck out a window."

Ellie laughed at the image of a thief carting off the chunky machine, which used alternate light beams to locate and scan fingerprints without powders or dyes. Then she stifled the grin. A woman *had* died.

"We're not Microsoft or Chase Manhattan, not a target for corporate espionage or identity thieves. No treasures to break in for and no prisoners to break out. Maybe we've been operating too long like we're some startup, a bunch of kids renting space in a basement. It always felt like that here. Feels like that here. I just never worried about it." Rachael leaned back against the counter, weariness clouding her face. "Maybe I should have worried about it."

"Maybe not," Ellie said. It *could* be just a heart attack.

"The only thing for which we *do* have a measure of security is the client files. Once a case is completed, we take everything related to it off the server and write it to a disk or a drive. Our IT guy is a bit paranoid about hackers. All of it is labeled with a system that makes Dewey Decimal look like an ABC primer *and* is stored in the vault."

"You have a vault?"

"Sounds fancier than it is—it's a huge safe in a closet in the basement, up a short hallway from the cafeteria. Lord knows what the school used it for. Security on that is OD, bells and whistles and cameras and weight sensors. Anyone who tried to dig up dirt on one of our high-profile clients would find themselves entombed until Tom came to slap the cuffs on. That leaves me little to worry about other than local teenagers cutting the fence to visit our body farms. The *CSI* craze is still going strong in this country."

"Has that ever happened?"

"Not so far. Had a dog hanging around today, but that's okay. I want to give our attendees every example of real-life hazards to the crime scene. Maybe a satanic cult dismembered your body, and maybe it was just the landlady's poodle."

Ellie didn't stifle her chuckle this time, then nodded at the pieces of broken glass in the superglue chamber. "Are you going to dye-stain those?"

"I'll use RAY if I need it." Superglue turned fingerprint ridges to a plastic white structure. The stain consisted of three dyes—rhodamine, ardrox, and Basic Yellow 40—and would change those white ridges to a fluorescent yellow, helpful to distinguish them from patterned or "busy" backgrounds. But if the white superglued ridges were well formed, they might be easily seen against a dark brown glass substrate, making the dye stain unnecessary. In either event the prints needed to sit overnight for the polymer chains to harden.

"What are you hoping to find?" Ellie asked.

"I don't know. Barbara's prints, and only hers, I guess, but we don't know that she even held the jar. She might have only knocked it over when she fell. And prints wouldn't mean much, anyway, since everyone in the building uses that chemical storage closet. Even the attendees—they've been here for a week and a half and mixed up reagents last week to collect DNA from guns. Or someone might have picked up the HCl to move it to get to something else. Those shelves are pretty packed." Rachael rubbed one temple. "I guess I just want to know how a coworker—even one I didn't particularly like—is here one minute and gone the next."

"That's understandable," Ellie said.

The chamber beeped. Rachael flicked the switch and cracked the door. The faint odor of hot superglue wafted out. "But not very professional."

"It is in our line of work."

She must have found that either comforting or amusing, because the crease in Rachael's brow flattened out. She left the chamber as it was, flicking out the light and closing the door to the lab. The women wound their way back around to the exit closest to the parking-lot walkway, dodging other staff wrapping up their days. Attendees who hadn't rented cars and needed the shuttle to the hotel loitered around the door. No one wanted to wait outside, where it had begun to rain once more in violent, heavy drops.

"Crap," Ellie said as distant thunder sent a tiny vibration up through the floor. "We're going to be dripping wet before we get near our cars."

"What are you doing tonight?"

"Unpacking boxes and cramming to be ready for tomorrow's lectures."

"How's the house?"

"Um." She'd been so eager to get out of her postdivorce apartment that she'd bought the house on nothing but one short visit and snapshots on Zillow. "A complete mess right now, but it will be great with a little TLC. Maybe a lot of TLC. And some paint."

"Got time for dinner? My mother is making her lemon chicken. Melts in your mouth."

Ellie opened her mouth, shut it, opened it again. "That sounds fabulous."

"Oh, believe me, it is," Rachael told her. "If you have any doubt, my mother will tell you so at least three times."

Chapter 8

Rachael lived in a tidy, two-story Colonial done up in medium gray with white trim, surrounded by wide lawns and a driveway leading to a rear garage. Ellie parked her Mustang at a respectful distance up the drive and wondered if the woman would mind if she, Ellie, stole her color scheme.

Her shoes squished slightly as she got out. They'd had to brave a monsoon to get from the Locard to the parking lot. It ceased, as if someone had turned off a tap, as soon as they pulled onto Rachael's street, but the reprieve wouldn't last. The clouds had more where that had come from and were keeping it zipped up, only to lull her into a false sense of relief. Ellie could feel them lurking overhead, hidden in the dark. Waiting.

The neighborhood smelled like wet trees and nothing moved on the block except the wind—occupants were inside their homes staying dry and out of the deluge.

The front door, with its elaborate inlaid glass design, flew open as soon as the cars stopped.

"Mamamamama!" A three-foot-tall blur of curly hair and

blue T-shirt streaked across the soggy grass and threw itself against Rachael's knees before Ellie could even get out of the driver's seat. Her new boss shifted her tote bag and picked up the child in a fierce hug. This lowered his volume only slightly.

"I apologize to your eardrums," Rachael said over his shoulder. "This is Danton. He is going to be three in five months. Look here, Danton, this is Ellie. Can you say hi, while we get off the wet grass that you're not supposed to be running around in your socks in?"

The boy dutifully lifted his head to gaze at Ellie, considered her carefully for a moment or two, but either her presence or the sudden boom of thunder overhead made him bury his cheek in Rachael's shoulder once again.

Ellie laughed. "Maybe later."

Rachael's mother, Loretta, greeted Ellie with a hug. She had Rachael's eyes, but a waistline that belied her talent in the kitchen—which did, as promised, smell divine. "Welcome, welcome. It's about time my girl had someone to talk to other than me and this little bundle of terror. I'd prefer someone of the male variety, single with a good job and a bit of charm, but you'll do."

"I appreciate it," Ellie said.

They'd arrived just in time to keep Loretta happy, and Ellie found herself enthusiastically devouring everything Loretta heaped upon her plate. It felt as if she ate more in one sitting than she had in months. But if nothing else, she knew how to be a guest, so she sang for her supper with a nearly nonstop description of her most interesting cases with the FBI's Evidence Response Team.

At first she hesitated, not knowing what might be appropriate dinner conversation. Then Rachael assured her: "My mother has heard so many descriptions of decomposed bodies, she could paint one—"

"Got better things to paint," her mother commented.

"—and has been sworn to secrecy so often, it's become second nature. I think most of her friends believe I don't have a job, since they never hear about it."

Loretta pantomimed zipping her mouth shut and tossing away a key.

"Plus, this one hasn't quite mastered three-syllable words. So I think we'll be okay."

Conversation naturally turned to the death of Rachael's coworker.

"That woman?" Loretta speared a noodle. "I thought she was kind of a bitch."

"You only met her once," Rachael reminded her.

"Once was enough. Cold as a day in February. Asked her why she only used medications for genetic abnormalities in her research instead of all illnesses, and she said she didn't have time to explain it to someone without a medical background. I guess I wasn't important enough for her to bother."

"It wasn't you." Rachael convinced Danton to try another bite of chicken, though he seemed more interested in the noodle salad. "She treated everyone that way. She used up all Gary's colored markers to make her charts. She told Hector that a crime analyst shouldn't be a real position—it could be done faster, and with less drama, by a computer. She never did the annual training course in cybersecurity until Cameron complained to the dean that she'd downloaded two viruses doing internet searches—get with Cameron tomorrow to get your keycard fixed, by the way."

"Will do," Ellie said.

"He's—he was—convinced that she was a spy for *Access Hollywood*. We did some work for that actress, the one in the latest superhero movie—"

"Lili Martin," her mother supplied.

"She had a stalker, and the tabloids found out that we proved her hairstylist had sent the letters. *I* always thought that Lili alerted the media herself, figuring that once the guy had been arrested and she felt safe, she might as well get a little publicity out of the whole ordeal. But Cam insisted he'd seen Barbara accessing the safe. Which isn't possible, only the director and I have the key and the combination. Cameron's a little . . . high-strung."

"Just don't wear green," Loretta told Ellie, and picked up her plate. "He don't like it."

Despite the gleaming dishwasher under the counter, she washed and Ellie dried while Rachael gave Danton a bath and read him a bedtime story. Then Loretta excused herself to "nap in front of *America's Got Talent*," and Rachael poured Ellie a glass of wine. Ellie wrapped her still-sensitive fingers around the cool glass and they settled onto a red leather couch.

"Your son is adorable." Ellie knew a lot of parents, and knew quite well the way to their hearts: admire their handiwork.

"Oh, he is. He needs to be. That's why God made two-year-olds so cute—it's protective coloring. Keeps you from killing them."

As Ellie tried to keep from snorting the wine up her nose, Rachael went on. "I adored him from the second he was born, but then I feel like that about all my nephews and nieces—I have five. When Isis died . . . I went to children's services to pick him up. I walked in, took one look at him, and that was it. There was no way I'd ever let him go."

"What about—"

"His father? He's a soldier, currently somewhere in the Middle East. Another one of Isis's brief romances. He's not a *bad* guy," she admitted with obvious reluctance. "But not able to be a parent."

Ellie said, "It's wonderful of you to take him on. That's a big step."

Rachael gave a sound like a snort. "Too big for my husband. He packed and moved out before I'd even moved Danton in."

"Oh my G—"

"We hadn't planned on having children. He's a defense attorney. Picture a type A, power-couple lifestyle of rooftop dinner parties and weekends in Aruba. No room in there for somebody else's kid." She gestured at the cushions beneath them. "That's why I have a leather Brabbu couch with a two-year-old, which is clearly insane."

"I'm so sorry."

Rachael peered into her wineglass, like it might divine the future. "Maybe it was a bad idea from the start . . . the marriage, I mean. Because Danton wasn't the final straw—it was when I said I was going to quit as medical examiner to go full-time at the institute. I'd only been an adjunct professor until then. ME meant too many hours, handling all the supervisory and administrative work and only occasionally able to get into the autopsy suite. Overtime, constant stress. I loved it like anything, but I didn't think I could handle it and still give Danton the attention he needs, that he deserves. The more I think about it . . . I wonder, did he marry me just to have an inside man at the MEs? I don't know. Maybe."

"That would be a bit extreme."

A slight grin. "He was a man of extremes. That's why he was fun—until he wasn't. What's that look? Sorry, I didn't mean to drop the Davies family drama on you—"

"No, it's just funny in a way. Your husband left you because you have a child. Mine left me because I wasn't ready to have one."

Rachael took a turn with the look of shock. "For real?"

"Mm . . . if I'm honest, that's probably only *part* of the reason." She summarized quickly: meeting Adam while in college at Georgetown, marrying him, and getting into the bureau. Adam hankering for a more traditional lifestyle, and just maybe not caring for the esteem Ellie garnered at the bureau. "He had an idea of what he wanted his life to be, and went for it, whether I fit in or not. Like you—maybe it was for the best, to find out early on."

Rachael held out her glass.

Ellie clinked hers against it. "To exes."

"May their souls rot forever in limbo"

Ellie laughed so hard, she nearly spit Pinot Noir all over Rachael's Brabbu couch.

Chapter 9

The storm had grown from nasty to wicked by the time Ellie made her way back to her home near Breezy Point Beach. The trip reminded her just how dark, dark could be. Not even the back roads in West Virginia had seemed as deep with pitch, but she hadn't been old enough to drive then.

She wound up passing her own driveway and having to turn around in the Breezy Point Campground's vacant parking lot. Rain dashed at her car from every direction and the trees seemed to be dancing with it—towering oaks, uniformly large and possibly unstable.

The white house had two stories, with a porch off the front of each, plus a screened-in sunroom, but its cheery exterior disappeared in the gloom of night. She had not left a light on. What was it real estate agents always said? Never buy a house you've only seen once and never buy a house you've seen only at night. She'd violated both, but the idea of morning coffee on the upper porch with the light dawning over the bay and the gentle sound of whispering leaves had clouded her judgment.

At least she'd gotten something with an attached garage and an automatic door opener, and thus made it into the house without having to stop and wring out her clothes.

The usual household tasks—plus changing into yoga pants, filing the last of the house-buying paperwork, picking out clothes for Day Two of her new job—kept her too busy to notice the violent activity outside, but later, seated on the couch staring at an empty fireplace, she heard every crash of thunder and dash of water against the glass in the windows. It seemed a fitting ending to a tumultuous day. But it was only water. It couldn't hurt her, right?

Plenty of other things could.

Ellie's upbringing had been tumultuous as well, in ways that made her predecessor dying on her first day at work a mere inconvenience. Elizabeth Carr had started out in a suburb of Cleveland, Ohio, with loving parents and a large extended family—at least on her mother's side. The Beck clan believed in family, education, and hard work, in that order.

But when Ellie was four, her mother, Claire, died in a car accident. Two days later her father, Jack Carr, decided he might not be cut out for life as a single parent. He didn't just slink away at least; he packed her things and drove her over to her grandmother's. There he'd crouched down to her level and, instead of goodbyes or apologies, said: "Whatever they tell you, it wasn't my fault."

She never saw him again.

Her grandmother had taken her over, with her mother's three siblings to help. Even her mother's cousin in Nevada would fold Ellie into her own gang of four during the summers. But Grandma's health failed long before her spirit did and she decided that Ellie should move three streets over to strict Aunt Rosalie's.

Living there, nine-year-old Ellie had no space of her own, but did have playmates—her cousins Maureen, Margery, and Glen. Uncle Wayne was a good man until the aftereffects of soldiering in the Gulf caught up with him. Rosalie moved the kids elsewhere for a while, without spelling out why. Her three cousins could eventually go back home, but Ellie did not.

Ellie moved instead to Aunt Katey's in West Virginia. She had playmates once again, but this time with totally *un*strict Aunt Katey and her mechanic husband, Terry. Her cousins Rebecca and Melissa were each within a year of the twelve-year-old and thrilled to have a new friend—so thrilled that Ellie became the rope in a pervasive, nonstop, fight-to-the-death round of tug-of-war. Each girl had an endless stock-pile of tears, screams, silent treatments, cutting nicknames, and icy glares in their arsenal.

A few years later she'd argued, as much as a shy fifteen-year-old could argue, when Uncle Paul and his wife, Joanna, wanted the bright Ellie to move in with them and attend a private school in Naples, Florida. But the space and peace quickly soothed any qualms.

The two doctors still had a house there, though they spent most of their time overseas with Doctors Without Borders—*after* they'd made sure Ellie got into her first choice, Georgetown University. But the scholarship didn't cover summer sessions, so she'd fly to LA and another of her mother's cousins, Tommy, with his wife, Valeria, and their two sons. There was no aging out of the Beck family foster care program. A couch would always be provided to flop on, whether you wanted it or not.

She'd met Adam at Georgetown, and finally had her own couch. Their marriage and careers took off from there. And changed. And ended, at least the marriage part.

But now she had a new place and a new friend and, well, a new life. Unlike poor Barbara Wright.

So let the rain dash. This house—other than a brief stay in the postdivorce DC apartment—was the first time she'd had a space that was entirely hers, and hers alone, like, In Her

Entire Life. She thought the roof had all its shingles—she hadn't seen any water damage, had she? And the foundation might be only ten or so feet above sea level, the beach *was* right across the street, for heaven's sake—but she did have flood insurance. Had the agent said anything about flood insurance? And the back door might rattle in the wind like someone was trying to get in—Uncle Wayne would say the whole house had too many access points, with a front door, a door off the dining area out to the screened-in sunroom, a door at the back of the utility room that led to the garage, a back door at the other side of the kitchen, and a door upstairs that opened onto the balcony. But hey, if the fifty-year-old wood caught on fire, she'd have plenty of options.

That back door really *did* sound like someone was trying to get in. She pulled herself away from the cold fireplace—she'd have to get some wood, there was a handy chopping stump in the backyard and an ax in the basement, and she had chopped wood before, right?—and made a circuit of the house. She checked every door and window with a thoroughness that would make Uncle Wayne proud and that she refused to chide herself for. Ellie considered herself never paranoid, but always sensible. Doors had locks for a reason, and no talent, even that of inanimate objects, should be wasted.

The front door entered into the long living room, with the stairs up to the right and an opening to the dining room and kitchen on the left, past the fireplace. The dining room opened to the kitchen on the right and the screened sunporch on the left. The kitchen sat behind the living room, on the other side of the wall. If she could take that wall out, the first floor would become open concept. Mental note: Ask contractor if that's structurally possible. Correction, find contractor first, then ask.

While the stairs to the upstairs led from the living room, the stairs to the basement were placed at the far end of the kitchen, next to a tiny half bath. She flicked on the light and made her way down the steep, bare wood steps. At least the basement didn't also have an exterior door, only high glass block windows, stone walls, and a concrete floor that appeared, to her relief, as dry as desert sands.

With the lower floors secured, she went up to the second. The stairs opened into a wide sitting room—which as yet had nothing to sit *on* except the decorative but uncomfortable straight chair that came with the small desk. She'd get a love seat and a coffee table . . . eventually, perhaps. She'd decorate the walls with the framed art prints and the travel-related hand-me-downs from Uncle Paul and Aunt Joanna's travels. The blowgun from Borneo sat propped against the desk, but she hadn't unpacked the headless statue of Nike made of such pitted and worn marble that Ellie often worried it had been dug up at the Acropolis *sans* permission of the Greek General Directorate of Antiquities and Cultural Heritage.

Double doors led to the upper porch; raindrops assaulted them now, rattling like BBs. A dead bolt had been installed above the knob, but the decorative squares of glass would make it too easy for someone to break one small pane, reach through, and move the thumb turn. Mental note: Switch this out with a keyed dead bolt.

That concluded the doors. She continued the survey with the upstairs windows, quaking as well against the wet wind off the bay, and found the three bedrooms and two baths were as she'd left them—the sparse furniture awry and stuffed with boxes, from which only the necessities, like toothpaste and bras, had been excavated so far.

A crack of thunder split directly over the house, so loudly that she yelped.

And even though damp foundations and damage from falling branches worried her far more at the moment than ghosts and serial killers, she decided one more necessity might be in order.

In one of the many cardboard cartons labeled BOOKS, there were, indeed, many books, but she'd also packed her best jewelry, a stash of three-hundred-odd bills, and a .32-caliber Colt Detective Special—because no one would ever look in a box labeled BOOKS.

It took several tries and many a distracted stroll through literature past before she found the right carton. The revolver and its sack of ammunition were sandwiched between a biology textbook and an Ann Rule paperback. She'd often wondered if her grandfather had bought it because it was cheap—at the time—or because he thought the name was cool. He hadn't had much interest in guns, per se, since this had been the only one he owned, and he didn't even have a holster for it, stowing it carelessly enough to accumulate scratches on the barrel and grip. But he'd died shortly after her fifth birthday—perhaps her grandmother had made him get rid of firearms when a toddler came to live in the house, and he kept this last one purely as a tool for home defense. With a two-inch barrel, it wasn't much good for anything else beyond close combat.

When Ellie had been nine, as her grandmother used her last bits of energy to pack up Ellie's things before moving to a hospice center, Ellie had snuck into the bottom drawer of her grandfather's toolbox in the basement. The box rusted away on a lower shelf among the jars of old screws and extra plastic tubing where Ellie had been looking one day for wire to make a bracelet for her doll. She had never told her grandmother about finding the gun. Maybe her grandmother never knew it was there, and maybe, then, she'd never miss it.

Ellie pulled it out and, with trembling, thin fingers, tried to aim it at the furnace. She knew better than to even put her finger through the trigger guard. A flange over the cylinder chambers covered them from the back, so she twisted her wrist to take a cautious, sidelong glance at the barrel. The chambers were empty. She even took the flashlight off the shelf over the stationery tub to make sure, but its dim, battery-failing light showed nothing in the round holes. The nine-year-old felt relatively certain that the gun was not loaded.

She also took the canvas sack with the jingling, cute little bullets. She didn't know how to load the gun and didn't plan to try. As long as she had it, she could figure the rest out *if* and *when* she really needed to.

Perhaps this was stealing, but she didn't think so. Grandma had told her to take whatever she needed. The house would be sold—indeed, she would be back there many times helping to clean and paint, toward that end—and her grandmother certainly wouldn't need the gun where she was going. Aunt Rosalie would find it and throw it away, or do whatever she had to do to destroy such an awful object. No one would want it, except Ellie; and no one needed it, except Ellie. That little girl was going to be on her own now, she'd heard the visiting nurse say to her aide.

Clearly, Ellie would need all the defense she could muster.

She'd wrapped the gun in an old T-shirt and put the bullets in a bag with some bangle bracelets, where the soft jingling would not be noticed. At Aunt Rosalie's it had never been a problem, buried under her bed where Maureen and Margery were too sweet to invade someone's privacy. When Uncle Wayne's oddities put the whole house on edge, Ellie sewed a false bottom into her backpack, her imperfect seams lost in the dark interior of the bag. It served her well in West Virginia, where even under the intense, pervasive scrutiny of her cousins Melissa and Rebecca, it remained her secret.

Uncle Paul and Aunt Joanna, of course, would never have thought to look through her stuff—she could have packed a couple of grenades, two cats, and a carton of cigarettes in the car to Florida without question. The childless couple had no reason not to trust her, and she never gave them one.

Now she kept the gun cleaned and oiled, paired with fresh ammunition in a nonmusty sack. Still, no holster, but she hardly needed one, wouldn't be carrying the thing around.

Back in her bedroom with the gun, sack, and Ann Rule paperback, she considered her options and found she really only had one: the small drawer in the nightstand. The headboard had no shelves or other compartments and she had seen too many head wounds to want the thing under her pillow. That could end badly.

She didn't truly expect a phantom to come sneaking into her boudoir in the wee hours. The house was quite secure, well lit, and might sit among trees and a backcountry road, but it was hardly isolated—on one side lived an aging teacher of high school physics and on the other an emergency room nurse, her auto mechanic husband, and their three highly energetic children.

Ellie slid the drawer shut and went to find her pajamas and some ointment for her fingers. She hoped her usual insomnia would take a night off. She needed to get to the Locard early in the morning, load up her presentation on genealogical tracing, and be ready for the attendees when they filed in.

It was going to be *such* a good day.

Chapter 10

Rachael did not go directly to her office the following morning, unwittingly postponing her introduction to the crisis of the day. Instead, she first used her passkey to open Barbara Wright's office and plan out what needed to be done. She had promised Ellie an office as part of her position, and while Ellie hadn't said a word about it, the lack of a ready one offended Rachael's sense of order. Rachael had a very firm sense of order.

Barbara had promised to have it largely vacated before Ellie arrived, but clearly hadn't made the effort. Barbara rarely made any effort that didn't directly benefit herself. Three framed photos of the woman with various bigwigs and captains of industry still sat atop the filing cabinet, snacks and juice boxes filled one desk drawer, no less than four sweaters and two jackets hung from a wheeled coatrack. A single box had been packed: a cardboard filing container labeled AAFS in black marker, perfectly centered on the desk blotter.

Rachael lifted the lid. Three thin binders of genetic conditions requiring medication, separated by colored tabs. Printouts—probably Hector's—of murder clusters in various areas of the country. A cute storage box filled with USB drives. It had to be the materials Barbara planned to present at the American Academy of Forensic Sciences' annual meeting, and/or the research she planned to continue at Caltech. Rachael replaced the lid. Clearing this office would take a lot more time than she had, right at that moment— maybe over the weekend. She could bring Danton with her. She'd been trying to make a game of washing counters and wiping windows to convince the boy that cleaning was fun, but so far he hadn't fallen for it. Rachael hoped that meant only that the kid was smart and not that he might take after his mother. Isis had never met a responsibility she wanted any part of.

Voices popped up in the hallway outside, her coworkers gearing up for the day's work. Footsteps and words bounced along the gleaming tiles.

Rachael unplugged and piled up Barbara's laptop, tablet, and cell phone, carrying them upstairs to Agnes's workspace. All three had been sitting on the desk and all three belonged to the Locard; she would have the digital analyst download everything relevant to Locard work. Anything else—personal items, presentations, photos—could be put on an external drive for any of Barbara's heirs or family members. The electronics could then be wiped, updated, and assigned to new staff. Like Ellie.

Any other forensic analyst might flicker an eyebrow in interest at what might be on a colleague's devices; electronic analysis, after all, was like a treasure hunt, you never knew what you might find.

Agnes did not flicker. She merely said she'd get to it, the only time frame she ever promised.

Next, Rachael went to the fingerprinting lab and plucked,

carefully, each piece of broken glass from the superglue chamber. She took her tray of broken glass pieces over to the magnifying lamp and flicked it on.

The magnifying lamp hung at the end of a gooseneck stand, a sort of crane, so that the lamp hung in space and could be raised, lowered, or twisted. Small lights were mounted on its underside for extra illumination—not only white light of varying intensity, but ultraviolet and infrared if needed.

Unfortunately, none of it helped. Rachael lifted each piece and turned it over in her fingers, searching for useful fingerprints, while unsure of what she expected them to tell her. Barbara Wright had had a heart attack and fell in the supply closet. Maybe she'd picked up the jar and dropped it, and the annoyance, the final straw when she had so much on her mind, had agitated her heart into seizure. Maybe she picked it up, then her heart began seizing and she dropped it. Maybe her heart began seizing and she pitched forward, knocking the jar from the shelf. Her fingerprints would or would not be deposited on the jar, depending on which had occurred.

Did it really matter?

But why, she thought as she rotated each chunk of brown glass under the bright magnifying light, *are* no one's *prints on the jar?* It hadn't been brand-new, since she hadn't found a cellophane seal clinging to the lid. Even if it had been new, whoever had stocked it in the closet would have touched it, unless they were cautious enough around acids to wear gloves even for that simple action.

Rachael groaned inwardly. What was she *doing*? The woman had a heart attack and died. Yes, Barbara had been relatively young and apparently healthy, but anyone could have a heart attack. High school kids occasionally had heart attacks. And Rachael had perhaps ten minutes before that morning's session should begin and she hadn't even dumped her purse in her office yet—

She pulled a white evidence box from a cabinet and began to stack the pieces in it. If it was evidence, she would wrap each in some paper towels or something so that they wouldn't break further, but it wasn't evidence at all. So, why was she even keeping it? She should just throw it out. Where was she even going to put it, when it didn't have a case number assigned? Really, the only thing to do now was to tell Shirley in purchasing to order another jar.

She picked up the piece with the label still clinging to it—part of a label, the left half, holding two shards of glass together. FISHER SCIENTIFIC/ 1 L/ C4H1—the rest of it had been torn off. Under that was TRIS HCL in bold letters, and below that, in small font, the company's address. Some Locard employee had added a handwritten notation in marker to record when the bottle had been received: *Rec'd 8/1.*

Nothing she didn't already know. She *did* wonder where the other half of the label had gone. Perhaps it had bounced away under a shelf and she'd missed it when she picked up the pieces. Or it had stuck to the floor and, again, she missed it. Could it have actually *dissolved*?

Rachael had had considerable training in psychology and, not for the first time, turned it inward. *This is just avoidance, obsessing over unimportant details because you don't want to face the fact that someone you worked with every day was here one minute and dead the next. You have seven minutes until class is supposed to start. Get moving.*

She scribbled *Rachael *Don't touch!** on the box and left it on an empty counter. Then she hustled back down to the anteroom on the first floor, hoping to grab a coffee before facing a room full of people expecting her to tell them something they didn't already know.

She didn't make it. The first—or second?—issue of the day presented itself, in the form of the two Saudi bodyguards. They stood before the secretary's desk in the open area outside the director's, Rachael's, and the dean of research's offices, and spoke in tones both agitated and pleading. What they said, Rachael couldn't guess.

Clearly, neither could the secretary. Blond, fortyish, generally unflappable Carrie turned to her. "I can't understand what they're saying. Something about Farida."

The two Saudi bodyguards unleashed another torrent of words, now directed at both women. Both were, as always, impeccably dressed and groomed in high-quality fabrics of, unless she missed her guess, British design. Their beards were clipped to uniform lengths, their torsos too thick and portly for their age, Rachael thought. Bashar seemed nearly panicked; Irfan, mostly annoyed. He had the thick neck and slightly pushed-back chin that signaled sleep apnea to Rachael.

"Do we have *anyone* here who speaks Arabic?" Rachael asked Carrie.

"Hector did some work in the Middle East during a sabbatical."

"Call him, please."

"Farida." Bashar, the less-distant cousin, spoke carefully.

Rachael gave him her full attention.

He held both hands out, fingers splayed, palms down, and swirled them around. "Not here."

She said slowly, with careful enunciation: "Farida is not here? Not at the Locard?"

"Yes!"

"Okay." Did he mean she would not be attending class today? Maybe Farida felt ill and was still back at the hotel? Perhaps they—or she—worried that credit would not be given for the course if she missed a day. "Okay. That's all right."

This neither reassured nor satisfied him. "Not. Here."

"Right."

Whatever he meant to convey, she had not gotten it, as his expression flicked from worry to irritation and back again.

Rachael considered giving him a computer and asking him to write out what he wanted to tell them. Then they could use a translation app to convert the words to English. But even though a word processing program could write in Arabic, they didn't have an Arabic *keyboard,* which surely would be a problem, unless they were spatially identical to U.S. ones and Bashar possessed excellent touch-typing abilities. He could write down his words and Carrie could type them into Translate . . . but the keyboard catch again, it might take her forever to find the right characters, even if his penmanship allowed her to decipher each unfamiliar character correctly.

"Do you have a translate app on your phone? Something they can just speak into?" she asked Carrie.

"No, but I'll find one I can download."

But when the secretary dug out her phone with the slightly oversized screen and went to the App Store, Irfan, the more-distant cousin, came to life. He plucked one of his two phones from a back pocket and frantically swiped through three screens full of icons before finding the one he wanted.

Bashar said something to him. He responded absently, tapping one foot while the program opened. Bashar spoke again, voice louder and full of incredulity. Rachael didn't have to know Arabic to know that he had just demanded, "Did you have that *this whole time?*"

He almost couldn't stifle his agitation in order to use the app, clearly forcing himself to speak slow and clear Arabic words into the rectangular electronic device that Irfan now held out to him.

Then nothing.

Irfan looked at the screen in alarm, muttered, and tapped one spot one time. A disembodied voice, tinny but pleasant, said: "Farida is not here and not at hotel."

Rachael frowned. "She didn't come—"

Irfan snatched the phone back, tapped some settings, and held it out again, toward her this time.

Rachael took a second to form her question. It needed to be simple. "She did not get on the shuttle this morning?"

The two men waited for the translation, then answered. "No."

"Is she in her room?"

"Hotel says no."

Rachael wondered if they had knocked, if the desk had called, if someone had actually gone in. She asked if they meant Farida had disappeared overnight. Had the girl run away? Defected, like a visiting Soviet in the 1970s? Had the lure of American-type freedoms proved too strong?

It didn't seem likely. Farida might be young, but not impulsive-teenager young, and she had not expressed any desire to stay in the U.S. She clearly loved her land, her family, and maybe even this fiancé.

Rachael needed more information. "When did you see her last?"

They needed a minute to work through that syntax, most likely different in Arabic.

"Last night, class over, waiting for shuttle."

A bad feeling—well, she'd already had a bad feeling, so a *worse* feeling—spread through Rachael, warming her insides and constricting her heart.

"Did she go back to the hotel on the shuttle last night?"

"No."

That was what they'd been trying to tell her.

"Do you know if she got another ride to the hotel?"

"No."

Was that "no, she didn't," or "no, we don't know"?

"What happened last night?"

Slowly, awkwardly, the story emerged. Hector arrived; though not fluent, he still managed to speed up the process. The two men and Farida had been waiting with the other attendees in the ground floor hallway for word that the shuttle had arrived—no one wanted to wait in the open parking lot in the pounding rain. Farida announced that she had to use the ladies' room, so all three of them moved downstairs to the cafeteria.

Rachael pictured the layout. A narrow hallway ran between the cafeteria and an inner wall, with entrances to the two restrooms, the gymnasium, the locker rooms, and two storage rooms, with the kitchen at the south end of this hallway and a door at the north. The door opened onto a brick pathway that eventually curved up the hill and merged with the path to the parking lot. Farida had dumped her tote bag on one of the long tables and entered this hallway to go to the restroom. The men had remained in the cafeteria and attempted to get cups of cola from the drinks station on the south wall of the room, but the machines had been turned off for the night.

"*Ffffft*" described the hissing sound the uncooperative soda dispenser made, according to Irfan. His tongue seemed a little too fat for his mouth. Definitely sleep apnea.

They then returned to the lunch tables, since there was no place to sit in the hallway. And they waited. And waited. For perhaps ten minutes—which did seem a long time, but they knew girls spent a lot of time primping, and they could hardly go in there to find out what kept her. A look of terror passed over Bashar's face at the mere thought.

They finally approached the ladies' room and called to Farida, asking what kept her and complaining that they would miss the shuttle and have to call an Uber. They heard nothing in return. The ladies' restroom, Rachael knew, had no door, per se, only a privacy wall to block the view of its interior.

Just then, a lone woman had come along, and they had tried hard to explain their plight. She did not understand them—Irfan sucked in his cheeks and used his thumbs and index fingers to make circles over his eyes, and Bashar drew himself up and looked down on them with a somewhat-cold air.

"Agnes," Rachael and Hector said in unison.

With hand gestures and pleading looks they let her know that they needed her to do something regarding the rest-room. She went in and quickly came out again with raised eyebrows and upturned palms. Clearly, there had been no one and nothing of interest in the restroom.

They thought perhaps Farida hadn't seen them, over by the drinks machine, and had gone back upstairs via the north staircase, which led from the hallway to the first and second floors. They did grab her tote bag from the cafeteria and poked their heads out into the rain first, to see no one on the brick path—well lit, Rachael knew, from the light over the door.

So they went upstairs, where the rest of the attendees were filing out the door on their way to the shuttle. They did not find her, just had to hope that she might be at the front of the line. Everyone was rushing and holding coats and bags over their heads to stay dry, making it difficult to distinguish one from the other in the dark and rain.

Nope, Rachael thought. No woman would leave the building for the night without her purse. She would have made sure her bodyguards had it before going.

The cousins got to the parking lot and piled on the shuttle to see that she was not there. They did try her cell phone before the shuttle departed, but the tinny ring tone wafted up from inside her tote bag.

They decided she had ditched them, gone off with some other girls to go to a bar, or out dancing—she had talked about it over the weekend until they'd threatened to call her father—and now the two cousins were cold, wet, and hungry. Farida would have to figure out her own way home. Served her right.

At the hotel they went to their room and spent the evening griping about the selfish girl, who would get them all in big trouble.

Hector said to Rachael, "I get the idea they *didn't* call her father. He'd want to know why they failed. They still haven't contacted anyone else. Came back here this morning, hoping that she'd have caught a ride back with whatever decadent slut she'd been hanging out with, but apparently not. Class starts in two minutes and every other seat is filled—except hers. They are positive she would *never* miss class."

"I am too," Rachael said. As fond as she had grown of Farida, her thoughts leapt to the Locard. Could Farida be somewhere on the property, lost, harmed, incapacitated? Had one of the staff seduced her away? A less dire theory— maybe she had left with a classmate who lost track of her, left her at a bar downtown—not good—or let her flop on their spare bed and sleep in this morning—better.

Try the simplest solution first. "Okay. Let me ask if any of the other attendees knows where she might be. If that doesn't get us anywhere, we'll have to grab all the staff we can and do a search. Can you stay here with them and see if there's anything more they can tell us? I'll be back ASAP."

As Hector and Carrie got the men settled, Rachael hustled over to the classrooms. Her Crime Scene Documentation students were ready to go, mostly in their seats with notebooks ready. Nearly everyone had stocked up provisions, raiding the table in the back to refill their travel mugs with coffee and tea and grabbing doughnuts, Danishes, granola bars, and cookies. All looked up when she entered, clearly expecting her to begin instruction.

"I apologize for the delay," she began, though two minutes remained until scheduled start time. "Does anyone know where Farida is?"

Blank looks, and no answers. One person suggested she

look in the courtyard, as Farida had spent a few breaks out by the fountain.

Rachael asked, "Did anyone give her a ride last night?"

"She takes the shuttle to the hotel," Oliver said.

"Was she on it?" Rachael asked, though she knew the answer.

"Dunno. I rented a car."

"She wasn't," someone else said, and two others agreed.

"And no one's seen her this morning? No? Or at the hotel last night?"

"What's the matter?" Stef asked with concern. "What happened to her?"

"Nothing." Rachael hoped that was true. "We're just wondering why she's not here this morning." She ducked out, to avoid more questions that she couldn't answer, and went into the next room.

Ellie stood at the front, powering up a projector, and smiled to see her. The scene matched the one next door, attendees snagging their favorite early-morning drinks and snacks before taking their seats.

Ellie said, "Hi! Hey, tell your mom thanks again for dinner last night, it was—is anything wrong?"

"I hope not." Rachael repeated her questions, receiving the same answers. Some in this class had spoken with Farida often during breaks, but most had only seen Farida in passing or at lunch. Those didn't recognize her name until others explained "the Saudi girl." The headscarf had made her memorable.

Rachael had seen Alyssa talking to Farida more than once, and asked her specifically if she'd seen the missing woman.

"Nope."

Rachael waited.

"I offered to take her out over the weekend, look at some monuments and get dinner in Georgetown, but she said her bodyguards had arranged for a tour. I invited her to karaoke too, but she said she couldn't go to a bar."

"Nothing last night?"

Alyssa shrugged. "I didn't ask. It was such a crappy night, anyway. I was soaked to the skin before I even made it to my car."

"She wasn't on the shuttle," someone else said. "Her bodyguards were, though, arguing with each other."

"About what?" Rachael asked.

"Hell if I know. It wasn't in English."

Rachael thanked them and turned to go. Ellie walked her to the hallway. In the interest of speed she boiled it all down to a single question: "Are we worried about this girl?"

Rachael drew in a deep breath. "I don't know yet. But I hope not."

"Okay. Let me know what I can do."

Rachael said she would and returned to the office.

Hector did not have much to add to what they already knew. The hotel had, indeed, made entry to Farida's room and reported it empty, neat, apparently unused since yesterday morning's cleaning. The cousins were also positive that Farida, probably like any other young person, would never have been voluntarily separated from her cell phone for more than a few minutes. But they seemed equally worried that, though Farida already had plenty of glamorous locales, restaurants, vacations, things to do in her own world, perhaps the appeal of *different* locales had proven too tempting. This seemed the likeliest explanation. But what if she had fallen in with bad people or intoxicants, so she could not return, or, worse, didn't plan to return at all?

Hector confided: "I don't know what the punishment is for failing in your male-protector role where they live. They might get an earful from a great-aunt, or they might be executed."

"Really?" Rachael asked in horror.

"I doubt it." Hector rubbed his chin. "But I'm not really sure."

Carrie had filled in the director of the Locard and the three of them conferred in his office. Gerald Coleman had not only the expertise, but also the looks for the position—tall, slender, distinguished-looking, with olive skin, the product of an Egyptian mother and a half-Japanese father. A furrow had grown between his eyebrows, illustrating how he felt about students disappearing from the Locard campus. "And nobody's got a clue where she is?"

"Not so far. We're going to have to search the place," Rachael said.

"Obviously," he said with some annoyance. "Building first, stem to stern, and if there's no love there, then the grounds."

Carrie said, "She probably ran away. Who would want to go back to wearing a burka?"

Rachael said, "She didn't wear a burka! And she never mentioned wanting to stay in the U.S., never even hinted." She held up a hand as Carrie opened a mouth to protest. "And why leave from here, last night? We're in the middle of nowhere and she's going to go hiking up these back roads in the pouring rain?"

Gerald said, "So she did get a ride from someone, and they're lying about it."

"Because they're helping her escape!" Carrie said.

"*Maybe,*" Rachael said. "Okay, *maybe* someone we don't even know about picked her up at the gate. We need to get every available person—housekeeping, kitchen crew, maintenance—to check every inch of all three floors. *Every* inch." She couldn't shake the picture of Barbara Wright's body lying on the supply closet floor.

Gerald said, "Get Cam in IT to review the video surveillance of all the external cameras. It'd be nice to know what door she used to leave."

If she left, Rachael thought, but didn't say. She knew Gerald had his fingers crossed, hoping that whatever had happened to Farida—abducted, defected, or just lost on her very first bender—had happened *off* the Locard campus. And through her worry about the young woman, Rachael hoped so too. Two deaths in the building in as many days . . . *No. Not doing it.* "I'll get the kitchen staff to comb the basement level—"

"Not you," Gerald said.

"Wha—"

"You have a class to teach. The other attendees can't lose half a day because this chick went AWOL. I'll handle it."

Rachael reluctantly agreed.

Chapter 11

"The practice of genealogical tracing," Ellie began, "is an amorphous, continually changing animal. The idea, of course, is ancient—from the Bible to *Burke's Peerage*, family trees have been vital in certain contexts. But in the U.S., it was Alex Haley's 1976 book *Roots* that prompted a fascination with tracing one's family tree. Suddenly you didn't have to be royalty to care who your great-great-grandmother was. Another couple of decades and there were computers and cotton swabs through the mail, which made things so much easier than having to comb through dusty records in some small town in Japan. But the two routes are different: The dusty records will take you back through time. The DNA swabs will find your contemporaries here in the present, since great-great-grandma didn't leave a set of buccals for you to test. But for a complete picture, both may be necessary."

She had a strong feeling her audience was falling asleep.

Alyssa's eyes had already glazed over, and two others sat with chins propped on their hands as their eyes slowly closed. Caleb watched her with a half smile, and the cop from Los Angeles took notes. Sun slanted in from a high angle, and warmed the room. Genealogy might not be the most titillating material, but there was nothing she could do about that. She had tried to make the slides as entertaining as possible, with odd photos and snarky captions. But sometimes, kids, forensic science *isn't* super fun.

"With Ancestry.com and 23andMe—and their copious advertising—bursting onto the scene twenty or so years ago, tons of DNA information began to accumulate. When and how law enforcement realized that it could be a tool to put names to unidentified bodies and maybe suspects as well, I couldn't tell you with any accuracy. But after genealogist Barbara Rae-Venter pointed investigators to the Golden State Killer, everyone in the country was introduced to the idea of finding a criminal because their relative uploaded a profile to GEDmatch or some such site. So I call this presentation, 'DNA and Your Great-Aunt Maisie.'

"In this scenario your great-aunt Maisie mailed off her mouth swabs to a testing service. She won't admit it, but Maisie has always believed that she is related to Mary, Queen of Scots. The testing service sends back her profile, but merely knowing that she has a short tandem repeat named DYS388 doesn't thrill Maisie. She uploads her own profile to a clearinghouse. They report back with a list of hundreds of possible relatives, usually third and fourth cousins. To put this in context, you and your third cousin would have a great-great-grandparent in common."

More glazing. Even the photo of the very old-fashioned woman grumpily churning butter failed to get a smile.

"Genealogists look for close relationships. The more DNA shared, the higher the number of segments shared, the more likely that the two people are related. They look at centimorgans."

"You made that word up," Caleb complained.

"I promise I did not. A centimorgan is the distance between chromosome loci. Every person has about sixty-eight hundred of these. So if you have thirty-four hundred, or fifty percent, in common with someone else, you're probably their child or their parent."

The forensic tech from Greensville perked up. She had three children, Ellie had learned over coffee that morning.

"If you have one percent, you're likely a third cousin. Now, also in this general database with Maisie, there is a sample from a stabbing three years earlier in Des Moines."

Now most others in the class raised an eyebrow or straightened a spine. Finally some relevance to their daily work.

"Blood was found at a distance from the body, didn't match the victim, and is presumed to be the suspect's. It has enough DNA in common with Maisie to be a third cousin, and the detectives want to know more. Clearly, it *isn't* Maisie, and no one would suspect the seventy-year-old of stabbing a coed and then climbing down a drainpipe outside her window three states away."

The last head-nodder now seemed to be listening.

Ellie switched the projector remote to her other hand. Her acid-singed fingers had returned to nearly normal overnight, but a trace amount of sensitivity remained. "Now, we need more than test tubes and a thermocycler—someone has to actually trace Maisie's family tree back to that great-great-grand who is the ancestor in common with the suspect. This isn't simple. Biologically speaking, you have four grandparents, eight great-grandparents, and sixteen great-great-grandparents. Researchers have to find all the progeny of those sixteen people to get a complete set of Maisie's third cousins."

"Lot of work," a lieutenant from Ohio groaned.

"It *is* a lot of work. That's why it's best to hire someone who's done this a few dozen times and knows where all the resources are. Anyway, from that large group of distant cousins, the investigation gets a little more like old-fashioned police work. Of this group, who lives in Des Moines? Sure, someone could have been there for a reunion or on business, but let's start with the obvious: Who's in the kind of shape to shimmy down a drainpipe? If there's a Y chromosome in our suspect blood, we can eliminate females. We'll check out their social media—maybe one was finding inner peace in Nepal that whole summer. Wring any last drop of information out of their genetic profile—maybe there's a partial description of the perpetrator, so who's got the genes for a certain hair color, eye color? Maybe two have a criminal record, let's put them at the top of the list. Let's say this all narrows down to Maisie's ne'er-do-well great-nephew Bruce. Once you have enough, you get a warrant to get a clean sample of Bruce's buccals and prove it was him in the Des Moines murder. Off Bruce goes to jail, and all because Maisie really wants to be related to Mary, Queen of Scots."

There were some chuckles across the room. "Damn, Maisie," someone muttered.

"But—" Alyssa said, and stopped.

"There's a ton of 'buts,'" Ellie admitted. "I said it's an amorphous topic, and it is. These genealogical services started out with the best of intentions, help adoptees find their birth relatives, reunite family members separated by war or time, maybe identify unknown remains. If it can also solve crimes, win-win. There were no particular rules for use by law enforcement, and if there were, sometimes they were disregarded through ignorance or subterfuge. It's a roundabout way of running someone's DNA without having to jump through the hoops of subpoenas and warrants, and resulted in accusations that the clearinghouses and the cops violated people's civil rights."

"Tough." The lieutenant from Ohio, one Matt Gold, did not sympathize.

"Technically, it does," a fortyish guy in a Glock T-shirt said. "It's searching someone's DNA without consent."

"Technically, it's not." The woman next to him smoothed her orange-tinted hair—Bettie, someone had called her. "The Fifth Amendment only applies to testimonial evidence. That's why we can collect fingerprints without subpoena."

"But we only collect fingerprints when someone is in *custody*, so there's an arrest warrant in existence or about to be in existence. Most places can also collect DNA under those circumstances. But you can't walk up to someone on the street and demand their fingerprints, unless they consent to give them."

"But this isn't their DNA. It's Great-Aunt Maisie's," Bettie countered.

"Why would people *not* want to solve crimes?" someone else asked.

"Luckily, we don't have to debate that as part of this course," Ellie stated firmly, "because it's a mess. Clearinghouses would first only allow law enforcement to search in cases of murder or sexual assault, then they allowed people to opt out, then they automatically opted everyone out, unless they opted in. Genealogists were in the middle of a firestorm they never wanted and were split down the middle themselves. The debate got very ugly, very quickly. Both the services and law enforcement needed clear rules about what they could do, and what they couldn't do, but that's taking some time and can still vary by state."

Caleb stretched, arms reaching overhead. "I don't care if they put my nephew in jail. He's a jerk, anyway."

A few more laughs. Then Ellie said, "So, why are we talking about this here? Because it's not going to go away. Surely, DNA databases will be used in some way in the future—just be very sure of the current state of the laws when you're making your investigation."

"Maybe that's why Dr. Wright wanted to search people through their meds," a cop from Topeka mused out loud. "Then you're not looking at subjects' DNA. Only unknown DNA versus subjects' meds."

Alyssa Cole said, "That's even worse. HIPAA laws would never let her get that off the ground."

Ellie tried to arch her back, stretching without appearing to be stretching. Time for a break. "Let's say she did, for the sake of argument. My point is that both genealogical tracing and Dr. Wright's ideas about finding medical conditions in unknown samples at crime scenes are all ways of narrowing down your suspect pool. We're accustomed to picking up a swab of blood or semen, uploading the profile to CODIS, and then searching it. If it doesn't match anyone, it doesn't, and we're out of luck. We need to be open to new ways of using the same evidence. And on that note, class, let's take ten minutes for restrooms and refills."

The people in the room rose slowly to mill about, some still debating the uses and abuses of DNA evidence. Ellie grabbed some coffee and couldn't help but replay Barbara Wright's lecture the previous day in her head. The woman had mentioned a preapproved grant, not "I *have* a grant." She was going to quit the Locard without a definite on the grant position? Bold move. Maybe an overconfident one, but Ellie had to admire it. She would never have jumped without the assurance of a net. Extended family had always been there to catch her when she had to leap, but only out of the goodness of their hearts, and even as a child she had never taken it for granted.

Somehow it made it all the more sad that Barbara Wright would never have the chance to find out how strong her net would have been.

Chapter 12

Rachael led her charges out the north door, heading for Body Site 1. The rain had gradually lessened all morning and stopped altogether during their lunch break, leaving the trees dripping and the ground saturated. They had to maneuver around puddles flooding the walkway and she hoped no one had worn shoes of which they felt particularly fond. She'd spent lunch checking with Carrie—staff had walked every inch of the Locard building, checked every closet, bathroom, locked office, and so on, with no trace of the missing girl. The maintenance man, a burly guy of mixed race named Stuart, had been consulting a map of the campus for the most logical way to cover the grounds.

While looking for Farida obviously took priority, Rachael had also asked him to keep an eye out for a small German shepherd–type puppy, or a means of egress for same. He'd been skeptical of finding any animal in those woods other than raccoons, squirrels, or the occasional beaver, but said he would keep it in mind.

Rachael told herself not to worry. Worrying was pointless, and not useful. She hated to waste her brain on nonuseful activities.

Yet she worried.

"What happened to the Arab girl?" Tony, the New Mexico detective, asked. The tiny red lines through the whites of his eyes, which hadn't been there the day before, made Rachael wonder if he'd enjoyed last night's happy hour at the hotel bar a little too thoroughly.

"Why were you asking us where she is?" another attendee asked.

Before she could answer, Stef said, "We walked out of the classroom together last night. But then she walked off with those bodyguards and I didn't see her again. Are they gone too?"

"No, they're here." Rachael glanced over at Oliver Suarez. He and Stef had sat on either side of Farida in class and had conversed with her the most during breaks. He had seemed to "*like* like" the young woman—one can always tell—and now Rachael expected him to be full of questions about her absence. But he only watched Rachael's face, waiting for her response.

"I bet she had a drink in the hotel bar or spoke to a man or something, and they killed her," Stef predicted. She clearly meant the cousins, not the unknown man at the bar.

"I doubt that. They came to us to find her."

The Californian Border Patrol agent had an answer for that. "Well, sure—they had all night to think about it. They'd want to look innocent."

"If they had all night," Tony argued, "they'd have gotten on a plane and gone back to Saudi Arabia. We wouldn't be able to touch them. They killed that journalist in Turkey and no one could do a thing."

A woman from Louisiana argued, "Yeah, but they were supposed to be protecting her. They were her cousins, and now they have to go back and tell their uncle or great-uncle or whoever her father is that they lost her. You can bet they're a lot more afraid of him than they are of U.S. law enforcement."

Stef's hands fluttered, as if she were jonesing for a cigarette. "Not if he's the one who ordered it."

Rachael didn't want the class to devolve into detailed speculation of what had happened to Farida. Supposing—hoping—the young woman had simply walked off for a bit of fun in the loose foreign country before returning home, and had been having a good enough time to blow off a day of class, Rachael would hate to see her return tomorrow to knowing looks and prying questions. They only had one and a half days to go, but still.

On the other hand, Farida had spent over a week chatting daily with this same group of people, so if anyone knew where she might have gone, they would. Even if they didn't know they knew. Rachael couldn't cut off such a font of possibly helpful information.

She wiped a fallen droplet of water off her check, shrugged more comfortably into her windbreaker, and took a deep breath of the rain-scented air. Then she asked Oliver: "Did she say anything about wanting to go somewhere in the DC area? In the U.S.?"

"No." He kept his eyes on the path, but to be fair, the puddles made that necessary.

"Any DC sight she particularly wanted to see?"

"No." But then he added, "The Lincoln Memorial."

Stef said, "Of course. The guy who freed the slaves. That would have had a lot of meaning for someone who wasn't free."

"She was free enough to come here," Tony pointed out.

Oliver said, "She said they'd gone there over the weekend, anyway."

Rachael said to him, "You have her number. You've been texting, right?"

"Yes." He didn't ask how she knew that, how she'd overheard them in class.

"She text anything about wanting to leave, to go out?"

"To go walkabout?" Stef added. "To defect?"

" 'Defect,' " Tony said with a laugh. "I haven't heard that word since the 1970s."

Oliver said they'd only talked about class information, reading suggestions, that sort of thing.

"Anything last night?" Rachael asked. He said no, which made sense. Farida's phone had been in her tote bag, with her bodyguards.

They reached the turnoff for Body Site 1, and a chorus of groans went up as heels and soles sunk into the softened earth or slid on layers of sodden leaves. Brush and weeds and branches grabbed at arms and legs as they passed, wetting the business casual attire.

It's all good, Rachael told herself. *Real-world conditions. Everyone here has seen worse.*

"This sucks," Stef grumbled.

"Yes. Yes, it does," Rachael agreed. "Okay. We are once again at the side of dear departed Chester, learning all about the joys of taking notes in a wet environment. If you're not accustomed to dictating your observations, using the Notes app or the equivalent on your cell phones, this might be the scene to start with. So, what do we see?"

Because the goat had not been completely buried to begin with, even more of the covering dirt had been washed away since the day before. Nearly the whole body could be seen, the fur easily standing out between fallen leaves.

"The water washed away all the maggots," someone said, a distinct note of relief in their voice.

"To some extent, yes. Insects generally like a little moisture, but not too much. This entire lot slopes from the road down to the bay, and with all the clay in our soil, the water doesn't drain too quickly. A lot of our maggots have been washed down the hill toward the Chesapeake."

"Could the entire body have shifted?" one attendee asked. "It looks different than yesterday."

"Like he rotated. He was lying almost directly north-south before," another said.

Rachael didn't think it had rained *that* hard, and in all the years she'd been doing this—often in rainy weather—she'd never had a body move. It did look a little different, but that had to be due to the mini flood washing away a great deal of leaf covering.

Since the course purported to teach documentation practices that met standards for accreditation, they weren't really there to observe changes in a buried body over time. It would be the job of *next* week's class to actually exhume poor Chester. "It's not likely. But since we're out here to document our observations, you could always measure his position again and compare to your previous notes. In the meantime let's talk about plants."

Most didn't seem any more enthusiastic about plant life as they had been about insect life, but they listened. Rachael crouched down and picked wet leaves off the fur, one by one, placing them in piles to her side, separating by size and shape. Again, since the course meant to teach documentation and not actual outdoor scene analysis, they weren't going to identify the various botanical samples or research their origins. She only wanted to discuss the basic reasons and practices for doing so for those occasions when botany could be relevant.

"You very rarely hear about botany being used in investigations anymore, when eighty or one hundred years ago, every lab would have a microscopist, who could identify pollen spores from every local plant. But it is still vital knowledge under certain circumstances. Plants are living things, and as living things, what is their primary function?"

"To live," someone said.

"After that."

"To procreate," Oliver said.

Rachael nodded up at them. "The name of the game, in the ecological universe, is to get as many of your genes as possible into the next generation. Plants *want* to disperse. They want to send their seeds over distances by outfitting them with hooks, hairs, breakaway parts, and sticky secretions. So you just killed somebody and you decide to dump them out in the woods, where, unless you are truly unlucky and some hiker stumbles on them, they'll just decompose and/or get ripped apart by coyotes or bobcats or ants. Your goal is, news of your crime never makes it back to the human world."

A few chuckled at her description. A few others saw where she headed.

"So you're dragging that body through the plants," Stef theorized, "while all those seeds and pollen and bits of leaves stick to it."

"The body and you, exactly. Even if you carry the body. Even if you wrapped it in a tarp or a duffel bag that you take away with you, you still have to unwrap it and get it into the ground. Even if you made it easy on yourself and forced your victim to walk in under their own power, then they're going to have items from low-lying weeds and brush on their shoes and lower pants and not along their whole body. Everything can tell us something, if we listen."

Tony said, "But those leaves are lying on the body because they fell from the trees overhead. With the way the wind whipped yesterday, probably all the leaves here right now are a mile from where they started and have nothing to do with the body."

Rachael said, "*Are* they from the trees overhead? What

trees *are* immediately around the body? Those are the details you don't want to forget to document. Maybe you find a bunch of maple leaves caught in the clothing, but there's only oak around the grave site. And what stage are they in? If it's April, but you find a great deal of fully grown, dead leaves buried with the body, then maybe they've been there since fall."

"Still," someone said, uncertain, "they're leaves. And it's a forest."

"Very true," Rachael said. "Like most forensic evidence, it can mean a lot or nothing at all, depending on the circumstances. Finding the victim's blood on the suspect's shirt doesn't mean anything if your suspect says she found the man with stab wounds and attempted CPR. Finding the suspect's prints on the vase means nothing if it's his house. So finding oak pollen on our Chester would not tell us much. But if we found sand spurs in his fur, that would indicate that he and/or our killer entered the woods from the beach and not the road."

Still, many appeared skeptical. "Would that really convict someone in court?" one asked.

"Once again, it all depends. If your suspect lives on the beach, then it's another nail in his coffin. It might be circumstantial evidence, but many cases are built on circumstantial."

Tony, surely accustomed to the open land of the desert, argued: "But there could be sand spurs all over this forest—raccoons, woodchucks, would carry them around on their fur."

"True also. That's why documentation is key. One errant sand spur is easy to explain away. Twenty, not so much. That's why you photograph the area, collect a few leaves from each tree, clip a branch of the brush. If you really are out in the middle of a woods like this, with no fixed reference points, you might need to pound in a piece of rebar—somewhere away from the body—and use GPS to geolocate your exact points. Use a compass to determine true north and south."

"Outdoor scenes are a pain," someone grumbled.

"But they smell better," Tony pointed out.

Rachael said, "Yes, there's a huge amount of detail added when you're working a remote-location crime scene—ninety-nine percent of which we're not going to go into here—but I can't stop myself from mentioning some. Anyway, during excavation your job is to collect all the plant life you find with the body so that a botanist can determine how likely or unlikely it should be to find creeping beggarweed in the victim's cuffs. Maybe it grows around the entire perimeter of the forest. Maybe it only grows in one meadow at the south entrance, the most direct route from your suspect's house."

"Or maybe it grows *at* your suspect's house," a woman from Iowa suggested, warming to the idea.

"That would be ideal," Rachael agreed. "If it's something that shouldn't be found in the entire forest, it's much more compelling. But the documentation has to hold up in court. That's why—"

Something nudged her foot, softer than a waving branch, and she looked down into a pair of huge brown eyes.

"Puppy's back!" Stef crowed.

At least three people said in unison, "He's so cute!" Two dropped down to pet him, despite the mud sticking to his ears and legs.

"What are we going to do with you?" Rachael muttered. She really didn't want him poking around the body sites—*real-world conditions be damned*—but it seemed silly to fuss about a dog when a veritable army of raccoons inhabited the trees. Depositing him outside the campus fence would be pointless, when the gate stood open all day, and the fence clearly hadn't been an obstacle so far.

If she picked him up to keep him from disturbing the class, what would she do then, other than trash her windbreaker? They had no place inside the building to keep him, nothing that could function as a kennel outside, and then what?

Home? Yes, Danton would go out of his mind, but her mother's asthma would rebel. Take him to the humane society? Could she rat out that face, condemn him to a stint in doggie jail? Surely, he'd be adopted, something so adorable—

Right now, she had to get him out of her class. Concentration had been completely shot. A medical examiner's investigator from Utah had pulled half a doughnut from his pocket and was letting the dog chow down on it, while a crime scene tech from Idaho complained how that wasn't good for him. To which, the investigator said that the dog was starving, so perfect nutrition didn't seem so important at the moment, and a detective from Nebraska nearly stepped on their buried body to pat the puppy's head, who, after downing the piece of doughnut, began to dig in the wet dirt.

"All right," Rachael said. "Let's get back to work. And unless you all want decomposed goat sticking to your shoes, I suggest you watch where you step. I'll take our stray back to the Locard—I'm sure Carrie can figure out what to do with him for the rest of the afternoon."

"Oh, but he's helping," the crime scene tech cooed. "Look, he's excavating."

Oliver sniffled, as if the damp weather irritated his sinuses. "If this was a real crime scene, you would have removed him immediately."

"Well, of course," she said. "But this is just practice, and he's really cute."

"What's that?" Tony said, leaning over the puppy. A flash of white appeared under the tiny paws.

"Goat bones," someone suggested.

"Don't let him eat those! They aren't good for him."

"That's chicken bones . . . or any bird, because they're hollow and they splinter. Mammal bones are fine."

"They can still chip and tear up his intestines—" the no-chicken-bones attendee argued.

"What do you think they eat in the wild—"

Tony cut them off. "I don't think it's goat." The homicide detective moved in a smooth motion for a large man. He crouched, gently held the puppy back with one hand, and with the other brushed dirt from the hole the dog had been widening. Conversation ceased. The woods grew silent, with no sound save the random drips of water from overburdened leaves. Foreboding gripped Rachael's throat and she waited.

Tony wiped another clump of sodden earth away, and everyone present saw the fingers at the same time. White skin with perfectly manicured, unpolished nails.

She must be cold, Rachael thought ridiculously.

Some of the attendees stepped back without thinking, others remained frozen in place; some kind of gasp or moan or wordless question hissed from each and every mouth.

The tech so fascinated with the puppy brushed at some leaves on the opposite side of the grave. Rachael recognized the green-and-blue pattern of Farida's headscarf, even as dirt mottled the colors.

Oliver let out a low groan, a cry of amorphous pain.

Rachael felt as if someone had pounded on her chest, hard enough to crack the breastbone, knocking the air out of her lungs with grief. But she also knew what to do next. "Everyone, step back. *Now.* Leave the equipment, take back only what is in your hands right now. Touch nothing else."

"Is that Farida?" Stef asked.

"Watch where you step, try to stay in a single or double file, try not to create any new tracks. Go."

The group obeyed her instructions without question, but

not, she knew, because she made a good drill sergeant. They didn't bother to ask, because they already knew what would happen next: Their mock crime was now a real crime scene, with all nonessential personnel removed. Whoever conducted the investigation, it would not be them, even though their training and expertise made them ideal for it. Local police would take over the scene and the attendees would be shut out.

A murder on her own doorstep, and Rachael would not be able to do a thing about it.

She took up the rear, even doing a quick, silent head count to make sure that every student who had entered the woods with her now left with her, that none could have hidden in the brush to circle back and alter the crime scene before authorities could arrive. It killed her to walk away and leave her scene unguarded, but she had no choice. Accounting for her charges had to take priority. They were not only witnesses, but from this point on, they were also suspects. As was she.

Her mind whirled. Go in the lower door and put the class in the cafeteria—they could use the restrooms, get some coffee to warm up, keep the mud on their shoes confined to one area. Tell Carrie to get in touch with maintenance man Stuart and his team searching the woods and call them back to the Locard immediately, and not by way of Body Site 1. Call Sheriff Tom Medina for the second time in as many days. Did she need to inform the FBI? The U.S. Diplomatic Service? The Saudi Embassy? Gerald would know, he had done more international work than she had.

How had this happened? *Farida*—that poor girl. Rachael had autopsied well over a thousand victims and examined hundreds of crime scenes, but those deceased had been strangers, not someone she'd spoken to every day for eight of the past eleven. She'd gotten really fond of the girl in that time. Farida had been bursting with youth, health, optimism, modest ambition. *Life.*

Clearly, the killer had moved the corpse of Chester, buried Farida, and put the goat back. The storm had made such a mess of the scene that it covered any tracks, made the disruption less obvious. But why the body site? The killer had ten acres to choose from. They could have dragged or carried her another twenty feet out and she'd have remained unfound indefinitely. Odors wafting through the woods would be blamed on the body sites. It would start snowing soon, things would freeze. Farida might not have been stumbled upon until spring—if ever.

And when had she been killed? It had to be in the sliver of time between the end of class and her trip to the cafeteria, and the boarding of the shuttle back to the hotel when her bodyguards had not been able to find her. Maybe during the boarding? Could she have walked off with someone? Been held captive by someone? Decided to go for a romantic stroll in the unlit woods in the middle of a monsoon? Or inside the building? Could she have had a quiet tête-à-tête in the gym, someone's office? The vault?

Having reached the Locard, she directed her attendees down the lower walkway into the cafeteria. There she asked them to please remain until further notice, help themselves to coffee and snacks. No one argued. Again the attendees knew exactly what would happen next, knew they could not help, *and* were glad to be out of the damp.

She asked the kitchen staff, still cleaning up from lunch, to get them whatever they needed, and if they could, make a note if anyone left. The two older lunch ladies and the temperamental chef stared at her as if she'd lost her mind.

They were even less pleased when she plucked the mud-covered puppy from Tony Altamonte's hands—she'd have to offer to pay the cleaning bill for his peacoat—and asked them to *please* rig up some sort of pen for him, with water and some leftover lunch scraps.

She escaped before they could protest and trotted up the south steps. *Keep calm. To-do list.*

First, have Carrie call Stuart and his crew in. Second, tell Gerald. Third, call Tom Medina. Fourth . . .

Rachael had no idea what to do fourth.

Chapter 13

A number of things then happened with what seemed like breathtaking speed, but relatively calm logic. The two Saudi men didn't need an interpreter to know the look on Rachael's face did not bode well, but perhaps they chose to believe it only meant that Farida had not yet been found. Carrie stifled her own questions until she and Rachael had ensconced the men in the conference room with plenty of hot tea and prepackaged snacks. Rachael then led the secretary into Gerald's office on the other side of the unit and closed the door, this very action prompting him to cut short his conversation with a natural-gas magnate in the Midwest amid reassurances and apologies. He waited with clear reluctance as Rachael delivered the four words no one in charge ever wants to hear: "We have a situation."

After Carrie unclapped her hands from her mouth, she got on the radio to Stuart and the searchers. Rachael called the sheriff, and, as she expected, Gerald knew what federal authorities to call in which sequence. As she disconnected her call, the director was saying, "I don't know anything more than that, the girl's still in the ground. Yes, there's a slight chance it's somehow *not* the Saudi girl, but we truly doubt that. I wanted to get you guys on board immediately, and Anita told me to call you." Pause. "I'm calling the FBI now." Pause. "She's in the *ground.* She didn't bury herself, so, yes, we're pretty sure it's murder." Pause. "I will." Pause. "*Yes*, as soon as I can, but I need to get off the phone to do it."

Anita Coleman was Gerald's wife. She was also one of the assistant directors of Intelligence & Analysis within the Department of Homeland Security.

"Sheriff's on his way," Rachael told him.

"I'll see if the FBI thinks they need to come out." He rubbed one hand over firm but aging skin, pressing fingers into his eye sockets. "Of all the students here, why her?"

"That's what I want to know." Rachael's tone sounded as grim as fine ash. "I'll get Hector to take over my class. He can explain coding for the national databases."

"I thought he already did that." Gerald always turned out to be more aware of the day-to-day operation of the place than she expected.

"He did the basics, but there's always more to say."

"Wish we could just send them home. It's only a day and a half, and the post test. We could give a small refund."

"I don't think that's a good idea."

"Why not?"

"Because they're our suspect pool."

Anne Arundel County sheriff Tom Medina stood at the edge of Body Site 1, his gaze darting around the small clearing. Next to him, Rachael said nothing and let him think. Stopping and thinking could be the most vital part of crime scene processing.

Space, perhaps fifteen feet in diameter. Trees and brush surrounding fairly thick, but not too thick, to pass through in any direction. No apparent trail other than the one leading in from the pathway. Evidence of footmarks, broken twigs, branches, pushed aside, but then course attendees had been stomping around out here for years.

The lieutenant next to him remained equally silent. He stifled a throaty cough, which made Rachael want to suggest a suppressant, maybe with an expectorant.

"Are we sure that's your missing Saudi girl?" Tom demanded.

Rachael said no, they couldn't be completely sure. "That looks like the scarf she wore yesterday, and the fingers look like a young woman's. But we've touched nothing."

"And that goat thing is on top of her?" He didn't wait for the answer. "We're going to need your surveillance videos, get our crime scene techs out here. This is a bit frustratin', Dr. Davies. We're a few hundred feet from the best forensic personnel in the country, and we can't use a one of you."

"It's not going to be easy for us either," Rachael admitted. Her hands itched to start stringing out a grid and dig in— literally—with a trowel and sifters.

The lieutenant with him asked, "Who's going to tell the Saudis?"

"I vote for them." Tom jerked his head toward the trail, up which Gerald Coleman led two men in suits through the wet leaves. Gerald led the way, watching the path carefully as he placed each step, scowling whenever the wet mud oozed up over his leather soles.

The suits were a dead giveaway. Rachael recognized the two FBI agents—she had last seen them only a few weeks before, and worked with them several times before that. She had technically lured Ellie from their bureau, but they didn't seem to bear any ill will. "You got here fast."

Michael Tyler said, "We were at a search warrant in Marlboro." He towered over Rachael at about six foot five, with the bulk to match. All of the bulk appeared to be muscle and not fat, though she would bet he needed more greens in his diet. He had short black hair and a scar on his temple in the shape of a rough, incomplete circle.

His wiry partner, with slightly longer hair and slightly shorter height, checked his non-department-issued shoes. Then Luis Alvarez joked: "Don't you have any place less . . . wet? Hey, Tom."

The sheriff introduced his lieutenant; then both he and the FBI agents peppered Rachael with questions she did her best to answer. Everyone there wanted to dive in and find the answers, but with such an already-compromised scene, patience became the better part of valor. Who would take point? Whose techs would be processing the area? Would the FBI be assisting or handling the whole shebang?

After a very short discussion Michael said he thought that given the international component, the FBI should take the investigation. "If we could assume whoever is in there is an American citizen, we wouldn't even be here. But we're going to need to get a couple different federal agencies on board—"

"I agree," Tom said. "It's all yours."

Rachael watched his lieutenant goggle at this. "What? You're just going to let them *take* it?"

"Yup."

"Without even—"

The sheriff cut him off. "They've got the manpower, the international contacts, the fancy equipment, and the teams of techs. And they are big enough"—he clapped Michael on the shoulder—"to take the heat from the diplomats and the media and activists when a frenemy like Saudi Arabia gets the news that one of their kids was slaughtered by a decadent American. Good luck with that, pal."

"Thanks," Michael said, his voice dry.

Tom bid Rachael an empathetic farewell and followed the director back up the trail. She heard the lieutenant continue to splutter objections as they left. "How do we even write this report?"

"We came, we saw, FBI took jurisdiction," the sheriff told him. "End of story."

"Beginning of ours," Luis muttered. "Okay, let's get the Evidence Response Team out here. Ironically, that would be Ellie, if you hadn't poached her."

"Sorry," Rachael said, smiling for the first time all morning. "Not sorry."

Michael unconsciously echoed what the sheriff had said about being so close to a building full of equipment and trained personnel and not able to use any of it, because everyone at the Locard now became their suspect pool.

"Yes and no." Rachael led them back to the paved pathway, wishing for the first time that the Locard had another route to the parking lot. "Of course everyone on the grounds is a suspect, but—if it doesn't sound too self-serving, putting the body under the goat doesn't make sense. Everyone at the Locard knows we were scheduled to dig up the goat next week in the Body Recovery course. Farida would have been discovered then. But these current two classes—"

"Would be gone and scattered across the country," Luis finished.

"It would benefit a student more than a staff member," she surmised. "I know that sounds like the knee-jerk reaction in every small town when there's a murder—'It couldn't have been one of *us*, it has to be some evil person from outside the community.' But it *is* true. Unless someone thought we could excavate the goat next week and *not* notice the body, blame any insects or smell on the goat, but I can't believe that. Obviously, she's not that deep . . . though the killer might have had a hard time estimating that in the rain and the dark."

"Why not just drag her deeper into the woods?" Luis asked.

"My question exactly," Rachael said as they made their way to the Locard. "Why kill her in the middle of a driving rainstorm? Unless he carried a handy shovel along with him, he—or she—had to dig out a hole with bare hands. He—or she—had to be covered with mud when they finished."

"Why kill her at all?" Michael asked.

Why, indeed, Rachael thought.

Chapter 14

Ellie knew none of this until Rachael interrupted her last hour of class with the shocking news. The interruption was necessary because the FBI had brought out a team of agents to interview each person and they wanted to get that done so the attendees could still leave for the day, more or less on time. Consequently, Ellie cut short her lecture on the latest advances in obtaining CODIS-eligible nuclear DNA profiles from hair shafts, something always thought to be impossible.

Perhaps not a great loss, as she found her audience to be less than captivated. They only needed to know that such a tool existed and to ask their respective labs to do the analysis. Beyond that, well, they didn't need to know how the sausage got made.

So she helped the agents and the attendees to rearrange the desks to create four separate interview stations. Then the attendees were ushered into another classroom to wait their turns. The group from Crime Scene Documentation were kept separate; no need for them to share details of the scene with Ellie's group. When an individual completed their interview, they were shown to one more empty classroom to wait, or, if they had their own transportation, to leave for the day—the preferable choice, since the less people the agents had to keep track of, the better. Everyone present was a known quantity and Rachael had a record of their names, addresses, phone numbers, workplaces, etc. They could leave, but they couldn't *escape*, not for long.

One FBI agent remained in the hallway at all times, to monitor bathroom breaks, usher attendees from one room to the next, and to stay aware of any problems. Bureau personnel behaved as they always did, with courtesy and professionalism, and the attendees remained more curious than agitated. They had been at many, many crime scenes in their time, and knew the process.

But still, it was weird. Ellie was used to processing crime scenes, investigating them, not being a participant in one. And she'd just *gotten* there. She didn't even have the floor plan of the building down yet, everyone in the building a complete stranger. Even Rachael, she barely knew.

Ellie took a deep breath. No matter. She had to hang in, see it through. She had no place to go back to.

Nor did she want to. She *wanted* to be at the Locard, and a series of unfortunate events were not going to drive her out.

Glancing through the panes in the classroom door, Ellie could see a much more animated conversation among Rachael's group. They had actually known the victim and would have more detailed theories of what had happened. To Ellie's group, though they had spent lunch hours with Farida, the crime seemed more of an intellectual exercise mixed with a potentially serious inconvenience. Would they be delayed going home? Would they miss the last day of class? Would they still be issued the all-important certificate of continuing-education credits?

With the interviewing system established, a fresh-faced young agent with a perfectly centered tie took Ellie first. Ellie couldn't help much, since she had never met or even seen Farida, though Rachael had mentioned her during dinner the night before. No, no problems had been mentioned from either Rachael or her own students. No, she did not recall anyone in her class discussing the Saudi student, though she'd only been there since the previous morning. "I was only supposed to guest-lecture a few hours each day, but then Dr. Wright died yesterday—"

"Wait," the young man said, "what?"

She explained about the instructor's untimely accident— apparent accident—and the medical examiner's tentative verdict of sudden heart failure.

"But this Farida Al Talel was not in her class?"

"No."

He made a note, then moved on.

Back out in the hallway, she headed for her new office and ran into Rachael. "Is there anything I can do?"

Rachael rubbed one eye. "Oh my G—my brain's running in a million different directions at once. I'm going to IT to see what the surveillance video shows." After the slightest of hesitations she added: "Come with me."

As they hustled along the shiny floors, she brought Ellie up to date on their current status. The FBI had brought an interpreter, someone much more fluent in Arabic than Hector, to interview the two bodyguards. As the two people closest to Farida, they were the best source of information, but also the most logical suspects. Rachael claimed not to see it—she'd never seen any hint of real conflict among the three—but they *had* been out to the body site every day, right along with Farida, and would know that the goat would not be excavated until they had left the country. "I never saw them argue with Farida. All three seemed to be truly comfortable with each other, exactly like what they were—kids who had grown up together. But on the other hand, who else could possibly have a motive?"

The Information Technology unit consisted of one Cameron, a skinny guy with light brown skin and honey-colored eyes, small tattoos on his neck and both arms. The worn quality of his obscurely worded T-shirt contrasted, somehow, with his meticulously trimmed haircut, and he had either had too much coffee or having four extra people crammed into his workspace messed with his comfort zone. His gaze jerked around toward them as much as it did toward his screens.

The IT "department," as Rachael had explained to her, served the needs of the Locard Institute, maintaining the (somewhat minimal) surveillance cameras, keycards, servers, individual laptops, voicemail system, and the other accouterments of a large office. Cameron's job was to keep the researchers and their research, and the instructors and their coursework, functioning and accessible. He did not conduct crime analysis or research himself.

Behind him stood Agent Michael Tyler and a young woman he introduced as another FBI special agent; Ellie didn't catch her name, because she was too busy reliving the last time she'd seen Michael—when he'd fished her out of the Potomac just as she'd been on the verge of drowning. She'd rescued the person she'd jumped in to save, but other than that, it had not been a very auspicious occasion and she felt awkward. Now he simply nodded at her, said "Dr. Carr" in that gravel-pit voice, and left it at that. She gave him a half smile back and then focused on the screens.

Cameron had three large monitors on his desk, all curved toward him in a gentle scallop. There seemed to be only five surveillance cameras, one over each of the four outside doors and one covering the parking lot. The door cameras covered the stoops and walkways immediately outside the upper and lower north doors, the south door, and the front entryway, which opened onto the courtyard. The north upper door opened from the first-floor hallway, and the north lower door, from the basement hallway next to the cafeteria. The south door opened from the south end of the first-floor hallway onto a sidewalk that circled the building; the wide grassy area where the gym classes used to play sports had long since overgrown. The parking-lot camera appeared to be on a pole at the southeast corner of the lot, aimed toward the gate in the northwest corner.

"We have no interior cameras," Rachael warned.

"Why not?" the female agent asked. She seemed about Ellie's age, with a perfectly light touch of makeup and blond hair in an equally perfect updo. She wore a dark green suit with a skirt, as well-tailored as those of her male counterparts.

"It's come up a few times, but we never saw the need. We do have alarms on all the windows and doors. The windows will alarm if they're opened between seven p.m. and seven a.m. The doors will alarm at any time if they're opened without a keycard. But cameras weren't a thing a hundred years ago when this was a boys' school, and drilling through the plaster to install them seemed more trouble than it's worth. We only put up external ones in case teenage *CSI* fanatics decide to explore—which has never happened. We've never had a break-in."

The agent didn't ask any more follow-up questions, but Ellie caught the slightest eye roll before she turned her attention back to the screens.

"Class ends at five-thirty," Rachael told the agents. "The hotel shuttle usually picks them up at five forty-five, but the driver had called Carrie—the secretary—to say he was stuck in a small jam on Fairhaven Road, where some large branches had fallen across the road. What time did you let yours out?" she asked Ellie.

"Slightly early, maybe five-twenty. I ran out of things to say about getting nuclear DNA from hairs without roots."

"You can do that?" Michael asked.

"So, where do your students go then?" The female agent had clearly shelved talk of hairs for another time. Ellie wondered where Michael's partner, Luis, was. She liked Luis.

"The ones who are local or who rented cars can leave. Since we're so close to DC, a lot of attendees get their own wheels so they can see the sights in their spare time. Those who need the hotel shuttle usually hang out around the first-floor door, or in the parking lot in good weather."

"Which it wasn't, last night," Ellie put in.

"It was *pouring*," Cameron intoned, scowling at the monitor. He had cued up the videos to five-fifteen the previous evening, and his words were instantly verified. Every camera showed a solid, twinkling gray curtain across the landscape, largely blotting out trees and pavement. Only by peering for a while, assisted by shifts in the wind, could Ellie determine which camera was which.

The first screen showed the south door and the front entry. The second screen showed the upper and lower north doors, and the third, the parking lot. The lot, truly larger than the Locard really needed, contained only a smattering of fifteen cars or so. The kitchen and maintenance staff would most likely be gone by that time, Ellie figured, along with any staff member who wanted to beat the storm.

The room became silent as everyone watched. Only the slightest sounds of cloth brushing cloth as someone shifted their weight and a commercially masculine scent wafting up in nervous puffs—Ellie bet on Cameron for the excess of Axe body spray—broke the stillness.

No one moved at the south or front doors. The occasional brave soul dashed out into the rain from the upper north door, pummeling up the sidewalk to the parking lot in a futile attempt to stay at least partly dry. Ellie knew that would not work. When she had arrived at Rachael's house, her pants had still dripped from the knees down. She'd left her shoes stuffed with paper towels by the radiator.

The runners showed up several moments later on the parking-lot cam, frantically opening car doors and collapsing inside. Then headlights would flicker as the lot slowly emptied. The vehicles became dark, shapeless blobs in the dim light and the heavy rain, making it impossible to tell a mini from an SUV. At least Ellie couldn't.

Michael said to the other agent, "Once we have all the statements from the attendees, we can cross-reference with this video, pinpoint who was where when."

"Of course."

"*Of course,*" Ellie mimicked in her head. *Just say "yes," sweetie, we all know you're terribly smart.*

Whoa. Instantly she heard someone else's voice in her head—Aunt Rosalie's saying, "*Cattiness is beneath you, young lady.*"

"There she is," Rachael said, and everyone focused on the middle screen.

The lower north door had opened—they could just see the sharp corner of it at the very bottom of the screen—and two people hustled out. Both wore long coats with hoods, but whether those coats were made of light plastic or heavy wool, Ellie couldn't guess. One figure had their right arm around the shoulders of the other, shorter figure. They walked straight ahead, briskly paced, but not at a run or even a trot.

"You think that's her? Why?" Michael leaned over Cameron's shoulder, earning an annoyed glance.

"It's about her height. And that—that flicker of material by her shoulders—that could be the ends of her headscarf."

"Time?" the female agent asked.

"Five thirty-nine and thirty-eight seconds," Cameron said with another scowl.

"That would fit with what the bodyguards said," she told Michael.

She probably debriefed them herself, being fluent in Arabic, as well as five other languages, Ellie's inner bitch griped. *Stop* that!

"Who is that with her?" Michael asked. He had to know that they didn't know, but hoped their subconscious would come up with something.

Ellie's didn't, and neither did Rachael's. "I have no idea. It could be practically anyone in my class. Farida wasn't particularly tall—I'd guess five-two, the second shortest in my class. That suspect could be anywhere over five-five, since they're hunched against the rain."

"Who has a coat like that?" the female agent asked.

Rachael and Ellie stared at the screen, where Cameron had helpfully frozen the clearest frame of the two people walking away from the lower north door. Farida—whom they presumed to be Farida—wore a knee-length raincoat with a hood.

"She just bought that over the weekend," Rachael said. "I don't know what kind of climate she'd been expecting, but Chesapeake in October was not it."

"The average temperature for yesterday is a high of seventy-three and a low of fifty-five," Cameron said. He stared only at his screens, so didn't seem to speak to anyone in particular. "The record high was ninety-two, and the record low was thirty-nine."

Michael said, "And the man? Or other person? Is the coat familiar?"

He or she wore a nearly full-length raincoat, also with a hood. The floodlight made it glimmer under the shifting rains, but without sunlight outside shades turned to gray-scale. The color of the coat could not be guessed. Nor could Ellie guess at the material, but somehow from the way the light reflected from its surface, she thought it might be some kind of nylon or plastic.

The school didn't have a coatroom or coatracks in the hallway. Ellie's attendees had simply draped their jackets and coats over the backs of their chairs, and a coat that long would have dragged on the floor. "I didn't notice anyone with a coat that length."

Rachael said, "I haven't either, but I haven't really paid attention. A number of them have backpacks or large tote bags. They might have brought it folded up, since it wasn't raining this morning . . ." Her voice trailed off as if checking off a mental inventory of each student and their belongings.

"It's not one of her bodyguards?" Michael asked.

"No," she said immediately. "They both wear black leather jackets, very fashionable. I suspect raincoats wouldn't fit their self-image."

"But she left with him—or her—voluntarily. Who would that be?"

Again, leaving the question deliberately broad, to see what they would say. Ellie knew the technique. She'd been trained in the same place.

She felt Rachael take in a breath, hold it, before answering, and Ellie thought: *Someone just popped into her mind.*

"I don't know. Farida had been friendly with everyone, but seemed to stick to . . . I don't know what you'd call it, rules of engagement, I suppose. She didn't flirt, any more than a beautiful twenty-three-year-old seems to flirt simply by being beautiful and twenty-three. I heard other students invite her out for meals, bar-hopping, even just girls' nights, but I never heard her accept. So to ditch her bodyguards and run out into a maelstrom? I don't know."

"But *is* she leaving voluntarily?" Ellie asked. "Looks like that person has their arm around her pretty tightly."

"She seems to be moving under her own power," the female agent said.

"Do they show up again in the parking lot?" Michael asked. They all waited, gazes locked on the third screen. Nothing moved except the torrential rains, turning the scene fuzzy with each gust, light quavering across the ground as the floodlights reflected off the churning puddles. Five forty-two. Five forty-three. Five forty-four.

Nothing.

A flicker at the bottom of the screen made Ellie think the door had opened again—probably the bodyguards, peeking to see if Farida might be outside for some reason. No one exited.

At five fifty-seven, the shuttle bus entered the lot from the road. It stopped at the lower left edge of the camera's view, obviously getting as close to the pathway as it could.

The other agent leaned closely over Cameron's shoulder, moving her face to within six inches of the screen. Ellie didn't think that would help, and the IT guy's shoulders twitched.

"We can't see who gets on," the female agent complained.

"Back *up*!" Cam snapped. "Back up, back up."

She straightened, stepping back. "We'd hardly be able to tell, anyway, with people wrapped up in coats and umbrellas."

Michael said they'd find out from the other attendees. They probably had a jolly ride back to the hotel, cold and soaking wet and exchanging bitter observations about rain, and would remember who else had been there. "Besides, she walked out at five-forty—"

"Five thirty-nine and thirty-eight seconds," Cameron corrected.

"A little before five-forty, yes. If the person with her killed her, then got on the shuttle, that means he dug up the goat, enlarged the hole enough to fit her in, put the goat back, then maybe jumped out at the end of the group going to the van so no one noticed . . . all in seventeen or eighteen minutes? I won't say it's impossible, but it hardly seems likely."

Rachael agreed. "Plus, they'd be digging through the dead leaves and dirt with their bare hands. I don't know how they would *not* be covered in mud when they finished. Everyone on the shuttle had to be wet, but surely they'd notice someone's pants or sleeves caked with slime."

"And the smell," Ellie said.

"And the smell. Also with the dirt and dead leaves would be dirt and dead leaves soaked in decomposed goat. You don't get that smell out easily. It clings to the clothes even when we try *not* to get too close to bodies. Sometimes I'd go home and take a shower and change and *still* be smelling it."

Cameron spoke up. "There are many compounds that produce different odors during decomposition, usually beginning with trimethylamine, then indole and hydrogen sulfide—"

The other agent made a face, as if suddenly queasy.

"Thank you, Cameron. The point is, other people on the shuttle would notice," Rachael finished.

"We don't know that they didn't," Michael said. "We'll see what the interviewers come back with. But if he was still digging, would the people on the way to the shuttle see him? Her?"

Rachael said she doubted it. "There's still quite a few leaves on the trees between the site and the path. They'd be rushing past in hoods and umbrellas, trying to move fast while avoiding puddles. Dressed in that dark coat, all he had to do was stay low, turn off any light source, and the brush would cover him—or her. Maybe not during the day, but at night? Easily."

"But it wasn't night," the other agent pointed out. "The sun hadn't gone down yet."

"Six twenty-one," Cameron said, both legs jiggling, toes propped on the wheeled spokes of his chair's base. "Sunset, last night, six twenty-one."

"So it was still light out."

"Not last night," Rachael and Ellie said in unison. Between the cloud cover and the trees overhead, Ellie remembered only dark during the trek to the cars. Yes, it had been later than the rest had gone, but the darkness had seemed complete. No gentle twilight to be found.

"Okay, so it was dark. That indicates someone familiar with the grounds," the other agent went on. "Would one of the attendees, even having been here for a week and a half, be able to find that place in the dark?"

Ellie had wondered the same thing. She hadn't been there and so could not picture how far the killer would have had to walk or drag Farida, or how much space he or she would have to work in once they got there. It somewhat cleared her students, frankly. The body site had not been part of their coursework and they had no reason to go there. On the other hand, the teaching schedule allowed for plenty of breaks and there were no restrictions on movement; attendees could wander around the grounds at will, were even encouraged to take in the surroundings and enjoy the beauties of nature. Crime scene investigators could work crazy and hectic hours and needed to learn to take breaks when they could get them. Most likely, the attendees in her class had also checked out the body sites at least once during the past ten days. A body farm to a CSI equaled a sculpture garden to an art student.

But would one become familiar enough with the location to both get there and bury a body in the dark, or even partial dark?

They continued to watch the parking-lot video. Cameron tweaked the speed to 1.25 and the seconds passed a bit faster. Watching surveillance videos took a lot of patience—watching it in real time made the minutes crawl, but a higher speed created the risk of missing something.

Two cars left at nearly the same time, six-four, then a third at six-ten. All three had been parked at the far south end, nearest the pathway, and their occupants appeared as vague blurs moving near slivers of even vaguer blurs at the very bottom edge of the screen.

Between six-ten and six-thirty, Cameron clicked the speed up to 1.5 and four more people, presumably staff, exited and drove away. These unlucky few had parked more toward the center, most likely in the morning when it had not been raining. At the end of the day this created twenty or thirty more feet of downpour to pass through. As with two figures at six-thirty.

Rachael looked at Ellie. "That's probably us."

Ellie agreed, though between the rain shifting the light and the distance covered by the camera, she could barely recognize the outlines of her prized 1965 Mustang.

"There's still three cars left. Who would that be?" Michael asked Rachael. "Director Coleman?"

"No, he'd left early for some dinner he had to attend with his wife and a couple of representatives. Formal thing."

"On a Wednesday?" the female agent asked.

Rachael stared at her. "You're not from DC . . . originally, I mean?"

She asked this so diplomatically that the woman frowned. "No! I'm from . . . a little place, you won't have heard of it. Why?"

"The senators and representatives almost always fly home to their districts on the weekends, to do their campaigning and fundraising and photo ops with their constituents. They're not allowed to do that on federal time. So pretty much everything that happens in DC happens on a Tuesday, a Wednesday, or a Thursday."

"Oh."

Cameron gave the monitor such a dark look that Ellie wondered why—then realized he scowled at the reflection of the female agent behind him. Perhaps he didn't like women, or *really* didn't like people crowding his space. Or—what was it Rachael had said about the color green? Maybe he didn't like the color of her suit.

Michael directed them back to the issue at hand. "Who else would be here late?"

"Hector's been hanging around waiting for the daily stats from overseas for a project he's working on. Barbara had too, until . . . Gary gets absent-minded sometimes and forgets to go home until his wife calls him. Angela is our second-shift maintenance person. She comes in about three, overlaps with Stuart to take care of two-man jobs, then finishes up. We don't have a night watchman; Angela goes around, makes sure all the rooms are empty, that no one forgot to turn off a hot plate or cranked the thermostat up too high or down too low, if they left the coffeepot on, that sort of thing. She checks that all the doors are locked and goes home about seven p.m. But if someone's waiting out an experiment or simply working late, she leaves them to it."

Michael and his fellow agent exchanged a glance, and Ellie knew they were making a mental note: *Talk to Angela.*

They had continued to watch the screens during all this conversation, but the three vehicles continued to sit, alone, in the rainy parking lot.

"Is that all you guys are going to need?" Cameron asked finally, speaking to his screens.

Michael said yes, and could they have a copy of every camera from, say, Tuesday morning until the time the body was discovered on Thursday?

This elicited an exasperated sigh from Cameron. "Do you have a USB with at least four terabytes of storage? Or an external hard drive? Because I don't have too many of them handy and I only use the solid-state kind, and Shirley always questions it when I order more, and—"

"It will be all right, Cameron," Rachael soothed, adding that the Locard would definitely front the FBI a four-terabyte flash drive and she would personally okay with Shirley the purchase of a replacement. Michael said the FBI would also repay them with a new one.

Ellie had the impression that Cameron in IT had a specific picture in mind of how he expected his day at work to go, and it didn't include handing out high-capacity blank storage media to any federal agency who happened to ask. This impression warned her that right now might not be the best time to ask him about her keycard as well.

They left Cameron in peace and headed back to the first floor.

"All right," Michael said. "Let's talk numbers. How many students from each class?"

Rachael answered immediately. "Twenty-three in Ellie's, twenty-four in mine."

"Staff?"

"Thirty-two . . . at last count. Plus, three adjuncts, none of whom are here this month."

"So there was thirty-two staff members and forty-seven students here yesterday?"

"Mm . . . no. Our frauds analyst is out on maternity leave. Our dean of research is at a possible mass grave in Venezuela. CiCi, our media manager, is out with the flu. As I said, Gerald left early yesterday. So—twenty-eight staff? But I can't be sure."

The female agent said, "We're going to have to search everyone, students and staff, for a raincoat that fits that description. And their cars, to look for mud, blood, and other physical evidence from the site."

Ellie tried to imagine how they'd get search warrants to examine vehicles and homes or hotel rooms for forty-seven attendees and twenty-eight staff.

Michael held the door to the stairwell open for them and didn't show enthusiasm for the idea either. "We'll try to eliminate as many people as we can first. Sounds like this is going to be one huge grid of timetables—who was where and when, and for how long, and can it be verified? Like the train schedule in an Agatha Christie."

"Look at you, quoting the master." Rachael smiled. The first smile Ellie had seen from her since finding Farida's body.

The female agent asked, with a sigh in her voice: "Do we even know the corpse *is* this Saudi girl yet?"

"We should soon," Michael Tyler answered, and asked her to check on the agents interviewing the course attendees. They needed to know who was on the shuttle, who wasn't, and how and when the others left the grounds. He would check in with his partner first—Luis waited outside to steer the Evidence Response Team—and then he would find Rachael to do the same survey of the staff.

Rachael headed for the office after asking Ellie to show Michael to the turnoff. Somewhat mysteriously, since Ellie had only become an employee the day before, and Michael had already been to the site. But without any other immediate plans she gestured toward the north door and they fell into step—uneasily, on her part. Their reunion felt awkward. The case they'd both been working, only a month before, had been upsetting for a number of reasons, though none had been his fault.

"By the way," she said. "I never did thank you formally for saving my life."

"Eh, you were right at the bank. You would have made it anyway."

She didn't agree, but let it go. "So, why are you on this case, if you don't mind my asking? The victim isn't a minor. Is it only because you were in the neighborhood, sorta?"

He shook his head. "I'm transitioning out of CARD. Luis and I are going to violent crimes."

She had met Michael at a home where the four-month-old baby had gone missing. As part of the FBI's Child Abduction Rapid Deployment team, he and his partner, Luis Alvarez, investigated kidnappings and disappearances of minor children. It was tough and sometimes heartrending work. "Wow . . . that's . . ." Questions crowded her mind: Had the stories of harmed children gotten to him? He was divorced, Luis married, and they both had children; working child cases could be particularly difficult for parents—they looked at the victims and saw their own kids. But there were plenty of other reasons to shuffle around at the bureau: unit tensions, promotion stalls, juggling schedules. And in reality, violent crimes work had a touch more social prestige. She didn't know him well enough to ask.

"Yeah. We start November first. So this is who you left us for." He glanced around at the deep woods, the still-damp paved pathway with a few lingering puddles. The birds had gotten over the activity and were singing away, ignoring the humans or perhaps talking about them. "Liking it so far?"

"It's been quite a day and a half." But she knew her smile answered his question.

They passed the small BODY SITE 2 placard and she stopped at the BODY SITE 1 marker. He couldn't have missed it—the Evidence Response Team had tied yellow crime-scene tape in two long strands on either side of the trail, designating where agents could walk without too much danger of destroying evidence—or at least any evidence that hadn't already been destroyed by the class's trip out there that morning.

"This is it," she said unnecessarily.

"What do you think of it? The scene, I mean. It's not a big area—suggest anything to you?"

She blinked. "I haven't seen it."

"The buried goat—"

"I haven't been in there. No need to be . . . and I *have* only been here for a day and a half."

"Oh, right," he said, and she wondered if that had been some sort of test. Probably not. She could hardly be a serious suspect—she'd never even met the victim.

He looked down at her. "I'm sorry, but—"

"I've got to stay behind the tape. It's okay. I know the drill."

"I know you know." He gave her a light ghost of a smile, then moved into the woods.

She watched him go, wondering who had been available to work ERT today. She would undoubtedly know each of them, and likely had processed scenes with them. Her ex-husband, Adam, might be right through those trees. Part of her longed to go see the body excavation, learn everything she could about this poor dead girl, get her hands in the dirt, and look through the insects . . . but another part didn't want to see any of her former coworkers. What was it Thomas Wolfe said? You can't go home again?

She turned and headed back to the Locard.

Chapter 15

Michael Tyler's socks were getting wet. The saturated ground and leaf cover had oozed up against his shoes just enough to creep through each tiny hole in the stitching. Days like this were why men used to wear rubbers, rubber covers made to snap over your outside shoes and prevent exactly that oozing. When had they fallen out of style? The sixties? The seventies? When had men decided to make fashion a priority over dry socks?

Only four ERT techs worked the crime scene, but that was all right; the space didn't allow for more. Luis remained on the path and stayed out of the clearing proper.

The techs had already photographed, videoed, sketched, and used string and spikes to create a grid around the body. They now prepared to move the remains of Chester to a plastic sheet, on one side of the grave.

"It's a mess," Luis told him.

"A complete mess," a tech echoed. "Don't know what part of the hole was already here, what part he added to make room for her, what bugs are here for that thing or for her—"

"They barely had time to start on her," another argued.

"What vegetation was on it, or what got caught last night when he moved all this stuff around?"

"Ready?" a third asked, patience clearly waning. They all wore no-longer-white Tyvek jumpsuits and latex gloves, with extra sleeve sections from the elbow to wrist for added protection. *They* had Tyvek booties keeping their shoes dry, Michael noted. He wondered how long those would hold out against the elements as the techs continued their conversation.

"Is this thing going to hold together if we try to move it? I can't even tell if it's still in one piece."

"Only one way to find out."

"It should hold up. Some guy did this last night in the dark and a monsoon and it looks like all the pieces are in the right places."

"Why here? Did he think they'd dig up this stupid goat and not notice there's a human under it?"

"Maybe it's insult to injury. She's probably Muslim, and putting a pig on top of her would be, like, the worst thing someone could possibly do to her."

"Worse than killing her?"

"Yes."

"Except it's not a pig."

"But we usually bury pigs. Maybe he assumed it would be a pig."

"The two-inch-long fur didn't tip him off? One, two, *three*."

All four of them had surrounded the dead goat, equally spaced, north-east-south-west, and they lifted and moved with their bare hands. Michael assumed they didn't dare use shovels or metal plates as they usually would, since that risked damaging the body underneath. Chester resisted at first, but then came loose with a sucking sound so they could swing his wet, mud- and leaf-covered body onto the plastic sheet, with only a few tufts of fur left behind.

"This thing has to come back with us, doesn't it?" one of the techs complained. The lab is going to reek—"

"No, no. The MEs. We'll take it to the MEs and process it there. Then they can dispose of it."

"Yeah, our facilities aren't meant for that."

The evidence examination rooms at the FBI had plenty of hoods and airflow equipment to deal with clothing, weapons, even vehicles contaminated with decomposed matter—but an actual *body*, human or animal? Not so much.

With that settled, the four techs gazed down into the partially cleared hole. Luis and Michael leaned forward, trying to find a safe place to put their feet, and craned their necks.

"That's her," Luis said.

"It's the scarf they described," Michael agreed.

"I checked her Facebook page. That's her."

The young woman lay on her left side—oddly, just as Chester had. Her arms were folded up, hands by her face, knees pulled up, her black hair still silky, even with twigs and dead leaves and clumps of mud tangled in the strands. She wore her new raincoat, pants and shoes sticking out from its lower hem. Michael could tell her skin had been creamy, even given the distortion caused by the strangling.

The blue-and-green scarf had been pulled around her neck and knotted. It nearly disappeared under her chin where it had dug so deeply into her flesh. One of the techs squatted on their heels and pulled, gingerly, on the right flap of the raincoat. "I don't see any blood."

"Strangled with her own scarf. So he didn't bring a weapon with him," Michael muttered.

"In a manner of speaking," Luis said, "if he was at all familiar with her, he knew she'd be wearing one."

"Mm, true."

"Nails are broken, some of them," the tech continued, prompting more conversation.

"Please have gotten some of his skin," another tech said.

"Bet it's hers. Scratches on her neck—she was trying to pull the scarf away."

"Maybe both?"

"You're such a dreamer."

With obvious reluctance the four workers tore themselves away from the body, which would have to remain until the ME investigator arrived—and they had lots to do first. Luis and Michael backed out of the trail as the techs carried Chester and his tarp back to their van, then returned to work the grid, poking through the leaves and twigs and mud for anything that looked like a clue. A leaf that didn't seem to belong, a mass of insects gathered around a dropped piece of flesh or food, something easy like the killer's driver's license, that sort of thing.

Luis asked what he'd learned inside the Locard, and Michael summarized his past hour. "Surveillance time stamps are accurate, so she walked out from the lower level at five-forty. My guess? She was dead by six."

"Me? I say five forty-four."

"I'd like to come back here at five-forty tonight, see how much light there really is out there."

Luis held up his watch, which read 2:35. "Probably not going to be difficult, dude. I'd guess we'll still be here at five-forty *tomorrow* night. She walked out under her own power?"

"It *looked* voluntary, from the back in the dark in a pouring rain. He could have had a gun in her side. He could have had a hand over her mouth. He could have said, 'Hey, the shuttle's here, your bodyguards said they'd take your purse and you'd better hurry.'"

"Would she go?"

"Why not? She's been hanging out with these people for a week and a half. Why would she even hesitate?"

Luis had a pensive look. "Rachael described her as pretty traditional, so I'm thinking she's a little—well, sheltered. Those girls are so closely monitored over there that they're . . ."

"Not warned about stranger danger?"

"Yeah, kinda. There's very, *very* little run-of-the-mill street crime in Saudi Arabia. I mean, if you tick off the royal family, you might wind up in jail or stripped of your assets or dead and never mentioned again, but mugged in an alley? Doesn't happen."

A bird sounded off in the tree above Michael, a sound so loud that he winced. "Risky, though—how could he know she wouldn't scream bloody murder, or at least refuse to go anywhere with anyone who wasn't one of her cousins?"

"He couldn't—but if she did, he could just shrug, say 'suit yourself,' and walk away. No harm, no foul."

Michael stifled a smile. Luis always reconstructed crimes in his head as if he were seeing a movie, including not just dialogue but gestures, facial expressions, and probably background music.

Luis went on. "Everything *about* this is risky. There's two classes, plus staff, going home, moving along this walkway. They couldn't know that Rachael or one of the instructors might decide to check on the goat, maybe worried that the hard rain could wash too much dirt or body parts away—though they'd have to be dedicated as hell to walk out here in that rain. I ran into Subway on the way home—twenty feet in, twenty feet back to my car—and my wife says my good shoes are probably ruined."

Michael agreed. "Not to mention they're committing a crime on the grounds of the best forensic institute in the country, occupied by not only the best experts but two classrooms full of trained investigators."

"Had to be spur of the moment," Luis said. "Over-whelmed by lust, he grabs her or at least makes a pass at her. Or maybe they're flirting, but he wants more than she's ready for. She turns him down, he goes nuts."

"The ground's already disturbed for the goat, so it might be easier to dig up than somewhere else in the forest. If he just drags her farther in—people are going to notice she's missing, going to know the Locard is the last place she was seen. The grounds would be searched."

"If he puts her under the goat, maybe, *maybe*, she won't be discovered until next week. The attendees would be gone. If it's a staff member, they've bought a few more days to pack a go bag or at least think up a decent story. He may have thought the body was more concealed than she actually was, in the dark."

"No one would have planned to murder someone while surrounded by the people who investigate when someone's murdered."

"Nah," Luis said. "It couldn't possibly have been planned."

Chapter 16

Inside, the interviews continued. By some weird form of psychic osmosis, the attendees and certainly the staff now had at least the basics of the plot: Farida had been found buried under Chester the goat. Clearly, a murder, and a murder that had taken place the night before after class. Perhaps while most of them had still been on campus, unless Farida had cooperated until after the majority had left, and only then had things turned sour.

Everyone who had met the dead woman professed to like her—indeed, the young agent with the perfectly centered tie thought to himself: she had been young, pretty, lively, both friendly and exotic at the same time—what's not to like? That said, it had been a short acquaintance, and these were people who investigated murders for a living, so along with pity for a too-short life came a virulent wave of curiosity. A brutal murder in utterly unique circumstances was way more interesting than checklists of what your scene notes had to contain in order to meet accreditation standards.

Every agent prefers cooperative witnesses or suspects . . .

but these were a little *too* cooperative. The agent found himself on the receiving end of more questions than answers.

"How deep was she buried?" a Border Patrol agent named Stefanie asked him.

"I don't know," he said with complete truth, and then tried to turn it around. "How deep do you think she would need to be buried?"

"It depends on when he planned for her to be found—if at all. Does it look like he used a shovel or bare hands? The ground was so freakin' wet out there—it was like soup, no, like . . . oatmeal, maybe. How'd she die? How'd he do it? Stabbing?"

"I don't have those details." Though he did. "Did you talk to Farida often? What about?"

"About Saudi Arabia." Stefanie—"Call me Stef"—had cropped hair, a deep tan, and hyperactive feet. With her right leg crossed over her left, her right foot danced a jig and sometimes her hands joined in with a gesture or a sketch in the air, waving a metal water bottle as if it were a signal flag. "Do you know women *just* got the right to drive there a few years ago? They only got to *vote*, like, not even ten years ago. Can you imag—well, *you* probably don't care."

Because he wasn't Saudi? Because he was a man? He didn't ask.

"But it's so bizarre. She only got to come here at all because her family sent bodyguards to make sure she wore her headscarf and that she was never, ever, alone with a man. They didn't even like me sitting with her on the hotel shuttle. Those two guys always looked at me like I'm some kind of whore who was going to whisk her off to a brothel to ply her with drugs and booze and . . . Ohmigod, *men.*"

He jumped in quickly while she paused for breath. "Did she say she was unhappy?"

"Well . . . no. But she wouldn't have dared, would she? People go to jail over there for criticizing the government.

It's, like, an actual *law.* It's on the books. And for sure those two goons would have ratted her out as soon as she uttered a discouraging word. It had to be them. She probably talked back to one, or let her scarf slip, and they did an honor killing. And there's two of them, so they could cover for each other."

"Did she say she was afraid of them?"

"No," she admitted. "But they grew up together. She probably thought she was safe because they were family. They're *really* into family over there. Her parents are trying to marry her off to some guy she's met once, and she was going right along with it."

"So she had a fiancé?" Maybe one of the bodyguards secretly loved her, didn't want her with another man.

"Not officially. Not yet—at least according to her. But let's face it, it's not like she had any real rights. If Daddy says you marry this guy, you marry this guy."

The agent didn't argue, both because he didn't know much about Saudi Arabia and because he suspected that most of what Stefanie Parsons "knew" had been assumed rather than learned. But he didn't dismiss a word of it. One or both of those two bodyguards could easily strangle a petite female, and close friends and family always make more likely candidates than a casual and recent acquaintance. "Did you interact with her outside this campus?"

"Sure. We're both staying at the hotel, so we met in the bar for drinks a couple times. Meaning *I* had drinks, she had cola, and the hotel bar is technically inside the restaurant so she could tell her parents she hadn't been in a bar. And, of course, the bodyguards were there, but . . . she could have snuck something into the glass if she wanted to—they weren't paying any attention. Those guys *love* sports. Any kind of game that was on the TV, baseball, golf, rugby, football, they were whooping it up."

"Anyplace outside the hotel?"

"Nope. I asked her a bunch of times, even just McDonald's, but nope. She and the goons did rent a car over the weekend to go see the monuments and the other stuff—she wanted to see Air and Space, they wanted to go up in the Washington—but that's it. That I know of. She could have gone out with someone else, I guess. But I can't see why she would, if she wouldn't go with me."

Maybe to give her ears a rest, the agent thought.

A half hour later the same agent had moved on to Oliver Suarez, from Montana. The smooth-faced man, of about his own age, immediately interested the agent more than Stef had. For one thing, he was the first person the agent encountered who seemed more sad than curious. Oliver Suarez, from Montana, didn't ask a single question, but he did repeat more than once: "I can't believe she's dead. I can't believe that could happen."

"What could happen? That she could be murdered, or that she could be murdered here?"

"Both, I guess."

"Why?"

The guy's mouth fell open slightly. "Well—because . . . it's a *school,* a school full of CSIs. How could someone here be a killer? How could someone murder somebody at the *Locard* and get away with it?"

"They haven't," the agent pointed out, feeling kind of slick with this observation. "Yet."

But Oliver didn't even seem to be listening. "And this is America, not a backward, repressive place like . . . She was *free* here."

Not that free, not with the bodyguards watching her every move. Though he had already asked about that, and Oliver had said that she didn't seem concerned. Her cousins didn't worry her—but then, she never did anything wrong either. She seemed really conservative. The agent assumed that meant no flirting with Oliver, a slender guy dressed in a neat flannel shirt and black jeans and well-trimmed sandy-blond hair. "You were friends?"

"Yes. I mean, we only met last week, but we talked."

"During breaks and suchlike?"

"Yeah."

The agent asked the same things he'd asked Stef, whether they'd met outside of class or anywhere other than the hotel lobby, restaurant, or bar.

Oliver didn't hesitate. "No."

"Did you ask her to?"

"Sure. Practically everyone offered to take her with them to see the sights. I rented a car so I could get around—I hit all the major museums over the weekend and have checked out a bunch of restaurants—but she always said no. She had to go places only with those two guys."

The agent sat back, rubbed one eye, affecting weariness with the long day, while his mind probed Oliver's wall for weak spots. He caught a whiff of the guy's aftershave or cologne . . . this could mean sweat had begun to pop out of some pores, always an interesting sign of agitation. "Well, she was from a different culture."

"You can say *that* again."

"Did she express any dissatisfaction with life in Saudi Arabia? Did she ever say that she'd like to live here?"

The young man seemed even more dispirited at Farida's lack of interest in defecting than in her death. "No."

"Did you ask her?"

"If she liked Saudi Arabia? Not in so many words."

The agent's patience waned. Time for a more direct approach. "Look, dude, I get it. This fresh, gorgeous, exotic creature comes into your orbit and you're hooked. Maybe you even felt sorry for her, thought to yourself, 'Let the poor, regimented kid live a little, taste life on the wild side before her parents hand her over to stay barefoot and pregnant for the rest of her days.' You're only here for a couple of weeks, then you'll part ways, never to be seen again. Your wife will never know."

Oliver had been looking away, refusing to agree, but not refusing to listen, but this last remark snapped his attention back to the razor's edge. He couldn't help looking down at his left hand, where the faintest tan line around the ring finger gave him away. "No. Farida had—she had standards. She had *morals*."

"You respected that. You didn't want to hurt her—"

"No!" Oliver's voice ticked a few decibels upward, enough that people at other interview stations turned to look. He noticed them noticing, lowered it again. "I know what you're doing, okay? You think I don't know? I wouldn't hurt her—she was a good person. Her religion and her customs and her family meant something to her, and I liked her. But that was it. She didn't flirt with me and I didn't flirt with her. She didn't flirt with anybody."

"Okay. Got it. But she got on *somebody's* nerves. Do you have any idea who that might have been?"

"No," he said, his words crisp and firm. "Not at all."

The agent had interviewed enough people to know when the interview had ended. This one had.

Next.

Across the hall sat a different agent, this one drawing close to the mandatory retirement age of fifty-seven, thinking how now that he didn't have to care about promotions and jots on his résumé and racking up the overtime, he could appreciate this particular murder for just how bizarre it was. First you had someone buried under a goat. Next that goat was part of a forensic institute's practice body farm. On top of *that*, the victim hailed from one of the most repressive, unabashedly gender-segregated societies in the world. Maybe *the* most, though doubtless their king—they still had a *king,* for cryin' out loud, and he wasn't some kind of sentimental figurehead like the rulers in England, he was an honest-to-God *"my word is law and I'll cut off your head if you even think of bitching about it"* king—this king would be deeply insulted to hear the agent's thoughts after the king changed all sorts of things, like letting women drive and allowing young men to listen to rock music and all that. The agent had spent a few years trying to infiltrate terrorist groups in the Middle East, and considered himself an expert on their culture.

At least more so than this guy in front of him, one Caleb Astor, a crime scene tech from Missouri. "Why do you think this particular victim?"

"I have no idea," the guy answered, reasonably enough, but then tried to answer the question, anyway. "She was young and pretty? She was female? She was available? How'd she die, anyway?"

"I don't have all the details yet." Information here was to flow in one direction, and one direction only.

Though he did have that particular piece of information, the mode of death, and it made him check out everybody's hands. As the ligature tightened around the girl's neck, she might have reached back and dug nails into the killer's arms or hands.

He saw nothing on Caleb Astor's hands or arms. The man wore a short-sleeved T-shirt, slightly underdressed for the weather, but clearly had no scabs to hide.

"Does seem kind of weird," Caleb said.

"What does?" *Other than everything?*

"She's the only one walking around with personal body-guards, and *she* gets killed. *Two* bodyguards. And they're not tiny dudes. They're kinda scary."

"Maybe the killer saw it as a challenge."

"Sounds nuts."

Don't know, the agent thought. It would be one heck of a challenge. "Do you think there's a political angle?"

"How would I know?" Caleb Astor said, but, again, went on regardless: "Got to be."

"Why?"

"There's other pretty girls in this building. There's easier girls in this building—I mean, ones who aren't terrified to be alone with a man and who don't have hired muscle following them everywhere."

"Why do you assume it's a man?"

The guy all but rolled his eyes. "Because it's a pretty young girl. But, okay, maybe they don't care about that, but then there definitely has to be a political angle. Why the *one* person who's a Saudi national? It's a big middle finger to the terrorists."

"Or a big middle finger to the Locard."

Caleb Astor considered this. "Like someone's using their training against them? Kinda like that BTK guy."

"Who?"

"The BTK Killer. He got a degree in criminal justice, learning all about how cops investigate crimes, forensics, everything—so he could get away with murder."

"Possible," the agent said, trying for a grave tone but inwardly giggling. The idea of a serial killer going to CSI school made him chuckle for no really good reason. "But why right now? Why this victim? Did anybody here talk about politics? Seem aggressive toward her or her cousins?"

"No," Caleb said without hesitation, as if the notion surprised him a little. "Not that I know of, but I only saw her at lunch. She was such a cute kid. Everybody liked her."

"Okay. So, when did you see her last?"

"Dunno . . . lunch yesterday, probably."

"Anything happen at lunch? The dead girl argue with anyone? Or seem buddy-buddy with anyone in particular?"

"No."

"What about at the end of the day? After class?"

"Eh, I don't know—if I saw her, I don't remember it. It was chaos—pouring like there's a hurricane coming through out there, and everyone trying to cover themselves up with their coats, when it would have taken a hazmat suit to stay dry."

"Did you take the shuttle?"

"No, I rented a car. I like my own wheels, and I wanted to see Arlington while I was here."

"So you left right away?"

"Yeah. No—well, we were all hanging around by the door, griping about the rain, and I was kinda hoping it would let up, but finally when they made a run for it—"

"Who's *they*?"

"The shuttle group. I figured I might as well . . . I could hang around here all night or I could get wet. So I got wet."

"And you didn't notice Farida in that group?"

"I didn't notice anybody. We all pulled our coats up over our heads, held bags over our heads, whatever. Didn't do any good. I've been drier in my swimming pool."

"You're all at the same hotel?"

"Yep."

"Did you hang out with anyone that night? See the body-guards? Anyone mention Farida?"

"Nope. By the time I got there, I just wanted a shower and delivery pizza . . . I did go down to the lobby to get a beer from their mini-mart. The chick from here, I think she works for you—Alyssa—she was there getting a wine. Some round-headed kid from the other class, Ollie, I think his name is. They were talking."

"About Farida?"

"No, about that teacher who died yesterday—"

"Doctor"—the agent consulted his notebook; he knew the name, but some instinct made him downplay it—"Wright. She didn't teach the victim's course?"

"No. She lectured our class. She talked to theirs about DNA collection once last week, while we got the digital analysis girl, for about two hours, but that was it."

The agent didn't try to wade through that syntax. He only knew that two dead people in as many days raised some red flags in his brain, but—what connection could there be? "Any interaction between the doctor and the Saudi?"

The guy shrugged. "How would I know?"

Again fair enough. "What did this teacher die of, again?"

"Acid. I guess she broke a bottle, choked to death on acid fumes."

"Ouch," said the agent.

Chapter 17

"Their chick," Alyssa, sat across from the agent next. She seemed vaguely familiar to him; he had probably seen her haunting the halls of Quantico or the Hoover Building. She rattled off her title, GS level, and current assignment with the narcotics task force, and added that she also worked ERT.

"So you should be out there right now," he joked. "In the woods with your friends."

"Yes." It did not seem like a joke to her at all.

"You probably know every one of them," he added more thoughtfully. If you were going to kill someone, it couldn't hurt to have your buddies working the crime scene . . .

"What did you think of this dead girl?" he asked.

"She talked a good game," she told him, after taking a moment to consider.

"What does that mean?"

"She was all bouncy and happy all the time. Like that would make us forget that fifteen of the nineteen 9/11 bombers came from Saudi Arabia."

Uh-*huh*. "So you didn't like her, then?"

"No, I mean . . ." She tucked a few brown strands of hair behind one ear. "I didn't *dislike* her. I felt sorry for her."

He said nothing. Waited. Always a good interrogation ploy.

"I mean, what else could she do? She's from a place where she's not allowed to go to the store unless Dad sends a brother along to make sure she's not flashing her boobs at crowds of guys. Sure, she can go to college and get a job and maybe even work with people of the opposite sex, but only as long as her dad or husband says it's okay. Her parents are making her marry some guy she's never *met.* Of course we all look at her like she's some kind of pathetic little brainwashed flat-earther . . . What else could she do but pretend it's all *great*? That her country is making such great strides because she can go to a mall, take off the burka, and, for your information, this whole marriage thing is just fine with her?" Alyssa sat back, crossed her arms. "No one wants to be *pitied.*"

The agent had listened to a lot of people rant over the years, and recognized the permanently scowled face of the permanently dissatisfied. But he didn't want to dismiss it. No matter how you stretched logistics and time, it still made more sense that the two cousins had killed the girl when she got out of line. That was their *job,* if taken to an extreme.

So he'd really like to know whether the recently deceased had been about to fling herself at the door of the State Department and ask for asylum, or if she'd been as proper and pious as everyone else had described. "You think she *was* unhappy? Didn't want to go home?"

"Would you?"

"Did she say so? When?"

"Not to me." A shrug, and he pictured her pedaling a bicycle backward, away from her statements. "I barely knew her. She probably didn't even know my name."

Thanks for nada, then. "Do you have anything else you'd like to tell me?"

She gazed directly into his eyes. "Nope."

By five o'clock, the agent was ready for dinner, a beer, and a cigar, in that order, but he had only one more interviewee to go and then he could get out of there and back to the city to write up his reports. It would be nice if they could wait until tomorrow, but with a Saudi national brutally murdered so close to DC, that would probably not be an option.

This last guy looked sensible enough, a brawny white guy with a weathered face and massive hands, calm but cautious, not hostile but a long way from puppy-dog eager-to-please. Cop, the agent bet himself. Large city, supervisory position. Smoker, from the smell of his clothes. He opened with, "Hi. Thanks for your help, I'll try to make this brief. Your name?"

"Craig Bennett, sahgeant. NYPD. I was head of homicide."

Two points, two points, two points, the agent thought. "Was?"

"I mean, I am still, but I'm taking over as forensic services lieutenant at the beginning of December."

"Ah. That's why you're here? What course?"

"Collecting Evidential DNA."

"Did you know the dead girl?"

"I *saw* her, in the hallways and at lunch. I don't believe I ever spoke ta her."

"But you know who we're talking about? Farida Al Talel."

"The Saudi girl." He pronounced the country as "soddy" rather than "sowdi." "She always had a headscahf on, you couldn't really miss her. Cute kid. Lively, always talking . . . the way girls are at that age."

"What did she talk about?"

"Don't know. I wasn't that close."

"Okay. Hear anyone else talking *about* her?"

"No. Other than 'I guess that girl's from Saudi Arabia.' That's about it."

"Nothing more personal?"

"No. I think people were mainly surprised—*I* was surprised—that she was here at all. Women aren't even allowed to drive over there, or weren't. I didn't think people there let their girls out of the house, much less halfway around the world. But then that's what the bodygahds were for."

The agent made some notes, thinking, *This guy doesn't know anything about this particular crime, reasonably enough . . . but he's got to know a lot about crimes, period.* "You've certainly investigated a lot more murders than I have, so, as a longtime homicide cop, if you had to make a wild-ass guess—who's our guy?"

Craig Bennett's face went a little flat, unimpressed by the flattery. But he was also a professional, and so appeared to give this careful thought. "Those two guys with her, Frick and Frack, I call 'em. Apparently, they're family, but also political guardians. A lot can go wrong with both those relationships, know what I mean?"

"I do. Anything else?"

The NYPD detective hesitated. "Next I'd say that guy who was in class with her. I don't know his name, little guy, blond hair, clean-shaven. He had the hots for her bad."

"Really."

"Always sat next to her at lunch. She seemed to like him too, but hahd to know how much from a distance. I only noticed them at all because he was so clearly gaga. Nothing wrong with that. Young love, all cute and sweet."

"Until she says no."

"Exactly." Craig Bennett spread his hands as if disavowing any concrete knowledge. "Whether anything like that brewed, I have no idea, I'm just glancin' at them from three tables away. But if it were my case, I'd talk to him right after Frick and Frack."

"Huh." The agent put a hand on his stomach to cover the rumble. Time to wrap this up. "We'll check that out, and, of course, Frick and Frack as well. Who *were* Frick and Frack, anyway?"

"They was an ice-skating slapstick comedy team. Skated with the original Ice Follies for forty or so years. The comedy was silly, but the ice skating was actually pretty impressive."

The agent stared. This guy was screwing with him. Cops tended to get prickly around feds.

But Craig Bennett smiled. "The only reason I know that is because Frack was my great-great-grandfather. It's my mother's family's only claim to fame. Lord knows, they never done anything else of note."

"Okay." The agent's stomach rumbled again. "Anything else? What do you think of this place?"

"The Locard? It's pretty good. The course is stringent— it's not all the instructor reliving their glory days or commercial product demos, like other places I've been."

"What about security? Is it possible someone wandered onto the grounds and stumbled on this young lady?"

"Anything's *possible*. But I doubt that. I don't know the grounds real good, but it feels like we're pretty isolated here. Some random killer would have to be out and about during a downpohr looking for a victim, catch her when she's outside for some reason, and then—is it true, she was buried under the goat?"

"That's what I've heard."

"They'd have to know about that too, or find it in the near dark. So I doubt it. But as for security, there isn't any, to speak of. Hardly any cameras and no guard. It's like, I don't know, a library or something... There's nothing here to steal, so they don't get too concerned about it. Plus, a lot of the staff are ex–law enforcement, and so are most of the students, and you know . . . there's no place *less* secure than a police department."

The agent cocked his head slightly, and waited for him to continue.

"It's a place nobody wants to come to, innocent and guilty alike, so break-ins aren't a big threat. *And* it's full of people who are armed and trained. Airports, medical examiner labs, and hospitals all have stricter procedures than places like this, but the Locard—they're comfortable and feel secure, and that makes them complacent. As far as security goes, the outer doors lock behind you, and that's about it. A child could murder someone here. Though that doesn't mean," he finished thoughtfully, "they'd get away with it. It *is* a school for CSIs, aftuh all."

Chapter 18

After Rachael's thorough debriefing—too polite to be called an interrogation, at least it had seemed so to her—she made her way back outside to the pathway and found Michael and Luis in conversation. The rain remained in the clouds, but refused to issue any guarantees or even reassurances. Instead it waited, watched, and debated whether to torment them with another deluge. The sky might be feeling generous . . . or it might be playing with them like a cat with a moth, ready to pounce the moment they took their first easy breath.

She recognized the identical look with which they regarded her—awkward but firm, concerned but cautious. As a technical suspect/witness/involved party, she should not be there, should not be near the crime scene, should not be given any information whatsoever. Except that the path formed the only egress between the school and the street. Their indoor headquarters, pool of suspects, and "affected areas" were all under the Locard's control. Rachael's control.

Of course she would make it as easy for them as possible. "I know I shouldn't be here," she began.

"It's all right," Luis couldn't help saying, though it wasn't. She could hear voices behind the trees, out of sight, as the Evidence Response Team worked the scene. Otherwise, the woods were as calm and peaceful as always. At least the moisture in the air kept the odors tamped down. She could smell only damp wood and someone's aftershave.

"But I thought of something that can't wait. Is the ME here?"

She meant the ME investigator, as the actual county medical examiner rarely came out to crime scenes, with too much to do, always, at the office. But the agents would know the shorthand.

"Yes. Her name's Deirdre."

"I'd like to talk to her."

The men stared.

"Farida was Muslim. I don't know a great deal about the customs, they tend to vary between countries and regions and sects, but—"

A stocky woman of about forty came up the path behind the agents, camera and backpack swinging from opposite shoulders as she scribbled notes on a clipboard. "Hi, Rachael."

"Hi, Dee. Look, I wanted to ask you and Mallory for a major favor." Mallory Givens was the county medical examiner. "The victim is Muslim, and seemed pretty strict about it. Can Mallory or maybe Betsy do the autopsy? It needs to be a woman."

Now Deirdre stared.

"And there needs to be only women in the room. From beginning to end."

"But . . . um . . . I can't guarantee that. It depends on coverage, and . . . victims don't get to pick their pathologists."

"I know, I know. But I knew this girl, for a short time, and I'm sure this would be really important to her and her family. They're going to be devastated enough without adding more pain. I know it's inconvenient, but surely you've made accommodations for religions before . . . If Farida had a dying request, I know this would be it."

Deirdre smirked. "I think it would be 'don't kill me.' But—you realize she's dead, right? She's not going to know who's cutting her open."

Rachael had performed over a thousand autopsies herself, but for the first time she winced at the thought. "I know that too."

"It's stupid."

"It seems so," she said diplomatically. "But just because I don't understand someone else's beliefs doesn't mean I want to disregard them. It's a favor, to her and to me."

"But—"

"Please. I don't know what else to say, but *please*."

Michael spoke up. "Actually, we'd appreciate it too. This already has the potential to become an international incident. We'd rather not throw any more gasoline on that particular fire, if we can help it."

Deirdre ignored him and spoke to Rachael. "Okay, okay, if you're going to give me the puppy-dog eyes. I'll tell Mallory and we'll lock Doug out of the autopsy suite. But you owe us a box of Krispy Kremes."

"Guaranteed."

"A *big* box."

"I promise."

The investigator turned away and began to shuffle back up the narrow trail. Then she stopped and added to Rachael: "Hey, we moved your dead goat. I assume you were using that to show the changes during the process of decomposition?"

"That was mostly the week before last. This current course is all about documentation, but, yeah, changes were part of it."

"Did you do anything, like, to speed up the decomp?"

The question stumped her. "No. Like—no."

"No acid or anything? I know it sounds weird, I just ask because—"

"Acid?"

The two FBI agents appeared as confused as she felt, and Deirdre gave an impatient wave. "There was a scrap of label between the goat and the girl. It was probably on the ground from when you were working out here, I don't know—"

No, she thought. *It can't be.* "Label from what? Can I see it?"

Now it was Deirdre's turn to stare. "Uh, okay. Hang on a minute."

"What is it?" Luis asked. "What does that mean?"

It would take too long to explain. "Don't know yet. Probably nothing." It must be detritus from the school, blown away from the dumpster or fallen out of the pockets of one of the staff, even a student. It could have been blowing around in these woods for months. It could be—

"Here." Deirdre had returned with a small paper bag, like an undersized lunch sack. With fresh gloves she reached in and pulled out a piece of torn paper, about two inches wide and one inch from top to bottom. Two borders of its edge were smooth, two were jagged, as if it were the upper right hand corner of—something.

Rachael handled it with a light touch, since the thin scrap of paper had been in the very wet earth for at least twenty hours. That was why the techs had put it in a paper bag instead of a plastic one where it would rot.

"That can't be," Rachael said.

Because under the wiped-away mud, the color of the paper remained a fresh white, because it had *not* been blowing around the woods for months, because the still-legible lettering spelled out: 1NO3 PH 7.5±0.1. The rest of the formula for Tris-HCL. The rest of the label that, until yesterday, had been on the jar of hydrochloric acid, inside the Locard's chemical supply closet, that had fallen and possibly killed Dr. Barbara Wright.

"That can't be," she said again.

Chapter 19

Once the team of FBI agents had finished their interviews, Ellie helped to herd the course attendees out of the building and out to the parking lot. The locals were glad to go and make an early day of it, but the out-of-towners would rather hang around an interesting crime scene than watch a short list of cable channels in a generic hotel room. She had herded cats before—literally, Aunt Katey always had at least five hanging about the house—but not a herd that had both scented the intoxicating aroma of bizarre yet frighteningly close crime, *and* had nothing better to do. They knew better than to violate the crime scene tape roping off the trail to Body Site 1, but that didn't mean they couldn't question the ERT tech stationed there to guard it. Who happened to be her ex-husband, Adam.

"How'd they do it?" asked a beefy guy. "Those feds wouldn't tell us how she was killed."

"You can't blame us for asking," commented the NYPD sergeant from her course, Craig Bennett. "The poor kid."

"Was she raped?" This from a skinny, fidgety woman wearing a too-thin windbreaker.

"That's cold, Stef," someone told her.

"Reality is cold," she shot back.

Adam held up two hands, his amiable self on view. Ellie knew better than to trust it. "Come on, guys, you know I can't tell you anything."

Caleb had fallen into step beside her as they walked. "I'm ready to head out. There's got to be a decent restaurant somewhere in this county and I'm going to find it. I've had so much pizza this week, I'm going to puke at the thought of tomato sauce. Join me?"

"Thanks, but I can't. I can't even recommend a place—I've only been here three days myself."

He didn't seem particularly appreciative of this, but didn't press the point. Ellie watched as he and the rest of the group meandered toward the parking lot.

She waited until they were out of sight, then spoke to her ex: "So—how *did* she die?" Then she laughed as his mouth fell open. "Kidding, kidding. It's just been a long day, and I couldn't resist."

"That guy hitting on you?"

She didn't bother reacting to this in any way. She didn't care whether Caleb had been or hadn't been, or what Adam might think about it. He had forfeited any right to know. "I doubt it."

He dropped it instantly, which told her that he didn't truly care either. "Let me get this straight. You start working here, and two people die."

"It sounds bad when you say it like that." She tried to keep the grin on her face, and knew she failed. It did disturb her. Of course the two dead women had nothing to do with Ellie—she didn't believe in curses—but she had always responded to the victims' crime scenes. They weren't supposed to come to *her*. "And the one yesterday was an accident."

"Maybe not."

She felt her eyes narrow. "What does that mean?"

"Ask your new boss."

She didn't expect him to tell her anything of their investigation. She no longer worked for the FBI, and she no longer slept by his side; she knew that. He *shouldn't* tell her anything.

But he didn't need to be so damn smug about it.

"I'll do that." She turned and headed back to the Locard.

With nothing more to do in the now-empty classrooms, Ellie made her way back toward the office. *Her* office, though it didn't feel like that. The first-floor northern wing appeared dark, lit with only the ghostly glow of the last of the day's light. It had to filter past deep trees, then a set of outer windows and through office spaces, before the last few photons could peek through the windows and doors of the inner wall, into the hallway, then across the hallway into her new room. The Locard building had begun as a school and still resembled a school in many ways, and anyone who had passed through the education system couldn't help feeling anxious to be there after hours. *You don't belong here,* the echoes said. *You're going to get in trouble.*

Lights flickered on as she progressed; the entire building had been fitted with motion-activated overheads. They illuminated the chilly hallway, but did nothing to make it more friendly. Instinctively, she headed for the bright glow at the end of the road: Hector's open office door.

The stocky man stood in front of a poster-size graphic taped to the wall opposite his desk. Ellie hadn't paid much attention the first time she'd been in his office, too occupied with other things, but now she saw that most of the room had been similarly decorated. Graphs, charts, lists, papered the solid parts of all four walls. Only the windows had been spared.

Hector noticed her presence. "Hey!"

"Hey, yourself. What *is* all this?"

"Nothing important—just my life's work." He laughed and waved for her to come in. "It's numbers, numbers, and more numbers. You've heard of the serial killer algorithm?"

"Yes." She strolled the perimeter of the room, noting the titles. *Uniform Crime Report 2000-2010. Supplementary Homicide Report 2015. VICAP Categories. Murder Clusters by County 2022.* "A journalist got interested in crime statistics and thought they could be used to identify serial killers, but couldn't get his editors on board until he published a story about discrepancies in infant death reporting."

"Yes!" Hector sounded pleased. "He wondered why so many more babies died of SIDS in one state versus another, and it turned out that MEs in that state tended to declare SIDS because it seemed a kinder diagnosis than accidental suffocation. Nothing to do with murder, of course, but the story prompted a national discourse on how infant deaths are treated and reported. After that, people started listening to him about serial killers. National crime stats had been too general and too inconsistent to really help much. He had to figure out, after a lot of trial and error, how to categorize the facts about unsolved murders into an algorithm to alert cities that they have an active serial killer in their midst."

"I read about that. He—Thomas Hargrove—used the Green River Killer as an example. He put in all the information about murders in the Seattle area and the algorithm pegged the Ridgway victims as the probable work of a serial killer." She refixed a loose piece of tape holding up a list of *Victim Characteristics in Cleveland.* The very, very single-spaced page listed victim's gender, age, date of death and manner of death, whether they were married, single, cohabitating, and if they had children. The data went back decades. Many were crossed out, a perfectly straight pencil line drawn through them.

"What are the crossed-out ones?"

"They don't have any obvious similarities to other deaths."

"So likely not the work of a serial killer, then."

"Right."

"So you're applying Hargrove's mathematics to the cases with similarities?"

"I'm expanding on his work. The algorithm can find serial killers' patterns to point out where they're operating. I think it should be able to predict those killers' future victims. Pivot from detection to prevention. Speaking of which, how's it going out there? With our own murder?"

She tore herself from the *Victims in Cleveland* page to come back to the present. "Not sure I know. The whole day's been pretty chaotic, and, of course, the agents can't tell us much."

"Yeah, well. Cops are really good at *not* telling people stuff."

Ellie couldn't help a defensive reaction to this. "I doubt there's much they really know, yet. The investigation is only a few hours old, even if it seems like we've been here for days already."

"True, true," he murmured, as if he'd already lost interest in the conversation. She joined him in staring at a two-color bar graph with years across the bottom x axis and homicides up the y.

Hector explained, "The total bar is the number of homicides each year, with the red bottom the solved ones. The top gray part is the leftover homicides that weren't solved."

Ellie saw it immediately—though the overall murder rate had steadily declined since a peak in 1990, the amount of murders solved as a percent of the total had also declined.

Hector said, "Law enforcement is reporting more and more homicides in which they have not even made an arrest, much less a conviction. Technology is getting better, we're getting the DNA analysis backlog dealt with, video cameras are mounted everywhere, yet over ninety percent of homicides were solved fifty years ago, and we're getting down to only fifty or sixty percent today."

"Do you think—" Ellie began, then stopped.

"I think lots of things. What are *you* thinking?"

"That there's probably a lot of factors at play here. There's twice as many homicides today as there were in 1960, but we probably don't have twice as many cops, relative to population."

"And for population, read caseload."

"Yes. So many departments are overworked and under-equipped. Also, maybe, maybe, criminals are getting smarter, watching the ID Channel a little too often."

"*Maybe.*" Hector smirked. "Overall, criminals are still pretty dumb. Even serial killers are rarely as smart as everyone thinks. They're supposed to all be geniuses, like Hannibal Lecter, yet in reality their IQs trend slightly lower than average."

"But . . ." Still, she hesitated.

"Go ahead. You don't have to be PC in my office."

"I'm wondering if the cleared-by-arrest rate has gone down due to changes in homicide investigation and prosecution rather than changes in homicides, per se. At least partly. Back in 1960, police officers were perhaps a little . . ."

"Cavalier?"

"Good word. Maybe I'm stereotyping a period, but we could make the guess that cops, prosecutors, and judges were maybe not as strict about search warrants or probable cause arrests."

"Round up the usual suspects. So maybe they made more arrests because they arrested the wrong people?"

"It could be. Or they had more freedom to arrest the right people—let's hope that's the explanation. Then there's prosecution today. Sometimes I feel like they're . . ." Ellie hesitated again.

"I said you didn't have to be politically correct."

"Gutless wonders," she confessed. "Like they won't prosecute anything unless a conviction is served to them on a solid silver platter with a side of parsley."

"Now, don't you feel better?"

She laughed. "It's probably unfair. I'm not a lawyer, so I don't know what they're dealing with. I know they're as overworked as anyone else, but refusing to prosecute anything that's not a one hundred percent slam dunk cannot be the answer."

"You'll get no argument from me. That might be one more grain weighting a downward spiral—the more homicides are not solved in a city, the more homicides you have. That's something that's been confirmed by this kind of work, by paying attention to the statistics. My plan is to find a new algorithm, one that can not only say 'these dead people were probably killed by a serial killer,' but 'these people who live between these three streets, and are between fifteen and thirty, and are male and live with small children, and don't have their own vehicle, are probably going to be next on his list.'"

"That would be pretty cool. *Will* be pretty cool."

"It's largely geolocation. Location and opportunity are *much* more important to a serial killer than the phase of the moon and whether the victim had her hair in a ponytail. But everyone is different. Their list of must-haves will vary."

"True. Again, like Gary Ridgway—he grabbed women and girls who were available. He wasn't particularly picky about what they looked like or what day of the week it was . . . they're never going to be one-hundred-percent predictable. So me predicting future victims is considered a long shot, but Barbara is invited to Caltech with her crazy idea about cross-referencing prescription drugs with genetic conditions in suspect samples. And using whose research? Mine. She swooped right across the hall to snatch it off my desk like I should consider it an honor to help her out."

"Which research did she want?"

"Mostly the murder cluster info. Her theory is to take a set of murders with bodily fluids left behind, find residue of some sort of drug in the fluids, and then figure out who in the area took that drug and might be a likely suspect. Talk about reversing the scientific method—instead of going from hypothesis to conclusion, take a conclusion, your suspect, and then work backward to find your hypothesis, your drug. If it doesn't work, start with a different conclusion. I can't believe she even found enough examples that the American Academy okayed her presentation."

"You didn't think much of it?"

"Barbara was great at making much ado about nothing. *And* not giving anyone else credit for that ado. You'll see notations on all my posters where I cribbed numbers from the Murder Accountability Project and the Uniform Crime Reports—*I* footnote where appropriate. But hers?"

"Your name didn't appear on the presentation, I'm gathering."

"You gather correctly. Not a mention of my original data. It became *her* original data. I would never have known if I hadn't volunteered to pick up orders at Cap'n Taco one day and she was still in class when I got back, so I went in to leave it on her desk. There were her charts—she'd managed to find five examples of apparent serial murders in five different places in which the killer is on some sort of med. *My* data—except for the med part—and *her* name. After that, she started locking her office."

"Wow," Ellie said. "That's awful."

"It's really not *important*," he said, though his tone told her it was very much so, "but it's annoying."

"It *is* important. I may not have spent much time yet in the research world, but I'm pretty sure neglecting to credit your sources is a fairly serious crime."

His face relaxed in the light of her concern. "I could have

made a stink, complained to the director, to the American Academy. I could have sunk her new job at Caltech. But that sounded like a lot of work, so I figured I'd handle it my own way."

She turned from the data posters to face him fully, a tiny catch in her breathing. "What did you do?"

One corner of his mouth turned up in a mocking grin. "Nothing."

A frisson of abrupt worry tingled along her spine. "Hector. What did you do?"

"Nothing." The grin widened. "I figured it was a small price to pay to help her out the door. She wasn't a very nice person. The type that takes the last cup of coffee and never makes another pot. The one that jams the copy machine, then walks away and pretends it wasn't her. I *wanted* her to go be a star at the academy meeting and then waltz into Caltech, because I just wanted her to *go.*"

He laughed merrily. Ellie forced a smile she didn't feel until a sudden blaze from the hallway caught her attention. The overhead lights had timed out, but someone had reactivated them.

She stuck her head out of Hector's door to see Caleb Astor cocking an eyebrow at her. "Hey, teach. Carry your books?"

"What?" She couldn't even sort those words out. "I thought you left."

"Circled back. I just wanted to lose that nosy fed." He rocked on his heels, almost like the schoolboy days his words echoed, skirting business casual in a pair of jeans, bright white sneakers, and a sweatshirt with a picture of the St. Louis Gateway Arch. "So . . . class ended early, got nothing to do tonight . . . you said you're new in town, too. Maybe we could explore the vast dining options of Chesapeake Beach together."

Hector joined her in the doorway, inadvertently push-ing her into the hallway, his electron-orbit personal space bumping up against hers. "Student-instructor fraternization is strictly forbidden at the Locard," he said, clearly enjoying himself.

"Aw, that's harsh, dude," Caleb said, also amused.

Ellie, not so much so. The guy was leaving town tomor-row night, maybe sooner if the Locard canceled tomorrow's classes. Did he think she'd jump at the chance for a one-night stand with someone she'd likely never see again? Not amusing at all.

Perhaps that was unfair. Maybe he simply didn't want to eat alone.

Maybe. She couldn't tell from the leering sort of smile he put out, and it didn't matter, anyway, she had way too much to do. "Well, that's kind of you, but I'm afraid—"

Her phone gave out a weak chime and she checked the screen. A text from Rachael asked her to meet in the direc-tor's office, and to please bring Barbara's box of presentation materials with her.

Saved, literally, by the bell. She ignored Hector's smirks and used Barbara Wright's keycard to get into her office— Ellie's "*sort* of her" office. "I'm afraid I'm going to be tied up here for a while yet."

Caleb followed. "I can wait. This place looks pretty comfy—at least compared to my hotel room. Seriously, Doc, I've been living on fast food all week. Here I am, far from home, right next to the Atlantic—there's got to be a place to get a decent lobster, doesn't there?"

She plucked the clearly labeled box from the desktop. Then she stood outside the door with a pointed look, until he picked himself up from the armchair he'd collapsed into and joined her in the hall. She pulled the door shut and nod-ded at her colleague, who had not moved from the doorway opposite. "I'm sure Hector here will know where to find the best lobster in town."

"Yeah, but he's not as pretty."

"I must protest," Hector said, "I'm very pretty. You just have to catch me in the right light."

Ellie told them to have fun and continued up the hallway, the overhead lights coming to life, one by one, as she passed.

Chapter 20

Rachael, meanwhile, head aflutter with confusing and dark thoughts, checked in with the director. She'd known him for several years and knew he would be nearing the point of apoplexy. Maybe he'd ask his wife to come out and help; she hoped so—Rachael believed that if Anita Coleman could get opposing leaders from any conflict in the world to sit down in a room with her, then that war would be over within fifteen minutes or less.

Instead, Carrie had done what she could, and the FBI had brought both an interpreter and someone from the State Department to deal with the Saudis, so Gerald only had to pace the length of his office and think up dire predictions for the future of the Locard.

"What are they doing? Are they done out there? Is she gone?" he demanded as soon as she appeared in his doorway. His medium-dark skin had the flush of elevated blood pressure—he should leave off caffeine for the remainder of the day.

"Working on it, no, and yes." Rachael had no idea how to tell him there might be some connection between the deaths of Barbara Wright and Farida Al Talel. "How are you doing?"

"Trying to think of ways to brush up my résumé. Which is pointless, since no one would look at it, anyway. No one is going to consider hiring the forensic director who had a foreign national mysteriously murdered on his own damn doorstep!"

"Gerald," Rachael said in the most soothing tone she could muster. "The situation isn't as bad as all that."

"It's *exactly* as bad as all that." He stopped pacing, but only to rest his hips against his desk and rub his face with one hand. "Who's going to come here after . . . this?"

"Are you kidding? These are crime scene people. They'll be flocking here just to—"

"Not the *students*! I don't care about . . . This place doesn't exist on the students. We *subsidize* the training. The Locard truly functions on the private clients and the research grants—and you know how fickle they can be."

Rachael agreed, with reluctance. All the events of the day caught up with her in one moment, and she sat on the counter along the windows—a cozy spot during cold weeks, with the radiator humming below it. Today it didn't warm her. The private clients, the ones with deep pockets and delicate problems and an abhorrence of publicity in all forms, would not find a campus murder titillating. She tried to think of something comforting to say and came up short. Gerald was right. They could all be out of their jobs soon, and the Locard—this amazing, beautiful experiment—could be abandoned to decay alone in the forest.

She refused to voice these thoughts. "What should we do about the current classes? Should we cancel tomorrow, mail them their certificates? It's only one day of instruction—well, day and a half, since this afternoon was lost as well . . . I don't think anyone will ask for a refund."

He considered this. "That would be best. Who's going to

be able to concentrate, anyway? And as long as they get their paperwork, they'll be happy."

Certificates were gold to the attendees, the proof of completion they needed to claim the Continuing Education Credits on résumés, certification applications and renewals, promotion opportunities, and to show their employers what value they'd gotten for the departmental funds. In any professional course of instruction the vast majority of attendees wanted to be there to sharpen their skill set—but there were always a few who just wanted to get out of town on their agency's dime. They'd spend the whole week at the hotel pool, if instructors weren't required to keep track of such things.

Carrie, possibly overhearing the word "paperwork," came through the open door. "What are we doing with them?"

"I say let them go," the director told her, "but the FBI might have other ideas."

Rachael agreed with the second half of the sentence, not necessarily the first. "I'd rather—and if I were the FBI, I'd rather have the students here, and staff as well. All their suspects in one handy spot. Once the nonlocal ones check out of that hotel, they're back to their home states, where the agents have to get on planes to do in-person interviews. Where getting a search or arrest warrant will be a much lengthier process."

"New cities, new judges, they might not have a field office nearby to work out of," Carrie said. "But are they even going to be here tomorrow, physically on campus? What if the feds wrap it all up tonight?"

"That'd be sweet," Gerald said, "but I doubt that's going to happen. But if we have class tomorrow, aren't we liable? What if someone else turns up dead? Everyone in those two courses will sue *us* for putting them at risk, not the FBI. They're not going to gripe over missing one day, not if they still get their certs. I say, screw the feds. I have to protect the Locard."

Rachael acknowledged this very valid point. "But if they could *solve* it—"

The thought cleared his brow of a few lines. "True. That's the best we could hope for, at this point: quick deduction, quick arrest, over and done with, and out of the media by Monday. And, yeah, keeping all their suspects in one place could help with that. Speaking of"—he said to Carrie— "what's happening with the cousins over there? Still lots of weeping and moaning and gnashing of teeth?"

"You could be a little more sympathetic! They've lost their relative!"

"They're probably the ones who killed her!"

Carrie did not fear to glare at the boss when she felt he deserved it. "I don't believe that. Those boys are *distraught*. They're begging the State Department guy to inform the next of kin, because they can't bear to do it."

"Sure. They're probably going to be executed for letting her slip their grasp. Or for killing her. Or for killing her, even if they were *ordered* to kill her."

"I don't believe that," she said again. "I think it's an emotion thing. They grew up with this girl, she was more like a sister than a cousin to them. They're pouring their hearts out through the interpreter over there. And thanks for taking care of the autopsy, that really helped them breathe a little easier," she added to Rachael.

"I'm glad." Poor Irfan was probably going to die of uncontrolled sleep apnea, anyway. "It's getting late—do you need to go home?"

"What, now? Not a chance! This is the most interesting thing that's happened to me since my sister got stranded ten miles offshore on a senator's yacht during a dinner party because the captain had a three-martini lunch and forgot to put gas in." Then she excused herself and took another box of tissues into the conference room.

Gerald had started pacing again, though with less agitation than before, apparently ignoring these last exchanges. "I get that about the two men. But, like it or not, they're still much more likely suspects than anyone here—precisely because they *were* close. There's a whole history there that we don't know. They're only a branch of the royal family, but that family is vast and their funds have been drying up over the years. The royals over there are always extorting, imprisoning, coercing, *and* killing other royals to move themselves up in the hierarchy. She could have been next in line for some inheritance. Maybe this marriage her parents wanted was some sort of power play. Who knows . . . What's she got?"

He posed this last question gazing through the windows in his office wall as Ellie entered the anteroom with her cardboard box.

"That's the other thing I have to tell you about," Rachael said.

Chapter 21

To Ellie's eyes, the scene appeared as chaotic as any other that day. The director seemed in a state of deep confusion. Then Carrie, his secretary—Ellie had met her on a brief orientation visit the previous week—emerged from a door to say that some guy from the State Department had a question for Rachael. Then Rachael asked Ellie to meet the agents in the cafeteria and said she would follow in a moment, presumably once she finished with the State Department guy.

Chaos. But chaos was an acquaintance of long standing, so she balanced the cardboard box on her hip and made her way down the south staircase.

The Locard Institute, which had rung with frenetic activity all day, now held only a deafening silence. And it wasn't even quite dinnertime—where had everyone gone?

Not to the cafeteria, where the tables sat vacant with half the lighting turned off. She dropped her box on one of the long tables and went into the inside hallway, with the doorways leading to the restrooms, the gym, the storage room, and the lower north walkway.

The walls were tiled from floor to ceiling, the subway tiles still glossy after all these years. Both were now covered in black fingerprint powder—not the entire walls, only from approximately three feet above the floor to seven or so feet above, the region where a human being's hand would reasonably land. Ellie saw many roughly rectangular, random patches of relative clean, where the fingerprint tape had been lifted, to be placed on a white card and examined because one of her ex-coworkers believed they saw a usable fingerprint there. She didn't envy them that job, an exercise—nearly an exercise—in futility, since everyone connected with the Locard had likely used the hallway that week. Even those who brought their lunches might come by for the gym, the locker rooms, or to get something out of storage. Or the vault.

And now the cleaning staff would have to wash it off. That would be a sucky job—the fine powder could be washed off the glossy tile with soap and water, but the grout might need a scrub brush.

She returned to the cafeteria to wait, feeling the chill of the damp October night creep into her muscles, her tendons, her bones, and wondered if it had gotten too late to scrounge up a cup of coffee. Over at the beverage station a tiny red light glowed on the urn—dare she hope?

Two steps in, she heard a sound. Very faint, like a scuffle, or the scratch of a shoe on the hard floor. When she stopped, it did too.

She turned, doing a complete three-sixty. No one. Not a shadow flickered.

It could be someone in the gym, working off their stress by shooting a few baskets . . . even though she could see across the hallway to the gym doors, and no light shone through the porthole-type windows. But then, shooting baskets in the dark could really improve your other four senses.

It might be someone in one of the restrooms. Those lights were definitely on.

It could be a machine—the room was full of them. She hoped the noise belonged to a coffee-making one.

Three more steps toward the beverage station, and she heard it again. A click, a swipe, a brushing sort of vibration, like stiff bristles against a softer surface. She spoke firmly: "Hello?"

No answer.

Ellie straightened her shoulders, feeling ridiculous. This institute existed to solve crimes and was currently populated by not only a team of trained investigators, but one of armed agents. Yes, there had been a murder, but that didn't mean she needed to fear another.

First of all, she might not be currently armed, but she was still an agent.

Second of all, she hadn't even met Farida. It seemed highly unlikely that anyone who had a motive to kill the young Saudi woman would also have a motive to kill Ellie.

Another sound, a scrape and sort of shuffle.

Unless it was someone who simply enjoyed killing people. And wasn't that exactly the kind of person the Locard existed to study?

Yes, study. Not *hire*.

But where better for them to be? Where better than a place that would teach them everything they *shouldn't* do if they didn't want to get caught?

"Hello!" she said aloud, more firmly. *I am not afraid of you.*

But she had never liked the dark. When she was little more than a toddler, one of her cousins had turned out the lights on her on the steps to her grandmother's attic, and she had screamed and screamed.

Then she heard a different sound, a definite voice, not a machine or a window frame quivering in the breeze. This sounded like a low, weak whimper.

Ellie strode into the kitchen, scanning the area while patting the wall for a light switch. Bright fluorescents flooded the room in an instant, reflecting off the clean stainless-steel appliances and a floor of gleaming brick-colored tile.

The whimper came again, and Ellie took a few steps forward without thinking. The kitchen consisted of two wide aisles, with stoves and cooktops and warming racks lining either side. In the rear aisle someone had formed a circle of boxes, cartons stacked two high all the way around. The cartons read TOMATOES, or in some places CORN, WHOLE KERNEL.

She couldn't see what the circle held at first—newspaper, a bowl—

Then its occupant caught sight of her and burst into a shrieking series of yips.

"Who are *you*?" Ellie demanded, but the puppy was too busy making its own wishes heard. It sounded as if *feed me* and *let me out* topped the list, followed by *rub my tummy.* The decibel level subsided only slightly when she stroked his head, which felt damp and more than a little dirty. He had tan fur flecked with black strands and a dark muzzle, ears that stuck up, but curled, and perfectly adorable little paws. "Okay, okay, stop shouting. What are you doing here?"

"I see you found our tracker." Rachael walked in and surveyed the enclosure. "Interesting fence. What's in those boxes?"

"Feels like cans." Ellie now sat atop one stack as the puppy licked her fingers.

Rachael addressed the dog. "You better not have peed on those, sealed or not. I'll be eating out of those cans one day."

To Ellie, she explained: "I asked the kitchen staff to take care of him. I can't believe they left him here . . . I'll give them the benefit of the doubt and assume they trusted I'd be back."

"What's this?" Michael Tyler came in and leaned over the cartons. His fingers smelled interesting enough to steal the dog's attention from Ellie.

"This is the guy who found your body this morning," Rachael told him.

"Why is he in your kitchen?"

"Because if we let him out, guess where he's going to go?"

"Not good," Michael admitted. "ERT isn't ready to let the scene go. We're going to hold it until tomorrow."

"Best practices," Ellie said. It was never good to let go of a crime scene too quickly. A question might come up as evidence and bodies were examined. Then returning to an already-released scene might require a new search warrant, or at a minimum removed any guarantee that someone hadn't entered the scene in the meantime and altered, removed, or added evidence.

Rachael hunted up some beef stew, cut the pieces smaller, and nuked it to slightly warmer than room temperature for the puppy. Ellie refilled his water and fluffed up the old towel one of the cooks had tossed into the ring. Surely, with a stomach full of warm stew, he would lie down for a nap while the grown-ups talked.

But instead of sitting down to confer, Michael continued through the cafeteria proper to the hallway. The lights there sprang into life as they entered the long, narrow corridor. He stopped outside the ladies' room, staring across the twenty or so feet at the exterior door. "So she voluntarily walked out that door . . ."

"*Apparently* voluntarily," Rachael corrected.

". . . while her bodyguards were right around the corner.

Why? Escaping with someone? He put a gun in her ribs? He gave her some cock-and-bull story about the shuttle leaving and her cousins had gone on ahead?"

"I doubt she'd believe that," Ellie said without thinking.

Dark eyes focused on her face. "Why?"

"Well . . . maybe she would . . . Who knows what anyone will do when an unexpected situation is thrown up—and she'd been here for a week and a half."

"She was comfortable and trusted those around her," Rachael translated.

"Yes. But her upbringing had been strict enough that her family sent not one but two male relatives to accompany her. I would think she'd balk at walking *any*where with *any*one, without them. But then again, who knows—it was the end of the day, she was tired, the storm was pounding, and she's probably accustomed to taking what people say at face value."

"Yes and no," Rachael mused. "She lived in a country where there are official rules and unofficial ones. And a great many of her gender, with whom she spent most of her time, walk around with their faces covered. She might have gotten a lot better at reading people than you think."

"Or the killer was a female," Michael said.

The two women agreed; that would have made Farida more likely to leave with the person, though she still might have doubted that her cousins would bail on her.

They stood outside the ladies' restroom. Michael said, "I'd like to see inside there."

Rachael said, "Uh-huh." Ellie merely waited.

"So, would you make sure there's no one in there?" he added with a lack of patience.

Ellie and Rachael looked at each other; then, in unison, they burst out laughing.

"Yeah, sure," Rachael said.

"I appreciate your attention to our delicacy," Ellie said, but softly, because, in truth, she *did* appreciate it.

They checked the chamber, found it devoid of humans, and called him in. All three of them were careful not to touch the walls, which were as full of fingerprint powder as those in the hallway.

Other than the dark powder, the room appeared to be a standard structure for ladies' needs, eight individual stalls with doors, six white porcelain sinks, slightly old-fashioned steel hot- and cold-water taps. No cabinets, the bare pipes clearly visible beneath. No windows, of course, as the gymnasium sat on the other side of the wall. No supply closet for housekeeping mops and cleaners.

Pushing doors open with a single finger, Michael began to inspect each stall for, Ellie assumed, signs of a struggle. As he did this, he asked no one in particular, "So you think she wouldn't have voluntarily walked away from her bodyguards? Unless she was, in fact, escaping?"

Ellie said, "Wouldn't it have been easier to sneak out of the hotel? She could have gone out a door or window there in the middle of the night, rather than walking up a single, narrow path at the same time that other people had no choice but to use it."

"Yes."

"It's impossible to know," Rachael reasoned out loud. "She was a human being with a host of thoughts and secrets and vulnerabilities. As we said, she most likely felt comfortable here and comfortable with the people here, attendees and staff. Not to mention the fact that everyone here is, in some way, working toward the goals of law enforcement."

"Yeah," Ellie examined the powder residue on a sink. "We're *supposed* to be the good guys."

"She might have believed anything anyone told her—why wouldn't she?"

"And they're used to doing what someone tells them in Saudi Arabia?" Michael asked, inspecting another stall.

Rachael didn't answer, so Ellie did. "Also impossible to tell. It's a complicated, interesting country. And it's gone through a *lot* of changes in only the past few years."

He paused in his movement, stared at Ellie for a split second. "Tell me about it. Seems like half of the students are insisting her cousins killed her—because maybe her family didn't want her back, maybe because she spoke to a man, any man, maybe because she came here at all."

"I'm no expert." Ellie paused, trying to come up with an analysis both concise and coherent—no easy task. She started to lean against a powder-covered sink, but then reminded herself not to. "Quick summary on the country of Saudi Arabia: It's still the most gender-segregated country in the world, and one of the most strict in terms of religious observance. That identity was rooted in its foundation back in 1744, when Muhammad bin Saud Al Muqrin, also known as Ibn Saud, formed an alliance with the Wahhabi religious movement.

"Nearly two hundred years later, in the 1930s, oil was discovered, and the royal family got even richer with the usual extravagances that can bring on. In 1979, radical Islamists occupied Mecca. The king at the time had to acknowledge this discontent and allow a crackdown on freedom—suddenly there was no music, no movies, no tobacco, women had to keep their faces covered around nonimmediate-family men, when all of that had been allowed before. And, of course, no alcohol," Ellie concluded.

"That would make me rebel right there," Rachael said.

"You and me both. There had always been no alcohol, but, like America during Prohibition, you could get anything you wanted, as long as you knew the mayor or the police chief or someone who could help you out if you got in a jam. But every bending of the rules was a risk in a country where religious police—an actual, full-time job—could throw you in jail for the least infraction. The populace put up with this because, first of all, they're believers, and second of all, the oil money kept things pretty sweet. Two-thirds of the workforce have government jobs. Education, health—everything is paid for by the government. Seventy percent are obese."

"Copy that," Rachael said. "I was dying to refer those boys to a brilliant dietician I know, but, surprisingly, people do *not* take it well when you give them unsolicited diet advice. I'm loving all this information, but why, exactly, do you know everything about Saudi Arabia?"

Ellie laughed. "I barely know a *fraction* of what there is—it is way too complicated a country. But my cousin Maureen spent some time embedded there with Associated Press and loaned me a book on it. I couldn't stop reading."

Rachael nodded and went back to checking the underside of all the sinks.

Ellie didn't add that it had been an audiobook, her usual refuge when sleep refused to come at night. One of the few side benefits of insomnia: a not-entirely-voluntary education in all sorts of topics.

"So, how did she get to come here at all?" Michael asked. He had reached the last stall, without, clearly, finding anything of interest.

"The latest crown prince . . . he's kind of a mixed bag. He consolidated power—and a whole lot of money—by rounding up three hundred of the most influential men and holding them captive in the Ritz-Carlton—gorgeous place, but not for them right then—until they signed over a ton of capital to the royal family. He seemed genuinely stunned when the other countries, not to mention business concerns, reacted so badly to the murder of the journalist Khashoggi, because he really thought Saudis killing a Saudi citizen in the Saudi Consulate in Istanbul would go largely unnoticed. He's very business oriented and believes oil will become a thing of the past, sooner rather than later. Without oil the country will go belly-up, sooner much rather than later.

"He also recognized that fifty percent of the population is under the age of twenty-five—things had to change. The abaya and face veil are no longer *officially* mandatory. There's a woman in the cabinet. Women can drive . . . though the protestors who agitated for it were still arrested, because freedom does *not* mean freedom to criticize the government. He's trying to rebrand the country as a tourist destination, building resorts, so suddenly there are movies, street festivals, sporting events. Girls can go to a café, and even meet boys there. City girls, usually. Those kinds of habits vary a *lot* by area."

"What happened to the religious police?" Rachael asked.

"Stripped of their power with one decree—I mean the power to arrest people for wearing colorful abayas, or their hair too long. It's still an extremely devout country—make no mistake about that. But with the whole land sitting on an economic precipice, the religious leaders had to face reality. If the country bankrupts, all those oil-rich people with houses in Switzerland and France could simply leave them behind to starve in the desert."

"So Farida got to travel." Michael gave up on the stalls, noticed the black powder on his hands, and moved to a sink.

"She's hardly the first, but, yes, things have changed a lot in a short time. We can't guess what Farida might have thought or wanted or planned. She might have been dying to escape to the West. She might have never considered it."

Rachael agreed. "Farida seemed so excited about working crime scenes in her own country, how they needed female workers so that crimes against women would be investigated thoroughly. And she adored her family. She mentioned them constantly."

Michael said, "You are right. Our techs didn't find anything suspicious on her phone. She sent her parents and siblings photos of practically everything, up to and including the coffeemaker at the hotel and the sunset over the Chesapeake."

Rachael said, "But at the same time—living in a place where what goes, and what doesn't, is still up in the air . . . she might be very good at keeping secrets."

"Exactly my thought." Ellie again began to lean one hip against a sink, and again thought better of it. "That's why we can't guess what she'd do or not do. And if her cousins, or anyone back in Saudi, knows, they're probably not going to tell us."

Michael dried his hands. "It's equally impossible to tell if she was attacked, approached, or abducted in here or in the hallway."

Ellie saw what he meant. Everything in the room was bolted to the wall—there was nothing to knock over or break open if two people were struggling, and ERT would have already found it if there had been. But she understood why Michael wanted to see the space. When trying to reconstruct a crime, you needed to be able to picture every step of it in your head.

They adjourned to the cafeteria and sat at one of the tables as Luis came in, carrying a steaming cup. The other three people demanded, with some vehemence, to know where he got it. The cafeteria urn had been drained.

"That lady outside the director's office? Carrie? Nice woman. Not bad coffee either." He gave them a smug look that made Ellie laugh even as she calculated the time it would take to run upstairs to see if there might be more. She felt chilled through to the bone marrow, and pulled her blazer more tightly around her torso.

Rachael asked what the bureau wanted, as far as the Locard's courses went. Would they prefer the Locard end the course, lop off the last day, call all the students tonight, and tell them not to arrive tomorrow? Or have them return to the scene of the crime? The Locard did not *have* to do what they advised—but she and Gerald were willing to listen to what the FBI had to say.

As expected, the agents wanted to keep all their suspects close at hand—under their control, somewhat. If they wanted more information from a particular person, they could pull them from the class, and that person would know that a refusal to cooperate would make them look suspicious: psychological coercion without actual psychological coercion. Once the attendees were back in their daily lives, it would be so much easier to find an excuse not to talk to the FBI: they were busy; their union wouldn't like it; their kid was sick; they were working undercover and couldn't surface right now.

Rachael told Michael that keeping the students for the last day did not seem to be in the Locard's best interests, possibly putting the students at risk, for which the Locard could be considered liable. However, they wanted the case closed ASAP and, of course, keeping the suspects together would help with that. So the director had a deal for them: They would let the students attend for their last day, provided the FBI maintained its presence on the campus and took responsibility for their safety. "We want armed agents here, looking out not only for the attendees, but the staff as well. To be blunt, if someone else dies, Gerald's going to blame you. Loudly and publicly. He's not being mean, he's just really scared. I am too."

An odd word in a professional setting, and it dug into Ellie's brain: "scared."

In many ways this situation had seemed like an unusually interesting crime scene, but now the reality of it stepped up and shouted in her face. This was her new *life*. She had given up her old dream job, her apartment, her city, for this. A place like the Locard existed on its reputation. If that died, the whole place might follow it into the grave. She would feel terrible for Rachael, who had given years of her life to the institute, but selfishly, she'd feel worse for herself. Where would *she* be?

Out in the middle of nowhere, with a new mortgage and no job to pay it with, and a résumé with only one reference: an ex-employer unhappy with her for bailing on them so abruptly.

She had closed her eyes and jumped off a plank into this job. Now she could only pray that someone hadn't drained the pool.

Chapter 22

Ellie listened as Rachael told the agents that it would be understandable if attendees did not *want* to return, in order to safeguard both their physical and emotional well-being. The Locard would never refuse to grant credit for the courses under those circumstances. They couldn't hold that over people's heads, simply to keep the FBI's suspects in the building.

Michael nodded, with a rueful expression. "Understood. We'll take the deal."

This left the FBI open to the same liabilities as the Locard, Ellie could see. If an attendee suffered additional trauma by being obligated to return, or if they fell to a similar fate, Michael and Luis would be held responsible. Meanwhile, the killer had another chance to hide, remove, or destroy any evidence he might have left behind today.

It would not be an easy Friday for anyone.

Michael began, "Tell me about this Barbara Wright."

When Ellie blinked in surprise, Rachael explained to her: "You remember when I picked up the pieces of broken glass from that HCl jar yesterday, the label was torn."

"Yeah. Did you—"

"No prints. I checked this morning, didn't even bother with the dye stain—there were no prints to stain. Not even smudges. I mean *nothing.*"

"Like someone wiped it off," Luis said.

"Maybe," Rachael said. "Not necessarily. Barbara might have only bumped it, knocked it off the shelf, rather than picked it up and dropped it. And whoever in the building unpacked it upon receipt, or used some of the acid since then, might have worn gloves to handle it—not unreasonable, with a caustic substance. But half of the label from the jar was found in the grave site, on top of Farida, under the goat."

"It . . . what?" Ellie asked. A piece of moon rock would not have been any more surprising.

"Yep. Doesn't make any sense whatsoever."

"Did her body—"

"No."

"Was there other—"

"No."

"Did anybody who—"

"Pretty sure not."

"Would you guys speak English?" Michael demanded. "For the rest of us?"

Rachael apologized and clarified: "No, her body showed no signs of having been in contact with acid. Neither did the goat's. No, there was no other use of acid at the scene while my class was there. And no one who would normally be using that acid in the building—like Barbara with the DNA buffers, or Gary with his inks, or Mickey in ballistics—would have been helping to bury the goat originally."

Ellie said, "Are you sure—"

"Yeah."

At Michael's dark look Rachael amended: "I'm reasonably sure it's the same label—I took a photo of the piece from the scene and just eyeballed it, but it looks to me like a jigsaw match."

Luis said, "But this Dr. Wright died of a heart attack?"

"Supposedly," Rachael said.

"Apparently," Ellie said.

"What does *that* mean?"

Rachael related what the pathologist had told her after the autopsy, that Barbara's heart showed some signs of arteriosclerosis and her lungs did not show damage from the caustic substance.

"But did show edema," Ellie remembered.

"Yes. Most likely related to the attack. Pulmonary and vascular functions are a complicated balance. Respiratory irregularities can trigger a heart attack, as in cor pulmonale—lung disease causes right ventricular dysfunction. A heart attack will restrict your breathing. When the heart stops pumping, the muscles don't have the energy to function, including the muscles that expand your lungs."

"So . . . breathing in the acid didn't kill her. The heart attack stopped her from breathing, which also stopped her from breathing in the acid," Luis said.

"Yes."

Ellie said, "Though she lived long enough to form a hematoma on her temple from the fall."

"Yeah," Michael said. "Is that important?"

Ellie turned to the former pathologist.

Rachael said, "I can't be sure. I wondered why she lived long enough to develop a clot, but not long enough to take a breath full of fumes. But she could have lived five, eight, ten minutes without breathing before brain death set in, and the bruise would have gotten underway immediately."

"Okay. So she died of natural causes?"

"Apparently," Rachael said.

"Supposedly," Ellie said.

"You're doing it again."

"I can't be *sure*," Rachael repeated. "I mean, solid one hundred percent for sure. Certain signs in the heart can result from heart seizure, or from someone being suffocated. Someone can suffocate because of a heart seizure. Most likely, Barbara's death was an unfortunate accident. But then, how did part of a label from near her body wind up in a grave with Farida?"

No one had an answer.

Michael said, "Turn it around. If someone purposely killed Barbara Wright, how did they do it?"

"Hit her on the head," Ellie said.

"It wouldn't have killed her, according to Betsy—the pathologist," Rachael said. "Unless it brought on the heart attack."

"Maybe it knocked her out, or at least stunned her so that he could hold her nose and mouth shut until she asphyxiated. Gently—if he'd pressed down on her face, it would have left marks on her inside lip."

"Betsy would have seen that," Rachael agreed. "But knocking someone unconscious is a lot more difficult than it looks on television. I would expect more damage to the skull."

Michael said, "For the sake of argument, let's say he hit her in the head. With what?"

"I don't know. Anything heavy, with a nonspecific surface—like something broad and flat."

"Like a floor."

In the kitchen the puppy let out a yip.

Rachael said, "I don't believe there was a fight. She had no other injuries and we saw no signs of a struggle."

"Anything in that room that would fit the bill?"

While the two women thought, Luis asked about the jar of acid.

Rachael said, "Broad enough, and maybe heavy enough, but I can't believe it wouldn't have broken if swung with enough force to do harm. There was no sign of cuts on her, and no sprinkling of acid over the upper shelves . . . unless she was already on the floor before being hit with the jar, and then we're back to 'no signs of a struggle.'"

"Okay. Let's try another route. Why?"

"Why asphyxiate?"

"Why Barbara? Why Barbara and Farida? What's the connection between them?"

"None," Rachael said.

"Other than location," Ellie said.

Luis asked Rachael, "Did she even *meet* Farida? You said she had been teaching the other course."

"Yes, she guest-lectured my class one day last week—Friday. Two hours on genealogical tracing and documentation of same."

"Were you there? Or did you take over her class?"

"No, Gary did. I had a meeting with Gerald and a client. That was why we picked that time slot."

Now the two agents exchanged a glance. "Good thing we didn't cut the students loose. We need to find out what happened in that class," Michael said to his partner. "Did Farida ask questions? Did the two women conflict? Did they converse about something? Anything?"

The puppy now let out a series of yips.

Rachael told them, "If so, no one said a word about it to me. They did say Barbara was condescending and a little dull, but no more than that."

"Is it possible," Luis reasoned out loud, "that a student or staff member caught part of this label on their shoe, and then went out to the site? Labels are sticky, and I would think acid would make shoes gummy."

Rachael considered. "It's possible. Because you're right, it would be sticky. But I don't see how that piece of label could have gotten out of the closet and onto someone's shoe, because no one went in there except me and the EMTs to pronounce death. The sheriff leaned over to survey the scene, but he wasn't wading around in the acid puddle either. The body snatchers got the body, and then I picked up the broken pieces of glass. There was no label there, other than the piece stuck to the broken jar. So I'd say no."

"In other words, the piece of label found in the grave was already gone from the supply closet by the time you found Wright's body?"

"To the best of my knowledge."

"So it was sticking to the killer?"

Ellie did a mental roll call of her assigned attendees, trying to picture if there had been a piece of white paper stuck to their clothing or shoes. No such image came to mind.

Michael's phone went off, the ringtone a series of low electronic beeps. *Even his phone,* Ellie thought, *is hyperprofessional. This is a man who gives nothing away.*

He glanced at the screen, then said, "Speaking of autopsies" and answered. After a few moments he looked around the table, evidently came to some sort of decision, and said to the person on the other end: "I'm putting you on speaker. Present is my partner, Luis Alvarez, along with Dr. Rachael Davies and Dr. Ellie Carr."

"Sheesh," a woman's voice said from the small device as he laid it flat on the laminate. "Is this being recorded? Aren't you going to swear me in?"

"Hi, Mallory," Rachael said.

"I did the autopsy on Miss Al Talel myself. With an all-girl crew, as you requested."

"Thanks, Mallory. I really do appreciate it."

"Eh, not a problem. The whole Bizarro World set piece made it too interesting to pass up. Long story short, no surprises. She was strangled with a blue-and-green scarf. We collected blood and skin from under her fingernails, but I wouldn't get my hopes up for DNA—she scratched the hell out of her own neck trying to breathe. Nothing else. No bruises or cuts, clothing all intact, no sign of sexual assault."

"Oh, thank you, God," Rachael breathed.

Luis echoed her. "Yeah. That would have made a horrible situation so much worse."

"Wasn't pregnant, and unless she had a superflexible hymen, almost certainly never had intercourse. Other than her sex life, or lack thereof, let's see . . . nothing. Completely healthy young woman. Heart good, lungs clear, apparently broke a rib a long time ago, I'd say a couple years at a minimum. That was it."

"Toxicology?" Michael asked.

"Takes weeks. What do you think we are, McDonald's?"

"I know, sorry."

"*But* I knew you'd all be dying to know, with an international victim like this, so I begged for some unofficial preliminaries. Also clear, no sign of intoxicants, narcotics, anything illegal. Nothing, nada, zip."

"That is also not a surprise," Rachael said.

"Nothing weird in her layers of clothing. Underwear, shirt, pants, socks, shoes, sweater, raincoat. No tattoos, talismans, class rings on a chain 'round her neck, love notes held next to her heart. A tissue in the raincoat pocket and a tub of lip balm in the pants pocket."

Ellie asked, "What are the shoes like? Muddy?"

"Coated. All the outwear is covered in mud—duh, she'd been buried—but her new Timberland boots had the stuff crammed into every tread."

Rachael spoke to no one in particular: "Not surprising—from our visits to the site during class."

"And she had tufts of fur sticking to the coat as well, which I assume is from the goat you also kindly sent along. Speaking of the goat, am I correct in assuming you did *not* also need me to do a necropsy on it?"

"Correct," Rachael said. "I know what killed the goat." She broke off to glance at the two FBI agents. "Though I assume the FBI hoped that your trace evidence techs could examine its fur, its exterior, for any item or substance the killer might have left."

"Yes," Luis said.

"He's taking a look at it, but I poked my head in there a few minutes ago and he didn't seem especially titillated by anything he'd found so far."

A pause ensued, in which the four people at the table tried to think of something else to ask, and failed.

"That concludes my remarks," the medical examiner said. "Thank you for coming. Transcripts will be available in the lobby."

"Wow, really?" Rachael teased.

"Pfft. *No.* And don't nag me for a report by nine a.m. tomorrow. Ain't gonna happen."

Michael said, "Got it. Thanks a lot, Doc."

Rachael said, "Yes, thanks so much, Mallory. I know this will make her parents feel at least an iota more at peace."

"Her parents will have other things on their minds," Mallory said, and hung up.

The end of a life summed up, Ellie thought. Nothing unusual. Except for some evil person knotting a scarf around her neck until she died.

Michael said, "The treads of her shoes. The crime scene crew looked like they'd been mud wrestling by the time they wrapped up for the day and insisted that the killer had to be covered in it. Unless they were in head-to-toe rain gear, like a Gloucester fisherman, and the rain completely washed it off by the time they got to their car—"

"It was coming down hard enough," Rachael muttered.

"—then their driver's seat and floorboard should be coated as well. It does seem to eliminate the people on the shuttle, we've got that list." He pushed a handwritten sheet toward them. "But we examined every vehicle that's left the lot today—"

Did someone touch *her baby*? Ellie sputtered, "Hey! No one asked me for my keys! That's original paint, you know. I hope someone didn't—"

Michael held up one hand, a slight grin appearing under this onslaught. "I'm sure it remains unmolested. We couldn't possibly get search warrants for them all, so agents waited in the lot as owners came out and asked for permission to search. So far no one has said no."

"Of course not. They'd be an instant suspect." It made sense, the least painful way to look inside a whole parking lot full of vehicles.

"Everyone had smudges of mud, dirt, leaves on their floorboards, but none seemed out of line, only the typical hazards of fall in the northwest. Somehow the killer murdered Farida, buried her, then walked away and drove home without leaving a trace."

"Or came back inside. There are lockers and locker rooms with showers," Ellie said without thinking, then winced at Rachael's miserable expression. Only the staff would be familiar with the gym facilities.

Michael said, "All were searched today, with nothing significant found. Of course someone could have bundled up all the dirty stuff and worn their gym clothes home or something, but they did it without leaving a trail of mud across the sinks."

"No sexual assault," Luis repeated. "The motive could still be sexual, could be anger at a failed romantic pass, or could have nothing to do with love or sex at all."

In other words, they were no further along than they'd been hours and hours ago, and now added in a possible connection to Barbara Wright to complicate matters.

The dog's whines now increased in volume and intensity, as if he were trying to convince his audience that a wild jackal had entered the kitchen and he—the puppy—was in grave danger.

"What is that thing?" Luis asked Rachael.

"It's a dog. I can't get more specific than that . . . Dogs all kinda look alike to me."

"Heretic," Luis said, and she laughed.

Ellie had been studying the list of students who took the shuttle to and from the hotel. Some she recognized from her class, like Sergeant Craig Bennett, Bettie Williams with the orange hair, and the lieutenant from Ohio, Matthew Gold. Some she didn't, most likely from Rachael's crime scene course. "Hey. Why is Alyssa on here? She lives in DC."

"Who?"

"Alyssa works for us—you. She does ERT sometimes too, that's how I know her. I mean, she *could* be staying at the hotel, but I'd assume she'd go home every night."

Michael drew an asterisk next to Alyssa's name, but then went on. "If we assume the same person killed both Dr. Wright and Farida, the only working theory I come up with is that Farida saw this murder, or knew something that would eventually make her realize who had killed Wright. He had gotten away with making Wright's death look accidental, but didn't have time to do the same with Farida."

"If someone killed Dr. Wright," Ellie reasoned aloud, "that had to occur between, say, ten forty-five, when she turned the class over to me—at least that's when *I* saw her last—and when she didn't show up to resume the class at one, and Caleb and I found her body."

"We'll have to canvass the staff, see if we can narrow that down," Luis said.

"But Farida would have been with me and our class that whole time," Rachael said. "Maybe a quick bathroom break at some point, but otherwise—what could she have seen?"

Luis said, "It could have been something someone told her, or something she overheard. Like 'I could kill that bitch'? And that could have happened before or after the actual death."

Michael said, "Back to this torn label—we have to presume our killer either murdered this Dr. Wright or was at least present at her death. They got the label stuck on themselves and then accidentally shed it at the second crime scene."

"Possibly," Rachael and Ellie agreed. Neither sounded convinced.

"Or he or she purposely took the label to leave at the second scene, in order to . . . what?"

The four people were silent. The puppy kept up his campaign to let them know that the jackal had now entered his enclosure with bared teeth.

Then Ellie said, "Because he wanted us to know."

"Know that Wright was murdered?"

"And that he killed both her and Farida."

Michael Tyler sat with his chin on one hand, looking at her. "That makes absolutely no sense at all." This didn't sound like an argument.

Rachael considered this. "On the surface, no. If we'd accepted Barbara's death as accidental, why rock that boat? Why call attention to your own crime?"

"Because it's fun?" Ellie suggested.

To accentuate his point, the puppy began to howl as if the jackal had already torn off one limb and had started to munch on a second.

"Fun?"

"To a killer, everything about murder is fun. All right—I can't stand it." She went into the kitchen as Luis called out that she would spoil the animal.

The puppy lapsed into tail-wagging, innocent silence as soon as she appeared. She complimented him on his clever escape from the ravenous jackal, picked up his old towel blanket, and wrapped him in it, to keep from being showered in flakes of dried, smelly mud. "You can sit on my lap if you're quiet. And don't pee on me."

But the meeting was breaking up, the fact that they were getting nowhere was plain to everyone. Michael and Luis would continue to monitor the crime scene, Rachael would see what Agnes had found on Barbara Wright's electronics, and Ellie would page through her research papers to see if they could possibly, in some unexpected way, have any connection to Farida Al Talel.

"What about him?" Michael said, referring to the bundle in Ellie's arms.

What, indeed?

Chapter 23

Afterward, Rachael went directly to digital forensics—she knew the habits of each and every Locard employee. Agnes professed a dim view of working overtime, and yet she always seemed to be at her desks—plural—at odd hours. The slim young woman had her hair in a short braid today, the end of it bound with a surprisingly whimsical elastic band in bright magenta, with dangling half-moons in neon yellow. The sunny colors did not match her mood. But then, Rachael never thought to use the word "sunny" to describe—

"Nothing scandalous," Agnes announced before Rachael could say hello. "No torrid love notes, irate exes, revenge porn active in Dr. Wright's electronics. Hector was pretty mad at her, though."

"*Hector.* Why?"

Agnes called up the emails to the monitor and let Rachael read for herself. They'd been using their Locard email accounts—hardly the move of people desperate to keep their exchanges a secret.

HAzores: I don't see my name on the materials you're planning to submit.

BWright: Why would you? It's my work.

HAzores: No, it's MY work, the sums of murder clusters by area, type, name.

BWright: All available online.

HAzores: But not compiled online. Come off it, Babs, you cut and pasted wholesale.

BWright: How would you know what I'm submitting? Break into my office?

HAzores: Not breaking when door's open. Same way you stole all my research, walked in while I was teaching. AA will be interested.

Rachael assumed he meant the American Academy of Forensic Sciences, at whose meeting Barbara planned to present her theories.

BWright: Go ahead.

HAzores: My name better be on that presentation.

BWright: Go ahead, whine to committee, won't care.

Rachael wondered if she meant the AA committee wouldn't care, or she wouldn't care. Or both. "Bit of bravado. Scientific communities take plagiarism charges very seriously."

HAzores: Committee will be the least of your worries, bitch.

"Timestamp," Agnes said.

Rachael checked it. Eleven twenty-five a.m., the previous day. Roughly an hour and a half before Barbara Wright was found dead. "Were they emailing each other from across the hall?"

Agnes giggled, a sound so unusual that Rachael started.

"I can just picture that," Agnes admitted, "two eggheads lobbing insults from their desks because they don't have the guts to walk ten feet to face someone in person."

"Somebody faced her at some point."

Agnes glanced at the monitor, over Rachael's shoulder, and clicked a few keys that brought up a hidden code Rachael couldn't decipher. "No, Hector was at his desktop, Barbara on her phone."

"That makes more sense."

"Can you really see Hector clocking Barbara over the head with a jar of acid?"

"We don't know that's what it was. Wait, how did *you* know?"

"Everybody knows."

True enough, Rachael figured. The staff had been informed of Barbara's death as a probable heart attack brought on by exposure to acid fumes. But once even the *idea* of murder popped into her head, it managed to leap into the rumor mill and disperse in every direction.

Maybe Hector came looking for Barbara, found her in the lab, saw his opportunity. *Maybe.* "I can't see it. I've never known Hector to have any kind of temper, much less a violent one. And over an academic credit? He hadn't even complained to Gerald—that I know of. And he could have made a formal complaint to the American Academy, and even Caltech. It might have caused her some real difficulties."

She'd have to inform the FBI agents of these emails, but that could wait until tomorrow. She would frame it as the minor squabble it was—as Agnes thought, a spat among eggheads.

Except this spat formed the only thing even close to a motive that she'd seen so far.

Agnes said, as if on cue, "Then there's this. On her laptop only, not the Locard system."

She angled Barbara Wright's laptop toward Rachael and clicked on a folder labeled WRIGHTGENE FORENSICS. It contained seven other folders, with labels such as MISSION STATEMENT, BOARD OF DIRECTORS, DEPARTMENT OF FINANCE, and PRICING.

Rachael explored each one. WrightGene Forensics' mission statement declared that WrightGene could "pinpoint suspects through their bodily fluids left at crime scenes, even when CODIS could not" and "existed solely to assist the law enforcement community in their efforts."

The pricing schedule, however, detailed the hefty costs collected for such assistance.

"She was going to start her own company," Agnes said.

"And turn quite a profit doing so. Well, good for her . . . I guess."

The board of directors, so far, consisted of one person—Barbara Wright, Chair, though the chart graciously allowed four slots for future members.

The finance report listed four venture capital firms, each providing different six-figure amounts for startup costs. One, Baudelet Capital Investments, had a question mark next to it.

"I wonder if these firms actually committed money, or if she hoped they'd commit money," Rachael said.

Agnes asked, "Either way, is this a motive for murder?"

"I can't see why. Nothing illegal about it. Unless she had a business partner she planned to cut out—and it doesn't seem to be Hector, who only cared about the academy presentation. Were there any references to WrightGene in her emails or texts?"

"Not her Locard account emails. Texts, kind of." Agnes woke up a third monitor and directed Rachael's attention to the downloaded texts. "It's this set here, but I'll summarize. She planned to meet someone called Dave in Seattle the day after she arrived for the American Academy. They could discuss his investiture. Not investment, *investiture.*"

"That's strange." The word "investiture" had nothing to do with investments, and rather to do with formally establishing someone in their role as high-ranking official or perhaps king. Maybe Barbara planned to fill in her board's organizational chart, beginning with Seattle's Dave. And she considered it quite the honor to bestow.

"Maybe it's a spell-check mistake, but hardly seems

likely, does it? Anyway, Dave's phone number belongs to a David Brubeck. Not the jazz musician, obviously. This Dave Brubeck is forty-three, married, three kids, and a quality control manager at Henderson Monitoring in Redmond, outside Seattle."

"How'd you find that out?"

Agnes blinked at Rachael as if both stunned and faintly disappointed. "Google. Ran the phone number. Then checked his Facebook and LinkedIn pages."

"Oh. And what does Henderson Monitoring actually do?"

"Quality control. Efficiency expert consultants. At least that's what their website implies. It's big on arty graphics and short on detail."

"I see. Well, unless this Dave flew across the country and snuck into and out of the Locard without anyone noticing, he hardly seems a likely suspect. But I'll turn all this over to the agents. They can contact Mr. Brubeck not-the-musician to let him know Barbara won't make their meeting, and maybe he can shed some light on whether this high finance was real or not. Thank you, Agnes. I hope you have a restful night. Oh—did you find any reference in her stuff to Farida?"

"Your Saudi girl? No."

"Nothing?"

"Not a mention. She didn't talk about young women, Saudis, Middle Easterners, Muslims, embassies, student exchange programs, or international matters—other than internet searches for crime rates, stats, summaries, and use of prescription drugs by country."

"Okay, then. Did you see her cousins downstairs last night? They said they asked you to check the ladies' room."

Agnes blinked. "By the cafeteria?"

"Yes."

"No."

Rachael had not expected this answer. "Are you sure?"

she blurted out, before remembering that Agnes was eternally sure of everything, and one would hardly forget being pressed into service by two men without aid of the English language.

"Why would I go two floors down just to use the restroom?"

A logical question. "I . . . thought maybe to go to the gym, or get something out of your locker . . ." Her voice trailed off in the wake of Agnes's blank gaze. Rachael didn't even know if Agnes had a locker, or if she had ever utilized the gym or its exercise equipment. Or, for that matter, the cafeteria.

"Not me. But there is one thing maybe you should check." Agnes used the same monitor to go to Facebook, logging into her own profile. Rachael could only glimpse several posts of book covers and what looked like a girls' night out, with a round of shots of some amber-colored . . . Was that a bottle of Jack Daniel's?

Rachael didn't dare ask, and Agnes quickly clicked on recent searches to bring up Oliver Suarez's profile.

"I went through the list of students and checked their social media—what I could. Some have theirs set to private, but not as many as you'd think." She frowned on this, literally, and shook her head. "People never learn. Of those students without private profiles, a lot posted in the past week about being here, photos of the water, *more* than a few of happy hour at the hotel. The standard tourist stuff of DC, monuments, Smithsonians. A few included photos of Farida—taken here at the Locard. It doesn't seem like she went out with anyone, not even to happy hour. Her profile *is* private. Most unhelpful."

"Okay." Rachael studied Oliver's page. Fabulous photos of snowcapped mountains, a close-up of an eagle sitting on a rock in the middle of a stream, for profile pics. But the four most recent posts were of Farida. The first, posted on the

Wednesday of the previous week, had been taken from the front of the classroom during a break. Some attendees sat, some milled about with their Styrofoam cups of coffee or reusable water bottles. Farida wore a blue headscarf and spoke to the woman seated next to her, apparently unaware of the photographer. Oliver had posted: *My crime scene doc class near DC. Going well. Girl in scarf is from Saudi Arabia.* This had garnered a few comments, one recommending a DC restaurant, two advising him not to miss seeing the Lincoln Memorial, and someone named Chaz asking, "Is she learning how to be a better terrorist?" Oliver and several others had responded to that with a mad emoji.

The second post showed the lunch bunch. He'd snapped a photo while Farida conversed with Stef, again unaware of the camera. Oliver's caption: *Farida trying a burger for the first time?* To which, a poster named Maddie said, "They do have burgers in Saudi, bro."

In the third photo, posted Monday, Farida smiled directly at the camera and stood alone. It had been taken in the courtyard, next to the fountain, and Farida wore the same headscarf she would die in. Rachael wondered where the two bodyguards had been. Photos were another iffy thing in Saudi, she had read somewhere. They were allowed, but frowned upon by stricter types. Though Taliban soldiers were now snapping selfies all over the place, women were not supposed to "advertise" themselves. Farida didn't seem nervous about it, however; her warmth and vitality shone through the lens. Oliver wrote: *My new friend, Farida.*

To which, people had commented:
Beautiful!
Hot!
Bring her home to Mama!
Looks like a sweet girl.
And Chaz advised him to check her suitcase for bombs.
Chaz, Rachael decided, *is a jerk.*

The fourth post had gone up at one-thirty that afternoon, with the sad notation: *This beautiful woman died today. An amazing life cut short. I was so looking forward to showing her Montana.* The photo showed Farida at what would become her own grave site, kneeling in the leaves next to, Rachael knew, Chester's body, though that had been cropped out, as had the people on either side of her. With her face turned up, she seemed to be laughing at something someone said with all the joy and hope of the universe concentrated into one young woman. The image broke Rachael's heart. It also chilled it.

"Is that the woods where she was found?" Agnes asked.

"Yes."

One-thirty . . . When had the attendees been informed? It would have been *right* around then . . . Oliver had immediately posted his grief. Not strange. He used a photo taken at what became the crime scene; yet it made an appropriate memorial in and of itself. A great shot with colors so vibrant you could touch them: Farida's dark eyes, red lips, the deep browns of the damp earth. Moreover, it captured her doing what she loved, what she hoped for and looked forward to in her own personal future. It was gorgeous—and clearly curated by someone who cared.

"He had it bad."

"But did she?" Agnes asked.

"How would we ever know? I very much doubt she confided in her cousins—though she may have. She could have texted a blue streak to friends back home, but that will be up to the FBI to find on her phone. She may have kept it all inside . . . For all the recent changes in her country, the modernizations, the new freedoms, she still must have learned to keep her thoughts to herself. And she might have thought Oliver was a nice guy, and that was all."

"Subsequently breaking his heart."

"Perhaps. We need to figure out exactly where Oliver was when everyone left last night. Using a photo taken at the same place her body turned up . . ."

"Insensitive," Agnes said.

"Weird," Rachael said. "Anything else you think I should know?"

"No. Pics of Farida show up in some other students' posts, but in group shots. No one singles her out in their comments."

"Okay," Rachael said again, feeling the weariness seep through her bones, from her head down to her toenails. "Thanks, Agnes. Enjoy your evening."

"I always do," the young woman sniffed.

Rachael wondered if it would involve Jack Daniel's, but didn't ask. A *"snootful"*—as her father would have said— *would taste pretty good right about now.*

Chapter 24

With the puppy under one arm, and Barbara Wright's carton under the other, Ellie still swung back to her new office before leaving the building, since on her desktop she'd forgotten the keys to her home and car. Rather than try to juggle both, while also unlocking the door and turning the latch, she let the carton slip to the floor. The carton wouldn't run away; she couldn't be sure of the dog.

Everyone else had gone. Hector's office was dark, the door shut for a change. She wondered why the FBI hadn't made both the students and staff leave the Locard campus. Investigation 101: Evacuate the crime scene of all nonessential personnel, promptly and completely. She knew her ex-colleagues held the Locard in great esteem, but the bureau had never let money, prestige, *or* esteem color their actions. It must be more along the "keep your enemies closer" theme, but still . . . unusual.

Everything about the current situation was unusual.

The puppy wriggled.

"Not a chance," she told him, entering the unlit room. "You

run off through these hallways and open rooms, I could be chasing you for the next hour. And I do not have the mojo for that right now."

The keys were right where she'd left them, on the desk blotter instead of clipped to her purse with a carabiner, like they should have been. She glanced at the windows—the sun had completely abandoned them now and the night outside sat in utter darkness. This turned the windows to mirrors, reflecting the light from the inner hallway. And against that light she saw two silhouettes, not only the one that belonged to her.

She turned around in a breath, clutching the dog a bit too tightly. He protested with a short *yip*.

"Oh," Ellie said. "Hello. Cameron—right?"

He stood in the doorway, next to Barbara's storage box, much taller than she had estimated when he'd been seated in his task chair. "You have Dr. Wright's card."

She breathed in. "Yes."

"You can't have Dr. Wright's card."

"I—I know, I'm supposed to bring it to you."

"This is yours." He held out a white plastic rectangle, pre-punched for easier attachment to a lanyard or key ring. "It's connected to your ID, in the system. You can't use Dr. Wright's card, that's not right."

She took the card and set it on the desk without taking her gaze off him. The young man wore the same grunge band T-shirt and loose-fitting jeans that she'd seen that morning, though his hair had grown less meticulously combed with the lateness of the day. His own gaze darted around the room without, it seemed, finding an interesting enough place to land. Or simply to avoid landing at all.

She unclipped Barbara Wright's keycard from her belt and handed it to him, clip and all. "Thank you. I'm sorry you had to make a delivery, I should have come by to get it."

"Yes. You can't have Barbara Wright's keycard. That was hers."

She started to say *I'm sorry.*

"*Stop,*" her cousin Maureen would say. "*You have nothing to apologize for. Stop being such a w . . .*"

"I'm sorry. Were you friends?" she asked.

"No. I didn't like her." He stated this like an observation of the weather, though his focus began to move about the room with even more haste than before.

"Oh." But since he didn't seem to mind brutal honesty: "Why not?"

"She wasn't nice. She made the director make me take the scan controls off her computer, when I said that wasn't safe. It's my job to make sure the server is safe. Because of her I did a bad job."

"It wasn't your fault that—"

"It's my job to make sure the server is safe. It's my *job.*" His left hand began to pluck at his pants leg, which she took as a sign of agitation. "I did a bad job, but it was *her* fault."

"Well, clearly—"

"And she always wanted my blood. Why do you have a dog in your office?"

"He's a stray. Why did she want your blood?"

"She wanted to test it. But why is he in your office? We don't have any other animals in this building. Dr. Simonds had a container of beetles to clean off bones and it broke and they all got loose and now we don't even have beetles here."

"We couldn't have him running around outside at the crime scene. What did she want to test it for?"

"To see why I am the way I am. I'm not like other people. But I told her, 'No, I don't like having needles stuck in me.' She said I was being a baby and needed to think about people other than myself. I thought that was mean, because I do think about other people. I gave my mother a card for her birthday."

"I agree," Ellie said firmly. She didn't specify what she agreed with, but it seemed to satisfy him. His fingers stopped pinching the denim seam.

"But I like dogs," he added.

"Oh." No, he wasn't like other people, but she felt stupid for feeling nervous around him, simply because she didn't know him and it had gotten dark out. And, yes, two murders, but still—any dog lover . . . She took a step forward. "Would you like to pet him?"

"No. He's dirty, and kind of smells. Goodbye."

And with that, he turned and left.

Ellie called "Good night!" but if he made any response, she couldn't hear it.

So . . . that was Cameron.

She checked the new keycard in the office door, and the electronic lock dutifully unlatched for her. After that, she managed to pick up the cardboard carton again, and then she and the dog were once again on their way to the parking lot.

Where, indeed, two FBI agents waited as Ellie approached the Mustang. The long day had not dampened their spirits— one seemed delighted to make a quick survey of the interior of Ellie's car, while the other assured Ellie that the puppy she held hailed from the Beauceron breed, herding dogs originating in France. They were smart and brave and made excellent guard dogs. Ellie needed to spend at least twenty minutes a day play-training with him for his first few years and he'd be amazing. Ellie wasn't sure what amazing thing she should train the dog to do, but didn't take time to ask.

The puppy agreed with this assessment, licking the agent's fingers as her partner checked Ellie's seat and floor mats for excessive mud or damp. She had plenty of smears on the carpeting from the last few days, but not enough to concern the agent, who said the dog looked like a German shepherd to him.

"Absolutely not. Beauceron." Then his partner squinted, gazing deeply into the puppy's eyes, and tweaked her assessment: "Maybe one-eighth Entlebucher Mountain Dog."

The man grinned, rolled his eyes, and mouthed "German shepherd" at Ellie before they moved as another person arrived to get in their car and leave for the day.

With the nearest pet supermarket forty-five minutes away, Ellie made do with a quick stop at a dollar store to stock up on all things puppy. They had food, flea collars, leashes, treats, and an impressive array of squeaky toys. She passed on the single available dog bed; she could find an old blanket or pile of towels for him as a temporary accommodation, and besides, from the look of his paws, she suspected he would have grown out of it by the following week. As serendipity or her lucky stars or whatever had it, she had bought a house with a fenced backyard, so at least she didn't have to worry about how he'd get enough exercise while she worked. He could run around to his heart's content. She'd figure something else out when the weather got really cold.

As she pulled into her garage, she saw her new neighbor out with her children. They chased each other in the dark yard, stopping only to catch lightning bugs.

Ellie had met the ER nurse supervisor once since moving in, but the efficient Daisy had hit the highlights: She and her auto mechanic husband had lived across from the bay for seven years, and had two boys and one girl, eleven, six, and eight, respectively. And also Daisy's father from Colombia. Summers were heaven—provided you had plenty of mosquito repellent—and winters an unmitigated bitch. But the water made it all worth it.

Still dressed in scrubs, Daisy watched from her driveway as Ellie approached. "Oh my Gawd, what did you do?"

"In my defense," Ellie told her, "I was left unsupervised. And he's so darn cute."

"He is that."

Kids and dogs belong together, and these kids and this dog were no exception. They promptly forgot about lightning bugs, usurped her pet, and tore up and down both driveways with delighted shrieks so earsplitting that the elderly man on the other side of Ellie's poked his head out his front door to see what in the world was going on.

"How is your job coming?" Daisy asked, never really taking her gaze from the three kids. "Your first day go well? Days?"

"It's been . . . interesting."

The four young beings sped past them again. "Be careful! He's only a baby, remember! You have to be gen—how on earth did he get so dirty?"

"That's part of the interesting bit. It seems he's been living in the woods around the institute, and we had that rain last night—"

"That was awful."

"What's his name?" the little girl asked Ellie.

"I don't know yet."

"You should call him Tiger."

"That's dumb," her brother insisted, now throwing the stick. "Because he's *not* a tiger. She names everything Tiger," he confided to Ellie.

"It does simplify matters."

He squinted at her. The idea that Ellie would even consider his sister's point of view lowered his estimation of the new neighbor. By several notches.

Daisy went on. "Other than picking up stray animals, the

job's okay? We're very proud of the Locard in this neck of the woods."

"I love it." She considered what the ER nurse had probably seen over the years, and decided to pick her neighbor's brains. "Let me ask a hypothetical. Do you know what kind of weapon could cause a hematoma on the skull without causing an abrasion or a bruise?"

If Daisy found this shift in topics odd, she gave no sign. Meanwhile, Sammy, her youngest, slipped on the grass while chasing the puppy and let out a wail. He showed his mother the barely scraped knee and she told him to go inside and get the antiseptic and a bandage. He considered the knee, the puppy, and the knee again, and decided the injury didn't warrant taking time out for proper medical care, not when his brother and the puppy played tug-of-war with a stick.

Then Daisy said, "A fall. A ball bat. Chain in a noodle. A lead pipe in the library."

"Mom, can we have a dog?"

"A chain in a noodle?" Ellie asked.

"Some of the ne'er-do-wells of the county—you know that foam that comes like a split tube for wrapping your PVC pipes? They like to get a length of heavy chain and shove it inside that, like a hot dog in a bun, then wrap the whole thing in duct tape. Swing it hard, it'll take even a big guy right down, but hardly leaves a mark. *And* it's not, technically, a weapon. Very popular."

"Mom?"

"The idea is to have something with weight, but a little bit of cushion."

"Mom!" Nico said, rubbing the puppy's stomach. "Can't we have a dog?"

"No, baby, are you kidding? There's you, there's me, there's Daddy, Alma, Sammy, and Papi too—where do you think we have room for a dog?"

"But can't we keep him?" Alma whined.

"*No*, of course not. He's Ellie's."

Three sets of eyes swiveled in her direction.

"Absolutely not," she said, to Daisy's visible relief. "You can play with him every day, but he's living with me. I need a friend. And a roommate with teeth is probably a good idea too."

Chapter 25

The still-unnamed puppy didn't care so much for the bath in the utility tub, but cheered up when rewarded with puppy chow and a chew toy. After that, he joined her upstairs at her desk in the sitting room—Ellie didn't know how else to refer to the extra space at the top of the stairs, outside her master bedroom and the guest bedrooms. Her desk faced a wide window overlooking the upper porch and the bay, a gorgeous view in the daytime; but in the dark she could only see her own reflection gazing back at her, a much less therapeutic sight.

With a bowl of salad, and a damp puppy sleeping on her feet, she spread out Barbara Wright's research.

The data seemed to fall into three categories: Lists of crimes, both solved and unsolved, by county. Lists of prescription medications on auto-refill, indicating these meds were necessary to maintain health in the face of chronic conditions. And third, murders and violent crimes with suspect DNA and/or bodily fluids left at the scene, where searching the DNA through CODIS had not helped because the suspect wasn't in that database.

A long listing, grouped by states in alphabetical order, put the three categories together:

Alabama: Four unsolved rapes, sickle cell disease found in semen samples. Five local pharmacies report standing orders of hydroxyurea.

Kansas: Two unsolved murders and one solved, in which the killer liked to spit on his victims. Thiazide had been found in the saliva residue. Virtually every local pharmacy dispensed thiazide diuretics to patients with high blood pressure, including the person convicted of the third murder. DNA analysis was currently pending to prove him guilty of the other two as well.

Maryland: Two child murders, victims eight and ten, unrelated to each other and apparently picked at random. Murder by strangulation, found behind fast-food restaurants close to the DC city limits. Tissues found, again, but not with nasal mucus—some other liquid, possibly tears, since it did not give a reaction for amylase (indicating saliva). The tissues analysis showed compounds consistent with valproic acid, prescribed for migraines, seizures, and bipolar disorder.

Missouri: Five murders by gunshot, associated by matching ballistics. At one scene the victim had put up a brief fight and died with the suspect's blood staining her diamond ring. The blood showed mutations in the RB1 gene that would cause retinoblastoma. Two local pharmacies dispensed cyclophosphamide.

New Mexico: Two separate armed robberies in which, while waiting for the store to empty, the suspect blew his nose at the scene and left the dirty tissue in a trash can. The cells showed a mutation in the NOD2 gene, which, along with the witness statements, indicated some form of lung disease, such as interstitial lung disease or sarcoidosis. One local pharmacy dispensed methotrexate.

All crimes were more than three years old, which didn't surprise Ellie. Barbara would have had to contact each agency and somehow talk them into further testing on the suspect samples to look for medications and/or genetic conditions. None of that would have been done in a standard investigation. DNA would be isolated and entered into the CODIS database, and if it didn't match anyone, you were out of luck.

To summarize, between the pharmacological information—either suspect samples had a trace of a drug that indicated a disease, or the samples had genes that indicated the disease and therefore a need for the drug—and the geolocation, Barbara Wright had believed that a suspect could be pinpointed. Her idea to make use of what they'd been throwing away all this time *did* sound intriguing—extra work, but worth it, right?

A fourth category of data appeared to help with this winnowing process. Any DNA left at the scene could also indicate a phenotype—eye color, hair color, gender. At this point Barbara's process melded with the genealogical tracing process that had pointed law enforcement at the Golden State Killer. Take your pool of potential suspects—for example, patients receiving insulin in the Boston area—and start eliminating based on their observable characteristics.

Then go to their Facebook page and eliminate those who don't fit the psychological profile. Maybe you're looking for an introverted loner, and one patient is an event planner with a spouse and five children in various sports, which didn't leave a lot of time for stalking victims. Or a cat burglar who specializes in high-rises, and your patient is in a wheelchair. Or the one you think might have burned down a chemical lab happened to post pictures from a teahouse in Nepal on the same day. There were no guarantees to these assumptions, but any narrowing of a large list of suspects could help.

As a test control Barbara had included information about Bruce Pension, a prolific killer who haunted the Marion, Oklahoma, area, murdering eleven women over ten years.

DNA had been found at two of the scenes, once when he'd cut himself on the window he'd broken to gain entry, and once when he'd had a cold and left nasal mucus on a victim's cheek. A CODIS search did not help, as he had no criminal record. But the bodily fluids showed tranylcypromine, a less common anxiety med usually prescribed to help with panic attacks. A worn piece of paper listed those receiving tranyl-cypromine.

After that, Barbara had applied the same sort of logic that helped eliminate possible suspects when using genealogical analysis. The bloodstain showed a Y chromosome, so she eliminated women. She eliminated the very old and the very young male patients. She did further genetic testing on the samples to determine the probable phenotype, if he was likely to have light-colored hair or green eyes. She located all social media profiles of remaining suspects, trying to guess at who might be less well-adjusted than they appeared, who might have been in the same area of the victims at the same time, who had the type of jobs that would leave them free at certain times of the day. Utilizing all those factors, she and her system focused on one single suspect: Bruce Pension, who had, at some point before this, proudly confessed to killing all eleven. It wasn't quite as impressive as the mur-der algorithm identifying Gary Ridgway's work as serial killing, since Barbara was a human being, not a computer. She remained subject to confirmation bias—she already knew Pension to be guilty and might have eliminated sus-pects differently, if she'd been truly unaware—but it was certainly interesting.

Interesting system, Barbara Wright, Ellie thought. Except for one thing.

Prescription histories were confidential, along with the rest of one's medical information. Insurance companies and medical personnel had databases they could consult, to make sure a patient's meds were being taken properly, were not conflicting with each other, and were not being abused. But Barbara Wright did not work in either an insurance company or a hospital, so where had she gotten this information?

Another dive into the cardboard box did help with this question, but only raised some more. Ellie found a thick printout of pharmacies, medications, and the patients to whom they'd been dispensed. Pages and pages of eight-point font. Certain entries were highlighted—most likely, the cases Barbara had used in her presentation. The pages had no header or footer, and didn't even look like normal copy paper. The edges had tiny nubs, as if they had been printed on an old-fashioned dot-matrix printer with the perforated, hole-punched, sprocket-feed paper. Ellie hadn't seen such a thing in many years.

She rubbed both eyes, and *really* wished Barbara Wright could be asked about it.

The puppy shifted his weight across her toes. What *was* she going to name him? Because she had grown up in other people's homes, the choice had never been hers to make. Her second cousins in Nevada had had three dogs, sleepy hounds who had never paid much attention to her and who had too many teeth for her to approach comfortably. Her mother's cousin-in-law Valencia, in California, had two cats and they'd sleep on Ellie's lap while she studied.

And they'd had a fairly pure-bred beagle at Aunt Rosalie's, named Brownie—not the most imaginative name, but the only one her three elementary-school-aged cousins could agree on. One day Ellie and Maureen decided that Brownie should be trained for carnival work. They spent the afternoon constructing a haphazard obstacle course in the tiny backyard, utilizing a tree stump and odds and ends from the worn, detached garage. One board created a hurdle for the short dog to jump over, one stretched between the stump and the lawn chair became a balance beam. A piece of wire was formed into a hoop. The same sort of thing with a window screen became Brownie's only balking point; in the dog's view the girls wanted her to walk on air, something even a dog knew to be impossible. Brownie got around as best she could, by sensibly keeping one set of paws on the frame and stepping on the screen only when absolutely necessary, not quite committing herself to that leap of faith. Otherwise, the good-natured beagle ran through her paces without complaint, as many times as the girls wanted; pats and pieces of Milk-Bones her only reward.

But beagles are vocal when bored or hungry, and when Uncle Wayne's Gulf War–induced PTSD kicked in, the dog's barks and whines got too much for him to handle. Brownie wound up shipped off to a friend's place in a roomier suburb shortly before the children were sent to the cousins in Nevada. Aunt Rosalie tackled the problem with her usual determination and copious prayers, and Uncle Wayne battled his demons, until the three biological children and even the whiny beagle came home. But by then, Ellie had already settled into her third home in West Virginia.

Not for long, really. West Virginia, Florida, California, DC—not anywhere for long. She *had* found a home at the FBI, until her split from Adam made that awkward. Maybe that tension would have faded in time—the bureau was a very big pond.

But now she'd found the Locard. And if people didn't stop dying, she might have to leave there too.

Maybe she really was cursed . . . Her cousin Becky had suggested that once, after her arrival in West Virginia. Ellie's mother had died; then her grandmother died; then Uncle Wayne went a bit AWOL.

But maybe not. Nothing bad had happened to Aunt Katey, not really. Until last month at least.

Ellie shook herself. There were no such things as curses,

and the Locard killer would be a very real human who had made very real mistakes. All she had to do was find them.

The puppy woke up and gave a tiny yawn, looking up at her from beneath the desk.

"I promise I won't make you jump through hoops."

The tiny tail wagged.

"But I'd still like to know where Barbara Wright got a listing of prescription med dispensations."

The puppy barked.

"That," she told him, "is an excellent idea." She checked her watch—not too late to call, Florida being in the same time zone—and picked up her phone. A few seconds later she said, "Aunt Joanna? It's Ellie."

"Sweetie! How are you? You doing okay?"

Ellie took the extra-solicitous tone as an expression of concern about the events of the previous month. It had been rough, but not why she called. "I'm just fine, thanks. I'm actually calling with a health system question, and figured who better to ask than two doctors?"

"Of course, darling! Ask away. Paul's on the lanai with a cigar, so he's more than available."

Paul was her mother's brother. He and his wife, Joanna, were both internists, and Ellie had spent her high school years at their home in Naples. Once she'd entered college, they'd signed on with Doctors Without Borders.

Ellie said, "I'm surprised to catch you at home—I thought you might still be in Somalia."

"They made us leave. There were some high-body-count attacks all around us and the government insisted they couldn't be responsible for our safety. Really annoying. We had so much there left to do."

"Sorry to hear that," Ellie said, not entirely true. Paul and Joanna might not spare much thought for their personal safety, but Ellie did.

"We hope it won't be long. What's your question, babe?"

"It's kind of complicated. A former colleague had this idea for a program possibly tracing suspect samples left at crime scenes by the medications found in those samples—specifically, not controlled substances or illegal drugs, but things assigned for chronic or genetic diseases, like diabetes or irritable bowel."

"O . . . kay."

"I assume there's a national database of prescription history for doctors and insurance companies to access. You need to know if someone is doctor shopping for pain-killers—"

"Or if something I prescribe might interfere with something they're already taking that they forgot to tell me about, yes."

"Right. And insurance companies need to know the medical history for underwriting purposes. But could someone like, say, me, or my colleague, or even a police department—could they access that information?"

"Short answer? No. Prescription meds are protected health information. Confidential under HIPPA."

"That's what I thought. But we could get the information with a subpoena?"

"You'd know more about that than I would. But I'd guess anybody could get anything with a subpoena, but it would have to be specific. No judge in the world would give you a subpoena to openly fish through lists of prescription meds."

"What if it was a specific med in a specific city?"

"Well, maybe. As I said, you'd know more about that than I would."

"But there *are* such databases?"

Joanna paused and Ellie heard a slight slurp—probably green tea. Her aunt drank gallons of the stuff. "There are databases, and there are databases. There isn't a one-size-fits-all, nationally accessible program, like what I think you're picturing. State lists will have the controlled substances, but if you're not talking necessarily controlled . . . still, the EMR—"

"The what?" The puppy had slept enough, apparently, and had begun a closer inspection of Ellie's socks. She felt his cold little nose on her ankle.

"The electronic medical record. That will connect to the commercial pharmacies so your doctors can see what prescription you're taking and even when you picked it up. I don't even know where that information comes from originally—maybe the insurance payment—because it's not limited to a specific hospital or pharmacy. I'm sorry, dear, I'm not sure exactly what you're asking."

"Say that I want to know who in the city of Naples takes meds for Parkinson's. Could you, as a doctor in Naples, find that for me?"

"Yes . . . no. I could easily find out who's in the EMR for the Naples Community Hospital system, but if they're going to the Cleveland Clinic, then no. Plus, if I'm doing research and want to publish my work, it would have to go through an internal review board at the hospital and have them sign off on me getting the information. Excuse my grammar."

"Okay. *I* couldn't get access to the patient records—" Ellie said.

"Of course not. Confidential."

"—but what if I got you to look it up? I mean, *you* wouldn't, but say I knew someone who's not such a stickler for legalities."

"Then I'd be very disappointed in you, darling," the woman joked. "Sure, someone could do that from inside the system. They'd have to use their own log-on, though, so it would eventually flag *if* the person doing the looking doesn't have a legitimate reason for pulling up charts, when they're not involved in those patients' care. Unless they're in quality assurance, or something like that."

Ellie didn't have a chance to ask what that might be, before Joanna anticipated the question and went on.

"If the healthcare worker's job is quality improvement, or if they're on a committee to track treatments versus outcomes, say, or monitor an issue like antibiotic stewardship . . . that person might be opening patients' charts constantly, without flagging, because that's their job. If a pharmacist is working with a neurology group to see the compliance rate of antiepileptics, they could pull a million charts without alerting any system."

Ellie considered this. "So someone in quality control could access all patient records without raising any red flags . . . but only in a single hospital system? What if, say, the CDC is doing some kind of survey, of most prescribed drugs, prescribed drugs by area, drug dispensation versus outcomes. They'd be able to access a national database?"

Another pause and sip. "There's no *one* system . . . that I know of. There are some huge EMRs, but they're privately owned. Epic is probably the biggest, over fifty percent of North America, but some worker bee there could never cruise through patient information. They'd be flagged immediately. A director of quality control? Who knows . . . maybe . . . and that's still only fifty percent of the country. Besides, if it was handed to law enforcement to look through, it wouldn't hold up in court, would it? Illegal search."

"True." Ellie shook her head, hoping to clear it. "Someone with a project here was going to present this to some of the best minds in the country. She must have had an explanation for the data. I just don't have it in front of me yet. Thanks so much, Aunt Joanna. Tell Uncle Paul I said hi."

"Come and visit us before we go back, dear."

"I'll do my best, but I just started a new job. You know how that is."

Joanna said she did. The Beck clan understood work. They might not be all-in for hot sauce, destination weddings, or talking about their feelings, but they *got* having to work for a living.

When Ellie set the phone down, the puppy took this as a sign that her attention was all his and leapt into her lap—or at least tried. She had to give him a boost over the last few inches.

A job that might already be lost if the Locard couldn't get to the bottom of these two deaths, leaving her out in the cold, unemployed, and alone in this noisily creaking old house.

But at least she'd made a new, if furry, friend.

Chapter 26

Friday

A furry, but noisy, unrelentingly inconsiderate friend with no appreciation for those who had to get up at zero dark thirty, or near enough, and head off to a paying job. Because the puppy, who should have been grateful for the chow and the soft blanket and the bath—well, okay maybe not the bath, but at least the warm, safe place to sleep in—did not show any sort of appreciation at all. Instead, he demonstrated a complete *lack* of same for the roomy utility area between garage and kitchen, and kept up a barking, howling campaign to either convince her that unseen demons were shredding him, limb from limb, with a slow, torturous method learned from the most prestigious legions of hell; or that sleep could not be truly necessary, since he felt quite energetic after his nap under the desk and she needed only a rousing game of tug-of-war to feel refreshed.

But each household of the extended Beck family seemed to have the same rules for house pets: They were to be loved and cherished and cared for; licensed, vaccinated, and exercised regularly. But they were not to be allowed in or on beds or any eating surface, including tables, countertops, and any cabinets in which dishes were stored. There were individual tweaks about indoor furniture in general: Uncle Wayne would not allow Brownie on the couch, but Uncle Roland loved to watch television with an oversized hound on his lap for company. Valencia allowed the cats on anything upholstered, but they could not eat off people plates—leftovers would be transferred to their own designated bowls, since in Valencia's opinion even an automatic dishwasher could not get all those germs off her porcelain.

After fifteen minutes or four hours and twenty, depending on whether she judged by the clock or her gut, just as she'd begun to weaken and think that perhaps dog hairs on her sheets wouldn't actually kill her, he finally abandoned all hope and either resigned himself to spending eternity in the utility room or at last fell into slumber.

Then at least her eyes could close, which was not at all the same thing as sleeping. There were few things more frustrating than feeling exhausted, yet unable to sleep. It became a spiral moving ever downward as the frustration brought anger, which ushered in agitation, that being the very opposite of the relaxation needed to shut down. Insomnia had kicked in with every new house, fading in its potency over time, but never really going away, so it did not surprise her to find it in this new place. To make matters even worse, the house had clearly been constructed as a rickety container of creaking boards, doors that moved with unseen drafts, and one loose shutter somewhere on the first floor, which had come loose and felt the need to swing wildly every time the slightest puff of air blew in from the bay.

So Ellie arrived at the Locard feeling not-exactly-refreshed. Deadweight atop zombie legs might be a more accurate description. She needed coffee, a touch of plastic surgery on the bags under her eyes, and for at least one workday to pass without anyone dying. The cause and effect seemed clear: Ellie had been hired and the lives of two people promptly ended. Any more, and the staff of the Locard would drain the fountain, pile the space high with sticks and dry leaves, and burn her as a witch.

There were two FBI agents—she assumed their provenance from the suits and the labeled jackets—in the parking lot, not checking cars, but simply watching them, and another at the building's entrance. Ellie greeted them, one face vaguely familiar; she had probably met him at some point during her time at the FBI. Ellie did not ask what the agents stood waiting to do, knowing that the answer would be some bland and noncommittal *non*answer. To her way of thinking, *Trying to make sure no one else gets killed* felt too harsh for that time of the morning.

At least her keycard worked. IT boy Cameron knew his stuff.

She saw Rachael in the rear hallway as soon as she entered. The assistant director-slash-dean of education waved her over, saying good morning. "How are you doing?"

Ellie forced herself to refrain from yawning or rubbing her eyes, especially since the dewy fresh woman next to Rachael could have stepped from the pages of *Vogue*. Or at least *People*.

Rachael said, "This is Renee Canard. She's our latent prints professor."

"You're Ellie! *So* nice to meet you," the woman said with flattering sincerity. She wore a modest yet shapely dress in lime green, with tights and ballet flats. Long auburn hair stayed back under a wide lime-green headband, its ends trailing down her back, along with the wavy locks. A title sprang into Ellie's mind: *CSI Barbie*.

And she meant that as an utter compliment. It wasn't easy to maintain a sense of fashion and still work effectively in their field, and Ellie guessed that Renee was quite, quite effective. Something about the keenness of her glance and the focus in her body language.

If I had the energy, Ellie thought, *I'd feel intense envy right now.* But as it was, she only envied the paper cup in the woman's hand, the one with steam and a tag on a string trailing over the upper edge. "Very nice to meet you too."

"I asked Renee to work magic on the broken glass jar from yesterday," Rachael explained.

Even a tiny frown only made Renee more stylish. "Unfortunately, I couldn't deliver any. I got nothing. After Rachael's superglue I tried RAY and CyanoBlue, and every filter I had, but—nothing. That jar is very clean."

"Or someone wiped it off," Ellie said, "before dropping it on the floor."

"I can't imagine someone wanting to kill Barbara," Renee said, hazel eyes open wide.

"I can't imagine someone *not* wanting to kill Barbara," Rachael said. "Everyone did, at some point."

Renee argued. "Oh, no, not really. I mean, she could be annoying at times. Abrasive and dismissive. Had a huge fight with Angela last year about her parking space, which was *not* her parking space, no one has a designated parking space here, so . . . Okay, maybe you're right. Anyway, I have the glass packaged—is the FBI going to want it? Are they going to be ticked that I already processed it?"

Rachael said, "I don't see why. Officially, Barbara's death is still an accident."

"Huh. All right—oh, I did find some little bubbly things, like from a latex glove."

Now Rachael frowned. "Which are available in every room."

Ellie said, "And a building full of people who know enough to put them on if they're going to commit a crime."

"But it could be whoever stacked the supplies in the closet." Rachael didn't sound hopeful.

Ellie said, "We could swab those spots. Maybe, just maybe,

there will be a trace of DNA from when the person put the gloves on."

The other two women considered this, then nodded. Rachael said, "Maybe we can use Barbara's theories and find prescription meds in the sample."

"About that," Ellie began.

"I have to go," Renee said. "I have a video conference in five. This guy in LA sent the script for his new TV show over because he wants to know who's been leaking its details to the paparazzi. Got his whole staff to hand over their ten-prints for me to compare."

"And?" Rachael asked.

Renee grimaced. "It's his wife. *Awk*-ward." She sashayed away.

"I saw her get a fingerprint off an ice cube once," Rachael told Ellie.

"Is she always so . . . fashionable?"

"One Sunday I happened to come in and caught her in jeans and a T-shirt, but other than that . . . yeah. What were you going to say about Barbara's theory?"

Ellie lowered her voice as staff and students veered around them, to summarize what she'd learned from the dead woman's papers. "What she *didn't* leave is any sort of chain of custody for the data—do you know how she got lists of patients on various prescription drugs? She had to know it would be the first thing the AAFS would ask."

"She told me it was from a pharmaceutical survey ordered by the CDC. I meant to ask her more about it, but . . . I guess I got busy with other things. This project of Barbara's, she didn't tell us, Gerald and me, anything about it. She sprang it on us only two weeks ago. I knew Barbara well enough to know that she wouldn't be throwing any credit Locard's way—I doubt we'd even be mentioned. So I guess I put it out of my mind. She might have discussed it with

Harry—he's the research dean—but then he went to do the work on that mass grave in South America and we can't get ahold of him without a three-day process. Though knowing Barbara, I'll bet she kept it all to herself."

"Hector said she wasn't the sharing type."

"We should ask Hector. If anyone knows where certain stats and lists and surveys come from, it'll be him. Okay. One more day before our suspect pool is released back into the wild. What do you have on tap?"

"Everyone is going to test their own DNA with your rapid system. It was in Barbara's lesson plan, and mentioned in the course brochure, so I figured I'd better go through with it."

"Absolutely. The attendees have already lost most of a day, I don't want them to be disappointed further."

"What about you?"

"Practice documentation with class critique. Sort of a final exam."

"Sounds great."

"They hate it. But we never claimed a course on documentation was going to be exciting." Rachael watched the first attendees to arrive stream through the door. "At least it didn't used to be."

Chapter 27

Ellie's students milled about in random, but quiet, chaos—not only unsure of the exact procedure, but also unsure of how to act. After two weeks of intense training they should be shifting into "home mode," thinking about doing laundry and spending some time with the kids before returning to work on Monday, or whenever their next shift began. They would be calculating how long it would take to get to the airport, whether they could find someone to share a cab or their rental car, whether they'd remembered to leave a tip on the pillow for the hotel's housekeeping staff. They would be torn, most likely, between leaving the city while Farida's death remained a mystery, and wanting to get to their homes and back into their normal life, where they would be both paid for solving crimes *and* get to sleep in their own beds at night.

So she understood why they listened with *not* 100 percent attention as she explained how Rapid DNA analysis had been developed for use in the battlefield. Short tandem repeats were nucleotide sequences, two to seven base pairs in length, that occur within the DNA double helix strands.

There were over half a million present in the average human genome. Their sequence, and the number of the same sequence present, varied by individual, making them a handy means of identifying one human from another. These most-well-understood sequences of STRs were used in forensic identification.

In traditional DNA analysis, after the DNA strands were isolated from the rest of the tissue or bodily fluid, primer sequences would be added to the isolated strands so that the STRs could be amplified. The sample would be incubated with added primer sequences in order to reproduce copies of each STR piece. This made it possible for very minute stains or amounts of DNA to be accurately analyzed.

After that, with either gel or capillary electrophoresis, the STRs would be separated to determine the number of duplicates of each STR segment. This set of numbers created the "profile" of the subject, which would, in turn, be compared to all available STR profiles. As with searching the impression of a fingerprint picked up at a crime scene against the fingerprint impressions on file in one or more Automated Fingerprint Identification Systems, the match algorithm would return the closest matches the AFIS had. As with fingerprints, this correlation between a profile from a crime scene and a profile from the subject would rarely be a perfect 100 percent—cell lines could be unstable and something called "genetic drift" could create small variations between cell lines from the same donor. The end result would be a profile of one or two alleles at each of the twenty "core loci" that could be entered into the CODIS database.

Rapid DNA eliminated the need for human beings to conduct all these steps separately, making the process less labor intensive and with much less handling of the sample, from a collection point back to the lab, to be signed over to an analyst; then labeled, pipetted into a microtube, and labeled again—with the possibility of a mistake at any step.

All the various stops a liquefied DNA sample needed to make through forensic labs could be done inside one flattened plastic maze, usually referred to as a "microchip"— but not the electronic circuits bonded to a flat piece of silicon that the word usually meant. The cells would be lysed in the first chamber, then move to a mixing chamber, and then to a polymerase chain reaction, or PCR, chamber to be combined with primers to grow copy after copy, or amplified. Then the analyzer could "read" the information off the DNA strands to produce the profile.

All in about two hours, instead of the ten or so required for conventional analysis by even the most expeditious laboratory.

"How*ever*," Ellie told the class.

Caleb groaned. "There's always a 'however.' "

"You are correct, sir. There's a big *however*—not a drawback, simply a clarification: Rapid DNA requires a decent-size sample, not so much those minute amounts I mentioned a minute ago. Taking a cheek swab from a suspect is great, but swabbing up a bloodstain from a dirty kitchen floor, or trying for touch DNA from the counter where an armed robbery just took place, not so great. Crime scene DNA swabs can have very small amounts of DNA and often mixtures of DNA, and the system needs a way to eliminate contaminants like humic acid from soil, tannins, clothing dyes. Like any technology, it's getting better every day, but still no one quite trusts a software to be able to interpret results like those. It can't be completely automated—we still need a trained DNA analyst for samples like that."

Craig Bennett, soon to be leading NYPD's forensic unit, sat back in his chair. "Bummuh."

"That's why it's used largely to identify people—soldiers on the battlefield, wildfire victims, unidentified bodies. Say you have a series of rapes in your town and a DNA profile has been established. You catch someone near the scene of one of the crimes and arrest him—you can run his DNA in your booking room while he drinks coffee in an interrogation room. It doesn't match, he's exonerated and on his way."

"Or it does, and he's on his way to Rykuhs," Craig said.

Alyssa said, "I thought they closed Rikers."

"Working on it. It's a process."

Bettie twirled an orange-tipped dread and stayed on target. "But the Rapid DNA results are eligible for CODIS entry, right?"

"Yes, absolutely. When and how and who you can get samples from, and under what circumstances they have to be expunged, can vary by state law. Whether or not you can ask or demand a sample from that detainee in the holding cell is something you'll want to check. Some states might require testing done only inside accredited laboratories. You'll want to make sure anything you get will be admissible."

"We've got one," Matt Gold from Ohio announced to no one in particular. Three words at once seemed to be his limit. The man had taciturn down to the finest of arts.

Ellie said, "Like any other technology, Rapid DNA will become more and more common. That's why a little introduction and practice now will help you make decisions in the future." *Wow, that sounds like the course flyer.* She smiled to cover her embarrassment and moved on to what they would be doing that morning—swabbing the inside of their cheeks, dropping the swab into a labeled plastic tube about three inches long, and plugging this tube into one of the slots in the blocklike plastic framework. "The Locard built this one from scratch and it's actually a little clunky— no offense to my bosses—because they wanted to study ways to make the analysis of those mixed crime-scene samples more accurate, not because they wanted it to look pretty or be easier to use."

"Oh, yeah, sure," Caleb teased.

She ignored him. "The most recent commercial models now have a much slimmer plastic folder for the swab that is fed into a slot on the top of the machine. It's easier for non-DNA personnel to use and produces less waste like this, well, chunk of plastic."

"Can't that be reused?" someone asked.

"This one will, because it's only for training. It would never be reused for casework. Let's get started—swabs are here, just c'mon up and start scraping those epithelials. Anyone not swabbing in this round can take a snack break, bathroom break, check-your-email break."

"Fabulous," Craig Bennett said, and headed for the coffee.

Chapter 28

Michael Tyler and Luis Alvarez had arrived early. The agents assigned overnight had met with them on their way out with nothing to tell, except that the hallways got bloody chilly after dark and the surrounding ten acres seemed to be inhabited by owls and invisible ghosts who paced around, making leaf-brushing and twig-snapping sounds until even a seasoned veteran rubbed the St. Michael medal around his neck and kept his hand on his holster. "Creepy? You don't know creepy, pal, until you've spent the night in woods so deep you can barely hear the cars on 423."

"You're not the outdoorsy type?" Michael asked the man, whose skin was shiny and body odor growing after the long shift. His partner didn't appear any fresher, but laughed at the description. Luis stayed uncharacteristically silent, more interested in his fourth coffee of the morning. His wife, pregnant with their third child, was about to pop and had had a bad night.

"Give me a bank robbery in Dupont Circle any day of the week."

"Okay. Hope we don't need you again tonight."

The man shuddered at the thought, and he and his partner left.

"He doesn't know how much I mean that," Michael said to Luis as they continued up the walkway from the parking lot to the building. Sea breezes wound through the trees, creating a low whisper that, Michael had to admit, *did* sound kind of creepy. He turned up the trail to Body Site 1, still delineated with crime scene tape. "In eight hours, half our suspects are going to leave this area. If we want any follow-ups, we're going to have to get travel approved, arrests will require extradition—"

"Not like we haven't done that before," Luis said, choosing his steps carefully. It had not rained again, the ground firmer than it had been the day before, but there were still plenty of damp, rotting leaves ready to either make him slip or to gum up his treads.

"Yeah, but our two most likelies will be in Saudi Arabia. Sure, we have agents there, but let's face it, even if we issued a warrant, we'd still never get them back. *Or* our victim's body, so I hope that autopsy didn't miss a trick because there won't be any reexams or exhumations."

They reached the excavated grave and he stared down at the hollow where Farida Al Talel had been. Why? Why that girl? Something against her or something against Muslims or something against Saudis or something against women in general? Maybe she stumbled on the guy doing what he didn't want anyone to know about, but Michael didn't think so—if this had been a murder of necessity, merely a cleaning up of a loose end, he could have put her virtually *anywhere* else in the ten acres of Locard grounds. She would have been concealed for a longer time if he'd stuffed her in a bathroom stall. *Anywhere* except the grave he had to know would be—no, not dug up, but at least closely examined by twenty-five well-trained forensic and police personnel. He *wanted* her to be found. Why?

"It's just dirt now, partner," Luis told him. Michael had been staring at it for several minutes.

They continued on to the Locard. There they met briefly with Rachael Davies and Gerald Coleman, but no one had much to report. FBI techs had examined Farida's tote bag and phone, along with all her belongings retrieved from the hotel. Luis roused himself enough to report: "I can tell you, she enjoyed your class, Rachael. She took pages and pages of notes. They're in Arabic, but our interpreters tell us they're strictly academic, with no personal information. Whereas her texts, and texts and texts and emails, and more texts, are strictly personal—she loved the class, enjoyed seeing the sights with her cousins, loved Mummy and Daddy—sorry, that sounds like I'm being sarcastic, but I'm not, she and her parents and siblings are, were, close-knit. No mention of worry about anything except remembering everything she'd learned and sometimes missing her daily prayers. No one threatening her or worrying her in any way."

"So if there had been a danger to her, she didn't know it," Rachael summarized.

"Not until it was too late."

Gerald said, "Her family's freaking out, aren't they? Anita keeps calling me because the embassy liaison at the State Department keeps calling her, because there was really no reason for them to be involved at all—as long as you guys aren't preventing it, the cousins can just take her body and go. But the guy at State decided to get a jump on it and called the Saudi Embassy to inform them, figuring the cousins would, but they hadn't even thought of it, so now a few ambassadors, State, and their diplomatic security service are all mobilized just to help these two guys get on a plane. Next time I might not be so quick to listen to Anita." He turned and added to Rachael: "Don't tell her I said that."

"The family is upset, of course," Michael said. "And the major news outlets have picked up the story."

"Don't I know it!" Gerald jerked his head toward his beleaguered secretary, whose phone had rung four times in only the few minutes they'd been standing by her desk.

"But so far it hasn't risen to the level of an international incident."

"*Yet.*" Gerald's tone stayed dark.

"Yet," Michael admitted.

Rachael told him about Agnes browsing through the attendee's public social media posts, and Oliver Suarez's apparent infatuation. "I doubt it means anything. I haven't seen anything in his behavior to alert me."

"Our digital forensics had actually done the same thing—seems they can never resist checking the socials, and Farida had posted quite a bit herself. As you said, nothing actionable in any of it, but we do want to talk to him again." A little psychological pressure couldn't hurt. If guilty, he might make a mistake, and if innocent, he might remember something helpful.

"Come with me," Rachael told them.

She gave them an empty classroom to use and guided Oliver Suarez out of the group of attendees without his fellow students' notice; they still milled about the room, removing coats, selecting doughnuts and mixing creamer into their caffeine of choice. Waiting in the hall, Michael noticed that Oliver Suarez didn't ask a single question; he left his notebook and electronics on the table and followed Rachael out the door.

Michael and Luis introduced themselves, explaining that they needed to follow up with attendees who might be able to tell them more about Farida than less acquainted students. First, for their notes, they'd need some housekeeping details.

The guy didn't show any alarm or annoyance at having to go through the information again. He was from Missoula. He worked for the Missoula County Sheriff's Department as a civilian employee in the forensic unit. He had rented a car for this trip, which the assigned agents had examined before he left the Locard last night. He was twenty-eight.

"And you're married, aren't you?" Luis asked.

A pause. "Separated."

"Really? Because your wife, Sonia, still lives at the same address, right? Your address."

A direct look, uninterpretable to Michael. Annoyance? Fear? Curiosity? "We're emotionally separated."

"But living in the same house? Yes? Is that because of the two kids?"

"Children," Oliver stated with an utter lack of emotion, "need stability."

"And showing up with a twenty-three-year-old Middle Eastern Muslim girl—how would that affect that stability?"

A blink sufficed as the only visible reaction. "What are you talking about? We weren't making any plans."

"*We,*" Michael said. "You and Farida."

An edge of the lower lip disappeared between two rows of teeth as they worried the flesh. Finally, a show of . . . annoyance? Concern? Fear? "I don't know what you guys are getting at. We were *friends.* She was a great person and I liked her. What else do you want me to say?"

Michael flipped through his phone to find the screenshot of Oliver's last social media post with the picture of Farida by the fountain. "You'll forgive my confusion, because here you announce to the world how you can't wait to show her Montana."

Oliver squirmed, his body quivering. He stared at the phone. The longer he stared, the more his body calmed.

He's not looking at the screenshot, or wondering what else we have, Michael thought. *He's staring at Farida.* "Was she excited about that trip? Were her parents okay with it?"

"There was no trip! There were no plans!"

Luis said, "So your post was just wishful thinking? What *did* you wish for when it came to Farida?"

The anger faded as quickly as it had sprung up. His shoulders deflated and breath poured out of him in a low, hopeless hiss. "I wished, for her, a good life. That she'd be able to realize all her dreams. That she wouldn't wind up boxed into a pretty cage, barely able to breathe."

A frisson crept up the back of Michael's neck. That was exactly how Farida ended up—unable to breathe.

The sadness of someone missing a friend? Or a Freudian slip?

Chapter 29

The Locard's Rapid DNA device, made for classroom use, had been designed to run more samples at once than commercial machines—but it still couldn't analyze buccal swabs from all twenty-three students in one batch. Ellie would run half now and let it process, while she discussed the latest technology for Rapid DNA of crime scene samples, and what state and county facilities could do for them at present. Then they would test the other half of the students and let the machine run during all of lunch and part of the subsequent lecture on the basics of interpreting the results.

This left half the attendees breaking open sets of sterile swabs, rubbing those against the inside of their cheeks, and placing those used swabs in the sample chambers. Twelve chambers, roughly the size and shape of a small test tube, were lined up like bottles in a case of beer in one six-by-six-by-six clear brick of plastic. A log was kept to know which sample chamber had whose swabs.

The other half could relax with midmorning snacks until the lecture began again.

"What if my sample has doughnut crumbs in it?" Caleb

asked, cruller in one hand, swabs in the other. "Would that screw up the profile?"

"Flour comes from a plant. Plants have DNA," someone said.

"I think if someone could get DNA from food, we woulda heard about it by now." Sergeant Craig Bennett peeled the paper wrapper from his set of swabs.

"Only one way to find out." Caleb dropped his swabs in one chamber of the plastic block.

Ellie said, "I don't know about DNA from the organic compounds, but as I said, Rapid DNA processing is less accurate when there's a mixture or contamination. That's why it's mostly used for identification only. So it's probably best *not* to have half the swab soaked in coffee."

Bettie peeled open fresh swabs. "It'll probably be another five years and all DNA analysis—known samples, crime scene samples, hairs, bones—will all be this quick. Another ten, and people will be amazed we ever had to wait two hours."

Ellie said, "Technology marches on."

"At an increasing rate," Caleb said. "Pretty soon there will be nowhere a criminal can run. If they don't keep up with the times, they'll be behind bars in no time."

"There's still a lot to be said for luck." Alyssa turned away to swab her mouth, as if it were a private thing. Then she dropped the swabs in a chamber. "Look at that Saudi girl. Somebody murders her at a school for crime investigators and walks away. Place devoted to crime, and all he needed was trees and a ton of friggin' rain to cover him up."

"How do you know it's a *he*?" Caleb asked.

"Not necessarily, but most likely," she said, unabashed. "Pretty, young, obviously virginal thing, kept away from men her whole life, so she's as innocent as a toddler. That'd be like catnip to a man. Maybe a woman, but, statistically, most likely a man."

"That's harsh," Caleb laughed. "On several levels."

"Murder is harsh."

"I need more coffee before I ponder that. What about you, Doc?" Caleb asked Ellie. "Want a cup? I'm buying."

"In another minute, thanks," Ellie said. With the sample chambers full, she slid the plastic block into its tracks on the interior of the machine, making sure the wide door shut completely. She pushed the button helpfully labeled START and gave Craig an apologetic smile.

"You mean I opened these swabs for nothing?"

"Sorry! Just toss 'em, and take fresh ones for the next batch."

He grinned and watched the machine for signs of activity, which, other than screen glowing with the Locard logo, it didn't grant. The Rapid DNA device was truly a black box. Items went in, results were printed out.

Alyssa headed for the door, but Ellie stalked the woman. She had a free moment and the coolness had been bothering her, like a gnat dive-bombing her ears. Ellie could handle being ignored—every woman grew accustomed to that—but active dislike threw her for a loop. For too many years it had felt like her survival depended on a family liking her enough *not* to throw her out, and childhood habits die hard. "I don't know if you remember me. We worked ERT at the same time, maybe four or five years ago."

"Yeah," the woman said. "I remember you."

Pointedly unencouraging. "What unit are you in now?"

"Narcotics."

"Wow. That can be a tough field."

No effect other than the same level stare. "And you're here. In the big leagues."

Is she jealous? "I'm not sure there's anything bigger than the FBI. A different league, I guess." *Are you downplaying it? Why are you downplaying it . . . It's the freakin'* Locard, *and, yes, I'm here and you're not.* Ellie didn't need a past acquaintance to greet her as a long-lost bestest friend ever, but the cool-verging-on-cold feeling seemed specific to Ellie.

So, what? she told herself. *Remember what Aunt Katey said. Not everyone has to be a big fan of everyone else . . . but . . .*

Alyssa said, "You pull a kidnapping that happens to be your cousin's kid, and now you're here."

A personal connection that should have hobbled my career, not enhanced it. "That's how I met Rachael, yes. I was lucky that Dr. Wright was about to leave—"

"Who's now dead."

What? Like, what, I killed her? I already had the job! "Yes, that's a tragedy."

"Adam," Alyssa said, referring to Ellie's ex-husband, "is doing a *great* job as ERT supervisor."

Which he had been for less than a month. "Of course. I knew he would." *If you think a mention of my ex is going to make me miserable, you've got another th—*

And then the room blew up.

Chapter 30

Rachael was in her office when she heard the sound, just as she came to the end of a twenty-minute conversation with one Mr. David Brubeck, of Redmond, Washington.

She'd debated whether to call him. Without knowing his exact relationship to Barbara Wright, Rachael couldn't guess if she was interfering in the FBI's investigation or not. She might be tipping off a suspect—in the motive at least, if not in the murder itself, since he couldn't have been physically present. Supposed murder. And she didn't know he *couldn't* have been physically present.

How did she know if any of the attendees were who they said they were? They listed their employing agency with its contact information, and payment came from corresponding business accounts, but really, that wouldn't be all that difficult to fake. It wasn't as if the Locard conducted a background check on every single person who arrived on the campus. Guests, like private clients, were escorted everywhere, but course attendees were accepted as peers. They were given a temporary keycard . . . to the outer doors only, but still. Why not? Other than a tabloid reporter or a foren-sic wannabe hyped up on true crime podcasts, who would want to infiltrate a research institute?

Okay, she thought. *Maybe some of our policies need an update.*

In the defense she had already mentally prepared, should the FBI agents complain of her phone call, she *did* need to inform the American Academy of Forensic Sciences that Barbara would not be able to make her scheduled presenta-tion. And according to the information on Barbara's Locard-issued phone—she'd come up with a separate defense for that—this presentation had been a joint project between Barbara Wright and David Brubeck. He deserved a chance to recover and prepare, if possible, to give the presentation himself. After all, she would not want to deprive the acad-emy of information it had asked to hear.

Besides, she had told Michael and Luis about the texts, given them all the same information as Agnes had given her. They'd had their chance. And they might have already called him, for all she knew, and her call could be a courte-ous follow-up.

But it *was* mainly curiosity. The same itchy, exhausting condition she'd been afflicted with all her life. Rachael thanked the heavens that she had not had the type of mother who said such curiosity would get her in trouble, or warned her that it had already killed any number of felines.

Though Loretta *had* predicted, once or twice over the years, that Rachael might not like what she found.

And sometimes she'd been right.

Holding the printout of Barbara's texts, Rachael dialed the number. She couldn't waffle all day about this; she'd left her students filling out practice documentation forms, but they'd finish that quickly—or should, if they'd been paying attention for the past two weeks.

After that, there would be the standard course evaluation. She could imagine how those comments would sound:

This course was great except for all the people dying.

A place dedicated to justice couldn't deliver same to their own murdered student.

The snacks were good, but don't ever come here. You might not leave.

Mr. Brubeck picked up on the second ring, just as Rachael remembered the three-hour time difference between coasts. It would only be seven a.m. in Redmond. She mentally apologized for interrupting his sleep/breakfast/commute.

"Barbara?"

Clearly, the FBI had *not* already made notification. "Uh . . . no. Mr. David Brubeck?"

"Yes. Who is this?" Forty-three, married, three kids, Rachael recalled. The voice matched the image in her head, fortyish, white-collar, professional male. Maybe a little paunchy from the way he puffed out his words, unless she'd caught him at his morning calisthenics. A heavy nasal overtone . . . a cold? Sinuses reacting to Seattle fog? Tears?

Rachael introduced herself and gently broke the news. She hated to do that over the phone, with no idea of the exact relationship. Perhaps they were long-distance lovers, though nothing in any text had been remotely romantic. Perhaps they were brother and sister; no text had seemed particularly personal, but then they'd been brief and to the point, as people who knew each other very well might be. Maybe they'd been friends since grade school, were in-laws, were pen pals, had never met. So she felt her way slowly, ever aware of her attendees alone in their classroom while she played detective.

The silence that ensued might have been stunned, devastated, or calculating. What she would give for video.

Then he sucked in a breath, the air whistling over the phone's mic. "Barbara's *dead*?"

"Yes. I'm sorry for informing you this way, but I knew time was of the essence." A slight lie, since she could have called him the previous evening. "What with the academy meeting coming up next week. You were going to copresent with Barbara?"

"Me? No." He seemed to find the idea faintly horrible. "I was just . . . just, um . . . helping her."

"Really?" Rachael's gut pushed her forward with a host of tiny devils' pitchforks. "I thought you were to be an officer of WrightGene."

"She told you that?"

"She dropped hints." As in a private text sent from her to you. Rachael was fishing, but didn't want him to know she was fishing. At any moment he could thank her for the notification and hang up.

"Nothing had happened yet. It was . . . after the academy she was going to . . ."

"Get WrightGene up and running?"

"Yes."

Rachael adjusted a framed photo that rested to the left of her laptop and blotter, her and Danton at Dollywood. She had to know the connections here, without flat-out asking what on earth Barbara and her plans had to do with David Brubeck and—"You're at Henderson Monitoring now?"

"Yes."

Unhelpful. She wanted to know what Henderson Monitoring monitored, but would have to make a WAG. A wild-assed guess. "We found the data you provided her."

"No." Immediately. "No, that—wasn't from me."

Aha.

Hector had provided the unsolved murder clusters, so

that left the other half of the equation. "The pharmaceutical surveys."

Another silence. Calculating? Panicked? Or simply occupied with altering arrangements to go solo in front of the academy audience?

She straightened the framed photo again, and guessed panicked. A little flattery—and greed—might calm him down. "You've done an amazing job for her. I had no idea it was even possible to obtain nationwide stats on prescription distributions for non-narcotics. I assume there's all sorts of stuff in place for opioids and other narcotics now, but I thought we'd be thirty years behind the times on other scripts."

It worked, to some extent. His voice lowered one pitch or two, but he admitted nothing. "There has been increased attention over the years since we've made preventive care a star priority in this country. Henderson has several ongoing contracts with the CDC, the FDA, and various House and Senate subcommittees to monitor insurance payouts for scripts. From that, those agencies can reach conclusions regarding antibiotic stewardship, quality outcomes for epileptics, applications of cancer research, and so forth."

He could have been reading from the company brochure. "And you could pull all that information for Barbara to cross-reference with suspect DNA from unsolved murders. That's the kind of thing that seems so obvious, you only wonder why it hadn't been done before."

Because PHI—protected health information—was confidential and couldn't be accessed by lowly law enforcement types. *Or* researchers who would have to get their results past an internal review board, and those boards would be sure to ask where it had come from.

Some worker bee at an electronic medical records facility wouldn't be able to pull patients' information without setting off alarms. But Dave Brubeck, hired to do exactly that for nearly all patients all over the country, who routinely requested protected information all day every day, could look at everything without issue.

He could even make a copy for a friend . . . in exchange for a cushy pay grade at her new company.

"Exactly," he said in answer to her comment.

Rachael kept her voice smooth and interested, without fawning. He had to wonder if he could make a deal with Barbara's replacements. "But to present this to the academy—how did she plan to answer their questions about her source?"

"Proprietary."

"I beg your pardon?"

"Proprietary. She had already incorporated, making the details of the process proprietary. She only needed the academy presentation to announce that the process worked. Questions about her source, she wouldn't need to spell out for them."

I doubt that, Rachael thought. If Barbara had figured she could stare down any academy critics the way she stared down course attendees, she'd been delusional. A full accounting of data sources would be required for any publishing or stamp of approval, and no amount of fast doublespeak would bamboozle the AAFS review board.

Maybe Barbara knew that and didn't care—even if rejected, it would still get buzz going. Maybe she truly *had* been delusional, or maybe greedy, enough to believe it would work. Either way, it didn't seem to matter now.

Keep up this charade of collusion? "What will you do now, without Barbara?"

A sigh, and the slight bravado faded. "I don't know. I was only supposed to be a silent partner. It was all her."

Rachael wanted to know how they had met, how this long-distance partnership had come about, but couldn't see the relevance and she needed to get back to her students. Yet she probed for a few last pieces of information. "If someone else could take over for Barbara—had there been anyone else on tap for WrightGene? Besides you and Barbara?"

He dashed that hope immediately. "No."

"Did she get—did she gather data from any other sources? Besides Henderson?"

He insisted, with a firm current of pride: "No one besides Henderson is currently doing work with this depth of scope. It was all her and me. But mostly her."

Then who had killed Barbara? If not a rival for the information or the theory or the company, then who had a motive?

Other than Hector? She pushed that out of her mind. No way Hector would murder someone over a publishing credit.

But then, who?

A rumble sounded elsewhere in the building, not rolling like thunder, but erupting in a sudden clap, a thudding boom that seemed both muffled and distant and yet bizarrely close. The windowpanes shuddered and the items and photos pinned to her bulletin board—Danton, Danton, Danton and Loretta, dentist appointment card, NCIC update, Danton, new Bluestar order sheet—quivered slightly, as if in a draft.

Her first thought pictured journalists landing on the roof. They might have rappelled down from network news helicopters and miscalculated the last bit of distance, choosing to leap down to their target as if on a heroic air-sea rescue mission. Picturing the bizarre scenario, she expected each one to break an ankle and probably damage the classic slate shingles, and she didn't care if they slid off and landed two stories down in the courtyard. Served them right. The Locard's revenge.

Rachael had heard many strange sounds at the Locard over the years—a visiting mathematician experimenting with music tones at high decibels, the weekly Research vs. Education basketball games thumping balls against the gym ceiling underneath her office, two experimental bomb squad robots racing each other through the hallways, and two scientists popping the corks from champagne bottles to determine which brand came with enough power to kill. That had been fun research, she recalled.

But she'd never heard a sound quite like this one.

"I'm sorry, Mr. Brubeck," Rachael said into the phone. "I have to go."

Chapter 31

The moment of the explosion burned into Ellie's memory as cuts, and burned into her skin as bruises erupted on her flesh. She had been standing by the inner wall of the classroom, a few feet from one of the two doors to the hallway. She had been looking—glaring, to be honest—at Alyssa, wondering what was up with this junior high "Mean Girls freeze-out." Caleb stood in the doorway. Bettie with her orange hair and the lieutenant from Ohio were between two of the long tables discussing Daubert versus Frye criteria for admission of scientific evidence in court—Bettie doing most of the discussing as she sidled toward the door, the lieutenant managing to argue via two- and three-word phrases. Craig Bennett, NYPD sergeant, studied the Rapid DNA machine, his back to the rest of the room. The cop from Los Angeles leaned against the whiteboard to check his phone and would probably walk away with smears of dry erase marker across the back of his shirt from Ellie's diagramming of the analysis process. The forensic tech from Greensville reapplied her lipstick, surreptitiously, by touch and without use of a mirror. Other attendees sat at "their" spaces along the tables, making notes or sending messages via various mobile devices. The part of Ellie's mind not involved with Alyssa and her attitude considered calling the class back to attention; she should go on to the admission requirements for CODIS profiles, now that the Rapid DNA batch was running and nothing more could be done on that project for another two hours.

And then . . . a loud noise rent the air. It seemed to come from everywhere and nowhere at once, blotting out all other sound, invading not only her ears, but her mind. She might have screamed, a visceral and automatic reaction to the deafening sound, but couldn't be sure since she was already falling back against the wall—and the old-fashioned school did not have walls made of wooden studs and drywall. It had brick, painted smooth but still brick, and getting body-slammed against it did not feel good.

She did not collapse all the way to the linoleum. She remained on both feet, but it was touch-and-go. Her eyes shut in an instinctive defense against the flying debris she felt pelting her skin, some with pricks of pain, some as soft as a brush with a feather. A gasp turned into a choke when there seemed to be no air to suck in.

The room disappeared into a fog of white. The sound faded as quickly as it had sprung up and the air returned, but as Ellie breathed in the grimy fumes, she realized it was not smoke, but dust. Ground-up plaster, broken ceiling tiles, the gaping hole in the counter and cabinets, and the now-vaporized boxes of gloves and swabs combined to fill the air as it rushed in from the shattered windows along the counter. The mini-fridge–sized Rapid DNA machine had disappeared.

Alyssa had also remained on her feet, her face bleeding from two small cuts. The cop from LA next to the smart-board appeared dazed. Bettie Williams cried out, low but steady, one hand to her ear.

Other attendees were on the ground.

Ellie forced her legs to move, leaning on the long table. The blast had pushed anything it could find through the space, driving some items into people's bodies. Ellie passed three people who, with dazed, slow movements, were gingerly plucking shards of glass from arms and necks. Hands went to injured spots, bright spots of blood seeping through fingers, rubbing bruises sustained where chairs and tables and floors slammed into them. None were unscathed, but all seemed to be moving under their own power.

All but one.

Craig Bennett lay still, between an overturned chair and a table, with which his bulk had collided and shoved several feet out of place. He had obviously taken the brunt of the explosion, which caved in and shredded his chest at the same time. As she'd already seen in others, his body had been peppered with spears of glass, metal, and laminate, as well as coated with various dusts. A three-inch shard of coated metal stuck out of one cheek. Glass pieces glimmered, embedded in his clothing, all of it quickly staining with blood.

Ellie knelt, feeling a twinge of pain in each knee as they ground into the sharp pieces of debris covering the floor. She had to shove away a torn box of pipettes resting against his shoulder and a chunk of laminate lying on his stomach. The windows and countertop had been broken open, but also the cabinets beneath the counter had flown open, the doors twisted on their hinges. The three or four sections closest to the epicenter had largely collapsed, shelves dislodged, supports broken. Contents were disgorged in a shredded mess more like an eruption than an explosion. Forms, cable ties, a cylinder of disinfecting wipes, individual serving thimbles of half-and-half, napkins, stirring sticks, a tiny vial of phenolphthalein reagent, swab boxes, a stapler, and glass slides had been tossed up in a salad of debris.

No fire, though. Light black streaks emerged here and

there around the center of destruction, but no soot or black-
ening of any surface. That seemed weird to the absently ob-
servant part of her mind—it didn't look to her like an
explosion had taken place. It looked like someone had taken
the entire room and put it in a blender on pulse speed.

The narrow backsplash between the counter and the windows had broken and peeled off the drywall, exposing patches
of cottony insulation. Ellie glanced up; some ceiling tiles had
sheared off and fallen, while others showed a peppering of
sharp objects. Those and the rest of the debris, the broken
surfaces, the churned-up supplies, had been overlaid with a
steady Modern Art–like stippling of red.

Craig Bennett's blood.

She put a hand to his neck, feeling the pushback of years
of training in universal precautions at the touch of her bare
skin against someone else's blood, but refusing to care. A
faint pulse rewarded her boldness.

"Call 911!" she shouted—as if that would not have already occurred to everyone in the room.

First aid. She tried to focus. Stop the bleeding—but it
seemed to come from *everywhere.* At least three gashes deep
enough to form rivers of blood, and one on his shoulder,
seemed to be spurting in weak gasps—an artery?

Was he breathing? Lungs expanding?

Sound remained muted in her stunned ears, but around
her, the others had found voices, moaning, crying, asking
frantic questions. And, she hoped, calling EMTs to the
scene.

"CPR?" Caleb asked, suddenly down on the other side of
Craig's body.

"Press on that wound. Here."

He did, folding one hand over the other and pressing the
man's shoulder into the floor with the weight of his upper
body. She tried to do the same with the breastbone, but first
she had to find it, lost in the bloody mess of Craig Bennett's

chest. She started compressions, feeling a prick in the base of the lower palm. Probably one of those shards had broken her flesh, so she now created a biological hazard to Craig, and he to her.

But some risks had to be taken.

She pushed downward. It might not have felt so familiar if she hadn't just done the same thing the month before, a different man.

Who had died.

One-two-three . . . steady, firm pulses, the way Uncle Paul had taught her more than once. She wanted to ask if anyone had called an ambulance, but couldn't take the time out from counting. Even if they had, the Locard sat a half hour from the nearest hospital . . . one of the things you check when moving into a new area.

Every press downward felt unresisted and made a crunching sound as if one were walking across a sea of potato chips. She knew what it was and wanted to weep—this meant Craig Bennett's torso was now full of broken ribs and torn cartilage. She might be doing further harm by dislodging them even more. She might be driving slivers of bone into his lungs and heart . . . but she didn't know what else to do. He had to breathe, wouldn't survive without oxygen before help arrived.

These same slivers might poke through the skin and stab her as well, a thought both selfish and nightmarish.

She reached thirty, checked for breathing—no signs—and put one hand under his neck to tilt his head back. Then she pressed her mouth to his limp, bloody lips and puffed into his airway. She tasted blood and tobacco and coffee, and tried not to gag.

Blowing the air in, she saw his chest rise, almost imperceptibly. She'd blown hard, it should expand more than that. Were his airways blocked? Were the lungs as perforated as a pasta sieve and now leaked the air into the intercostal muscles?

She let the lungs deflate that small amount, then tried again.

No response. No cough or sudden intake of breath, a poignant resurgence in the last few seconds before a commercial break. Craig Bennett gave not the slightest indication of life. Was he already dead? He seemed dead. Most likely, dead.

Voices around her settled into actual words.

"What happened?"

"You okay?"

"You're bleeding! You're bleeding!"

"I know that!" said with a tone of great annoyance. "So are you!"

"What *happened*?"

Ellie shouted, more loudly than needed, but it was hard to tell with her ears still feeling as if they had plugs in them: "Did someone call 911?"

At least three answered with a chorus of yesses.

Behind her, new voices added to the cacophony and she knew it had to be Rachael's students, crowding across the hall to find out what that noise had been.

"What happened?"

"You're bleeding!"

"Is there fire? Did something catch on fire?"

"Oh my G—let me help you with that."

"Did you call 911?"

Ellie heard someone say, quite calmly, "We need the school nurse," and then burst into a short-lived, manic laughter.

"What *happened*?"

And then Rachael was there, unceremoniously yanking Caleb out of the way. She also didn't wait for gloves as she pried one of Craig Bennett's eyes open, felt his neck, opened his mouth. Then she looked up and shouted to someone named Stef to run and fetch the director. And to tell Carrie to coordinate responders.

Ellie reached thirty again, stopped, and puffed two breaths into the limp man's mouth. The chest rose and fell, that same nearly imperceptible nanometer or two. The large cop from New York gave no sign of returning to consciousness. His skin had gone deathly pale beneath the light coating of smeared blood.

Two sets of pounding feet echoed in the hallway, and Michael Tyler's deep baritone rang over the cacophony. "What happened? Where's . . . Sit down here. Are you all right?"

Rachael took over compressions, did a set, then stopped to check the pulse. With an increasing sense of despair, Ellie puffed in two more lungfuls. This couldn't be happening. Who on earth would want to blow up her classroom? First Barbara Wright, then Farida, now . . . everyone? Anyone? Had someone specifically wanted to murder this sergeant of the NYPD?

Ellie looked down at him, more objectively this time. He wore jeans and a beat-up plain leather belt. The shirt ripped open by the blast was a dress shirt in dark blue, no tie, cuffs neatly buttoned over a traditional analog watch with a leather band. Black athletic shoes, which had seen better days, twisted up beneath him. The treads retained some small clumps of dirt and a piece of a dried leaf, but no stains or still-wetness that would make her think he'd been bury-ing Farida Al Talel during a rainstorm the night before.

"Is there any word on the ambulance?" Rachael asked, her efforts making the same crushed-potato-chip sound in Craig's chest as Ellie's had.

"I called," a voice in the back said. "They didn't give an ETA."

"Ellie," Rachael said, arms stiff and pumping. "Are you hurt?"

"No." Was she? She couldn't be sure. Her ears were recovering, and when she looked down, she could see oozing cuts on her arms and thighs, but they were small and superficial. Everything seemed to work—bones, muscles. Everything except her brain, which, overloaded, had gone out to get some air.

Her tone equally stiff, Rachael gave her orders. "Take everyone who can move and get them out of here. Go to the cafeteria—both sessions. Tell them class is dismissed."

Chapter 32

The attendees from Rachael's course, whole and unharmed and accustomed to violent and inexplicable situations, stepped in as temporary EMTs. They served as human crutches for those who limped, and grabbed paper towels to apply pressure on oozing wounds as Ellie guided the slow-moving group down the south stairwell.

Like a nuclear explosion, damage depended largely on proximity. Ellie had been on the other side of the room and suffered only superficial cuts from flying debris—she could swear it had been someone's notebook that hit her in the face, the wire of the spiral binding cutting her cheek. She also had a deep cut in her right bicep that, fortunately, wasn't bleeding much. Alyssa had scratches and said her wrist hurt, flung against the wall as another student bumped into her. Lieutenant Gold cradled one arm in silent pain. At least three had dislocated fingers and Caleb limped; he told Ellie a falling chair had landed on his ankle. Bettie had a folded-up paper towel clamped to her tinted hair, the stain of bright red blood spreading from a wound on her temple; the wad reached saturation point just as the group reached the bottom of the stairs and left a trail of small droplets from the steps to the cafeteria. They were creating a swath of biohazards through half the building, Ellie thought. And the cleaning staff thought the fingerprint powder in the ladies' room had been a pain in the butt.

A dangerous bubble of hysteria welled up in her throat, but she swallowed it.

The wounded settled into chairs in the wide and silent cafeteria as Ellie informed the two bewildered kitchen staff of the situation.

The unwounded ferried water bottles back and forth. Ellie saw one sending a text for another, whose hands shook too badly to cope with a touch screen.

The kitchen staff didn't seem happy to find people around at an unscheduled mealtime. Ellie thought they should at least be pleased they no longer had a puppy in their kitchen—she and Rachael had even put the boxes back where they'd been. But the chef said only that lunch was not ready and wouldn't be for another three hours. Ellie assured them that wasn't a concern; since with luck, the students would be gone by then. Which created more consternation—were they preparing food they'd only have to throw out?

Ellie couldn't tell them, and cut through the din of protests to point out that they now had a room full of injured parties and could they please see what they could do to help? Then she walked away to let them figure it out.

She forced herself to speak firmly as she informed the attendees that they would wait there and the director would come to give them more information very shortly. She hoped that would be true. She also prayed to sound relatively competent, and not like a bewildered and very worried brand-new employee, both selfishly concerned for her own job *and* terrified for the safety of everyone around her . . . since both seemed to be in grave danger.

"Are you all right?" Caleb stood with all his weight on one foot.

"Yes. How is your ankle?"

"It just hurts. Nothing significant. What *happened*?"

"Somehow the Rapid DNA machine turned itself into an IED." She meant an improvised explosive device. Ellie had no doubt it had been the source; she hadn't had a lot of time to observe the room, but crisis had sharpened her observation; and even if it hadn't, the gaping hole in the counter and window where the machine had sat would have clued her in.

Bettie pressed a clean paper towel to her scalp. "So their homemade machine went kablooie?"

"I imagine it went right," Ellie said, "in someone's estimation."

The woman blinked. "But this is the *Locard*!"

That hits the nail square on the head, Ellie thought. How could someone be murdered, in a room crowded with trained forensic personnel with no prior acquaintance and, presumably, nothing to gain, at the nation's premier research institute?

She didn't for a moment believe that some flaw in the design had led to such an exothermic reaction. Not after two other deaths in as many days. Someone wanted to kill people at the Locard and weren't fussy about who. Barbara and Farida had been isolated, and any killer knew they had killed those two women, and those alone. But the Rapid DNA machine—anyone could have been standing next to it when it went off. Whether or not it had been his intention, Craig Bennett had done the same as a solider throwing himself on a grenade—he'd absorbed the brunt of the explosion, possibly saving lives while losing his own.

If Ellie hadn't been annoyed at Alyssa Cole, it would have been her in front of the machine. She'd likely have stayed by the counter to field more questions about the lysing buffers and the different designs of sample chambers. Instead, the blunt force and accompanying shrapnel had been absorbed by Craig Bennett's body.

Caleb snorted. "Where the hell are those FBI guys when you need them?"

She wondered that herself as she pondered what to do next. Emergency services had already been called. The woman named Stef arrived, reporting to her friends: She'd completed her mission, informed the director of the explosion, and advised the institute secretary to, once again, cope with and guide non-Locard staff on the property.

It sounded as if the maintenance crew would have their hands full trying to get the right people through the gate, while holding back the tidal wave of reporters hoping for a word about Farida Al Talel. Wait until they heard about today's tragedy. The Locard would never recover, Ellie thought, and felt horrible that this thought filled her with more despair than had Craig Bennett's death.

For death it had to be. She'd known that before starting compressions, but, of course, still had to try.

What to do . . . Tape off the scene, photograph, measure the site of the blast, and note what piece of the room had wound up where—the work of the ERT, of which she was no longer a member. They would have to do all that, and she could not be part of it.

Because she was, technically—no, not technically, quite *plainly* a suspect. As was everyone else in the room. Though she had not been trained for guard duty, it now became her job. She had to make sure that no one left, and if they did, know where they went. She had to listen for statements that implied more knowledge than an innocent party should have.

She had to make sure no one else got killed.

Chapter 33

Over the next hour several things occurred.

Ellie waited in the chilly cafeteria. Medical help arrived—the local stations must have coordinated resources to send everyone they could. Wheeled stretchers were brought in for the broken bones and three people with palpitations, while the cuts and bruises made do in straight chairs. The place where they'd all eaten lunch for two weeks now resembled a mass disaster exercise.

She escaped to the ladies' room—still covered in fingerprint powder—long enough to wash Craig Bennett's blood off her hands and face. Smears of it clung to her clothing, along with a thick layer of plaster dust. She needed an hour or two in the hottest shower, but clearly that would not be an option. She might have had supplies in a gym locker—if she hadn't only been working there for three days—and it didn't matter because there were much more important things to do right now, weren't there?

Rachael arrived and, of course, pitched in to treat the wounded, the Hippocratic instinct undiminished.

FBI backup also arrived in record time and a team set up

interview stations right there. They'd even brought temporary desk dividers so each very long table could have two or three semiprivate spots for the agents to question each attendee. The cafeteria formed a somewhat ideal place for it, built to hold an entire school full of boys in one lunch period and ringed on three sides with windows. No one felt claustrophobic *and* remained within sight of everyone else.

Ellie saw the female agent who had been watching the surveillance videos with them the day before. Her expression seemed a bit flustered, but the rest of her remained in perfection, her non-green skirt suit slim and unwrinkled. Ellie felt sweaty and dirty and anything but perfect, but then there were more important things to think about just then, right?

And there, the woman's pen had just run out of ink, anyway.

From her distance Ellie watched the agents talk with Rachael's students whenever she wasn't ferrying bandages around the room. The interviews moved quickly. Ellie could guess the answers: Many of them knew nothing about explosives, had never really spoken to Craig Bennett, and, of course, had been accounted for in a room across the hall when he died. Talks began with Ellie's students, which took more time, but from where she stood, she could see many shaking heads and a couple of shrugs. Everyone must be as bewildered as she felt—and if they weren't, they'd hardly wanted to tell an FBI agent about it.

All were asked to remain until the agents were finished, in case one attendee told them something that called for a follow-up with another attendee. They couldn't be stopped if they wanted to leave, but no one tried. They were professional CSIs who wanted to contribute. Or professional killers who didn't want to single themselves out for suspicion by running.

It meant that traumatized people were in for a long wait of sitting around and doing nothing except checking social media on their phones and trading fruitless theories. They even kept that to a minimum in terse, hushed conversations. No one wanted to look like a slavering conspiracy theorist, like the looky-loos they criticized for hovering around crime scenes . . . but on the other hand, they didn't want to seem uncaring, and had a more than legitimate interest in the situation.

Mostly, they just waited, faces reflecting the gray sky as it, in turn, reflected off worn terrazzo.

The staff would have to leave when done as well, Rachael told Ellie, for two equally uncomfortable reasons: In one way they were suspects, as anyone on campus had to be, so could hardly continue to kick around their own crime scene. And in another way they were potential victims. A bomb had been purposely set and had gone off. There could be many others lying in wait, anywhere in the building.

"I don't even want to think about that." Ellie winced as a nurse put two stitches in the cut on her bicep. She'd talked the woman out of putting bandages on her face, the scratches didn't warrant the discomfort of the adhesive. "They're going to have the bomb squad sweep the building?"

Rachael told her yes.

"Strangling a young woman, then bombing a classroom."

"Exactly. What could one *possibly* have to do with the other? And where does Barbara fit in?"

Finally Rachael could speak to the attendees. She kept it succinct: Due to obvious and recent events, the courses had ended and the attendees thanked for their cooperation and emotional maintenance over three very trying days. Anyone with their own vehicle could leave now and the hotel shuttle had arrived in the parking lot to pick up the rest.

She seemed amazingly together, Ellie thought. Ellie had encountered billionaire CEOs who collapsed into shuddering husks under much less dire circumstances.

The attendees were more than ready to vacate. "Do not

pass Go, do not collect two hundred dollars," she heard a student murmur to the woman with orange hair.

"I'm not even going to use the restroom. I'll hold it till I get back in my hotel room," Bettie returned.

"Mm-*hmm*."

The last few days had been an emotional roller coaster, no matter how battle-scarred an investigator might be. They were professional enough to be very curious and hungry to find the solution, but they were also more than intelligent enough to know that they themselves were suspects. Finding oneself on the other side of an investigation had been an experience none had bargained for or wanted. *Let's get while the getting's good.*

Not to mention: *Let's get out before someone else dies.*

The attendees filed out in near silence, heading directly for the basement-level outside door in the hallway. The same door through which Farida Al Talel had gone to her death.

Several stopped to tell Rachael how much they'd enjoyed the class before yesterday, and how sorry they were that the Locard . . . Well, how sorry they were.

Two said the same to Ellie, perhaps not realizing that they'd had a longer tenure there than she had.

Director Coleman had threatened to blame the FBI for a third victim, but Ellie didn't see how that would be possible. The building had been monitored all night, and no one had come in from outside. The bomb had been placed there by a student or a staff member. Knowing that, Ellie figured it could have been that morning, yesterday, last week—no way to tell.

What Ellie would give for a surveillance camera in that classroom.

"Yeah, we'll be criticized for that," Rachael said as they watched the attendees trickle out. "But honestly, why on earth would we have cameras everywhere? We're not open to the public, there's nothing to steal, and there're no children around. Everyone in the place is a trained professional—okay, granted, that doesn't guarantee nonviolent behavior—"

Ellie chuckled, a slightly hopeless sound. *That* had been proven, in spades.

"—but we're not likely to have staff stealing from the register or getting in fights. As I said, the only thing we've ever worried about is vandalism by bored teens, and we've never even had a problem with *that*. Hell. We're lucky we have locks on the doors. How are your stitches?"

Ellie gently redirected Rachael's hands before she could pull the bandage off. "It's fine, just a small cut. How is Director Coleman holding up?"

Now Rachael smiled. "It's okay, you can call him Gerald. The media is losing its collective mind, as you can imagine. You passed the trucks on the way in this morning?"

"A few." Several news vans had been pulled off the road by the gate—not easily, since the two-lane road had no shoulder and wet trenches along both sides.

"Stuart's been guarding it since six, convinced some podcaster will scale the chain link. He said the sheriff's department had to come to deal with the traffic hazard, and CNN had to call a tow truck to get their van out of the ditch."

"And it's about to get worse."

"A, I don't think it can get much worse; and B, chances are good even a bomb won't command the same level of attention. Craig wasn't a young, beautiful, foreign girl."

Luis Alvarez approached them. Stationed behind him, the FBI interviewers were packing up their forms and desk dividers.

"That was fast," Rachael said.

"Answers were pretty uniform. No one saw anything, heard anything, barely knew Craig, and had no idea why someone would want to kill him, if he had been the target. Hardly anyone in your class, Rachael, had ever spoken to the guy. A Border Patrol agent talked to him a couple of times . . . she said on 'smoke breaks.' "

"Stef," she said. "Yes, I did see them together . . . I'd kind of hoped he'd be a cautionary tale to her, since he'd already progressed to the pursed lip breathing. Hypercapnic respiratory failure."

"Uh . . . yeah. Your class, Ellie, chatted with him here or there, but no one became his best friend in the past two weeks."

"I can understand that. I'm not a super big mixer when away at training." She never saw the logic of becoming fast friends with someone she'd likely never see again.

"Antisocial," he deadpanned. "Plus, they just want to get out of here. And that's *if* he was even the target—which sounds possible yet unlikely to me."

"Me too," Ellie said. "I did have a short conversation with him before class, about Farida's death, more or less. We were talking about the Middle East and he told me about a past assignment to a human-trafficking task force. They'd rescued a group of migrant workers. The coyotes they'd hired to get them over the border instead trapped them into prostitution and forced labor."

"They were smuggled into Saudi Arabia?"

"That happens too, but this particular group was smuggled *out*. In some countries when foreign workers arrive, their bosses take their passports. The workers actually need their employers' permission to leave the country. If their employers are abusive, they escape from the house, but then can't get out of the country, so there're camps of homeless people who can't leave and don't want to stay. This particular group escaped, only to be brought to the U.S. instead of their home countries and forced right back into slavery and prostitution."

"Frying pan into the fire."

"Pretty much. He said it has gotten better the past few years, after a government crackdown."

That was all he'd told her before she needed to get the class going on DNA profiles and how quickly they could be obtained.

Michael Tyler arrived for the tail end of this conversation, tie perfectly centered, but with dark circles under his eyes. It reminded Ellie how tired she felt, and she didn't even want to think about what she looked like. "Were you hurt? Are you okay?"

She wanted to chirp that she was never better, but couldn't, just couldn't. She couldn't even add a note of conviction to her reply of "Yeah."

"I called his captain. He'll make notification to his family."

Ellie felt the usual punch-to-the-gut shiver at the thought of a family receiving news like that. "He was married?"

"Twenty-nine years, three kids. They *are* mostly grown now," he added.

He spoke from the human tendency, Ellie thought, to mitigate pain as much as possible. People look for ways to tell themselves that it isn't *that* bad, it could be worse if the children were small. At least they're adults. Teens would be worse, and elementary school age even worse. Maybe better if they were babies and wouldn't even remember their father. Though harder on his wife, to be left alone.

Humans always try to fit each event into a relative scale, slide it up or down so maybe they won't have to feel so awful. When, of course, it's *exactly* that bad.

Ellie didn't often curse, but she wanted to just then.

Michael went on: "Been with the department for twenty-five, could retire but had no interest in that. Started out in Queens, moved to Manhattan, rose slowly through the ranks, no major reprimands in his record. Patrol, vice, organized crime, white-collar, trafficking, armed robbery, homicide—

did them all, at one point or another. Was about to take over supervision of the forensic services unit."

Ellie exchanged a look with Rachael, figuring their thoughts ran along the same lines. If the victim had somehow not been chosen at random, and Craig was killed because Craig *was* Craig, Ellie thought, was it because of something he'd done or encountered in his past NYPD work? Or something he might do or discover in the future?

Or because of something that had happened at the Locard?

Michael looked at them both, the dark eyes direct enough to startle. "What's going on here?"

"I wish I knew," Rachael said.

"What do you *think*?"

"I think," Ellie said slowly, "someone really hates the Locard."

Chapter 34

"If there might be more bombs in this building, partner," Luis said as they walked back to the mangled classroom, "shouldn't we, like, avoid the area? Let the bomb squad do their jobs? Get the hell out of Dodge?"

"Yeah. Probably should."

Their shoes tapped along the tiles once worn down by schoolboys. "Not gonna, though, are we?"

"Scared?"

"No."

"Good. So am I. Anyone who's not scared of a bomb is an idiot. Besides, they already swept this floor."

The doors to the affected room had not been damaged, both open at the time of detonation. Inside, three technicians worked the scene. Michael had already conferred with them and knew that two were ERT techs and one, an explosives expert. The techs had photographed every inch of the room and now worked on a sketch of each piece of furniture and debris, with one using a tape measure and calling out numbers that the other wrote down. How far each type of item had moved from its original location would be important to reconstruct what had occurred.

Although it was pretty easy to figure out what had occurred, Michael thought. Someone had planted a bomb on or inside the cabinets along the window, and it went off.

He and Luis moved over to the gaping hole in the glass, carefully picking their way through the spots of blood and torn things. They didn't want to move what the techs were measuring any more than it had already been moved by the stampede of injured bodies. The damp breeze floated in from the broken window; they were lucky it wasn't a windy day, and neither too cold nor too hot.

One of the techs in the inner corner of the room noticed the caution. "We're finishing up the measuring. You don't have to worry that much about where you step."

Michael checked the woman's face for signs of sarcasm. Techs could get touchy.

The explosives expert leaned over one of the long tables. In a wide, empty spot he pushed around shiny pieces of a deep green material. His feet, with disposable booties over the shoes, stayed just off the edge of the slowly drying pool of Craig Bennett's blood.

"Where's the body?" Luis asked.

"They took him." The expert spoke absently, as if they'd know what he meant—which they did—and as if the body were a minor, peripheral event that had nothing to do with his work—which it didn't. Technically.

Still, it annoyed Michael. "Find the source yet?"

"I think so."

"Really?"

The expert looked up at his surprise. He was about sixty, with mostly gray hair, bad skin, and preternaturally light blue eyes. "It's not that hard. Well, I mean it *can* be that hard, but not in this case. Your DNA whatchamacallit box blew out, kinda forward, but most of the damage was on the front and back sides." He gestured at a pile on the other table, where a cohort of pieces, chunks of black and light-colored composite, had been semiorganized. "That thing is mostly made out of plastic—don't ask me how it works—and the entire interior of it is largely empty space. I don't get it," he added, shaking his head at the other table, as if both mystified and not pleased at what passed for technology in some fields.

"Okay," Michael prodded.

"So the blast came from *behind* the machine, not inside it."

"Or all four sides would be fractured equally," Luis finished.

"You get a gold star. Whatever the bomb is in usually winds up in the most pieces, relative to what's around it."

"And this is the most pieces?"

"This," the expert said, poking a shard of shiny green metal into its place as part of a bizarre jigsaw puzzle, "is in the most pieces. Everything else is broken, torn, dented. *This* is diced."

Michael stared at the debris. Reflective metal in a deep green color had been bonded to a thicker black plastic with some sort of coating in between the layers. He noticed a narrowed piece with threads along the edge. "It's a water bottle."

"You get a bronze star. Too wide at the top for a water bottle."

"Travel mug," Luis said.

The expert nodded vigorously, shaking gray locks over his eyes, which he pushed back with one hand. "So much more innocent-looking than a pipe bomb or a hand grenade but, for his purposes, equally effective. From the look of this place, though, everyone in here had one. I think our guy tucked it behind the DNA whatchamacallit, between it and the pillar between these two windows. You can see the divot it took out of the plaster. That kept more blast in the room instead of going out the window."

Michael started to poke at a piece of green metal, but stopped before his finger made contact. "Is that printing? A logo?"

WA could be seen, the rest of the word twisted off. Upon closer inspection, he saw traces of the white printing on other pieces, some letters, some shapes.

"Maybe we can trace it to its source," Luis said.

The expert waggled his eyebrows. "That's a great idea! You know what, though? I think, before it was blown to smithereens, I think maybe it said, 'Washington, DC' over a silhouette of the eponymous monument."

With that image in his head, the pattern assembled itself for Michael. An *ing* here, a triangular tip of the obelisk in another. This was not good news. "Sold in every cheap little tourist trap in town."

"Most likely. He was just going to blow it up—no point in using his custom Yeti. Those damn things cost too much."

Luis could picture the situation as well. "One of those places, stuffed with trinkets from China, guy paid cash, clerk never even looked up from his feed. How'd he set it off? Timer? Cell phone?"

"Timer. Wireless receiver *would* be a little bit much to fix up in a hotel room . . . if we're assuming it's an out-of-towner. If the guy lives here, with a whole workroom in his basement, no trick at all. But I found that."

He pointed to a tiny clock or a watch without a band, Michael wasn't sure. "Is that a wristwatch?"

"I don't think so, there's nowhere to attach a band. I think it was a clock set in something else and he pried it out. Probably another piece of cheap tourist crap. Attached to this."

This was the upper half of a partially melted 9-volt battery.

"I'm not entirely sure of that," the expert went on. "It

could have been some component of this DNA whatcha-macallit. But whoever installed it attached it to bare wires and added some glue just to keep it in place, which doesn't speak to sophisticated scientific technology. At least I hope not."

Luis said, "Didn't anyone notice some guy walking around with a bottle with wires and a battery sticking out of it?"

Michael said, "I doubt he waved it around."

The expert said, "He probably tucked it all inside, glued the top down for good measure to keep the force contained. That's why there's so much damage to the battery. From the outside it's just another cheap, innocent coffee mug. Inside, demons of hell."

This prompted Luis to make another survey of the room. "All this, from something the size of a travel mug?"

"Oh, that's not hard." He moved to pick up a piece of the green metal, then seemed to notice his own hand and scowled at it—or rather, the latex glove covering it. He even shook it, the wrist flopping loosely, but then picked up the piece, anyway. "I hate these things. My hands always sweat. I'm guessing ammonium nitrate. Guys like this always use ammonium nitrate, maybe with powdered solder for extra oomph. Ten or twelve ounces tucked up in a nice contained structure could easily do this because, relatively speaking, this is nothing. If that guy hadn't been standing right in front of it, probably wouldn't even have killed anybody. You might have gotten off with a ton of bad gashes."

"Staff," Michael said shortly, speaking to his partner.

"You don't think a student would have the time to construct a bomb?" Luis asked.

"How is someone from out of town going to be powdering solder and making up a detonator in their hotel room? I would *hope* that they couldn't get that stuff on an airplane."

"Checked bag," the expert said. "Besides, it *wouldn't* be that tough to mix up in a hotel room. Just clean it up before housekeeping comes by."

"Aren't there a bunch of restrictions on buying that stuff nowadays?"

"Sure, if you want enough to spread over a whole crop or blow up a building. If you only need enough to perk up your rosebush, go to Walmart. Or, if you're worried about nosy Walmart clerks and the taggants that manufacturers now put in fertilizer since people started using it to destroy buildings rather than grow food, you could bypass the garden department and go right to the health-and-beauty aisle."

Michael waited. He had spent years listening to experts. Rushing them only made the process longer.

Luis had also learned, but didn't care. "You've lost me."

"Ammonium nitrate is also used in instant cold packs— the ones you squeeze until you hear something pop like a glo-stick and then it gets cold? Load up on those and the clerk will just think you're accident prone. Cut them open, and figure out which of the activators can be detonated. Not all will be. It might take a little trial and error, but no one will flag the purchase."

"Can you tell how long it was there? The bomb?"

The expert stared at Michael as if he'd asked where babies came from.

"Okay, okay. Just asking. I thought maybe the components might only be stable for a certain period of time."

"Oh, I see. It's not that stupid of a question, then."

"Thank you."

"Because those would have been pretty stable. As long as you didn't toss a match into it, it could sit there for years."

"A match? It needed a spark, not an electric current?"

"Just a tiny spark. One little igniter, less than you'd need to light a cigarette." His gaze swept the room for the object, clearly expecting it to spring to his attention on command, then had to admit with some reluctance: "Haven't found that yet."

"How do we know for sure? What they used?" Luis asked.

"Not one hundred percent right away, I can tell you that. To really be sure, I need to take some samples, get them . . ." He brought one of the larger pieces as close to his nose as it could get without touching, then sniffed.

If he licks that thing, Michael thought, *I'm going to puke. Or shake his hand, not sure which.*

"It might be ammonium ni . . . but might not. Maybe. What is it they do here?"

"In this room?"

"In this building."

"Forensics . . . training . . . research. It's the *Locard.*"

The gray-haired man gazed around as if surprised. "Oh. I see. Huh. Expected this place to look a lot fancier. Well, good for them. What kind of—what's through that door?"

He didn't wait for an answer, but stalked over the scattering of items on the floor to a door to the right of a smartboard and a bookshelf. The knob turned easily and he flung it open.

For a bomb guy, Michael thought, *he's . . . It's a little bit amazing that he's survived as long as he has.* But when there were no further explosions, he and Luis joined the expert in staring at the inside of a supply closet.

"Isn't this where they found that teacher?" Luis asked. Sure enough, the tile floor within the horseshoe of shelving had been pitted and browned by the spilled acid.

"What teacher?" the expert asked.

Michael explained about the death of Barbara Wright, which had appeared to be an accident. It might still be, if he could think of an innocent reason why half a label from the jar next to Dr. Wright could have wound up on Farida Al Talel's body.

Not that the expert appeared to listen, occupied as he was by examining every single jar and box and bottle on the shelves.

"Lucky none of this fell," Luis said.

"Probably quivered a little, but the door protected it. Yep. *Yep!*" The expert straightened up with a medium-size bottle of brown glass. "This might prove interesting."

Michael stood back, expecting the man to exit the room, but he didn't. Instead, he unscrewed the top and peered inside. He shook the jar, and peered some more. Then he threw his head back and took a slight whiff—a much less robust inhaling than he'd done of the metal fragment.

"What is it?" Luis asked, and Michael couldn't blame him for, once again, forgoing the technique of waiting the expert out. It didn't work, anyway.

The man checked the label again, as if not sure. "It's sodium azide. Used to sterilize medical equipment, along with many other uses. What do they do with it here? They ain't doing operations or anything, are they?"

The FBI agents confessed that they didn't know, and that they'd never heard of sodium azide.

"Nice little white powder highly reactive to sparks. *Highly* reactive. Pellets like this are what make your airbag explode and smack you in the face."

"Yeah, but airbags don't take out a room," Michael said.

"You won't be so dismissive if you ever get your nose broken by one of them." The guy examined the label of the bottle, squinting at the fine print. Then he screwed the lid back on, carefully, and put it back in its place. "It might not be as easy to find at Walmart, but then, they didn't need to. It was right here, in their closet."

"So we're back to staff again," Luis said.

"Door isn't locked," Michael pointed out. "And most of these students *work* in labs. They'd know one chemical from another. Aren't you going to examine it, or whatever?" Michael asked when the man moved to leave the supply closet.

"Cross-contamination, my man." The expert closed the

door behind him and even stripped off the latex gloves he
disliked. As predicted, sweat dripped from the thin plastic
coatings and he shoved them in a pocket. "It can stay there
until we're completely finished out here, and then I'll have it
picked up for comparison. The people who work here,
they're not getting back in this room, are they?"

"No," Michael said firmly. "The building will be closed
until we're done. And guarded."

Chapter 35

That was the plan, but it didn't quite work to perfection, because Ellie made it back to her office without interception by a stern monitor type directing her to the exit. So, apparently, had Hector, who stood in his office making notes on a dry erase board, and Caleb, who peered through her office door window with his hand on the knob as if she might be inside, hiding under her desk. A tempting idea, right then.

"Help you?" she asked as she approached.

Through his open doorway Hector spoke without turning from his board. "Yeah, he's hanging around here again."

Caleb smiled at her. "Hey, Doc. Thought I'd see if you're free for a drink or three. I could use one—bet you could too. My flight's not until ten tomorrow, and I'm pretty sure you're going to have the day off, right?"

She should find this attention flattering, but didn't. It had been too exhausting and bewildering of a day and she couldn't feel attractive under a coating of plaster dust. "Don't either of you remember a bomb went off here earlier today? And we have no way to know if there aren't more?"

"Don't *you*?" Hector asked, still absorbed in his notes.

"I need my purse with my car keys, or I *can't* leave."

"The FBI did a sweep," Caleb said. "But you're right, we should get out of here, especially before that rain starts. Let's have dinner and some drinks. We've been blown up together. It's a bonding experience."

"The only thing I want to bond with tonight is my bed. No—don't say something cute. Don't even think it." She unlocked the door and entered her new office.

Of course he followed her right in, yet promptly accepted defeat. "Well, sorry my timing's off. Story of my life. The feds getting anywhere with the pieces of us left behind in that room?"

"I don't know."

He took a short turn around the office, not that it had a lot of pacing room. "Do you think the bomb has something to do with that Saudi girl getting killed?"

She hauled her purse out of a desk drawer and rubbed one temple. "I don't see how. But I don't see how two such bizarre incidents in two days could *not* be related."

"Exactly. They *have* to be connected. If her cousins were around, I'd suspect them—maybe getting revenge on the degenerates they believe killed her. Middle Easterners love bombs, don't they? It's in their genes."

"Terrorists everywhere love bombs, but I don't think her cousins are terrorists, and they weren't anywhere near the classroom after her death."

"Maybe *she* planted the bomb, and someone found out about it and killed her trying to make her tell him where the bomb had been planted."

Ellie considered this—at this point she was willing to consider anything. "But then they came into the building the next day without warning anyone that there might be a bomb here?"

"They couldn't say where they got the information without confessing that they'd murdered her."

It made as much sense as anything she'd come up with.
"Well, okay. It's a theory. But how did Farida plant the
bomb? Her class didn't use that room."

"In the mornings we all wander in and out. On Monday I
had to steal more creamers from the other class—no one
paid attention. But it's just an idea. Mostly, I wanted to let
you know that I really *was* enjoying the course—very helpful—until the, you know, explosion. Hope I can come back
for another session someday."

"Thank you." She hoped the Locard would *have* another day.

"Maybe then we can make some beautiful music together."
He delivered the corny line with such a goofy smile that she
had to laugh. And then, with a little wave, he left. She heard
his shoes padding up the hallway and then promptly forgot
about him, and instead glanced around the office. Was there
anything else she would need? The agents might keep the
building closed for weeks. Or months.

It *might* close forever. What attendees would want to
come to training in rooms that might blow up? What clients
would trust a foundation that had murders and bombings on
its own campus?

Where the hell would she go if this dream job evanesced
before her eyes?

Unwilling to leave, for fear she may never return, she
drifted across the hall, drawn to the *Victim Characteristics in
Cleveland* sheets like a moth to a bug zapper.

"Lover boy finally give up?" Hector said, scribbling another note.

"Yup."

"I'm not complaining about you being hot and all." He
turned then, and with one flick of his eyeballs swept her

from tip to toe. "Not complaining at all. But we're not going to make a habit of this, are we?"

"'Habit'?"

"Of eligible gentlemen forming a line outside your door. Because if you think I'm going to fill in as your social secretary, then I want a raise and paid medical."

She shifted her weight, doing almost a chair pose position to read the bottom entries on the long sheet. "Hector, you are as sophisticated as you are urbane."

"That's a terrible thing to say. What about death in Cleveland fascinates you so much?"

"It's where I'm from. And maybe my subconscious, the other day, noticed . . ."

Hector waited, then gave a sigh loud enough to signal that being hot would not always make up for interrupting his work. "Noticed what?"

"There's a Claire Beck listed here, but crossed out."

"So?"

"That's my mother's name."

Hector blinked, and the impatience left his tone. "Oh. I'm sorry, I didn't know your mother was . . ."

"She wasn't. Murdered, I mean. She died in a car accident."

Now his *Oh* had a completely different tone. "So that's not her, then. Is Beck a fairly common name in Cleveland?"

"Yes, very. Millions of people from central Europe emigrated to the industrial centers in the last century and the one before that."

"What about the date of death?" Verifying data had clearly become second nature to Hector.

"It's the right year, but—I can't be sure about the day. I can't believe I don't know that." Ellie pressed her hand over her eyes as if that would help her see the marker over the grave her grandmother had taken her to every weekend, rain or snow or sun. Ellie remembered running her tiny fingers over the carved letters of her mother's name, but the dates, the numbers in the stone had not meant much to her. At four, she could not comprehend the utter tragedy of a life spanning only thirty-four years. The visits had become more seldom as her grandmother grew ill, and Aunt Rosalie had too much on her plate to spend much time with the dead. Ellie hadn't been to the grave in a decade or two, and with that thought guilt crashed in on her like the walls of a mine giving way.

The slightly impatient tone returned to Hector's voice. "So it's not her."

"No. No, of course not." She should go, let him get back to work so he could finish and leave before another bomb went off, and she should as well. Rachael would be waiting for her. But she felt strangely reluctant to leave the place where a woman who had the same name as her mother existed as one crossed-out footnote. "What are you working on?"

"New batch of UCR stats." The Uniform Crime Reporting Program. Hector had written some case numbers on the board and now added red dots alongside some of them, referring to a sheet in his left hand.

"What are the dots?"

"Cases where there's CODIS information from the suspect."

When DNA had been left behind in cases that really were murders. She stared at the board, her eyes getting weary.

What could be the connection between a scientist whose death first appeared to be an accident, a young foreign national whose death certainly did not, and an explosive device with no particular target in mind?

Caleb's words echoed in her head: *It's in their genes.*

CODIS information.

Unsolved crimes.

It is *in their genes.*

An idea formed in her mind, inconsistent, contradictory.

*   *   *

When Rachael saw the phalanx of news vans still parked outside the gates, she changed her mind. She spoke out loud to the empty car, instructing her phone to call Ellie, then watched in the rearview mirror as the woman driving behind her held an object to her ear. That ancient Mustang predated any thought of Bluetooth-capable mobile devices. Hell, that car predated gas without lead.

"What?" Ellie answered.

"Some of these guys will follow us, and I can't lead them straight home—Danton's going to be skitterish enough with this storm rolling in. Let's go to your place instead."

"You're so sure they'll follow us?" The gate hadn't fully opened yet, the chain-link section rolling back at a snail's pace.

"I've been through this before. When we were investigating that football center for the murder of his girlfriend, news crews followed me into my garage, the grocery store, and church. Why? Is that okay?"

"Sure." She didn't sound sure. "But . . . I'm not as good a cook as your mother is. Fair warning."

Rachael laughed, then quickly stopped. Cameras were rolling. "No one's as good a cook as my mother, so don't worry about it."

The gate stopped and Rachael rolled through, barely touching the gas. Driving past a crowd always made her think of scenes in *The Birds,* the characters gingerly stepping among a temporarily calm flock. One sharp movement and they might swarm. They would overwhelm you and pick the bones clean before help could even think about arriving.

Keep calm, and your foot on the brake.

"Dr. Davies!"

"Dr. Davies! Who killed Farida? Is the Locard protecting her killer?"

"Have the Saudis vowed revenge?"

"What about Dr. Wright?"

"Are there any other deaths you're covering up? Dr. Davies?"

As she nosed the Audi past the last van, she heard them calling the same questions to "Dr. Carr!" So they knew who Ellie was too.

When she reached a free spot in the road, she pulled to the edge to let Ellie pass her, then followed. It didn't take long to reach the woman's new home, perhaps ten or fifteen minutes. Ellie had certainly gone all in for her new career at the Locard—if she left and went back to work in DC, the commute would be hellish.

Rachael hoped it wouldn't come to that . . . partly for Ellie's sake, but mostly for her own. Rachael had put her heart and soul into the Locard. Gerald had founded an amazing facility, but Rachael had put it on the global map, beginning when she'd only been there part-time. Perhaps *because* she'd only been there part-time—without her livelihood on the line, she'd been more able to think long-term. The institute went from being one more think tank to the go-to for everyone with a thorny problem, and/or for those who already knew pretty much everything and needed to know even more. Fourteen patents had come out of the Locard in the past six years. The team had saved a little girl's life and a big man's reputation, pinpointed a terrorist cell and proven a multimillion-dollar judgment against a national conglomerate.

She couldn't stand to see it go down. It would be like losing her sister, all over again.

The bay came into view, the sky turning it to silver as the sun set somewhere behind the gathering clouds. Rachael felt a tiny hint of relief; with that view, at least Ellie couldn't lose too much money if she had to resell the house. Of course, that would depend on what she paid for—

Ellie turned into a drive and Rachael followed.

Cute popped into Rachael's head. Two stories, white with navy trim, upper and lower porches, with white wooden railings. Rachael parked next to a narrow, screened patio, with a small table-and-chairs set and a grill built into the brick wall, as Ellie put the Mustang in its garage. Two little boys played Wiffle ball behind the house next door. One of them stopped to stare at Rachael until the other one threw the plastic ball at his ear. This produced an unconvincing cry of pain and a chase around the two trees.

Ellie's backyard seemed to be fenced, and Rachael heard the familiar screeching bark of a small animal torn limb from limb. Or that of a puppy wanting attention.

As soon as she got out of her car, she said, "I hear someone settling into his new home."

Ellie laughed and they went inside. She brought the dog in via the utility room door and, when asked, said she hadn't thought of a name yet. The puppy greeted Rachael with nearly as much enthusiasm, as if to assure her that the ring of boxes in the kitchen incident would not be held against her. "Have you named him yet?"

"No! Poor thing running around here all nameless."

It didn't seem to bother the dog, now attacking one of his new squeaky toys.

Cardboard boxes formed towers along several walls, but beyond that, the place was clean and bright, ivory walls trimmed with brilliant white. Navy curtains over white sheers gave it a nautical air, but the previous owners might have left those behind. She wondered what Ellie would do.

As if she'd heard her thoughts, Ellie patted the drywall that separated the living room, with its oddly angled brick fireplace, and the kitchen. "I'm thinking of taking this wall out, but then I lose a lot of cabinet space. And I'd have to move the refrigerator."

"And find out if that's load-bearing. But open concept

would be great," Rachael said, as big a Home & Garden Television Channel aficionado as the next girl. "New flooring?"

"I doubt there'd be a way around that. Want to look at the printouts? Or should we . . ." Her voice trailed away as she glanced around the kitchen. "Open a can of soup?"

"Don't worry about food. I can't stay long—Danton gets really upset by thunderstorms and they're predicting a bad one tonight. That boy's not afraid of much, but thunder is his Kryptonite." As if to emphasize her words, a flash of lightning brightened the dark gray clouds just as the first few drops of rain struck the windowpanes. "Besides, after the day we've had, I don't have much of an appetite."

"Good. Me neither."

"And you're probably dying for a shower."

"*Oooohhhh*, yes. But we've got to . . ."

Her voice trailed, and Rachael finished the thought. "Figure this out? We will. We definitely will."

Ellie struggled for a tiny smile.

Not confident, Rachael thought. *Not that one can blame her; neither am I.* She took a careful look out a front window, moving the sheers aside with one finger. "Two cars are out there now. Be warned, more will probably show up. It's not illegal for them to walk up and knock on the door. My advice? Don't answer it."

"Not a problem! Want to come upstairs? I spread it all out up there."

The narrow steps wound up from a corner in the living room into an airy sitting room, with double doors to the upper porch, and several doors to bedrooms and baths. Numerous cardboard boxes lined the walls up here as well, tidily stacked. An ornately framed print of Frederic Leighton's *Flaming June* rested against the chair rail, and a six-foot-long wooden stick leaned on the frame. The top of it had been carved to resemble a dragon. Rachael traced a flourish etched into the wood. "What's this?"

"It's a blowgun." Ellie paused, with that slightly worried look that white people get when they think you're going to say something about race. "My aunt and uncle brought it back from Borneo after they were there with Doctors Without Borders."

"Can you hit anything with it?"

Now she laughed. "I doubt it, though I used to be pretty good."

Rachael gave the dragon's head another pat, wondered for a moment how an animal that didn't exist managed to appear in wildly diverse cultures and locations around the world, and then moved on to the desk. Ellie had positioned a lightweight table with drawers under the window, so she could look out and see the water through the trees as she worked. Rachael spared a moment for the view, though it grew darker by the second. That evening's sunset had been accelerated by the cloud cover. "This is nice. You actually bought this sight unseen?"

"More or less. Reckless, I know." Ellie grinned. "It's the first place I've been in that was all mine. It's exhilarating and terrifying all at once."

"I know what you mean." Rachael had felt like that when she'd, albeit unofficially, adopted Danton. She adored him, but there would always be that worry behind the joy, wondering if his biological father would show up one day and steal him from her. Ellie had thrown out everything old and taken on everything new for the Locard. Rachael hoped they'd both have the futures they wanted.

Though in some ways they were very different, she thought. To Ellie, the Locard was a fabulous new job, but still just another job. To Rachael, the Locard had become her overriding purpose in life. Along with Danton, of course.

To see the institute go down in ignominy would mean more than needing to brush up her résumé and buy some interview clothes. Rachael hated to admit a weakness, but knew that failure would cripple half of her psyche for the rest of her days.

Ellie had spread out Barbara Wright's work, covering the table and extending in piles across the floor. She took an audible breath, one sharp intake, and then began. "If we take out Farida, maybe the other two deaths come back to DNA. Barbara Wright was about to unleash a new kind of biological tracing of killers—"

"Maybe."

"Maybe. In her mind, anyway, and she certainly sounded convincing."

Rachael leapt to it. "And you think someone didn't want her to do that."

"*Maybe.* Maybe someone is also working on a system, and wanted to head off competition, wanted to be the trailblazer themselves and not someone who simply rode behind the wagon."

"Murder among eggheads *seems* extreme—but it isn't nearly as rare as we'd like to think."

"But who's the other victim? The Rapid DNA machine."

Rachael leapt again. "Because you were going to run the attendees' DNA."

"Yes. What if one them is in here?" Ellie patted a pile of four or five sheets with the handwritten title: *Murders/ Violence w/DNA CODIS neg.* Cases in which the suspect had left bodily fluids at the scene, but a CODIS search had come up empty because the suspect's profile wasn't in CODIS.

"That eliminates staff," Rachael burst out.

"Except for me, because my sample was blown up along with the others," Ellie said, but absently. "It also eliminates your students, because they would have been in no danger of having their DNA exposed."

"But wait. How does Farida fit in?"

"I have no idea."

"That, young lady, is not helpful."

This brought the ghost of a smile to Ellie's face. "The only thing I can think of is total distraction. They got away with killing Barbara, but then we started to worry it like—like pups here with a bone. So the killer decides to throw us the most controversial, photogenic, newsworthy victim available."

"They might have heard me talking about fingerprinting the jar. Then they knew we weren't quite writing off Barbara as an accident." Rachael pinched the bridge of her nose, her stomach looping through a sickening circuit. "It was me. I got Farida killed."

"Don't be ridiculous!" Ellie spoke so firmly that the puppy stirred, uneasy. "A vicious killer murdered Farida. For all we know, *that* was the plan from the start and the other two incidents were distractions. Because even with Barbara dead, they still had a problem. When we ran everyone's DNA on Friday, we might see that it matched a suspect profile from an unsolved crime. Then killing her would have been a waste of time."

This sounded like grasping at straws to keep her, Rachael, from feeling guilty, and she tried to find a hole. "But you wouldn't—unless you sat there in class and compared every single profile in this stack right then—because you were going to give everyone their profile results. We were never going to keep them."

"So they could take them home as a little souvenir," Ellie admitted ruefully. "But they still must have been worried that their DNA would expose them—otherwise, why blow up the thermocycler? But then, they could have destroyed it yesterday."

"They could have set a timer so it would go off during the night and *no* one would have been killed."

"But they didn't. Because they enjoy seeing the havoc, enjoy seeing the pain and confusion. Someone has been having a really good time," Ellie finished, her voice lowering with the last sentence.

"That's a scary thought. Especially if you're right about the premise that says we have a killer who works for a law enforcement agency."

"Wouldn't be the first time. The Golden State Killer. Le Grêlé, in France. Gerard Schaefer. The Russian Werewolf. BTK. What better place to learn what *not* to do?"

Rachael couldn't help a shiver at the thought of someone sitting in the Locard's classrooms, absorbing all their knowledge only in order to use it against them. Someone she considered a colleague, a kindred spirit. One of *us*. "If that's true, how do we catch them? They're already gone, their DNA profiles with them."

Ellie gestured at the scattered papers. "I'm hoping there will be a clue in this, somewhere. I know it's a long shot."

"At this point I'll take any shot. These deaths have to be solved, and let's face it—it's vital to both of our futures that the Locard solve them."

"Copy that."

Chapter 36

They divided up the lists and printouts and sat on the cream-colored area rug, spreading the papers out around them. The puppy, of course, had to investigate; Ellie warned him that these were not newspapers and he was not to use them like the ones in the utility room. Fortunately, he showed no signs of thinking of them in that light. His tummy full of snacks, he flopped next to Ellie and went to sleep, while the two women threw out any idea that popped into their heads and let them bounce about the room.

Rachael continued to eye Ellie with concern, trying not to let the woman catch her at it. The crime scene expert seemed too absorbed in the materials to notice either her scrutiny or her minor but still-oozing injuries—but that might not be a good thing. Ellie might be so strong that she'd already forgotten a near-death experience. Or the full impact of that trauma might be waiting behind the draperies, planning to pounce as soon as Ellie took a breath. People were rarely as bulletproof as they appeared.

But unless the woman asked for help, Rachael would keep

her worries to herself. Ellie was a colleague, not a daughter. Or a sister.

"We don't have the DNA," she said. "But we have location. We could cross-reference the states and towns. Smart serial killers travel a wide area."

"It doesn't have to be a serial killer. They'd go to jail for one, as well as ten."

"True. Do you have a roster of your students? That should list their agency."

Ellie retrieved the two sheets of names and contact information from her tote bag. She also fired up her laptop to check online maps. Some location names were not at all familiar and she had to check what county they might be in or what cities they might border.

She read out a name and home location, and then both of them checked the various lists of violent crimes for ones in that area.

At the same time they continued to poke and prod the theory. Rachael said, "Okay, say we have a killer panicking about giving a DNA sample. Why not invent an excuse? They have to leave the course early and fly home for a family emergency."

"There's a strange death, then a murder, and they take off? It would single them out, invite attention."

"But they knew from the start, the Rapid DNA sample was part of the course—it's mentioned in the flyer. If they were nervous about that, why come at all? Or at least leave on Tuesday or something, don't kill Barbara, don't kill Farida. That would have been better." A flash of white lit the sky outside, turning the trees to silhouettes. A sharp crack followed, with an earth-rumbling *boom* after that. The puppy woke long enough to whine, then tucked his head against Ellie's hip and went back to sleep.

Danton had the same reaction to thunderstorms, except for the going-back-to-sleep part. The boy would howl as if the lightning had struck him. She'd have to get home soon.

Ellie stroked the dog's now-clean fur. "I think they *weren't* worried about the DNA test. The course description specified that our equipment is a closed unit and the profiles wouldn't be uploaded anywhere—I checked. That couldn't have been an issue, or the killer wouldn't have come. They didn't worry until Barbara discussed her system for cross-referencing unknown suspect profiles with dispensed medications."

"They had to get rid of Barbara before she interested the national forensic community in looking at meds. Then they had to get rid of the thermocycler to hide their DNA profile, while all Barbara's research was still sitting around."

"Except we never would have known that, because they would have taken their profile home with them."

"Maybe they didn't trust us not to keep copies. Criminals tend to believe that everyone else behaves criminally as well," Rachael said. How well she knew that. Her sister's taste in men had brought more than one career ne'er-do-well around the house.

"True. But then, why not just fake the DNA sample? They could have wet the swabs with water, but that would look even more suspicious—the profile coming out totally blank. They could grab someone else's water bottle—someone not in the class, so it wouldn't come up as a duplicate—and swab the neck."

"But they collected the swabs from their mouths in front of everyone else, you said."

"Yeah, right there by the sample chamber. I didn't want them walking around the room or shoving them in pockets, to minimize contamination."

"That would be tough to wiggle out of without, again, attracting attention. But blowing up the entire lab is a bit overreactive. No pun intended. Who's next?"

"Jaime Trellis, from Oklahoma City."

Ellie perused *Murder Clusters by County*, while Rachael thumbed through *Uniform Crime Reports*, after checking with the internet to find the right county. "Two men killed here, not specifically linked, but similar circumstances. You know, this bomb—someone had to first know how to make one."

"Google," Ellie said.

"Assuming Barbara's death got this started and the person didn't come here *intending* to kill Barbara and destroy the thermocycler, they'd have to find all the bomb components in one or two nights."

"Google."

"Maybe you find YouTube videos more helpful than I do! When I watch one, it seems they're always telling me to use something I don't have or click on something that's not there. We should at least find out if any of our attendees have experience in arson and explosives investigation—Carrie should be able to run down everyone's résumés tomorrow."

Then she remembered that Carrie would not be in the office tomorrow. Neither would Gerald, and neither would she. Indefinitely.

"Lieutenant Matthew Gold, from Columbus, Ohio. The man of few words," Ellie added, and they again checked sheet after sheet of printed data.

But there were also plenty of murders in that fair city. Geolocation could not help. There seemed, unsurprisingly, no spot in the country untouched by murder. There also seemed to be no spot where citizens did not have numerous varieties of chronic illness requiring medication.

Barbara—or Hector—did not have data for either murders or medications in Saudi Arabia, which was equally unsurprising. This prompted Rachael to wonder again: "Farida was in the other class. Some mixed during lunch, but who would she know well enough to walk out into a rainstorm with?"

Ellie shrugged. "Who from my course would even know where the goat was buried?"

"Well—they've all wandered in and out of the building during lunch and breaks. Especially last week when the weather was nicer. It wouldn't be strange for anyone to take a look at the site at some point." They weren't getting anywhere. She and Ellie needed a faster path to a narrower suspect pool. "Someone in the class got scared when Barbara spoke about cross-referencing meds and murders. But how could they *know* she'd find them?"

Ellie considered this, nodded slowly. "Either they didn't, and they're a supercautious type that takes no chances, *or* . . . she used their crimes as a case study in lecture."

"Exactly," Rachael said. "It could be either—life in prison is a fairly good reason for crossing every *t* and dotting every *i*, yes. But it *could* be that she detailed their work in front of the group, without any idea that the person she had pinpointed as a suspect by their medication actually sat in front of her. What examples did she use in class?"

Ellie grimaced as if someone had stuck her with a pin. "I came in, in the middle, so I didn't hear all of it. I know she talked about a suspect in Boston having Huntington's and a suspect in Arkansas with possible sickle cell anemia."

Without another word they both snatched pages from the list and scanned. In the sudden silence Rachael noticed that the noise of the rain had increased to a dull roar, pellets of water hitting the window glass like bullets. She hoped this home's construction was as solid as it looked.

Of the wide variety of cities listed, however, no one came from within two hours of Boston or the small city in Illinois.

"We'd have to ask the other attendees," Ellie said.

"And hope they'd even remember. Or took detailed notes."

"She'd probably have used the same case studies she meant to present to the academy. I didn't know Barbara, but she sounds like someone who always put her strongest foot forward—"

Rachael couldn't resist saying, "Usually in someone else's face."

"—especially when she's practicing to present to the academy *and* start up her own business. The meeting starts Monday, so she'd hardly worry about someone stealing her ideas at this point. She could put all her cards on the table." Ellie pulled some old-fashioned printouts down from the desktop. "I found these listed in the digital presentation on one of the USBs. Four rapes in Little Rock showing sickle cell disease. Two unsolved murders and one solved in Wichita where thiazide had been found in the saliva residue. Five murders by gunshot in St. Louis with the suspect's blood showing mutations in the RB1 gene—how did he leave blood at *five* . . . oh, I see. He or she left blood at *one* scene, but all five were connected by the ballistics."

"That makes more sense."

Ellie went on. "Two armed robberies in Phoenix where the suspect's mucus had a mutation in the NOD2 gene, and two murders in Adelphi with a killer on valproic acid. So let's say one of these five suspects is in my class," Ellie said.

"Probably should have led with this," Rachael said, trying to tamp down her irritation by reminding herself that finding this killer wasn't Ellie's job. It was Rachael's.

"I know. But these weren't in the class notes I found on

her desk, and I didn't hear her mention them . . . but then, I got there late."

"No worries. Anybody list those cities as home base?"

They snatched up the attendees list again. Rachael didn't hide the disappointment in her voice when she muttered, "No."

"No," Ellie agreed. "Every other city in the country, but not these."

Another crack split the air and Rachael jumped. "My boy's going to be screaming at that one. And once he starts, he can't stop."

"Do you need to go?" Ellie asked.

Rachael thought, *Clearly, she doesn't want to stop our work—and clearly, she doesn't understand why one freaked-out toddler grabs priority over three murders. I didn't used to either. She probably thinks, as I did, that people with kids overemphasize their importance, use them as excuses to get out of all sorts of work and obligations and overtime.* Rachael didn't want to be *that* parent—

But as she hesitated, Ellie doubled down on the understanding. "It doesn't look like we're going to get anywhere tonight, anyway. We've got to call all my ex-attendees to see if any recall details of what Barbara said in class, and most of them are on planes at the moment. If that doesn't work, we'll have to comb through every suspect profile from near our students' locations, trying to figure a phenotype to go with the genotype to see if it corresponds to that student. It may take weeks. This will now be a long-term investigation whether we like it or not."

Still, Rachael opened her mouth to say no. She didn't want to give up so easily and felt sure that Ellie would work at those scattered sheets all night. The woman had that same driven intensity when on the trail as she did. Or had, until Danton had fallen into her life, the cutest little distraction there could be.

But just then, another bolt creased the black sky outside and she changed her mind before the rumbling could begin. "I'm afraid I do. Let's sleep on it—I'm ready to drop, and maybe our brains will come up with a plan after some rest."

"Sounds good. You're going to get soaked in the ten feet to your car. Do you have an umbrella?"

"It's just water." Rachael picked up her bag and shrugged into her light jacket, which—bad choice for the weather— didn't have a hood. "I'll survive. Besides, it will keep those reporters from following me."

Chapter 37

Ellie needed a shower. She really needed a shower. But the answer might lie on the next page, and besides, her grandmother had always prohibited showers or baths during thunderstorms. Ellie didn't remember the exact logic, something about the water might attract the errant electricity ... It didn't make a lot of sense, but it did make a good excuse to keep working.

She *did* wonder if this monsoonlike rain would be a regular characteristic of coastal living. She took a break to check all the windows for leaks, plus the basement, but the house must be tougher than it looked, because she didn't find any. Standing in the dark living room, she looked through the front window for cars. The storm had convinced the media to give up on her ever doing anything interesting, and they'd abandoned her street, except for one nondescript sedan parked in front of her elderly neighbor's house, tucked nearly out of sight under the willow. Perhaps he or she had fallen asleep. Perhaps it belonged to an unlucky motorist who had broken down and had nothing to do with her at all.

She shrugged and went back to work. She didn't know

whether to resent or envy Rachael, so involved in raising her little boy. Ellie had spent a few years trying to conceive with Adam, consistently swallowing her disappointment and refusing to acknowledge the growing despair—but now wondered if she might have dodged a bullet. She felt no desire to take on that burden without a partner; how much better to be able to live as you wanted without having every minute dictated by a tyrant in Garanimals. Especially now that she didn't even have to share it with another adult.

So she could do things like work all night, staring at sheets of unhelpful paper, arranged and rearranged across the floor in front of her. Some showed wrinkles from the puppy walking over them.

"I *am* going to have to give you a name," she told him. "How about Alastair? After my favorite author."

The dog glanced at her over his rawhide chew toy, noticeably unimpressed.

"You're right. Then I'd start calling you Allie, and I'm Ellie, and we'd be Allie and Ellie and that would just get weird. Like I'm some crazy dog lady—no offense—without any hope of a normal adult relationship ever again."

The dog continued to chew.

They were never supposed to assume in forensics, but without some assumptions she couldn't choose a path forward. She could call every single sponsoring agency on the sheets to see if a) it really existed and b) the attendee really worked there. Though there was no reason to believe the killer wouldn't be who they said they were. It seemed unlikely they could pick out this class to attend purely to deal with Barbara, when Barbara had kept her secret formula under tight wraps until the end came into sight, hoping for a windfall of both prestige and money.

She could pinpoint a phenotype from the prescription meds dispensed near murder clusters, but she and Rachael had already explored that idea and come up with nothing—

or everything. There were simply too many murders, and none seemed to be in the right place. And since students didn't pop their pills during class, Ellie had no way to know who might need scripts to stay healthy.

Ellie slapped down the papers in her hand. "The heck with it."

The puppy froze.

"No, not the name thing. I had one person in that classroom who is not currently on a plane somewhere, because she lives in DC. So what if she can't stand the sight of me because she's jealous of my job and she covets my ex-husband, or maybe because I grievously wronged her at some point in the past by borrowing a pen and never giving it back."

The attendee list had each person's name, address, and phone number. Alyssa answered on the fourth ring. Her hello sounded distinctly unenthusiastic, but Ellie couldn't blame her for that. It seemed like 80 percent of unknown numbers these days were calls from scammers.

"Alyssa," Ellie began, thinking, *Please don't hang up on me.* "I just have one quick question. When Dr. Wright explained her theory in class about tracing killers by their prescription meds, do you remember what cases she cited?"

A pause, then a low drawl: "*What?*"

Had she been asleep? Had she gotten home to dive straight into the liquor cabinet? If so, again, Ellie couldn't blame her. It had been quite a week.

Ellie repeated the question, more slowly, and explained her goal. It could greatly narrow the possible scenarios to know . . . provided, of course, that Alyssa wasn't the killer. There were certainly enough unsolved murders in DC to make her a suspect.

Another pause.

"Alyssa," Ellie said, making her tone much more calm and quiet than she felt, "I know you don't like me, although I don't know why—"

"It's not that."

Oh, so you don't—

"I just don't remember verbatim what she said. I remember a guy blew his nose in Phoenix and the snot had something in it, some genetic abnormality. Something about Kansas. What looked like a series in St. Louis by gunshot, the casings found right by the bodies, which we all thought was weird because usually gunshot serial killings are, like, from a distance, like Son of Sam and the Beltway Snipers. When some a-hole is killing women, they usually strangle or maybe stab. Up close and personal."

"True," Ellie said, trying to sound encouraging. "Anything else? Any other case histories that she mentioned?"

"I think so, but I can't remember." She sounded as though she was really trying, which Ellie appreciated.

"Okay. Thanks a lot." A vague memory came back to Ellie. "One other thing—she was late for the afternoon session on Wednesday, right? Do you remember how late? Were all the attendees in the classroom?"

"Late?"

"I had the impression the students were all assembled and wondering where she was. Can you recall if the room was full, if everyone was there?"

"Hell, I . . . I don't know. It was *fairly* full, but I don't know who was there and who wasn't. You're figuring any missing person was off killing Dr. Wright? I dunno, because it was right after lunch and people were trickling in and out. If anyone noticed it was time for class to begin, I doubt they cared."

That had not been Ellie's impression. Why hadn't it been?

"Wait," Alyssa said suddenly. "The Kansas thing. She said samples from three murders had some thia-something that was prescribed for high blood pressure. The guy caught in the third one did take it, so they were testing his DNA to see if he did one and two. And Craig said that didn't prove much because everyone had high blood pressure. Bettie told him to speak for himself, and Dr. Wright looked all snooty at Bettie and said something. I can't remember exactly what she said, but it meant that Bettie must be lying because no way someone that big wouldn't have blood pressure issues. You want to talk pressure, I thought Bettie was going to do a Vesuvius right there."

"Okay," Ellie drawled, rethinking this approach, since sniping at someone's systolic pressure hardly seemed—

"But Wright said, about the thia-whatever, it *was* important because, otherwise, the guy wouldn't have been connected to murders one and two. Craig said it would all have come up once he was entered into CODIS after arrest and she looked even snootier and said it was much faster to do a direct comparison than wait for a routine search. At lunch we were talking about it and Craig said it wouldn't be *much* faster, and then the girl from Greensville said maybe it wouldn't be where he lived, but it depended on the lab submitting it. She didn't think much of hers."

Thiazide. Ellie tried to fit that into a useful scenario.

Then Alyssa said, "I gotta go," and hung up halfway through Ellie's thank-you.

An odd person. But then, some were, and it seemed best not to overthink any motives because she'd probably get them wrong.

Provided, of course, Alyssa wasn't the killer herself.

Then there was the elephant in the room: Farida Al Talel. Why, if this all had to do with a killer covering the tracks they'd left in a previous crime, *why* kill a young woman who could not possibly have a thing to do with it?

Farida's murder could not be due to greed or envy—she had no material possessions or a position anyone would want. Or wrath—she hadn't infuriated anyone to any great extent that had been noted by others, unless it really *had* been her cousins as a result of some personal dispute, and Ellie couldn't believe that, since only one person had left the building with Farida and did not appear large enough to be either of those two men.

She might have incurred wrath made of fear if she'd witnessed something incriminating about Barbara's murder, but how could that have happened when she was in the other class and her cousins rarely let her out of their sight?

That left the most obvious motive when a beautiful young girl was killed: lust. It *could* be pride, if she turned down someone's advances, but they'd only be advancing out of lust so—back to lust.

That did nothing to narrow her suspect pool.

Legs crossed, Ellie dropped her face into her hands. Round and round. Two murders that might point to one killer, and a third that pointed nowhere in particular.

"I think I need some rest," she said to the dog, who already had slumbered, and began to gather and sort the papers. She'd get into bed and let her brain work on it.

Yeah, right. She'd get into bed and stare at the ceiling. But, okay, her brain could work on it like that. It's not like she had to get up for work the next day, so if the clock glowed with times like 2:15 or 4:40, so what?

Besides, it *had* to be here somewhere. How often did one get a crime with such a defined set of suspects? The Locard might not be an English country house, but in this drama it fulfilled the same role.

The killer could be on the staff—surely, Hector had a better motive to kill Barbara than anyone else. Cameron's feelings seemed complicated and intense. But the attendees were the ones present, so to speak, at all three deaths.

She picked up Hector's lists of unsolved murder clusters—or rather, Hector's lists that Barbara had been using. Dr. Wright had highlighted and annotated several cases, mostly notes about the corresponding DNA profiles and possible dispensed medications. Maybe Ellie and Rachael had given up on the geolocation too soon. Or started from the wrong end.

"I am not going in circles," she told the puppy, quietly so as not to wake him. "Really."

Four rapes in Little Rock. Problem was, no one in the class hailed from any place in the entire state of Arkansas. And its capital sat right smack in the middle, not even close to a border, where a clever killer could slip over.

Five murders of females by gunshot in St. Louis. A quick internet search taught her a few things about the city she'd never been to. Geographically more interesting, St. Louis sat on a state border, separated from Illinois only by the Mississippi River.

Ellie checked the attendee lists. No one from St. Louis, and the four from Illinois hailed from the Chicago suburbs at the other end of the state.

At first she wondered why this cluster had attracted attention—as a large city, St. Louis had close to two hundred homicides every year. But less than a quarter were females, and most of those had been strangled by a spouse or significant other.

No one had been killed by a gun at the Locard, but then, a St. Louis resident could hardly have brought one on the plane.

St. Louis. Population over three hundred thousand, second in size only to Kansas City. Known for music, barbeque, and the Gateway Arch. Numerous Fortune 500 companies and a basilica with the world's largest mosaic installation. Sports teams, the Cardinals and the Blues.

The baseball team used, unsurprisingly, a red bird as their logo—the Ohio state bird, Ellie knew, as well as the state bird of six other states, none of which were Missouri. The Blues logo consisted of a blue musical note with a wing for a flag.

She had seen that logo recently—where?

A bell began to ring at the back of her mind, sending vibrations through her nerves until the hairs on her arms quivered and rose.

On her first day at the Locard, she'd ducked under the arm of a man to get inside when her keycard wouldn't work. The jacket sported an understated flying blue note embroidered into the material.

Caleb Astor. He'd said he was from Missouri. From a small town that she would never have heard of.

What was it? Ellie scrunched up her face with the effort of remembering, as if that would help. It was something with a *b*. Bomber? No, she had bombs on the brain. Baldwin? *Ballwin.*

She checked the online map of Missouri. She couldn't find the name, but he'd specified a *small* town. She did a general search for the name. There—Ballwin, Missouri. Nine square miles, thirty thousand people.

A scant twenty miles outside of St. Louis.

Caleb Astor. Who kept hanging around her—Barbara's—office. What if it wasn't Ellie he sought?

Caleb, who said he came to find Barbara because students were waiting for her, when Alyssa said the class hadn't even fully assembled.

Could it really be that simple?

Stop, she told herself, step back. Three hundred thousand people in St. Louis. A bit of a stretch to think a suburban crime scene tech *happened* to come to DC for a class and *happened* to hear the teacher talking about how she planned to get a search warrant regarding the murders he committed, because he left a trace of a medication in *one* blood sample at *one* scene—what was the medication again?

She grabbed up a different stack of papers. Obviously, his affliction couldn't be something obvious. He'd seemed perfectly healthy to her. Medium height, trim. Exactly the size of the person who had left the building with Farida Al Talel.

Just then, the lights went out. Her new home plunged into darkness.

Oh, hell. Please don't tell me the power went out.

The puppy, formerly slumbering away with his warm little body tucked up against her thigh, sprang to all fours, legs stiff. A low growl rumbled in his throat, a sound Ellie had never heard before.

Oh, hell. Please tell me the power went out.

A creaking board sounded from downstairs. Someone else had entered the house.

Chapter 38

Rachael drove the dark roads, rain dashing across the windshield in gusts. There weren't nearly enough streetlights, but she hardly needed them, since lightning crossed the sky almost constantly. The thunder sounded like a kettledrum solo. She wanted to call her mother—even getting on the phone with Danton might give Loretta some relief from the drama—but Loretta kept the ringer volume all the way up to avoid missing any calls. If, a big if, Danton had fallen asleep, a phone call might inadvertently elevate the situation to DEFCON 2.

In the meantime she should concentrate on the road. A fallen tree limb could appear around any corner, and an impatient pickup behind her insisted on crowding her bumper.

Of course her mind received and acknowledged the warning about proper focus, then immediately went back to thinking about the murders. Farida's killer had most likely boarded their plane, on their way back to their normal lives, without consequences.

She felt her face get hot. That poor girl, snuffed out just as she stood on the cusp of her future—and for what? If she and Ellie were right, Farida's life had been discarded purely because it had been convenient to do so. The killer needed to distract them from Dr. Wright and her theories, and the exotic young woman suited his purposes perfectly.

What if she and Ellie were wrong? Perhaps they'd gone too far out on a limb with the DNA theory. The prescriptions didn't have the names attached, so why would a killer be so concerned that Barbara had begun tracking meds? So she knew that someone in, say, St. Louis had retinoblastoma. She'd have to talk a judge into giving her confidential HIPAA information on several patients. That, in itself, would be a labor worthy of Hercules. Medical information had always been considered sacrosanct, and a court order like that would bring comparisons to *1984*'s Big Brother.

Retinoblastoma. Rachael had seen several cases of it over the years. Eyes were miraculous organs, amazing feats of biochemistry and engineering, and she avoided them as much as possible. Fortunately for her, most autopsies required only an external examination of the eyeball, unless the victim had consented to corneal donation. Rachael didn't beat herself up about the aversion—everyone had something. She'd known a pathologist who barely noticed maggots, but couldn't stand ants. Danton had thunderstorms. Rachael had eyes.

She slowed down to cross the small river of water that had accumulated in a low spot. Retinoblastoma came in two types, hereditary and nonhereditary. It usually surfaced in childhood from a mutation in the RB1 gene. When photographed with a flash, patients might appear to have a white pupil instead of the red one seen in so many casual snapshots. They might have two different-colored eyes. It could be treated with surgery—not only to stop the cancer from spreading, but save the vision as well, and after that with cyclophosphamide to prevent reoccurrence.

No one in either class seemed to have an eyesight issue.

Hardly surprising, as crime scene work would require decent sight. No white pupils, though those would likely show only in flash photography. No—

Wait.

One student did have different-colored eyes. She stopped at a red light, trying to fill in the face around one blue and one pale brown iris . . . the one who was with Ellie when she came to tell Rachael about Barbara. What was his name? Something with a *C*.

The driver behind her honked the horn, clearly impatient to get home and out of this storm. Rachael hit the gas, felt the car slide as the tires fought for traction in the small flood of the street, and looked for a place to turn around.

Chapter 39

It took work to overcome that first instinct to freeze, but Ellie made herself rise to her feet in one smooth roll, the puppy tucked into the crook of her left arm. Then she padded, as softly as she could, across the wide area rug. The floor remained silent until she ran out of carpeting and stepped onto the hardwood—then the planks gave a modest creak that came as a gunshot in the sudden vacuum.

She didn't let it stop her, but kept going into her bedroom, making her feet plant themselves as softly and as evenly-weight-distributed as she could. Around the bed, over to the nightstand: *Don't look behind, keep going.* The drawer slid open, but not, of course, without resistance. A castoff from her mother's cousin in Euclid, the wood had too much weight and not enough lubrication. Not much of a problem when you had both hands free and didn't care about noise. But she only had to free three or four inches of the drawer to pull out her grandfather's revolver.

She turned back toward her bedroom door.

She could see from there the top of the stairs to the first floor. The opening appeared as only a darker black within the black of the second floor, but when a flash of lightning lit the room, she could see—nothing. Railing, wall, top step. All right, then.

The puppy squirmed and whined. She didn't know if he was uncomfortable or scared or simply wanted the freedom to go investigate this new scent. Juggling a dog in one hand and a gun in the other hardly seemed the best way to confront an intruder; but if she set him down, he'd probably charge out to do the confronting himself, and he needed six more months and some training before he'd be ready for Mighty Dog duty.

She stayed in the doorway, slightly inside her bedroom, hoping that the dark interior would keep her hidden from the view across the equally dark sitting room.

And she waited.

Ellie had always thought the biggest mistake protagonists made in movies and television shows came as they stalked through their own home, often with a gun or knife in hand, wondering where the dangerous one might be. *Stupid*, she thought. *Let them come to me. Even if it takes all night.*

Even if she needed her cell phone, which sat across the room on the desk. She should have snatched that up when she rose, but she'd been too focused on getting the gun. Now she had the gun, but how to call for backup?

The shadows in the stairwell, as shadows do when stared at for too long, seemed to shift and move of their own accord. But when a streak of lightning lit the room, nothing appeared there, except the wainscoting and the white balustrade.

Perhaps she'd overreacted. This house produced a symphony of squeaks in the high winds, as she'd learned the previous evening. And how could he have broken in without some sort of crashing sound?

Rachael could have left the door unlocked, but as she'd gone downstairs, Rachael had specifically said she would lock the door behind her. Ellie didn't believe the former pathologist would forget that quickly, even distracted by concern for Danton or a plan for getting to her car without a complete dousing.

Caleb Astor—if Ellie was correct—had no reason to come to her house. He should be on a plane back to Missouri, accepting a stamp-size bag of pretzels from the stewards and laughing to himself over murdering three people at the prestigious Locard, only to walk away, utterly free.

The storm had most likely knocked out a transformer and that had killed her power, not someone turning off the main breaker at her electrical box. *The electrical box isn't outside, is it?* She had at least scouted that out since moving in, hadn't she?

Uncle Roland would be shaking his head at her. *"Your home is your castle, young lady, your fortress against injury and violence, as well as repose."* Then he'd add *"Edward Coke"* as the source of this wisdom, which had only confused her more, since she didn't know what the soft drink company had to do with houses.

She could look out the window to see if Daisy's lights still worked, but that would require crossing the room and turning away from her vantage point overlooking the stairwell. One she did not feel quite ready to abandon.

Yes, she'd probably overreacted.

Still she didn't move, and held the increasingly restless dog close to her torso.

No, the electrical box was properly inside her unfinished garage, mounted on the two-by-fours separating said garage and kitchen.

The garage, however, had an exterior door leading to the backyard. It was an old-fashioned wooden door, with two large panes of glass in the upper half: Its glass could be easily broken during a thunderclap functioning as a sound buffer; then the culprit could reach through, open the door, cross the garage, kill the power, and enter the kitchen. The garage-kitchen door would not have been locked. After she'd stored the Mustang, she'd sped through the house to open the sun-room door for Rachael.

The shadows moved again. She did not react, having been fooled that way once.

And then, as electrical light from the heavens lit up the bay, he was there.

"*Freeze!*" She heard her voice quaver. The dog yipped, either from the involuntary tightening of her fingers or because of the phantom materializing at the top of the stairs.

"'Freeze'?" His tone low, mocking, not at all like he'd sounded before. "Or what?"

This time she didn't quaver at all. "If you move, I will shoot you."

A sigh, as if a favorite student had disappointed him. The room illuminated slightly, backlit by the vague heat lightning that hides in the clouds. His hand rested on the newel, one foot on the landing, one on the step below it. His face seemed shiny, no doubt slick with rain, and he wore a light windbreaker and those bright white sneakers.

"You had to get new shoes," she noted.

She saw his head dip down toward the objects in question, as if he'd forgotten whether he had or not.

"Because," she said, "burying Farida really did a number on your old ones."

"You can say that again."

The puppy growled, and so did Ellie. "*Why?* Why did you kill her?"

Caleb Astor let out a short, small groan that sent a tremor of animal instinct through her body from scalp to calf.

"How could I *not*? I'd listen to her every day at lunch, watch her—so exotic. That little laugh, that perfect skin, that utter naiveté." His voice grew thick at the memory. "I wasn't sure it would be possible, not with those two goons hanging over her every second, but that made it even more tempting, way too tempting to pass up. The idea of doing it right under their noses, right in the shadow of the Locard—how could I *possibly* resist that?"

She needed her cell phone. But only four feet separated them; if she moved forward, she would be within his range to attack or grab for the gun, another trap TV protagonists tended to fall into. She had to get him to leave the stairwell, enter the sitting room, and back away at least ten feet.

"But how did you get her to leave with you?"

"Ah, yes. That was the trickiest part. The goons were on the other side of the cafeteria, trying to get coffee out of the machine, so as soon as she exited the ladies', I grabbed her around the shoulders and told her the shuttle had arrived and cousins had left, they thought she'd gone ahead. Kid was startled, but *so* trained to do whatever a man tells her. Of course she'd *also* been trained to never be alone with a non-related man, but—by then, we were out in the rain and I'm sure she just wanted to get out of it. We were heading toward the parking lot, so she probably told herself it was okay. They always do."

The puppy squirmed, and so did she.

"If we'd encountered anyone else on the path, I'd have just let her go, let the whole thing go . . . but, no one. That goat stunk, though. Man, I thought I'd never get that smell out from under my fingernails."

She needed him to move away from the steps. But even if she could get past him, where would she go? "You had to know she'd be found the next day."

"Of course."

"*Why*? Why not drag her deeper into the woods—"

In the dark she couldn't see his expression, but she saw the outline of his head as it tilted to one side. "Well, that wouldn't have anywhere *near* the same drama, would it? That wouldn't have been interesting at all."

"And that's your interest here? Drama?"

Finally, a pause. "That's kind of hard to explain. Does it really matter?"

No, she decided. *It really doesn't.* She didn't care about whatever flaw of his psyche prompted him to cruelty. Stopping him—*that* mattered.

She could simply shoot him, right here and now. He had broken into her home. Surely, the DNA from his dead body could be connected to Farida's scarf, sales receipts to the components of whatever he'd used to blow up the lab.

But she'd rather find another way. "Move over to the window. There by the railing."

"Or you'll shoot me?"

"Yes."

"Really? I thought we were getting along so well."

"*Move.*"

"I don't know what you're complaining about. All those fine people came to learn and, well, they learned. They learned there's no way to fight a fox that's already in the henhouse. I killed that girl and just drove away."

"In your rental car."

"One econobox, currently parked up the street. My city's pretty cheap."

"The agents checked all the cars. How did you—"

"Keep it so clean? The thing about rain that hard, it's like being in a shower. *Just* like a shower. It washed most of the dirt and leaves off my new cheapo raincoat before I even made it back to the car. Then—since I parked under the camera—I took the coat off, turned it inside out on the backseat, piled my shoes and pants and tied it up into one bundle, to be tossed in the dumpster behind a McDonald's on my way back to the hotel. Sure, I was soaking wet and freezing, but nothing got on the upholstery, except a little water. I *did* have to come in the back door and hustle my cold little buns to keep from getting caught in the hotel hallway in my skivvies, but October in Fairhaven is not a big tourist draw. A hot shower and I was right as, well, rain. Don't you love those in-room coffeemakers?" He leaned one elbow on the newel, put a hand to his chin, the picture of relaxed contemplation. "You know, I'd never strangled before. This trip truly *has* been an education."

"Yes. You prefer to use a gun."

Lightning let her see his slight shrug. "Couldn't get it on the plane. And I *had* meant to make this a working trip. Learning only. No side tasks. But then—"

"Then you heard Barbara explain how she intended to track you down through your cyclophosphamide."

"Yes. Yes, indeed." He straightened up from the newel, bringing his other foot up to the landing.

"Move over to the window," she ordered again.

"Right, right. Or you'll shoot me. It doesn't have to be like this," he told her in a whiny, patently false voice. "I don't want to hurt you. I didn't want to hurt anyone. I only came here to learn."

"How to be a better serial killer?"

"Education is the key to success, isn't it?"

"Move."

He moved. After an initial jerk, perhaps meant to unnerve her or test to see how itchy her trigger finger might be, he walked over to the window against the north wall. The muscles in her torso relaxed by a nanometer or two—this left her path clear to the desk and her cell phone. Puppy still in hand, revolver clenched in a palm beginning to sweat, she began the walk to the east wall, one step at a time, her gaze never budging from her target. She let the nerves of her sock-clad feet and her peripheral vision guide her.

She wasn't used to this kind of work. FBI agents were trained for hand-to-hand combat, but rarely had to engage in it, an arrangement she preferred. Despite what one saw on television, cops, not agents, chased suspects up dark alleys.

She really didn't want to brush up her skills tonight.

A soft sheen of light rested on him, similar to moonlight, but even fainter. It must come from a lamp at the house of the elderly man next door, she deduced. So she *would* have power, when and if she could get to the garage. Good to know, but not particularly relevant right now.

Let's keep him talking, she thought, while she figured out how to pick up the phone without putting down the dog. Or should she put down the dog? Would he stay out of kicking range or immediately go for Caleb's ankles? "What did you hit her with? Barbara?"

"Those rolls of butcher paper? They're pretty heavy."

Yet, with enough cushion to keep from forming blunt force trauma, just as neighbor Daisy had suggested. "Then you pinched her nose and mouth until she died, broke the jar, and backed out. Why the sticker? Why connect the two deaths if you didn't have to?"

"Oh, but I *wanted* to. It was so fun . . . I simply couldn't resist. Watching you and Dr. Davies and those feebs scurry around in complete confusion—merely killing people is going to be such a letdown after this."

She'd reached the desk, her hip brushing the edge. "And coming here? You couldn't resist that either?"

"No." His voice sounded chiding. "I'm not interested in killing you—not trying to hurt your feelings, but you don't tempt me at all. If I can't do it on the Locard campus, it's not a challenge, is it?"

"Then why—"

"I'm not here for you. I'm here for that box." He waved his hand at Barbara's research, most of which still stretched across the rug.

Something else clicked in her mind, a sequence she'd been putting together without realizing it. "That was why you came to her office at lunchtime on Wednesday. You had killed her and taken her keycard. But you couldn't use it, because Hector and I were right there."

"Yesssss," he said, exhaling a slow hiss of disappointed breath. "You were supposed to be at lunch."

"Then you guided me to 'find' the body, so you could drop the keycard on it." That clinking sound she'd heard when he pulled her back, supposedly out of concern for the fumes—she'd thought it came from her jacket buttons hitting the door, but it had been Barbara's carabiner hitting the floor near her feet. The illogic of it had been tickling her brain ever since. The card had been clipped to her belt loop; so, how would it have gotten free, unless someone deliberately unclipped it?

"I circled back to the office Wednesday night, but it was still locked, and I didn't have time to wait for you."

"No. You had to get to killing Farida."

"I couldn't go back in the wee hours or something, because the outside cameras would pick me up, *and* I wouldn't be able to get into her—your—office, anyway . . . not without leaving a trail of broken glass that would show exactly what I was after."

"That's why you came back to my office Thursday night." But she had been there, talking with Hector. Then she'd scooped up the box on her way to meet Rachael and the FBI agents.

"Now I *have* hurt your feelings, and I truly do find you attractive—but, yeah, I wanted the box. I came here and waited, but your neighbor and her brats were running around outside. I eventually ran out of time; I had to get going before all the stores closed, had a bomb to build."

Ellie crouched in a smooth, sinking motion, turning out the fingers of her left hand to pick up the flat, rectangular phone, while keeping the arm under the puppy. He twitched wildly and gave her fingers a gentle nip in a bid for freedom, so close to his goal, the floor. She ignored him and floated back up. "Blowing up the thermocycler? That was a bit extreme. Where did you learn to build a bomb?"

"Forensic training is available across all sorts of topics. And my boss got a grant to pay for it."

"You really do work in the police lab?"

"I really do. Don't bother calling anyone, Ellie. Just let me take my box and go."

"What would be the point of that? Everyone already knows. Rachael knows. The guy in Seattle who provided Barbara the pharmacy information knows. Hector knows. Killing Barbara was pointless. Killing me would be pointless. You're not going to get out of this."

The puppy licked her phone's screen. *Yuk, dog.*

He stepped away from the window, only one small, flowing step, then stopped. "Staying free to hunt one more day is not pointless. Your pals will have to get subpoenas for all the unsolved cases with a medical connection, and the feds are still looking for Saudi assassins. I'll have more than enough time to close up shop and start over somewhere else."

One more step. A brilliant flash lit the room.

"You might as well stop. Rachael knows your name," she told him, thumb entering her password on the illuminated screen, and she prayed to get it right on the first try. Working with only peripheral vision . . . "She's talking to the FBI agents right now."

Okay, a lie, but he can't possibly know that.

"Sure. If you'd really known it was me, she'd still be here, and you'd *both* be talking to the agents. You're not going to let someone else take credit for your discovery, are you?" He made a *tch-tch* sound. "Not the way to manage your career, Ellie. But then, you're not so good at that, are you? I checked you out. Your husband dumps you, you dump the FBI for the Locard, and people start dying."

One more step.

"Stop." 911.

"Why?"

One more.

"Because if you don't, I will shoot you. If you checked my history, you know I was a bureau agent for years. It's not like I haven't shot people before."

She hadn't, but he couldn't possibly know that either.

A tinny, distant voice said, "911, what is your emergency?"

"Go ahead," he told her, and took another step. "Shoot."

He honestly doesn't believe I'll pull the trigger.

So she pulled the trigger.

And the gun went *click*.

Chapter 40

Ellie froze, dumbfounded. That couldn't happen.

She pulled the trigger again.

Click.

"I *told* you, I came by last night." His voice slithered through the darkness.

She didn't waste time wondering why he hadn't stolen the gun—his weapon of choice—instead of only the bullets. She didn't waste time berating herself for not noticing that the revolver had been abnormally light because it lacked ammunition. She didn't waste time talking to the 911 operator.

She threw the gun at him, crouched to drop both the puppy and the phone from a safe distance to the floor, and picked up the blowgun propped next to the desk.

The puppy growled. Caleb said, "What, you're going to kill me with a poison dart?"

"No. I lost all the darts in our backyard in Florida. But I hung on to this."

"Another empty gun?" He touched his left cheek. "Seriously, that hurt."

"I kept it because it makes a good *bo*."

He seemed to stiffen. Perhaps the ancient term for a long staff was familiar to him. Perhaps it wasn't.

The puppy growled again, sprang forward, and sank its tiny teeth into his ankle.

Ellie swung the stick clear of the desk, circled it, and brought it down against Caleb Astor's neck.

It did little to incapacitate him. He put a hand to the spot, but seemed more occupied with shaking the dog off his leg until the puppy flew several feet and rolled, with a sharp whine. This sparked enough rage for her to swing the staff around and strike again with every ounce of force a five-eight, 130-pound human could produce.

He ducked, but not quickly enough to avoid it altogether. The stick bounced against his head, rebounded, reverberated a single shudder through her arms to her toes, and broke in two.

He straightened, blocking high with one arm, and she brought the other end of the staff up between his legs.

He grunted and leapt for her, but slipped on the loose sheets of paper underneath his feet—the research by which Barbara Wright had intended to become rich. And for which, she had died.

He went to one knee, but sprang up again as quickly as the lightning that lit the room. In that one flash before he reached her, she saw the hate, the anger, the depravity—and the animal instinct not only to survive, but to conquer. To conquer her. To conquer them all.

A sound banged somewhere else in the house, like a door slamming shut. Rachael's voice came, harried, agitated. "Ellie?"

He grabbed her hips to pull her to the ground. The puppy attacked again, not bothering to growl a warning this time, biting the now-accessible thigh.

And Ellie drove the piece of broken staff down into his

back. The jagged wooden end speared the flesh, driving splinters into muscle.

He screamed.

A light pounded up the steps—Rachael, with a small, powerful light, which turned out to be her phone's flashlight app.

The puppy, startled by a different animal's animal sounds, backed off and scooted over to Ellie's legs. Caleb reached for her as well, one powerful arm sweeping toward her ankle.

"Stop!" Rachael shouted.

And he did. Stretched across the area rug, spurting blood onto Barbara Wright's pages, moaning and then crying from the pain in his gored back, he lost consciousness ninety seconds before the ambulance arrived.

Chapter 41

"I think you hit a kidney," Rachael told her.

"Don't expect me to feel bad about it. I'd be okay with rolling him *and* Barbara Wright's research up in that rug and dumping it in the bay."

"You should know that the Locard takes a dim view of littering. I'd have to put a note in your file."

That got a laugh. A weak one, but a laugh nonetheless.

Ever the doctor, Rachael had made Ellie sit in her desk chair while the paramedics got Caleb Astor stabilized. She'd done as much of an examination of Ellie as she could by cell phone light, checking pupils and temperature and pulse for signs of shock, looking for blood or broken bones. Only after that, did she go into the garage to reset the breaker.

The house sprang back into brilliance, which the paramedics, at least, appreciated.

Ellie blinked in the illumination. The killer's blood stood out in sharp relief, scattered across the papers, the floor, and even her socks.

"I suppose my rug is toast," she said as Rachael returned with the two FBI agents on her heels.

"Holy crap," Michael said. "Are you all right?"

"What'd you *do* to that guy?" Luis asked.

An hour later, as they regrouped around Ellie's dining table, all questions were discussed and answered as best they could be. This included why bright, exotic Farida Al Talel had to die, despite having nothing to do with tracing DNA via prescribed medications.

"He was right," Michael said. "We would never have been sure that her death didn't have something to do with her still-very-controlled society, or with honor or terrorism or anti-Muslim sentiment or half-a-dozen other possible reasons."

"And she was a beautiful young woman." Ellie stirred her tea, clinking the spoon against Aunt Rosalie's china cup. "That was his preferred choice of target. Barbara and Craig were purely practical homicides. So this is my new place. What do you think?"

"Uh, nice," Luis said. "You sure you're okay?"

"The view is great, in the daylight. Yes, I'm fine, really. I've got my guard dog here with me." She hauled her furry champion to her lap.

"Does he have a name yet?" Rachael asked, reaching over to tickle the pup's ears.

"He does now. Kai. *Kaitiaki.*" At their blank looks Ellie added, "It means 'protector' in Maori."

"I'm not even going to ask how you know that," Michael said. "Just remind me not to tick you off. You *or* Dr. Davies here."

Rachael spoke with confidence. "Don't worry. We will never let you forget it."

"Nope," Ellie said. "Not ever."

Notes and Acknowledgments

As I typically do, I scoured a variety of resources to flesh out this story, including articles such as "The Messy Consequences of the Golden State Killer Case" in *The Atlantic* by Sarah Zhang; podcasts such as *Algorithm, Foreign Affairs, FBI Retired Case File Review, Demystifying Saudi Arabia,* and *Majd's Diary: Two Years in the Life of a Saudi Girl;* and books such as *Behind the Kingdom's Veil* by Susanne Koelbl and *MBS: The Rise to Power of Mohammed bin Salman* by Ben Hubbard.

Also, it should be noted: I have no idea if either of the Swiss comedic ice-skating duo Frick and Frack had any descendants, and certainly not one named Craig Bennett. There is no Marion, Oklahoma, or a serial killer named Bruce Pension, which I know of. I am also unfamiliar with the sheriff's department in Ballwin, Missouri. The American Academy of Forensic Sciences meeting is usually in February, not October.

I would like to thank my fabulous agent, Vicky Bijur, and all the staff at the Vicky Bijur Literary Agency, as well as my wonderful editor, Michaela Hamilton, and the marvelous crew at Kensington Publishing.